KING OF WANDS
Kings of the Tarot, Book 2

Cover Design and Interior Format

KING of WANDS

KINGS OF THE TAROT • BOOK 2

Love is in the cards.

ANNA DURBIN

DEDICATION

To Maizy, the muse who came back to me.

PROLOGUE

Wheel of Fortune: Destiny, fate, continual change, the peaks and valleys of life, turn of the karmic wheel . . .

LATE APRIL, 1807
BENTHOWER HOUSE, GROSVENOR SQUARE, LONDON

THE CANDLE ILLUMINATING THE CARDS on the table in Grandmamma's room flickered as Julia walked by it—for the fifth time. She was wringing her hands now—in addition to pacing the floor—waiting for her grandmother to render her interpretation. The old lady still hadn't spoken, and that made Julia all the more nervous, especially given her furrowed brow and the grim expression on her face as she stared at the cards. Was it really as bad as it looked? Or was Julia overreacting? Just to be sure, she glanced at them one more time as she passed by the table. Her eyes landed on the card in the ninth position, causing her gut to clench. She hated that card. It spooked her more than any other card in the deck.

Unable to stand the suspense any longer, she stopped pacing and threw her hands up in exasperation. "Well,

Grandmamma?"

"Sit, Julia."

"Sit? How can I possibly *sit*? It's horrible, isn't it? Just tell me. I can take it. It's going to be wretched, isn't it? I just know it is."

"Sit, my dear."

Julia groaned but obeyed the old woman nonetheless. She squeezed her eyes shut and held her breath, waiting for the bad news.

"It's going to be wonderful."

She opened her eyes in shock as the air whooshed out of her lungs. "It is?"

"Eventually. In the end."

Distressed beyond words, Julia shot up from her chair. "I knew it! I knew it was bad. It's dreadful. It's hideous. It's going to be just awful, isn't it?"

"It's not all that bad."

"Well, how bad is it?" She didn't really have to ask. Julia and her sisters had learned early on to read the Tarot from their grandmother, who had the extraordinary gift of second sight. When she was just a young girl, Grandmamma had received a deck of Tarot cards from an old Strega woman in Florence after she had shown the ability to read the cards with uncanny acumen while traveling through Italy with her parents. She had passed her knowledge of the cards to her children and grandchildren, so Julia knew as well as Grandmamma did how bad it was.

"Sit, my dear. Calm yourself. Now, it's true. You've drawn the Devil, Death, the Five of Coins, the Ten of Swords, and the Tower."

Julia gulped. "Those are the worst cards in the deck."

"Still, don't despair. It's not the whole reading."

"But it's half of it."

"But most of those cards are in the beginning. You've drawn some others that are wonderful—toward the end." Grandmamma pointed to the other cards one by one. "There's the Star. And the Page of Coins and the Ace of Cups. And look. See there? The Lovers! You know that's my very favorite card in the deck."

Julia pointed to ninth card. "What about that one?"

Grandmamma's smile flattened into a thin, grim line. "Yes. The Tower is indeed worrisome. Don't fear it, however. You mustn't give it that kind of power. Just be wary of it. You can be certain that everything will be fine . . . eventually . . . because . . ." She tapped the last card. "Look. You've drawn the King of Wands in the end, and he will rescue you."

Julia clucked her tongue, while her vocal pitch rose an octave. "Rescue me!"

"Indeed."

She raised her arms in the air again. "Oh, my lord! From what?"

Grandmamma patted her hand, and Julia took some solace from her reassuring smile. "There's no reason to worry about that right now. Just know that the King of Wands represents a kind and honest man who, when he loves a woman, he does so with his whole heart. He is a man of light hair, light eyes, and fiery passions. He represents the season of Summer, the element of Fire, and the direction of South. You may not recognize him as the one for you when you first meet him, but the moment you realize it, you will know it was him all along. He is your destiny, and he will make you happier than you could ever imagine yourself being."

Her mood brightened, if only a little. Perhaps the future was not so bleak. She smiled with guarded optimism. "Really?"

Grandmamma nodded. "The cards never lie." But her deep sigh revealed a caveat. She reached across the table and grasped Julia's hands in her own bent fingers. "Have patience, my dear child. Your happiness will be a few years in coming. You have many challenges ahead of you in the meantime. But be brave. Be tenacious. And you will survive even your worst nightmares. Remember, you are the clay vessel, and the misfortunes that befall you are but the fires of a kiln. They will strengthen you and transform you into a radiant work of art."

Julia nodded, taking some comfort from Grandmamma's words of encouragement.

"Now, sweet girl, I have a gift for your debut tonight." The old woman reached into her reticule and pulled out a small black box, which she handed to Julia.

She took the box and raised the lid. Inside lay a fiery orange cameo attached to a golden chain. She removed the necklace from the box and lifted it to her face to examine it more closely. "Is this . . .?"

"Yes. It's The Lovers. It's just like the cameos I gave Phoebe and Cassandra when they debuted. I had one carved in sardonyx for each of you girls to guide you each to your true love."

"It's lovely, Grandmamma. I shall cherish it always."

"Turn around, and I'll fasten it around your neck."

Julia did as instructed and then stepped over to a nearby mirror to inspect the pendant as it hung from her neck. So like her hair, the coppery orange sardonyx glowed in the candlelight.

"You look stunning, my love."

Julia stepped over to her grandmother and hugged her tightly. "Thank you so much, Grandmamma."

"You're very welcome." The old lady led Julia to the door of her chamber. "Now, remember. You will find your happiness and your true love. Maybe not tonight, but on some night in the future, you will find him. And when you find your King of Wands, you will know him by the love that shines in his eyes for you."

CHAPTER 1

*The Hermit: Withdrawal from the outer world
and meditation on the meaning of life; predicts a
meeting with one who will assist the seeker . . .*

JUNE 23, 1817
VILLAGE OF SOUTH KINDALE, HAMPSHIRE, ENGLAND

LADY JULIA LACEY GASPED IN blatant disbelief as the clerk at the Queen's Cross Inn handed
her a small parcel. Shocked, she stood motionless for
a moment, heart pounding, mind racing over what
the package might contain. Though it was clearly
addressed to her, she didn't trust what she saw. Surely,
it was a mirage and would soon vanish before her very
eyes. When it didn't, she brought it in for a closer look.

With a smile, the clerk said, "If you'll excuse me, my
lady, we've a situation in the kitchen, and I'm needed
in the back. Good day." He then disappeared through
a door behind the counter, leaving her alone with her
box.

It was very ordinary, as boxes went, rectangular
in shape, wrapped in brown paper, and tied up with

string. The only remarkable thing about it—other than the fact that it was in her possession—was its stamp of origin: Calcutta. She had long ago given up hope of receiving an answer to the inquiry she had sent her friend Kitty Blake in India last year. In fact, she had thought stopping at the Queen's Cross this morning to check her mail, as she did every Monday, would yield nothing more than the usual letters from her sisters in London. Yet, here was a package that could either answer all her prayers or dash all her hopes into the fire.

Tentatively, she shook the package. Several items rattled around inside it. She debated for a second whether to open it right there or wait until she got home. Curiosity prevailed, and she ripped the string and tore at the paper to reveal a wooden box. Again, heart pounding, she gently lifted the lid. She peeked into the box to find a folded letter sealed with wax and resting on top of several other items wrapped in tissue paper. She closed her eyes and drew a deep breath to steady herself. She held that breath as she took the paper and broke open the wax seal to read what it said.

December 15, 1816
Dearest Julia,
You cannot imagine how happy I was to receive your letter two months ago. I had begun to despair that something dreadful had happened to you when I didn't hear back from you after all this time. I can only think that Niles must have destroyed my letters to you or else you would have written me before now. I am just glad that you found Sidney's letter to Niles and decided to write me with your questions about his

friend and doctor, Renesh Sengupta. Sadly, yes, it's true about Dr. Sengupta. He was not dead when you and Niles left Calcutta, but Sidney believes that Niles had him poisoned shortly after the two of you left for home.

As for Niles, I was not surprised to hear about his demise, given how sick he was when you and he left India. Nor can I say that I'm sorry he suffered. That is un-Christian of me, I know, but there it is. I do hope this letter finds you in good health, however.

And now for the good news: I am thrilled to report to you that, yes, Camille is indeed alive and well and living with Sidney and me here in Calcutta! I am certain she would love nothing better than for you to come and stay with her in India at long last, as you said you would do in your letter if you found out she were still alive. I know I would welcome your return. As for Camille, she is a lively, precocious child with a great deal of curiosity. She is thoroughly lovely, and though she looks very much like her father, I daresay she also resembles her mother about the eyes. You can judge this assessment for yourself, however, as I have enclosed a miniature portrait of her that I commissioned for you when I received your letter in October. I hope you like it. Please do write me and let me know when you plan on returning to Calcutta. I can hardly wait to see you again!

Your devoted friend,

Kitty

P.S. I have enclosed some incense from the market in Calcutta for you. I remember how much you liked it.

Anxious to see the miniature of Camille, Julia pawed through the items in the box and found an oval-shaped object wrapped in tissue paper. She ripped away the tissue to reveal the gilt-framed portrait of a little girl with dark hair and big, bright eyes. Though she did not frown, the child's expression was still somber and sad, almost forlorn. Julia teared up and covered her mouth to stifle a sob as a thousand emotions rushed over her. Love, hate. Joy, anger. Happiness, grief. Gratitude, betrayal. Relief, disbelief. Resolve, uncertainty. And as each emotion played over her senses, hundreds of questions raced through her mind, not the least of which was how? How was it possible that sweet, precious Camille was still alive? Had Niles not told her before they left for England that the child had died of a fever?

She needed to get back to Calcutta. Now. To see the girl for herself. But how? Overcome with the sudden urge to do something, anything, to set in motion her return to India, Julia whirled away from the front desk, oblivious to her surroundings, and in doing so, ran directly into the gentleman standing right behind her, knocking him into a pile of luggage that stood waiting for the arrival of the next stagecoach. The luggage toppled, the man fell backward on top of it, and Julia fell forward landing on top of the man—practically nose-to-nose with him. Knocked breathless and stunned into silence, she could only stare insipidly into the most beautiful pair of blue eyes she'd ever seen. Aquamarines they were, and they stared back at her with a look of utter surprise and . . . something else.

Irritation, perhaps? He squirmed and huffed. Yes, irritation. It was definitely irritation.

Had she been less perturbed herself, she might have admitted that a woman could get lost in those blue eyes, but her skin bristled with abject annoyance at the fact that he had been standing so close behind her. Had he no regard for her personal space? And though his intoxicating scent—a mixture of bergamot and cedar wood—teased her senses, vexation coiled through her veins at their predicament.

After what seemed like an eternity, he clasped her arms in an attempt to right himself. The very nerve of the man rankled her. How audacious to grab her in such an intimate manner. It was simply not done.

"Sir, if you don't *mind*." Shocked and embarrassed, she could not hide the indignation in her voice. She glanced around the lobby for someone to assist her to her feet, but not a soul was present. As she lay atop the man on the floor, the situation grew more awkward with each tick of the clock hanging on the wall.

"Madam, brace yourself." His voice betrayed his own exasperation as he grasped her arms even tighter.

Julia squealed as he began to sit up, knocking her to the floor beside him.

"Oomph." She landed on her side, and as she did, she lost her grip on the box and watched as it sailed through the air, landing several feet from her. The lid flew open as it hit the tiles, dashing the contents of the package all over the floor.

"Oh, no! My box!" Panicked that she might have lost something valuable from the parcel, she shot him her most withering glare.

The man ignored her as he rose to his feet and held out his hand to help her stand. Seeing no other alternative, she took his hand with severe reluctance and plenty of asperity, and he pulled her to her feet with much ado and very little grace.

Once upright, she dusted off her dress. "I certainly hope nothing is broken." Only a simpleton would have missed the accusation in her voice as she bent over to pick up a couple of things that lay strewn across the tiles.

He picked up his own hat and set it on his head. "Allow me to assist you."

"No, thank you. You've done quite enough as it is," she snapped.

"But I insist." He clenched his chiseled jaw, and without waiting for her permission, he bent down and picked up a heart-shaped, silver locket that had come unwrapped from its tissue and handed it to her.

She took it from him and popped it open without thinking. Inside was a lock of dark hair curled into the shape of a heart. Camille's, no doubt. Her heart melted as she stroked her finger over the girl's hair. She was too engrossed in examining the memento to notice him as he continued picking things off the floor. Finally, he stood in front of her once more holding the box, along with a handful of other items, most of which were still wrapped in tissue. He placed everything inside the box and handed it to her. She snatched it from his grip with very little gratitude and no attempt at civility. She rummaged through the box's contents searching for the portrait, but it was not there. She picked through everything again more carefully, certain the portrait was lying on the bottom and she had just overlooked it. When she couldn't find it, she gasped audibly and clutched her chest. Frantic, she glanced around the floor for the missing picture but didn't see it. "Where is it?"

"Where is what?"

Panic set in. "The picture! The portrait. It's not here. It's gone!"

"Well, what does it look like?"

Again, she directed a withering gaze at him. "It's a picture. It looks like a picture."

He raised a brow and tipped his head to the side. "You don't say." His mouth quirked into a moue of annoyance. "A picture of what?"

"A little girl. Not that it's any of your business, sir."

His eyebrows drew together into a scowl, and he appeared to be holding back a comment. "Well, how big is it? What's its shape?"

She continued scouring the floor for the portrait. "Small-ish. It's not big. Oval. In a gilded frame."

They both paced the lobby tiles searching for the portrait. He went this way; she went that, but it was gone without a trace, as though the floor had swallowed it whole.

Finally, he threw up his arms in obvious surrender. "I don't see it, madam."

Tears threatened to spill from her lashes, but she managed to hold back a sob. "I just don't understand. Where could it have gone? What could have happened to it?"

He watched her for a moment, his features soften-
ing just a little. "Don't despair. Surely, it will show up."

She shook her head and swiped at a few tears that
had fallen from her eyes. "No. I fear it is lost. Gone
forever."

"Let's tell the clerk. He can watch for it, and if it
turns up, he can save it for you."

Julia closed her eyes. She should just nod and say
nothing, just walk away, but the last of her patience and
civility slipped away as her ire rose. "If only you had
not been standing so close to me, sir, I would not have
collided with you and dropped everything."

He narrowed his eyes, as he caught her meaning.
Again, only a simpleton would have misunderstood
the accusation in her words. And while it was true that
she was laying the blame for her situation squarely at
his feet, she couldn't muster a scintilla of conscience for
it. He took a deep breath, obviously struggling with his
own loss of patience and civility. "Well, madam, may I
suggest that you watch where you are going the next
time? Had you not been twirling blindly about like a
whirling dervish, you might have noticed me and not
run me over."

"Run you over!"

"Yes, run me over. Like a postilion at high speed."

"That is rich. You were standing so close behind me
that I couldn't have avoided you had I turned on my
tiptoes. Why *were* you so near me? It was really quite
unseemly."

His outrage was palpable. He huffed as he crossed

his arms in obvious indignation. "I was reaching for the bell on the counter. I was anxious to ring for the clerk because I am locked out of my room and need him to let me in."

"Humph. Well, then, don't let me keep you. If you'll excuse me, sir, I will leave you to it." Raising her brow, she gave him one final haughty sweep with her eyes as she waved her hand in dismissal and stalked off toward the door.

"Madam," he said behind her. "Good day."

She sensed, rather than saw, him bow. And from the main door of the hotel, she turned and caught a glimpse of him out of the corner of her eye as he straightened his cravat and strode to the front desk. He rang the bell for service as she opened the door and stepped out of the lobby into the brilliant sunlight of the summer morning.

Embarrassment vied with outrage for uppermost spot in her mind as she climbed into her gig and sat next to her maid Burton, who'd accompanied her into town. She took several deep breaths to calm herself. She had been a graceless oaf, it was true, and should have apologized for bowling him over, but his own testiness and ill humor with the situation had provoked her. Then, she had been so upset over losing Camille's portrait that she had forgotten her breeding. Perhaps if they ever met again, however, she would say she was sorry to him. Perhaps. More likely, though, she would never have the opportunity to apologize to him. He was probably on his way out of town this morning and she would never see the gentleman again. Though she should not have taken consolation in that fact, she did, in fact, take consolation in the notion that they would never cross paths again.

Charles Rodman stepped away from the main desk and peeked out the window of the lobby to watch the flustered, albeit bewitching, redhead steal away in her carriage. He had not known what to do about their predicament as she lay atop him in the lobby minutes ago. Irritation had prickled his skin at her clumsiness, however, and he had wanted nothing more than to rant at her. He'd been about to scold her when he'd gazed into her lovely eyes, with irises the color of cinnamon, and his mind had gone blank.

Well, not blank exactly. But he couldn't remember his name while he stared at her, so he said nothing. Dangerous, those eyes. Altogether too beguiling. For several seconds, they had left him too feebleminded for words. Then, as her lovely jasmine scent washed over him, it only served to further obliterate his faculties. His irritation finally spiked into anger over his body's inappropriate reaction to her as he lay beneath her. Had he not already been so annoyed at having managed to lock himself out of his room a while ago, he might have behaved more civilly toward her, but when she had crashed into him, he had lost all patience. He had been downright rude and offensive to her. Still, if he were honest with himself, he would have had to admit that his bad behavior toward her was driven more by resentment for the unsettling effect she'd had over him than by the accident. He had despised himself for being so consumed by her natural charms that he took his frustration out on her, blaming her entirely for running into him when he had clearly been standing too close to her in the lobby.

He dismissed his reaction to her as idiocy as a porter emerged from the door behind the front desk, presumably in answer to the bell. The poor man's jaw dropped when he saw the luggage strewn all across the floor.

Charles attempted a smile as he cleared his throat. "I'm most sorry, good sir. There was a small accident just a minute ago with the lady who was at the desk before me. She turned and collided into me, and we ended up knocking into the bags."

Unamused, the other man frowned and huffed in obvious frustration as he began to right the bags.

"Here. Let me help you." Charles bent down to pick up a satchel, but the porter merely shooed his hand away.

"That will not be necessary, sir. I have everything in order."

Not knowing what to do in this awkward situation, Charles scratched his head as the other man continued righting the bags. He hovered about while the porter worked, waiting for the man to finish with the luggage. At last, after all the bags were in a neat pile, he cleared his throat once again.

The porter raised a brow. "Is there something I can help you with, sir?"

"Yes, if you please. I am locked out of my room and need to get in to retrieve my watch."

The porter nodded and strode to the front desk and

opened the half door to let himself back behind the counter. He stepped toward the cubbyholes holding keys and other miscellany for hotel guests. He reached toward the key slots. "Are you in Room 201, Mr. Rodman?"

"No, that's the duke's room. I'm across from him in Room 202."

"Ah. Yes." The porter plucked the extra key for Room 202 from its compartment and handed it to Charles.

"Thank you. I'll return it shortly."

The porter nodded and then disappeared through the door behind the counter without further conversation. Charles, meanwhile, jogged up the flight of stairs to his room and retrieved his watch and then ran back down to the lobby. As he walked past the pile of luggage, the light in the room glinted off something on the floor, catching his eye. He stopped and looked down to see a gilt-framed, oval portrait of a little girl. This had to be the woman's lost picture. It must have slid beneath one of the bags when she dropped her box. He bent to pick it up and examined the likeness of the child. She had very dark, almost black hair and light brown skin. Though animated, her ebony eyes seemed to convey a sadness a child her age shouldn't know.

He looked up from the picture and searched the lobby for the porter who had given him the extra room key, but he then remembered that the man had retreated into the back. He decided that rather than ring the bell and wait around for someone to answer it, he would stow the portrait safely inside his pocket and give it to the porter or desk clerk when he returned from his errand.

That decided, he strode toward the door and stepped out into the morning sun. He wanted to get a sense of the village of South Kindale, since he would likely be spending the rest of his life in this little town if he were appointed vicar of St. Blaise's Church. To that end, he walked toward the square, which wasn't far from the coaching inn on the main road into town. He took in the early morning air, which was still cool and refreshing, not yet as warm as it would get once the sun climbed higher in the sky. When he arrived at the center of town, he looked up and searched for the church spire.

Spying the steeple standing up from the church's tower high above the rooftops in town, he turned south down a quiet lane where he saw the church itself. It was a modest structure of Gothic architecture, constructed of local stone from the looks of it. A graveyard stood to the left of it, while a house, which he assumed was the parsonage, stood some ways on its right. The whole aspect gave him a sense of peace and serenity. He liked this church. With luck, it would be his, and after ten long years of hiding away from the world as a curate in a small parish outside London, he would once again have a living to call his own and a flock to minister to.

And for the first time since he'd left London, he began to feel nervous about making a good impression on the patroness of the living. Would he be able to inspire the lady into bestowing the living on him? He hoped so, though according to his brother who had told him about the position, it was essentially his for the taking, for the patroness's brother was interceding on his behalf.

He took a deep breath and walked down the lane toward the church so that he could survey the outside of the building from up close. When he got to the building, he walked around the perimeter of the grounds and the well-kept churchyard. The old vicar must have been a stickler for the lawn because there was hardly a weed in sight. He strode to the graveyard, which was also well kept, and walked amongst the headstones, many of which were ancient. Much of the carving had worn away with the years, and the headstones themselves stood at odd angles to the ground, rarely upright, a testament to the ravages of time. A newer one, belonging to a Mr. Niles Lacey, caught his eye. From the looks of it, it had been erected within the last few years, judging by how fresh the carving upon it looked and the fact that it stood upright at ninety degrees from the ground.

Lacey. That's interesting. Could Niles Lacey be any relation to the patroness he would see later today?

He tucked that thought away as he finished strolling the graveyard and turned his attention to the church itself. The stone and rubble used to construct the building appeared to be in decent enough shape, while the stained-glass windows appeared to be newer than the rest of the structure. He attempted to look through one of the windows to get a glimpse of the nave, but the glass was far too opaque to enable him to see into the darkened church. Instead, he peered through clear glass windows into the vestry, which was a room of decent size. He then walked around to the end of the building and tried the doors there, but they were locked.

Unable to gain entry to the church, he walked several yards to where it bordered the parsonage, a quaint, though sturdy, two-story structure with a thatched roof. The well-kept lawn in front of the house was a deep, verdant green, and he walked the narrow stone path leading up to the front door of the parsonage. He rapped on the door several times but received no answer. Supposing the house to be vacant, he looked through one of the windows to the right of the door and spied a well-appointed study with a large desk and several tall bookcases. This would be the perfect room for him to compose his sermons, if he were appointed vicar of St. Blaise's, and he was now more eager than ever to meet the parish patroness.

He checked his watch then. It was time to return to the hotel to see if the duke had awoken yet. The duke, with whom Charles had traveled from London yesterday, was the patroness's brother and would make the necessary introductions. To Charles's knowledge, His Grace had still been abed when he had awoken at the first inkling of dawn. Impatient to see some of the village before going out to visit the duke's sister, Charles had shaved and washed and taken care of some correspondence in his room.

He had then headed down to the lobby, intent upon

stepping out to have a brief look at the church before the duke awoke. He was halfway down the stairs when he realized he'd left his watch in his room. He would need that watch so he wouldn't lose track of time. Irritated, he backtracked up the stairs only to discover that he had locked himself out of his room. Even more frustrated with himself, he had gone to the lobby to get a spare key from the clerk or porter when he had seen the woman who had run into him this morning.

Humph. *Her.* Even now, as he walked from the vicarage back to the inn, he shook his head in annoyance when he recalled their encounter earlier. It dawned on him then that if she were receiving her mail at the inn, she was likely from around the area, which, of course, meant that he would see her in church when he assumed his new post as vicar. He groaned aloud with the realization that he would have to apologize to her next time they met for his incivility today. Hopefully, their next meeting would not be so awkward as today's. Hopefully, she would not try his patience as she had done this morning. And hopefully, she would not affect his senses with her cinnamon eyes and jasmine scent as she had also done earlier. As he recalled his visceral reaction to her previously, he wondered where she was now and what she was doing at that particular moment.

Tendrils of smoke curled upward from the censer sitting on the floor in front of Julia as she sat in the special corner of her sitting room that she had marked out for the purpose of meditation. She crossed her legs one over the other in the lotus position, as Renesh had taught her to do in India, and rang the chime next to her on the floor, and then, as she had done a thousand times before, she closed her eyes and breathed deeply several times while concentrating on the rhythm of her inhalations and exhalations. The ethereal sound of the chime cleared her mind as it cleared the atmosphere, and the sweet smoke of the myrrh incense she had just received in Kitty's package this morning perfumed the air while transporting her to another time and another place.

As she relaxed, she gently held in her hand the precious locket containing Camille's hair that Kitty had included in the box she had sent. The girl's curl was so dark, as dark as her father's hair, that Julia was briefly overcome with tears at the thought of them both. She swiped them from her eyes, and as she refocused her mind on the task at hand, she chanted quietly, rhythmically, *"Om gum ganapatayei namaha. Om gum ganapatayei namaha."*

She concentrated on nothing but the words, dedicating her mantra to Lord Ganesh. Kitty had included a small statue of the Indian god in her package, and he now sat on the floor next to the censer, his smiling elephant head reassuring her, as she repeated the words to him.

"Om gum ganapatayei namaha. Om gum ganapatayei namaha."

They were a balm to her soul, and with any luck, they would help remove the obstacles facing her.

"Om gum ganapatayei namaha."

Soon oblivious to the world outside, she retreated within her quieted mind. Her whole mind focused on the chant as minutes passed, perhaps even an hour. Time and place became immaterial to her, as the sound of the ticking clock faded away. Such a state of tranquility enveloped her that everything outside her mind ceased to be. Utterly serene, with all consciousness focused on her one goal, she was connected to the material world only by her breath until she was jarred out of her deep peace and her rhythmic chanting by some intruder calling her name and shaking her shoulder.

"Julia!" said an obviously aggravated male voice. "Ho there, Julia, you're talking in your sleep. Wake up."

Jolted from her meditation, confusion flooded her brain. Her eyes fluttered open, and irritation bristled through her veins when she recognized the intruder standing directly before her arrogantly awaiting her attention, a smirk on his face.

"Bloody hell." Groggy from meditation, she tried to regain her sense of the present. "What are you doing here?"

"Language, my dear. Is that any way to greet your brother? Besides, you have a guest." His arrogant drawl irked her as he stepped aside to reveal another gentleman standing behind him.

Julia glanced up briefly past her brother and then did a double take when she recognized the man who stood behind him. Lord, if it wasn't the same gentleman she had gracelessly knocked over in the hotel lobby this morning. Heat rushed to her cheeks as she swallowed her incredulity—and her embarrassment—

at meeting him again. If the look of sheer horror on his face was any indication, he too recalled their earlier encounter. His eyes flashed with what seemed like alarm as his jaw tautened into a hard line and his brows drew together in obvious and utter panic. How curious. What could his reaction mean? Did he think she would rise off the floor and bowl him over again?

He didn't even attempt a smile as she turned her attention back to her brother. "I would say it's nice to see you, Benthower, but it isn't. It never is." She tucked Camille's hair safely into a pocket in her *kameez* so as not to lose it and then glanced to the entrance of the sitting room where her maid stood nervously wringing her hands. "And look. You've frightened poor Burton. What do you want? And how did you find me?"

"It wasn't easy, let me tell you. I've been all over Hell and half of Hampshire searching for you. It's lucky I found you as it is."

"That depends on your point of view."

Not surprisingly, he scoffed at her. "What, pray tell, are you doing living out here in the middle of nowhere? In your husband's hunting box, no less?"

"Lexington House is otherwise occupied."

"Humph. So I noticed. We called there first thing when we arrived last evening. I was hoping you would put us up for the night, but we ended up having to stay at the inn in town. Imagine my surprise at seeing all those strange women milling about your house and you nowhere to be found. They barely let me cross the threshold and absolutely wouldn't let me past the entryway to ask questions. Me, Julia. They wouldn't let *me* in. Your own brother. A duke, no less. The only information I could get from anyone was that you were staying in the hunting box. What are all those women doing at your house anyway?"

"They are friends." It was all the explanation she was willing to give. To change the subject, she asked him once again what he wanted.

"Aren't you going to offer us tea first?" he asked, glancing back at the maid.

"I wasn't, no, because as you can see, you've interrupted me unannounced, and I am not receiving guests. Now. If you will excuse me . . ."

He did not take her hint. "Just what in the hell were you doing anyway, Julia?"

"Language, Michael, we have a guest." She made the remark to avoid the question of what she had been doing. She then looked from her brother to the blond man with the eyes so blue who was still standing behind him. He was a handsome man, she had to admit, and her cheeks blazed with heat once again when she remembered that she had been on top of him earlier this morning. He still wouldn't smile at her as he regarded her, though. She tried to read his expression again, but unlike a few second ago, his thoughts were not clearly written on his face. He did lift a brow, giving her the impression that he was still alarmed over something. Perhaps he, too, was recalling their earlier predicament and their unfriendly exchange afterward.

Eventually, she stood after giving up hope of her brother leaving her in peace. "Aren't you going to introduce us, Benthower?"

"First tell me what you were doing down there on the floor. And, my God, Julia, what on earth are you wearing? They appear to be trousers."

"These? They are *shalwar*. They are trousers of a sort, I suppose. From India." She stuck her leg out to demonstrate. "And the top is a *kameez*, also from India. Together, they are *shalwar kameez*. I am wearing them because they make it so much more comfortable to sit on the floor than a dress."

"Just exactly why were you on the floor? And what strange language were you muttering?"

"Hindi, if you must know, is the language," she said with indignation, and though she didn't really want to explain to him what she had been doing in front of the stranger, she squared her shoulders to project the confidence she didn't necessarily feel. "And I was using yoga to meditate."

"Using *what* to what?"

She harrumphed. "I said, I was using yoga—y-o-g-a—to meditate."

"Yoga? Never heard of it."

"It's something you wouldn't understand, Ben-thower. I learned it in India."

He put up his hand. "Say no more. If it's from the Orient, it's a mystery to begin with."

"Tea is from the Orient, yet you say you would like some."

"Yes. Please. Order us some," the duke commanded.

Reluctantly, she requested tea from Burton, who left the room to prepare it. Julia then led her brother and the other gentleman out through the hallway to a small parlor done up in hues of evergreen and gold. It was definitely a man's sitting room. She had made no changes to it since moving into the hunting box over two years ago, though she had a mind to do it up in feminine pinks and frilly laces just to spite her late husband.

"Now, will you please introduce me to your friend?"

"Of course. Rodman, may I present my sister, Lady Julia Lacey. Jules, this is Mr. Charles Rodman. He's a curate at St. Mary's in Sunbury-on-Thames, just south of London."

"It's a pleasure making your acquaintance, Lady Julia." The man spoke so softly that she wasn't sure she heard him as he gave her an obligatory bow. When he stood upright, his chiseled jaw relaxed into what was without a doubt a forced smile.

"Likewise, I'm sure." She was certain from his mien that he was anything but happy to make her acquaintance. At the same time, however, she sensed his reaction to her was not out of annoyance with what had happened between them at the inn this morning but out of . . . anxiety, maybe? Odd. Why was he so alarmed? She flashed her own fake smile at him and made an equally obligatory, if not equally elegant, curtsy.

After the introductions, Julia offered both her brother and her guest a seat. Tea was brought in by and by. After she served the duke and Mr. Rodman, she poured herself some along with a teaspoonful of sugar and a little cream.

"Pray tell, Benthower," she said as she stirred her

tea. "What brings you all the way out to Hampshire in the middle of June?"

"Well . . ." The duke rubbed his jaw in hesitation as if he were choosing his words carefully. "I have a solution to a problem of yours, Julia."

CHAPTER 2

Ace of Coins: New venture or career opportunity bringing with it a new relationship . . .

JULIA COULD NOT PREVENT HER eyes from rolling. They spun in their sockets of their own volition. "Lord, help me. I remember the last time you had a 'solution' to a so-called 'problem' of mine, Benthower." *I ended up married to the loathsome Mr. Lacey.* "What so-called problem are you talking about now?"

"The problem of your parish not having a vicar."

"Oh, my goodness, yes!" She clasped a hand to her heart for melodramatic emphasis. "You simply have no idea how often I lie awake at night contemplating a solution to that very dilemma."

"Precisely." Apparently, sarcasm was lost on her brother. "Which is why I've brought Mr. Rodman with me to meet you. He is your solution— the perfect candidate for the position. And seeing as how the patronage goes with your husband's estate, I thought I would make him known to you as soon as I could."

Julia narrowed her eyes at her brother. "Benthower, may I see you in my sitting room for a moment?"

He waved away her request. "That's not necessary. Just say whatever it is you have to say. Rodman won't mind."

Irritated that he would not submit to a private inquest, she gazed at him with more boldness than she felt. "Very well. What is this really about?"

He narrowed his eyes at her this time. "I'm not sure I take your meaning."

"My meaning? I'll tell you what I mean. You do nothing without an ulterior motive, and I want to know what it is in this case. Why have you really brought Mr. Rodman here? Do you stand to turn a profit from the venture?" She peered out the corner of her eye at Mr. Rodman. He quirked his head to the side, as though the question perplexed him. Interesting. Though he said nothing, his cheeks colored slightly as his lips flattened into a grim line.

Benthower, on the other hand, stood as he harrumphed loudly and with severe annoyance. "May I see you in your sitting room for a moment, Julia?"

"Oh, I'm sure whatever you have to say, you can say in front of Mr. Rodman. He won't mind."

Neither the curate nor the duke smiled.

"Julia. Your sitting room. Now." Her brother spoke the words in his duke voice, a voice even she could not ignore. She scowled at him but stood with reluctance to lead him into the sitting room. He closed the door behind them.

"I want you to appoint Rodman as your vicar." His ducal tone once again indicated that he would brook no opposition.

"And I want to know why, all of a sudden, you think I need a vicar."

"Every parish needs a vicar. You don't have one here. Rodman is the perfect choice."

"But why, Benthower? Why him? And why all of a sudden?"

"Because if you do not make a presentation to the benefice soon, your rights as patroness will lapse, and you want to get a man of your own choosing, don't you?"

"In truth, I hardly care. Besides, our vicar died barely a month ago. I still have a while to nominate someone. What's the hurry? Tell me what's really going on."

Benthower doubled down on his insistence. "You have to act on Rodman sooner rather than later."

"Why should I be in such a rush to nominate Mr. Rodman? Is there something in it for you?"

"Why won't you just appoint him vicar?"

"Because I need an explanation for your involvement. We can go round and round on this, Michael." She used his given name here because it bothered him so much when she did. It gave her great pleasure when he glowered back at her. "But unless I know why you really want me to appoint Mr. Rodman as vicar, I'm saying no." She crossed her arms to affirm her stance.

Benthower's frown deepened. He stood for a moment with a comical pout on his face as though he were debating how to answer her question. Finally, he huffed and threw his arms up in apparent defeat. "Because I owe his brother, Lord Pruitt, a rather sizeable gambling debt, which he agreed to forgive if I could get you to appoint Rodman as vicar of St. Blaise's. Livings are hard to come by, you know, and ever since Pruitt learned that this parish living was vacant and that you had the right of advowson as patroness, he has been after me to assist his brother or pay the debt I owe him."

"Aha! Just as I suspected. It does have to do with money, your ever-persistent motivation."

"Well, I would've been flush now, had Cassandra not run off with Kingspointe last year."

"You mean you would have been flush now by cheating Cassandra out of her dowry, had she not run off with Kingspointe."

She was referring to the situation with their sister Cassandra who had pretended to elope last year with the Marquess of Kingspointe in order to thwart Benthower in a scheme so base that Julia hardly believed him capable of such infamy. He had conspired with a nitwit knave to bilk their sister out of her fortune of fifty thousand pounds by having the man compromise her in public and thus force her to marry him. He and Benthower then meant to split her money. Cassandra, however, had outwitted them both by running off with Lord Kingspointe instead, before she was forced to marry the knave.

Benthower now crossed his arms in obvious exasperation and irritation. "None of that would've been necessary if the courts would just do what is right where Bess is concerned."

Julia nearly choked on her irritation when her brother mentioned another of their sisters, Bess, who had been missing and presumed dead these past eight years. "And just what is that, Michael?"

He scowled when she used his given name once again. "They need to make a final ruling on her death so that her money can be distributed amongst her rightful heirs. Then I'd have my share. However, they've done nothing with the petition I filed last year to have her declared dead."

"But we do not know that Bess is dead."

"She drowned."

"Oh, honestly, what evidence do you have of that?"

"Her hat and spencer were found floating in the Serpentine. What more evidence do you want?"

"A body would be nice, but hers was never recovered from the water."

"It's down there somewhere, I'm sure."

"Well, why don't you go diving for it, if you're so sure? Perhaps the courts are reluctant to declare her dead without a corpse. I myself am still holding out hope that she's alive somewhere and just ran off before you could force her to marry the nasty Lord Strawbridge."

"Why would she object to Strawbridge? That was a good match."

"A good match for *you,* maybe. You'd have gotten half her dowry in the deal you made with that disgusting degenerate by convincing her to marry him, while all she would've gotten, more likely than not, was the French disease, given the man's habits. You know, the trouble with you, Benthower, is that you treat everyone—especially your own sisters—as chattel. You bargain away our dowries—*our* fortunes, Michael—in these horrible matches that benefit none but you and the men you conspire to split them with." She saw red as she spat the words at him.

Why Julia was surprised at Benthower's ignominy with Cassandra and Bess was beyond her really. After all, he had conspired with his old school chum, Niles Lacey, to get his hands on half of her own dowry ten years ago by duping her into marrying the rotten blackheart. She had been no more than a naïve little debutante when her brother had deceived her about Lacey's affections for her, telling her that Lacey was deeply in love with her and convincing her that she was his heart's desire. All too eagerly, she agreed to the marriage, unaware that Lacey was only after her fortune and family connections to satisfy the grandiose vision of his father, a common shipping merchant who wanted desperately for his son to purchase a vast estate and achieve the social status he had never been able to do. As part of the deal, Lacey agreed to split Julia's dowry with his good friend—her brother—for his complicity in getting her to marry him. Her mood curdled—even more so than it did in her brother's presence—when she thought of her dead husband.

Benthower dispelled the unpleasant memories when he cleared his throat. "Well, however you choose to interpret the past, I could really use your help now, Julia. Please. I'm in dire straits. I will have to use the girls' dowry funds to satisfy the gambling debt and other outstanding obligations otherwise."

Julia couldn't hide her shock. She gaped at him in

utter astonishment at his confession and honest appeal for help. "You know, Benthower, you might actually get some sympathy for your plight now and again if you were always this forthright in your dealings with people instead of trying to manipulate everyone for your own means."

The duke clenched his jaw. He stared down at the floor but remained silent.

"How much?"

He raised his head and furrowed his brow in apparent confusion. "How much what?"

"How much do you owe Pruitt?"

"Ten thousand."

"Good lord. That is quite a lot." She took in a deep breath to steady herself. "And this Mr. Rodman? Do you honestly believe he will make a good vicar for our parish?"

"I don't know him personally, but his brother has vouched for him. And all Rodman has talked about since we left London is how much he would like to serve the parish. I'm convinced that he would do well as vicar."

She pursed her lips as she considered her brother's request. It wasn't so much that she minded naming Mr. Rodman vicar of St. Blaise's. He seemed as good a candidate as any to do the job, she supposed. In any case, it didn't matter to her who held the office, as long as he was a decent person toward the other parishioners and didn't bother her about her lack of participation in the Church and her practice of Eastern rituals. No, her hesitation had more to do with her resentment of her brother's machinations and how he always managed to manipulate her for his own ends than any other reason. And here he was doing it again. In the end, however, she took pity on him, at the look of utter desperation on his face.

She also thought about the plight of his poor daughters who would suffer the most from their papa's insolvency, and after a moment's consideration, she capitulated. "Very well, Benthower. I suppose I shall nominate him for the position, but I want to ask him a question or two."

He positively beamed as he took her by the arms and kissed her on her cheek. "That will be no problem."

She rolled her eyes at his show of gratitude and stepped back from him. "So, does Mr. Rodman know of this arrangement between you and his brother? Or is he in the dark?"

"He does not know."

Julia raised her eyebrows. "Anything? He does not know anything?"

"Nothing. And Pruitt would rather he never found out about it. Rodman knows only that Pruitt talked to me on his behalf and that I agreed to introduce him to you as a favor to Pruitt."

"Surely, he must have an inkling that it is more than a favor, Benthower."

"I think not. I think he is truly in the dark and believes this is just a gesture of goodwill between nobles."

"Can he be that naïve?"

"He's a genuine man of the cloth, Julia. Pruitt said

he is virtuous and trusting and all that moral stuff. He's too trusting for his own good. It is not in his nature to doubt people's motives or suspect their actions, even after what happened to him with his wife."

"Why? What happened with his wife?"

"I think she cuckolded him. I don't know all the sordid details, mind you, but I do know that he was outraged when he found out about her betrayal. It was not a pretty situation. He wanted nothing to do with her, so he sent her away to live with her parents, while he left a living he held near Dover and moved to Sunbury to become a curate. She died a few months later, though Pruitt never said how. He just said that Rodman was a broken man after his wife's affair and has never quite recovered from the pain of her infidelity."

Stunned, Julia could not speak. She lost her breath and her ability to form words as the room spun for a moment at the irony. She hated irony. Detested it. And in this case, the Fates had been quite perverse in their mockery.

Charles took one last sip of tepid tea and regarded the dregs remaining in his cup as he contemplated the concept of irony. How ironic was it that the one woman in the world he least wanted to ask for assistance was the one woman who held his fate in her hands? His chances of obtaining this living now had essentially evaporated like the steam from his now-cold tea. He might as well go wait in the carriage for the duke. There was very little hope that Lady Julia would appoint him parish vicar after their unpleasant interaction this morning.

He winced the moment he realized she was the duke's sister. Why her? Why did it have to be the woman who'd knocked him over this morning? As he relived the embarrassing mishap in the Queen's Cross lobby, he mentally kicked himself again and again for his unfortunate, irritable response to her. He had told her to watch where she was going next time, for the sake of all things holy. Of course, she had provoked him with her comment about him standing too close to her, as if she were questioning his propriety. Still, the possibility that he might have mucked up his chances for this living by being ill-tempered with her earlier churned his gut.

He listened for signs of activity in the other room. Hearing none, he began speculating about what they had been discussing behind closed doors these last twenty minutes. If he were a suspicious man, he might have believed something more was afoot between his brother and the duke. Something more than a simple favor between lords, at any rate. Lady Julia's inquiry of Benthower about whether he would turn a profit from Charles's being appointed vicar struck him as particularly odd. How would one stand to profit from such an arrangement? The question bothered him as much as it boggled him. He would have to ask his brother for an explanation of that little piece of information.

In the meantime, Charles thought it more likely that Lady Julia was recounting for her brother the scene in the hotel lobby earlier this morning. No doubt she was berating him as a rude, improper, insensitive dolt and questioning his fitness for a position as vicar, a role that required tact and compassion in dealing with people. Would she even appear again in person to reject his application, or would she leave it to the duke to deliver the bad news?

The door to Lady Julia's sitting room opened, interrupting his thoughts. *Finally*. He stood to greet her brother at least, and to his surprise, she walked into the parlor alongside him. Charles held his breath as he glanced between them searching for any indication of how their conversation had gone.

His gaze landed on Lady Julia, and not for the first time, he was struck with the unwelcome realization that she was an attractive woman, with hair the color of burnished copper, offsetting her cinnamon eyes to perfection. Those eyes. Never had he been so captivated by a pair of eyes in his life, and this thought bothered him. Not even Eleanor had captivated him so with her simply brown eyes, and a strange pang of guilt hit him at the thought, as though he were betraying her. He quickly banished the emotion as rubbish, however. Eleanor had betrayed *him*, not the other way around. Still, even more troubling than memories of his late wife's unfaithfulness were these inappropriate thoughts of Lady Julia as a desirable woman. It was wildly improper to think of her in those terms, especially if there were the slightest chance that she would become his patroness.

At that, he laughed to himself. Likely, he would not have to worry about becoming Lady Julia's appointed servant to the Church. Likely, she had rejected her brother's wishes. Still, he searched her face once again for any hints of how things had gone. Not well, if her stoic, somber—almost sad—expression were any indication. In fact, he was about to grab his hat to take his leave as he regarded her cheerless eyes, certain that all was lost, when he glanced at her brother. As he watched the duke saunter into the room, he had the strange and wonderful feeling that it had all gone his way. The duke's confident smirk gave away his self-satisfaction, revealing he had gotten what he wanted.

A moment later, the duke confirmed the notion as he took Charles's hand and pumped it up and down in a firm handshake. "Congratulations, Rodman! You are to be vicar of St. Blaise's."

Charles let out the breath he'd been holding. Was it true? Was it real? He could hardly believe it. Consequently, he had no words.

"Yes, congratulations, Mr. Rodman. I want to welcome you to our parish," said Lady Julia in a tone far more subdued than her brother's.

He breathed deeply, attempting to regain his composure. "Thank you. Thank you, Lady Julia. I am most grateful for your trust in me. You won't regret it. I promise to be a good and faithful servant to the parishioners."

"Yes, well, I hope so. However, I do have a couple of questions for you before we make it official."

"Yes, yes, of course, of course. Anything. Anything you want to know. Just ask." *Good lord, Rodman. Rein it in. You don't want to alarm the woman.*

She flashed him an icy glare before speaking. Then

she drew herself up regally and looked him in the eye. "Tell me, Mr. Rodman, are you a judgmental man?"

Taken aback, Charles gaped at the question, not knowing fully how to answer it.

"Forgive me, sir. Let me rephrase that. Suppose someone—a woman, let's say—who'd committed an egregious sin in the eyes of the Lord came to you for solace, how would you handle the situation?"

He still did not know how to respond.

"What I mean is would you banish her? Berate her and tell her she deserves her suffering? Or would you have compassion for her and show her comfort?"

He hesitated. Perhaps a little too long, for Lady Julia's expression soured as she lifted a brow. Apprehensive about offending her, he ran his fingers through his hair as he formulated a response. "I suppose much would depend on the woman and the sin. Perhaps she deserves some censure."

Blast it all. How was that the wrong answer? Surely if a woman committed murder, she deserved some consequences, didn't she? But evidently, he had replied incorrectly, for Lady Julia narrowed her eyes and gave him a moue of disgust, while sweat trickled beneath his cravat.

"So, you take more of an Old Testament view of Eve and her so-called sin than, say, a New Testament view of the adulteress whose stoning to death Jesus prevented?"

Why did he have the feeling that he was well and truly had at that point? "I, uh . . . to tell you the truth, I never thought of it like that." It was all he could say.

"Ah." It was the only answer she gave.

The duke chimed in with his opinion. "So, as you can see, Julia, Mr. Rodman will make a fine vicar."

Lady Julia's countenance spoke volumes on how mistaken she thought her brother was, but His Grace seemed blissfully unaware of the dour expression she gave him.

The duke rubbed his hands together with obvious delight. "What are the next steps in the process of appointing him, Jules?"

She paused a heartbeat as she looked Charles in the eye once again. "Since you have recommended him so highly, Benthower, what I should do now is to write the bishop in Winchester notifying him of my selection of Mr. Rodman. Then I'll draw up the formal presentation deed as soon as possible. He should be installed as vicar of St. Blaise's in no time." Her tone was flat, betraying no emotion. Yet, her demeanor shouted her antipathy with the situation.

His Grace, however, actually clapped. "Wonderful!"

Charles looked between the two of them, vaguely curious as to why the duke was so thrilled with Lady Julia's recommendation and why she was so *not* thrilled. And though his appointment seemed all but sealed, he thought he ought to offer her some references at least to try and salvage what he could of her good opinion. "Would you not like to see the recommendation letter I have from my bishop, Lady Julia?"

She shrugged.

Interpreting that as a soft yes—or at least not a firm no—he reached into the inner pocket of his coat for

the note from his bishop. He also found the miniature portrait he'd recovered from the lobby floor this
morning and placed in his pocket for safe keeping. He
had forgotten to leave it with the clerk at the hotel
before he and the duke left the inn earlier. He handed
her the letter first.

She scanned it briefly and then returned it to him.
"Very good. I believe all is in order."

Benthower rubbed his hands together once again
in apparent satisfaction. "Good. It's settled then. Why
don't you pen that letter to the bishop right now, Jules,
while Rodman and I have a drink to celebrate? You do
have some whiskey around here, I presume?"

She rolled her eyes at her brother and then moved
toward a desk in the corner. "Over by the bookshelves
you'll find some."

"Rodman, let's toast, shall we?" Benthower poured
a glassful of whiskey for himself and one for Charles.

Though he took the drink with some hesitation,
Charles wanted more than anything to indulge in
something that might alleviate some of his apprehension. He didn't feel perfectly comfortable imbibing
at such an early hour in front of Lady Julia, however.
Would she think it at all improper? He looked to her
brother for guidance, but His Grace seemed oblivious
to his sister's sensibilities, leaving Charles no choice but
to make his own best decision.

"To your appointment as vicar of St. Blaise's." Benthower raised his glass and clinked it against Charles's.

Charles sipped his drink, while the duke downed
his in one long gulp.

"Julia, care for any whiskey to celebrate?" asked Benthower.

"No. Not at this time of day, thank you." Her clipped tone left no doubt as to her position on drinking so early.

Charles set his glass down, resolving to drink no more. He only hoped that having had a sip in the first place was not another black mark against him, like this morning's encounter with her at the inn. And the obviously wrong answer he had given her a moment ago about the fallen woman.

"Have you finished with that letter?" asked her brother.

"Almost. I'm just letting the ink dry."

"Good. Rodman and I will deliver it ourselves to the bishop in Winchester on our way back to London. We want to make sure he is installed as soon as possible."

While His Grace poured himself another drink, Charles took the opportunity to step quietly over to his new patroness. She stood dripping hot wax on the folded letter and pressing her seal into it. Her eyebrows rose in surprise when he neared the desk. He inclined his head to direct her attention toward his hand. Then, as discreetly as possible, he opened his fingers and held out the miniature portrait in his palm. "I believe this is yours, Lady Julia. I found it on the floor of the inn after the baggage had been cleared away."

She gasped when she saw it, her face brightening at once. He was so taken aback by her stunning eyes as she raised them to meet his gaze that he struggled to catch his breath. Truly, this was not an appropriate re-action to her now that she was his patroness. She stared at him for a moment, her expression filled with some-thing like astonishment and gratitude. Afraid that his own gaze might reveal something even he wasn't ready to grapple with yet, he looked down at the portrait once more. He watched her as she took the miniature from him with trembling fingers and ran her fingers over the glaze. He nearly came undone at her smile. It lit everything around her.

He glanced down at the portrait again. Who was this little girl? Someone very dear to her, obviously. Lady Julia sniffled as she stared at the likeness. After a moment, she recovered her composure and stashed the picture in the pocket of her shirt. Her *kameez*, had she called it?

"Thank you, Mr. Rodman," she whispered. "I'll never be able to thank you enough."

"No need to thank me at all, my lady. I am only happy to have found it."

CHAPTER 3

*Two of Swords: Stalemate, conflict of two equal
and opposing forces, difficult choice between dis-
parate beliefs . . .*

TWO WEEKS LATER, CHARLES STRUGGLED
to identify the reason for the vague sense of disappointment and irrational anger pestering him as he
stood outside St. Blaise's Church following his induction and institution ceremony. Family and friends
surrounded him offering congratulations and wishing
him well after the pomp and circumstance of the rite
were over. He also received countless introductions to
the parishioners who had attended the ceremony. It
was almost perfect, and as he breathed deep the fresh
summer air, he tried to feel the joy and satisfaction the
situation occasioned, but something was missing. Or
more precisely, someone was missing: Lady Julia. With
increasing indignation and annoyance, he had felt her
absence throughout the celebration. Why was she not
here? She was his patroness, after all. Her absence and
apparent lack of concern for matters to do with the
Church sent a clear message not only to him but, more
importantly, to the parishioners that spiritual affairs did

not signify to her.

It was simply insupportable, and he would have to talk to her about it. When the crowd around him dissipated somewhat, he stood alone at the top of the steps to the church mentally composing the speech he would give her the next time he saw her.

"Charles?"

Ugh. That voice. He cringed at the shrill and familiar sound, so much like a fork screeching across a plate that it disrupted his concentration and disturbed his peace. And as his sister approached, he searched for a place to hide. Turning, he paced toward the church doors to take cover inside the narthex.

"Charles! There you are."

Too late. She had seen him.

"Where were you going? Didn't you hear me call your name?"

"Yes, Caroline. I heard you. They probably heard you all the way to London."

She shooed away his comment with a flick or her hand. "Oh, nonsense. But if you heard me, why were you heading into the church? Oh, never mind. You must meet Mrs. Chamberlain. She is the widow of the former vicar. Mrs. Chamberlain, may I present my brother, Charles Rodman?"

"How good it is to meet you, Mr. Rodman." The petite, elderly woman made a small curtsy and then stood, but not entirely upright. She remained bent slightly at the waist, her white hair and a dowager's hump imparting an air of aged wisdom.

He bowed to her in return. "The pleasure is all

mine."

"What do you think of South Kindale so far?" asked the older lady.

"I like it, from what I've seen. It's a charming little village, and I'm looking forward to getting to know it better."

"I understand Lady Woodfield is going to remain with you for a few weeks to help you settle in. It must be wonderful to have your sister here with you."

"You can have no idea what it's like." He glanced at his sister to see whether or not his subtle jab had hit its mark. Based on her narrowed eyes, it had. Good. "But that's Caroline for you—always looking out for us younger brothers." He couldn't hide the annoyance in his voice, and truthfully, didn't even try. The next few weeks promised to be a special kind of perdition with her in residence meddling in his business on the pretense of helping him "settle in."

"Someone has to watch over you." His sister, like him, did not even try to hide her sarcasm.

"Careful, Caroline, or you'll give Mrs. Chamberlain the impression that I need a chaperone."

Mrs. Chamberlain laughed. "Not at all. But you very definitely need a woman's touch in setting up your household."

"What you need, Charles, is a wife."

And that was the real reason he did not want his sister staying with him. She would be forever busy with her matchmaking schemes in an effort to get him remarried. How many times had he told her—and the rest of his family—that he would never marry again?

Not after Eleanor. He would never involve himself with another woman. Arguing with his sister, however, was futile, so rather than try it, he bit his tongue and clenched his jaw as he shot her his most menacing glare.

"You needn't look at me like that, Charles. It's obvious you need a wife, and I intend to have you married by the time I leave South Kindale."

He could only roll his eyes as he shook his head.

Mrs. Chamberlain laughed, probably at the both of them. "Finding your brother a wife shouldn't be too difficult, Lady Woodfield. We have a number of fine women to choose from in our little village. There are the Misses Brookes over there, Miss Ryder behind them, Miss Denny by the spruce tree, and Miss Smyth with her parents, to name a few. Then there are the widows Mrs. Davidson there in the blue, Mrs. Rush in green, and Mrs. Wendell talking to Mrs. Rush." In what seemed to be more an afterthought than an actual suggestion, she said, "And, of course, there's Lady Julia, I suppose, but I don't know that she's not spoken for."

A strange and unwelcome sense of displeasure settled in Charles's chest on hearing that his patroness might be spoken for, and he wasn't sure which disturbed him more—the actual *notion* that she might have a love interest or his absurd *reaction* to the notion that she might have a love interest.

"Is Lady Julia here today?" asked Caroline. "I would like to meet her."

Mrs. Chamberlain shook her head.

"She is not ill, I hope," said Caroline.

"Oh, I don't think so. I heard that she was off to London a week ago today. She should be back the day after tomorrow, I'm told."

Caroline's lips turned downward in a frown. "It's odd that she missed Charles's ceremony today. She's the parish patroness, is she not?"

Mrs. Chamberlain nodded. "Indeed. But, you know, she never does attend church."

"For heaven's sakes, why not?"

Mrs. Chamberlain shrugged. "I hardly know. All I can tell you is that when Edgar was vicar, he could never convince Lady Julia to do her duty and return to the fold, so to speak. No matter how many times he talked to her, she never once came to church. It was quite disheartening to him—and to the other parishioners as well, he felt."

Caroline shook her head in apparent disappointment. "Well, that's a shame. But, if she doesn't attend church, I have to rule her out as a potential mate for Charles. We can't have a vicar's wife who won't attend church. However, I suppose it is a moot point. You said she might be spoken for anyway, did you not, Mrs. Chamberlain?"

Once again, an odd sense of discontent settled in Charles's chest as his heart produced an eccentric little thud at the question. If he were honest with himself, he would've said he was more interested in the answer than the situation merited, which was absurd. Why should he care if Lady Julia belonged to another, after all? Moreover, the conversation was beginning to feel more like gossip than anything else, and since he wanted to keep himself above such prattle, he only half-listened to Mrs. Chamberlain, until her assertion that Lady Julia frequently had a man staying alone with her at the hunting box. Then she had his full attention.

Caroline's theatrical gasp at the scandalous news echoed his own shock, but he remained silent.

"Oh, but it is true, Lady Woodfield." Mrs. Chamberlain made a distasteful moue with her mouth before leaning in to continue her account. "He's frequently out there with her. *Alone.*"

Caroline whipped out her fan and cooled her face with it. "Goodness."

"I suppose it's not fair to jump to conclusions with Lady Julia not here to answer for herself, however," said Mrs. Chamberlain. "The man may be a relation, after all."

Caroline nodded but didn't answer, and though Charles was insanely curious to hear more about Lady Julia and her frequent male guest, he decided it best not to engage in hearsay about his patroness. "Well, if you ladies will excuse me, I'm going to speak with the bishop before he leaves. It was very nice meeting you, Mrs. Chamberlain."

"The same here, Mr. Rodman. I wish you good luck in your ministry."

He merely nodded and bid them farewell. In the back of his mind, though, he decided that he would see whether or not Lady Julia attended services next Sunday, and if she did not attend, then he would do his duty as her vicar and visit her to discuss her absence from church—and perhaps inquire about her regular gentleman visitor.

A week later, as he drove his gig out to visit Lady Julia, Charles contemplated how he would broach the subject of church attendance with her. She had missed services this morning, and that irked him more than her absence from his induction and institution ceremony last week, especially when he heard from his sister that she had returned from London on Friday. She could have come to church today, and when she did not, he could draw no other conclusion than that she had intentionally avoided services.

His only regret now, as he turned the gig up the lane to the hunting box, was that he had announced his intention to visit Lady Julia after church to his sister. Caroline, naturally, had insisted on accompanying him so that she could meet the woman and offer her friendship. He guessed, more likely, that his sister had an ulterior motive, something to do with appraising Lady Julia's potential as a match, unless he misread her intentions.

She had nattered away non-stop, talking of nothing but Lady Julia the whole way to the hunting box, of Lady Julia having spent four years in India with her husband, Mr. Niles Lacey; of her husband's untimely death a couple of years ago from the ague that he contracted while in Calcutta; of how well she was regarded in the community, regardless of the fact that she often had her male "friend" staying alone with her; of her charitable works in London and in the parish here in South Kindale; and most of all, of the mysterious women living at her home for reasons unknown to the general community, while she lived farther out of town in her husband's remote hunting box.

How his sister had come by all this knowledge about Lady Julia was no real mystery. No doubt she had uncovered these details through gossip. She was nothing if not notorious for her ability to unearth information from any source, in this case from parishioners, many of whom she debriefed daily when she visited them on his behalf, ostensibly.

As he pulled the gig to a stop in front of the hunting box, he asked the Good Lord for forbearance this afternoon in dealing not only with his sister but also with Lady Julia. He only hoped he could tamp down his annoyance with Caroline as she intruded on his business and rein in his displeasure with Lady Julia as he questioned her about why she had not attended church this morning.

He stepped down from the gig and assisted Caroline down as well. They walked together to the porch of the hunting box, and he rapped on the door.

"Mr. Rodman!"

He turned toward the voice behind him to see Lady Julia emerging from a wooded area with a gentleman beside her.

"To what do I owe this honor?"

She approached the porch, and Charles's breath hitched as he took in her stunning beauty. Blast it all. That she affected him this way unnerved him, and he silently upbraided himself for his reaction. He redirected his attention to the tall gentleman walking next to

her and attempted to school his features into something like indifference, but resentment sliced through
him at seeing the other man with her. Who was he?
Was he the one who often stayed out here alone with
her? And just what was his relationship with Lady Julia?
And moreover, must he be so blasted good looking?

"Lady Julia." Mr. Rodman bowed in greeting, and
as he rose, his face clouded over with some emotion,
one she couldn't quite put a finger on, but which she
sensed was disapproval. "I ventured out to visit you this
morning hoping you might be able to spare some time
for a little chat."

Oh, lord. She stifled an eye roll. What could this be
about? She feared she knew.

She approached him on her doorstep and regarded
his chiseled features. Lit by the afternoon sun, his fair
hair and face glowing in its light, he looked like a veri-
table god. She laughed a little to herself at the blasphe-
mous notion. As a minister of God, he really shouldn't
be looking like a god, after all.

She turned her attention to the attractive woman
by his side. Who was she? "Of course, Mr. Rodman.
Won't you join us for some tea? And may I present Mr.
Arthur Drake from London? Arthur, this is our new
vicar, Mr. Rodman."

As Arthur and the vicar bowed to one another, Julia
reflected that nearly three weeks had passed since she
met Mr. Rodman and appointed him as vicar to the
parish. In that time, she still had not formed a firm
opinion of him. She didn't know what to make of

him. Their initial interaction at the inn had been antagonistic, and his admission that he might be a harsh judge when he answered her question about the fallen woman still bothered her. However, in the weeks since their introduction, she had received so many testimonial letters from his former parishioners endorsing him and praising his service as their curate that she had been, quite frankly, a little shocked that he was so well loved. In general—and on principle—she disliked men of the cloth for their proselytizing and their severity, but perhaps he wasn't such a bad person after all. He might just prove to be a true find, a real treasure for the parish.

Pity, however, that she wouldn't be partaking of the spiritual counsel Mr. Rodman had to offer, but the Church of England and she had parted ways three years ago. The Church—or rather, a very judgmental vicar—had failed her when she had most needed succor in her life, and she didn't want it—or this new vicar, Mr. Rodman—meddling into her spiritual affairs these days, not when she had her yoga and her meditation to bring her closer to her concept of God—and peace.

Arthur and Mr. Rodman stood on either side of her as they sized each other up, and that unidentified emotion she had sensed from the vicar earlier—disapproval, was it?—played over his features once again. What was he thinking? Did he object to Arthur's presence? Surely, Mr. Rodman had heard from the locals that she had a male guest staying alone with her from time to time at the hunting box. Did he condemn that arrangement? She smiled to herself at the notion. Was it wrong to take delicious delight in shocking the vicar? She didn't care if it was. She would like to try offending him once, just to see his reaction.

She regarded the woman by his side once again. Had he remarried, and was she his new wife? Odd that Benthower had not mentioned it, if so.

The woman smiled broadly and elbowed Mr. Rodman in the ribs as though prompting him to speak. He scowled at her instead.

"Charles?" She smiled sweetly at him. "Where are your manners? Aren't you going to introduce me?"

The vicar rolled his eyes heavenward for the briefest second. Clearly, whoever she was, the woman provoked him. He answered in the flattest, most unenthusiastic monotone Julia had ever heard a person use, and she almost laughed aloud. "Of course. Please forgive me. Lady Julia, Mr. Drake, this is my sister Caroline, Lady Woodfield. Caroline, may I present Lady Julia Lacey and her companion, Mr. Drake?"

Lady Woodfield's enthusiasm, on the other hand, was almost comical. She curtsied and then gushed. "I'm so pleased to meet you at last, Lady Julia. And you, too, of course, Mr. Drake. I've heard so much about Charles's patroness from his parishioners since I've been in South Kindale that I had to meet you. When Charles said he was going to visit you this afternoon, I, of course, begged him to let me go with him."

"I'm honored, Lady Woodfield." Unsure what to make of the vicar's sister, Julia looked to the woman's brother for his reaction. He said nothing, but he had crossed his arms over his chest in what appeared to be intense vexation, if Julia were reading it right. He also scowled so severely that his lips disappeared from his face leaving just a thin, grim line. Again, Julia almost laughed aloud.

"Are you staying with your brother then, Lady Woodfield?" Arthur asked.

"Yes, for a little while, at least. I'm helping him settle in at the vicarage. I'm also reaching out to his parishioners on his behalf. I can't tell you the number of social calls I've made since I've been in town."

Mr. Rodman scowled even more deeply, if that were possible. Taking pity on him, Julia thought to rescue him from further irritation. "Let's all go inside, shall we? I'll have Burton put on some tea." She led them both through the front door past the small entryway into the parlor and instructed her maid to bring refreshments. She then invited her guests to sit, while she seated herself on a chair near the mantle.

An awkward silence settled over everyone until Julia spoke. "What brings you out to these parts, Mr. Rodman?"

He cleared his throat. "As I said earlier, I was hoping to talk with you."

"Yes, of course. About what?"

"It's more of a conversation we should have in private."

Julia couldn't help herself from laughing at his very ominous expression. "My goodness. You can't say whatever you are going to say in front of your sister and Arthur?"

He pulled at his cravat as if the thing were too tight. "I'd rather not."

Arthur rose at that moment. "Julia, dear, why don't I take Lady Woodfield out to the garden and show her around for a bit? That will give you and Mr. Rodman a chance to chat. We'll be back after a while."

Lady Woodfield leapt off the settee. "I'd be delighted to see the garden."

Arthur stepped over to Mr. Rodman's sister and offered her his arm, and the two of them left the parlor without further ado.

Once they were gone, Julia shifted in her chair. So, here she was. Alone in the parlor. With the vicar. Warm suddenly, she snapped her fan open and waved it over her face. She dreaded the discussion to come but declined to make the first comment, letting him take the conversation where he would.

He tugged at his cravat once again but took her cue. "I wanted to thank you for getting my presentation deed to the bishop as quickly as you did, Lady Julia. The institution and induction ceremony was scheduled faster than I could have imagined possible."

"I hope it was not all too fast for you."

"No, the timing was perfect." He paused a heartbeat and looked her in the eyes. "But I'm sorry you missed it."

She glanced away. "Yes, well, I suppose it is I who should apologize to you for missing the ceremony, but I'm afraid I was in London last week, visiting family." In truth, she was anything but sorry she had missed the vicar's installation into the parish. She had not wanted to attend and play loyal church hypocrite at the show, so she had left town on purpose.

He cleared his throat one more time. "I'm also sorry you missed my first service this morning. I would have liked to have had your opinion on how everything went and what the parishioners thought."

Burton brought tea in at this point, and Julia served the vicar and offered him a fresh biscuit. "I'm sure the service went just fine, Mr. Rodman. You seem like someone very capable of handling the duties of vicar. Fine weather we are having, is it not?"

"Very fine, but I would like to have your opinion— as my patroness. Do you think you will attend next Sunday's service?"

Ah. He wasn't having her attempt to divert the subject, was he? She didn't answer him at first. She was too busy trying to determine what to make of Mr. Rodman. The old parish vicar, Mr. Chamberlain, had stopped out to the hunting box on numerous occasions to encourage her to return to the Church. She had not been comfortable discussing her churchgoing habits—or lack of them—with the former vicar, and she did not wish to discuss them in any fashion with the new one either.

She suppressed an eye roll when he reiterated his question as if she had not heard it. She regarded him more closely then, and not for the first time, she noted that he was a handsome man. Alarmingly so. Were he anything other than a vicar and she anyone else but his patroness, she might have found herself attracted to him, in fact. The wildly inappropriate notion amused her while also sending a warm wave throughout her body, and she fanned herself again as she laughed aloud. Embarrassed by her sudden outburst, she managed to sober herself before speaking. "Next Sunday, you say?"

"Yes, next Sunday. Why do you laugh?"

Nerves, she supposed, and then she laughed again. "I don't really know."

"You don't really know whether you'll attend church next Sunday, or you don't really know why you are laughing?"

"A little of both, perhaps." She laughed yet again, and when he did not, she sucked in her cheeks in an attempt to stifle more laughter. "Forgive me, Mr. Rodman. In answer to your question, I don't know whether I'll be in church next Sunday. I could be back in London then, for all I know."

"Well, if you're still in Hampshire, will you not consider attending church?"

A small eye roll did escape her this time, along with a hostile huff. "Why is it so important that I attend church next Sunday—or at all, Mr. Rodman?"

He leaned forward in his seat and rested his arms on his knees. In doing so, he looked so thoroughly handsome and masculine as to nearly beguile her into stupidity. "Because it is your duty to attend church on Sundays."

After a moment of staring at him, she regained her senses, along with her consternation and her voice. "Oh, really? I don't understand. Why it is my duty?" She tried to contain her growing irritation with the vicar, but it was the same argument Mr. Chamberlain had given her so many times.

"Because it is the duty of every good Christian to honor God on the Sabbath and because you are the patroness of the living here in South Kindale. Your absence from church sets a very poor example for all the other parishioners."

"Rubbish!" The word was out of her mouth before she could stop herself. His eyes widened, while her hand flew to her mouth. She had crossed the line of propriety and regretted the outburst at once, as she tried to rein in her anger. "Excuse my language, Mr. Rodman, but I don't see how my churchgoing habits should have any affect one way or the other on the other parishioners."

"I believe your habits do affect the other parishioners."

She huffed once again. "Why?"

"Because you are the parish patroness and the daughter and sister of a duke. People look up to you. They admire you. They want to be like you. If you were to cut your hair as short as a man's, why, it would soon become all the fashion around here. Don't you see, Lady Julia?" His voice filled with obvious emotion. "You are not only an official of the church, you are also a paragon in this little community, and people follow your example." He then sat back in his seat.

"Let me ask you this, Mr. Rodman. Has there been poor attendance because of my absence?"

"Well, not directly that I am aware of, but you never know what people will do in a close-knit community like this."

She inhaled deeply, trying to calm her agitation. "Well, until such time as people stop going to services because I don't go, I am sorry, but I must tell you that I don't attend church as a rule."

"May I ask why not?"

"I . . . I just don't like to. May we leave it at that?"

"No, we may not. It's important that I understand your viewpoint. Why don't you like to attend church, Lady Julia?"

How could she put into words her feelings about the Church without offending him—or revealing too much? "Let us just say that I get nothing out of it, for one thing. I feel no connection to the Church." Although this was the truth, it was by no means the entire truth. "I have no need of the Church—or God, for that matter. At least not your Christian God."

"No need of God?" He shot out of his chair and stood before her in obvious alarm and indignation. "Why, that's blasphemy. Everyone needs God."

She shrugged. "I don't."

He shook his head as though she had just slapped him. "Then whom do you offer your prayers to at night? And who provides you solace in times of need?"

She shrugged. "Lord Ganesh, I suppose."

This time, he scrubbed his hands down his face in obvious exasperation. "And who is Lord Ganesh?"

Uncomfortable with his question, she rose and strode to the window, which overlooked the backyard and garden. Pulling back the curtain, she spotted Arthur and Lady Woodfield strolling amongst the plants. "He is a Hindu deity, the breaker of obstacles. The son of Parvati and Shiva."

Startled by his sudden footsteps, she turned as he stomped toward her at the window, his arms stretched wide in obvious dismay. She nearly laughed as he regarded her with sheer horror. He huffed out his breath while staring at her for several seconds in distress before responding. "You mean to tell me that you worship an *Indian* god? Because that violates the First Commandment."

"Don't look so alarmed, Mr. Rodman. 'Revere' is more the word. As I would revere a Catholic saint or Martin Luther."

He narrowed his eyes as though he didn't trust her explanation. "So you do not put this Hindu god above the one true God? I absolutely could not condone that, if you do."

She wanted to laugh at the level of torment this conversation was causing him, not because she was happy to see him suffer—well, maybe she was just a *little* happy about that—but because it was so entertaining to see him bothered by something so very trifling. "Not if it will make you feel better. In truth, Mr. Rodman, there is only one God among them all anyway. Even the Hindus with their many gods revere Brahman as the one source of the phenomenal universe."

He shook his head in unqualified disbelief. "The one source of the phenomenal . . . *what*?"

"Universe. The tangible world. The physical plane, which is truly only an illusion."

"An *illusion*?"

"Yes, an illusion. Nothing—none of this is real. We

are all caught in the grips of our own misunderstanding of the true nature of reality."

He appeared horror-stricken. He also appeared to waver between wanting to discuss further what she had just said and wanting to ignore it completely. Finally, he scrubbed his hands down his face, as he had done before when he seemed to be at the end of his wits. "What about our God?"

"I would hardly call him mine, but I believe *your* God is the same as Brahman." She could have smacked herself across the forehead for that remark. She should have known better than to say something that could only incite argument.

Indeed, he inhaled in abject shock. "You mean to say that you believe that *our* God is the same as this Indian god?"

She shrugged. "Yes, essentially. *Your* God is the same as the Indian God. Whom I prefer to pray to."

He regarded her for a moment, his head cocked to one side. Then he threw his arms up in what appeared to be hopeless exasperation. "That—that's heresy, Lady Julia."

She merely laughed at his indignation.

"Do you still believe in Jesus Christ?" he asked with caution.

She shrugged once again. "In a fashion, I suppose. I believe Christ is an avatar of God—or Brahman, if you will—who died for our sins so that we wouldn't have to suffer in death any longer. So that our journey from one lifetime to another could end and we could become one with God once again."

He stared at her in true revulsion this time. "Where on earth do you come up with these notions?"

Again, she shrugged.

"You do realize, of course, that they're heretical?"

"Probably so, Mr. Rodman. But I'm fortunate in that there's not a thing anyone can do about it these days."

He shook his head once again, and then his features softened. "Yes, not to worry, Lady Julia. Thankfully for you, the Kingdom no longer executes heretics."

His emphasis on that last word amused her, and she smiled at him once again. "You think me a heretic?"

"Completely." He put his hands on his hips and turned away from her briefly, as though she stymied him. Then he turned back to her. "So, tell me, where did you learn these heretical beliefs? Who taught you to do—what was it you were doing the day your brother brought me by to meet you?"

"Oh, you mean yoga?"

"Yes. What is that, and where did you learn it?" His question sounded more curious than derisive this time.

"It's a relaxation technique I learned to use in India to meditate and calm my nerves." She hoped he would not ask her whom she had learned it from in India because she did not wish to discuss Renesh.

Fortunately, he didn't ask her to explain who had taught it to her. Instead, he asked, "To meditate?"

"It's difficult to explain to the uninitiated, Mr. Rodman."

He quirked a brow at her. "The uninitiated. I see. Well, what were you muttering as you 'meditated'?"

"*Om gum ganapatayei namaha?*"

He merely nodded.

"It's a mantra."

"And what exactly is a mantra, if I may ask?"

"Again, it's difficult to explain, but I suppose you could think of it as a 'prayer.' Yes, indeed, I was praying."

"To this Lord Ganesh?"

"Yes."

"Why him? Why not our God?"

She turned away from him and walked back to her chair where she sat once again. "Because Lord Ganesh is the remover of obstacles."

He joined her, sitting in the chair next to hers by the mantle. "You were praying for the removal of obstacles?"

She nodded and looked down at her hands.

"What obstacles, if I might ask?"

Ought she to tell him? Ought she to confide in this man, this potentially very judgmental man of the cloth, what her goal was and the obstacles that prevented her from achieving it? No. Absolutely not. Not yet, anyway. Taking him into her confidence now would not feel appropriate when she hardly knew him. "I prefer not to discuss them, if you please."

"Will you at least tell me why you don't pray to *our* God for assistance in removing your obstacles? He will help you."

She raised a brow at him and weighed her words, trying to keep them from sounding too caustic. "Because *your* God has failed me on more than one occasion. I have no confidence in His willingness to help me. He hasn't so far."

He put his hand to his heart. "You wound God with your words, my lady. And me as well." With pain etched across his features, he continued, "As His representative here on earth, I can tell you that God will take care of you according to His plan."

She fisted her hands as her ire rose. "His plan! His plan? What about my plan?"

"Ours is not to question the will of the Lord, but just know that He will help you, if you will but ask Him for His succor and trust in His Church."

"Never." Nearly shaking now, she stood. "Never again will I trust in Him, in His Church, or in His clergy—*especially* not His clergy."

Mr. Rodman also stood at that statement with obvious zealousness. "Why not? How is it that have we alienated you so much, Lady Julia?"

It was an impassioned plea for her to tell him all that had gone wrong in her life, but she did not wish to go into the reasons why the Church had alienated her. Not with the vicar. There would be tears and pain on her part, accusations and judgment from him most likely, and she couldn't stand to see the censure in his eyes. She did not wish to display that level of vulnerability to anyone, but especially not to him. She turned her gaze away from his too-intense scrutiny. "I'd rather not discuss it, if you please."

"As you wish." He was silent for several seconds until, finally, he cleared his throat, probably to get her attention. "Lady Julia?"

She turned back to find him scrutinizing her,

his eyebrows drawn together in obvious concern, as though he were reluctant to end the discussion. "Yes?"

He lifted his hands in supplication. "Is there anything I can say—or do—to persuade you to come to church next Sunday?"

"Not a thing, I'm afraid."

He raised his hands in surrender then, resignation evident on his features at her adamant tone. "Then I suppose I should be on my way."

At last. Relief flooded her senses—and her expression, most likely.

"I should try to find my sister. Where do you suppose she and Mr. Drake are?"

"I saw them out back in the garden a minute ago. Why don't you wait here while I run out to fetch them?"

He nodded but said nothing. She dashed out of the parlor to escape him and made her way through the kitchen to the backyard. She opened the back door and scanned the yard for Arthur and Lady Woodfield, but neither was anywhere in sight. Odd. How could they have wandered off in so little time? She ran down a couple of paths through the garden past flowers, shrubs, and herbs, but could find them nowhere. Exasperated, she returned to the parlor.

"I am sorry, Mr. Rodman. I couldn't find them, but I'm sure they're around here . . ." Breathless from running, she stopped short when she saw him paging through a book with one hand, while he held it in the other. ". . . somewhere . . ." Startled by her voice, apparently, he jumped back nearly a foot. "Oh. Please forgive me, sir. I didn't mean to frighten you."

He lifted his gaze from the open book, as a deep, crimson flush blossomed across his cheeks. Eyes wide, he stared at her in unmistakable embarrassment.

"Is something the matter?"

He appeared unable to speak as he slammed the book shut. Curious, she stepped closer to investigate what had him so alarmed. Ah. Well, no wonder he blushed. Heat rushed to her own cheeks as she stood there not knowing quite what to say. They stared at one another for what seemed an eternity, his thoughts inscrutable, until she finally cleared her throat and said, "I see you've found the *Kama Sutra.*"

After several seconds, he recovered his voice. "*Kama* what?"

"*Sutra. Kama Sutra.* I must apologize. I'm terribly sorry, but I completely forgot about it. Arthur must have left it out here with the other books on the shelf after he was done with it. It really belongs in my private collection." She held out her hands waiting for him to give her the book. "I'll just put it away." When he didn't immediately hand it over to her, she quirked her head to the side and smiled. "Unless, of course, you'd like to read it. I have to say, it *is* fascinating. It's an instructional manual from India, mostly on the art of pleasure, though it also counsels a man on how to be a good husband and citizen."

He blinked but didn't reply.

She laughed nervously, not knowing whether she should continue explaining the book or simply drop the subject. His expression of mild horror amused her, however, and provoked her to badger him further. "I found a very old, very worn copy of the manuscript at a bazaar in Calcutta, and a very dear friend had it translated and re-illustrated for me into what you see now. You're welcome to borrow it."

"No, no," he choked out. "No, I thank you, but, uh . . . I shan't need it." He thrust it toward her.

His distress was comical, and the urge to tease him—just a little more—seized hold of her. "Did you happen to see the illustration on page forty?" That was bad of her. Very bad.

He shook his head, apparently at a loss for words.

Smiling, she reached for the book. "I'd be happy to show it to you. It's one of Arthur's favorites." Oh, what wicked fun. She was taunting him without mercy now, she realized, but his reaction was so entertaining—almost adorable—that she couldn't help herself. When he said nothing, she plucked the book from his hands and flipped it to page forty, revealing a couple in a pose so erotic that even she raised a brow when she saw it again. She stepped closer, turning the book toward him as she tapped the illustration. "This is the one."

As he peered down at the picture, his eyes widened a fraction. She suppressed a grin as she sensed this very staid and proper vicar's inability to look away, ensnared by his own carnal instincts. He examined the image for several seconds and then lifted his eyes to hers. Something unexpected—something primal—flashed in his expression then, and her knees wobbled and nearly buckled under the intensity of his gaze as it smoldered and bored into her soul. He gently tugged at the book, removing it from her grip, and in so doing, inadvertently brushed her fingers with his own. She wanted to pull away from him, but so help her, she could not break the contact, and suddenly, the tables turned. Suddenly, this was no longer her little game, her amusing trifle. Suddenly, it was very real. All humor vanished as she realized the joke was now very much on her.

As their fingers lingered one atop the other, he caressed her, subtly, ever so slightly. Or had that been her imagination? Whatever it was, it sent a flutter throughout her lower belly. Their eyes locked. The air between them crackled with unmistakable desire, and Julia's breath hitched as the sparks flying between them threatened to ignite into a conflagration.

Even Arthur and Lady Woodfield's sudden entrance into the parlor was barely enough to douse the fire burning between them. And even though he dropped his hand from hers and slammed the book shut, her heart pounded and her pulse throbbed in uncomfortable places throughout her body as he continued to stare at her.

"Charles?" Lady Woodfield's voice still did not break the spell between them.

Though he backed away from Julia, he did not drop his gaze, and she burned under his scrutiny. "Gather your things, Caroline. We should go."

He still did not look away from her, and she could not force herself to look away from him.

"Leaving so soon?" Arthur asked.

Mr. Rodman did not answer, as though he had not heard the question. Or perhaps he was just ignoring it. He continued to hold her gaze for two heartbeats. Two very astonishing and intense beats of the heart. "Yes, Mr. Drake. Let's go, Caroline. We must be on our way. Now."

"Oh, but I didn't get to talk to Lady Julia."

Finally, the vicar shifted his eyes away from her, and she could breathe again. He set the book back on the shelf and stepped over to Lady Woodfield. "Perhaps you'll find another opportunity to visit." He took her arm and began leading her out of the parlor toward the front door.

Arthur raised his hand in protest. "Nonsense, nonsense. You both must stay to dinner. Shouldn't the vicar and his sister eat with us, Julia?"

Too affected by her silent but powerful interaction with Mr. Rodman, Julia could only nod.

"Won't you join us then, Mr. Rodman and Lady Woodfield?" Arthur said jovially.

"Oh, yes, let's do, Charles!"

The vicar's mouth formed that thin, grim line Julia had come to recognize as his look of disapproval. She had seen it enough during their earlier conversation about her beliefs to know when he was displeased, and he was displeased now. What was he thinking? Had their unspoken exchange upset him? It had surely upset her. She only wanted him gone so that she wouldn't have to examine her reaction to him with too much honesty. And hopefully, she would not see him again for a very long time.

After a few seconds, however, he finally replied, "Yes. Yes, of course. I—we—would be delighted to join you."

His somber expression belied his words, and Julia wagered he had just broken the Ninth Commandment.

CHAPTER 4

Seven of Wands, reversed: Backing away from challenge, avoiding conflict, unwilling compromise, avoidance of disagreement through reluctant truce . . .

WELL, WHAT WAS HE SUPPOSED to do when faced with an invitation to dinner? Turn it down? He couldn't very well do that. Not with Caroline standing there in raptures over the notion, eagerly encouraging him to accept the offer. He sensed, however, that Lady Julia had not been particularly pleased when Mr. Drake had invited them to stay, and even less so when Charles had accepted the invitation. More likely, if her humorless features were any indication, she would have preferred that he be on his way and never darken her door again.

In truth, he would have preferred that as well. Lady Julia unsettled him, wholly and completely. He didn't know what to do with her. He hadn't courted many women in his youth. Two perhaps, other than his wife, and as a consequence of his limited experience, he had never developed the exceptional skills at seduction that his brothers and friends had. Nor was he as adept as they were at stirring a woman's passions or even knowing when a woman was receptive to his advances. Still, he knew enough about a woman's desire to know that she had been as affected by their silent interchange as he had. The heat in her eyes had only increased the hunger raging inside him. He could barely contain it or his arousal. And that scared him.

He had not been with a woman in six years. Not since his wife died. He had pursued no one in the intervening years for fear of being hurt again. He had, therefore, become something of an expert at tamping down his sexual appetite, an ascetic almost, but he had nearly lost all control with just the brush of her finger against his. It was ludicrous how aroused he'd become at just a touch. He probably would have exploded with a kiss or an embrace.

This attraction to her was not good. It was entirely inappropriate given the circumstances. More than inappropriate, it was insane, and he needed to rein it in before complete chaos ensued. What a conflict it would be if he were to act on his desire. She was essentially a heretic, for one thing. How could he preach the word of God to his flock when his own wife sat in a corner somewhere repeating her pagan mantra to an Indian deity? She was his patroness for another. How would it look to the Church and his parishioners if he were to marry the woman who gave him his post? And third, he sensed a passion so unbridled in her as to frighten him. How would he be able to satisfy a woman of her nature when he hadn't been able to please his first wife?

Even without the conflict of becoming involved with her, Lady Julia was far too tempting. Remaining rational while he discussed—or rather argued against—her beliefs with her earlier that afternoon had been a monumental challenge, especially when he was so tortured by an unparalleled urge to take her in his arms and kiss her until she couldn't speak any more about the illusions of the physical world.

Then there had been that book. That—that damned book from India. What had she called it? *Kama* something? What was a gently bred noblewoman like herself doing with a book of plates depicting human sexual congress? In varying positions? Some of which he had never even imagined, and of course, never tried. And when she had shown him the illustration on page forty, he'd nearly lost his mind. Though he knew her game, though she had clearly been teasing him—mocking him, toying with his sensibilities—he had been unable to regulate his body's response to her taunt. As he examined the image, the thought of imitating that pose—particularly with her—had him so aroused that he had almost succumbed to temptation and his baser impulses and ravished her there and then. Thank God Caroline and Mr. Drake had entered the room at that moment. He shivered when he thought about what would have happened between him and Lady Julia had they not.

Half an hour later, after he had cleared his mind of all improper images and regained his senses, they all sat around a modestly appointed table in the dining room. The meal was an informal affair. Lady Julia did not even dress for it, wearing instead the gown she had worn that afternoon. Drake also wore his day clothes, and as Charles accepted a bowl of sautéed carrots from him, he asked the man the one question that had bothered him most since meeting him. "So, what brings you out to Hampshire, Mr. Drake?"

"Oh, I happened to meet up with Julia when I was in London last week tending to some business with my publishing company, and I decided to accompany her back to the hunting box because she has offered to help me plan and host a party that I'm having in August at my house in Somerset, not far from Glastonbury. I wanted to be here for her birthday celebration, as well."

He turned to his hostess. "When is your birthday, Lady Julia?"

She wouldn't look at him. "In twelve days."

Drake would be staying with her for nearly a fortnight? Insupportable. They weren't even married. But were they engaged perhaps? "Hmm, I see. So tell me, Mr. Drake, how do you know Lady Julia? And what is your relationship with her?"

"Charles, really. How rude," Caroline scolded him. "Such impertinent questions. You'll embarrass poor Mr. Drake."

Poor Mr. Drake? Charles wanted to punch the wall at the image he couldn't get out of his brain involving "poor Mr. Drake," Lady Julia, and the *Kama* whatever-it-was.

"Mr. Drake is Lady Julia's cousin. He told me on our walk through the garden that his father, the Earl of

Tremain, is her late mother's eldest brother."

The most irrational—and irritating—sense of relief washed over Charles upon hearing there was nothing romantic between Drake and Lady Julia. He relaxed his grip on the knife and fork he was using to cut his roasted chicken until he realized that just because they were cousins did not mean they weren't romantically involved. His thoughts soured again, and barely able to control his outrage at the idea, he grasped his utensils until his knuckles turned white. "Do you have any intention of marrying Lady Julia, Mr. Drake?"

He could've smacked himself for blurting out the question, but it needled him to think that the pair might be lovers. Nearly everyone gasped, and Caroline chastised him once again for his impertinence.

Drake, however, merely laughed. "Julia and I have known one another far too long to become romantically involved now, though I do believe she had a slight tendre for me when she was eleven—and still might, even to this day. All my cousins did, you know. Have a tendre for me, that is." He winked at her with something like insouciance. "I'd marry her if she'd just consent to it."

Lady Julia gasped and then swatted her cousin on the arm. "Arthur. Please. Quit teasing Mr. Rodman, you conceited oaf. You know perfectly well that the only one of us ever to have the slightest tendre for you was Phoebe. You also know perfectly well that I would never marry you—or *any* man, for that matter, ever again. Vile institution, marriage." The woman visibly shuddered as she took a sip of her wine.

"Oh, dear," said his sister. "Why are you so opposed to marriage, Lady Julia?"

Charles cleared his throat. "Now, now, Caroline. How rude. You'll embarrass poor Lady Julia with such an impertinent question. Marriage isn't for everyone. You know full well that I myself never intend to marry again, for instance."

His sister dismissed him with a cluck of her tongue. "Nonsense, Charles. You'll marry again. That's why I am here. You do not belong alone. You just haven't found the right lady yet."

"Ah-ah-ah, Caroline. What have I said about meddling in my personal affairs?"

Rather than answer him, she shook her head and shrugged in insincere ignorance.

He was not falling for her affectation of innocence. "I have told you not to even attempt to match me to anyone. I am happy with my situation as it is."

She raised a brow as she speared a carrot with unmistaken hostility, and in a clear effort to avoid further discussion of the matter, she turned her attention away from him toward their hostess. "Lady Julia, the garden behind the hunting box is lovely."

"If you think the one here is nice, you should see the gardens at Lexington House," Drake said.

Caroline clapped her hands together. "Oh, I would so love to see them. Do you suppose you could show me the gardens at your estate sometime, Lady Julia?"

The woman's hesitation seemed odd. "I'm not sure that's possible. I have some guests staying there and wouldn't want to intrude on their privacy with a visitor."

Caroline's smile drooped in what was no doubt disappointment. "Oh, I see." She cocked her head to the side. "I'm curious about the women living in your house. Though I have heard about them, I haven't heard why they are there."

"Your brother told you about them?" Lady Julia shot him an accusatory glare, which he deflected with a shake of his head. Clearly alarmed, she turned her attention back to his sister. "Then who told you about the women staying at Lexington House?"

"Oh, practically everyone I have visited. The entire town knows about them."

Lady Julia's eyes shot open. "Exactly what do they know?"

"Not very much. Only that they are living at your estate while you stay at your hunting box. Naturally, everyone is curious as to why they are there."

"Naturally." Lady Julia made no other comment, leaving the obvious question on everyone's tongue unanswered.

Silence settled on the table then. No one said a word until Caroline addressed the question still hanging in the air like a criminal on the gallows at the Old Bailey. "Why *are* those women staying at Lexington House?"

Drake and Lady Julia exchanged a meaningful glance, and she released a weary breath of resignation, as though she were surrendering to the question. "I shouldn't tell you. I mean, it is meant to be a secret. If word got out about all the women living at the house clandestinely, some with their children, we would have no end to trouble."

Charles thought to relieve her from the stress of explanation. "Then we shall pry no further. Right, Caroline?"

"Oh, but you can trust me, Lady Julia. I will not say a word to anyone about why those women are living at Lexington House."

Lady Julia scrutinized his sister, as though she were assessing her trustworthiness.

Caroline put her hand to her heart. "On my word. I promise."

Lady Julia sighed once more. "Very well. They are there seeking asylum from their husbands. Protection from them, if you will. They have run away from their situations to escape the men who beat them. My sister Cassandra runs a similar home in Essex. We provide these women with food and shelter until they can make their own way. We help set them up in new homes with new identities where they can start over without the fear of having to go back to their husbands and face continual physical torment."

Astounded, Charles's mind reeled at her revelation. Essentially, she was separating married couples, keeping husbands from their wives. He didn't quite know how he felt about that. Was it even legal? Unable to formulate a coherent response, he remained silent.

Caroline clasped her hands together with apparent respect. "How very noble."

His sister's remark perplexed him. Surely, she did not approve of someone intentionally keeping a man from his wife, did she? It was an improper state, one he was certain God would not tolerate.

"Thank you, Lady Woodfield." Lady Julia smiled, and her smile affected the rhythm of his heart. "Now you understand why we must keep everything secret."

"Yes, of course, I do. I understand completely, and I admire you and your sister for your aid and generosity toward these poor women. Don't you, Charles?"

She would ask him to reveal his stance on the matter, wouldn't she? He cleared his throat and thought a moment about how best to answer. "While I understand Lady Julia's concern for these women and appreciate the fact that her intentions are out of the goodness of her heart, I'm not sure I can condone separating husbands from their wives. It's not natural. God would not approve it, and therefore, neither would the Church. And the law of the land would certainly never allow it."

Caroline gasped. "Charles, I cannot believe what you just said. God most certainly *would* approve of keeping these women out of harm's way."

Drake, meanwhile, scowled at him in obvious antipathy as he crossed his arms over his chest. As for Lady Julia, she threw her fork down on her plate with considerable force and narrowed her eyes at him. "Oh, but Mr. Rodman is *right*," she said heatedly. Her statement was more of an accusation than an acknowledgment. "The law and the Church are not on our side. They stand by a man's right to discipline his wife. In fact, they condone it. Though they may not openly approve severe brutality, they do nothing to stop it. Women are beaten every day, some within inches of their lives. That's why we must operate in secret. We have no other choice. Women—mostly from London, but some from other parts of the kingdom as well—come to us bruised in body and broken in spirit. It is a most vile situation, one without immediate remedy."

She spoke passionately, as though this cause was very dear and personal to her. Which begged the question, had she herself been beaten by her husband? If so, how despicable. Physical violence against another person, especially a woman, was a punishment too repugnant to consider. "You are right, of course, Lady Julia. Disciplining a woman with one's fists is never allowable and something that God most certainly would not sanction. However, you and your sister are wrong in separating wives from their husbands. That is not the answer."

She rose from her chair, her face flaming red, her anger palpable. "Then, what *is* the answer, Mr. Rodman?"

He stood immediately, as was polite when a woman stood. "Please, Lady Julia, I did not mean to upset you so. Please. Won't you sit down again?"

She sat. Reluctantly, he could tell, but she sat. She also crossed her arms over her chest as though she were greatly perturbed with him.

He took his seat also, and silence once again fell over the group, until Caroline once again broke it. "So, Charles," she began acerbically, "how would *you* suggest addressing violence in a marriage?"

He took a deep breath and exhaled it forcefully. "With the help and counsel of a clergyman, the couple should be able to work out their difficulties within the confines of the law through prayer."

His sister and Drake both scoffed.

Lady Julia's eyes nearly popped out of her head. Then she leaned back in her chair and uncrossed her arms to raise them in outrage. "Why am I surprised? As a man, you side with the law, of course, which makes a wife chattel to her husband. A legal non-entity. And as a *holy man*, you offer prayer as your only solution to every problem instead of recommending meaningful action." She clenched her jaw after her speech and appeared to hold herself back from saying more.

Caroline clapped. "Brava, Lady Julia! I commend you. You must continue your good work."

"Thank you, Lady Woodfield."

"Of course, my dear. But please tell me, what made you and your sister take these poor women in and give them refuge?"

Lady Julia hesitated once more with her answer, as though she were uncomfortable telling them her reasons. She looked to Drake, as if for his advice.

He nodded. "Go ahead, Julia." Anger—or something like it—flashed across his features "You should tell them. People should know what happened to Phoebe."

She inhaled and then focused her vision on something across the room. "A portrait of my eldest sister Phoebe hangs over there on that wall. She would have been thirty-two this year. She was good and kind and saw only the best in people. Trusted their motives entirely too much, believing them to be truthful and sincere in dealing with her. Our conniving brother, however, manipulated her trusting good nature for his own benefit by arranging a horrible marriage deal for her." She paused to sigh. "She had planned to marry a man whom she loved deeply the year she debuted, but when our mother died unexpectedly that spring, Phoebe went into mourning and had to postpone her wedding for a year. She promised her heart to her beloved, and he pledged to wait for her. His father, meanwhile, sent him to Canada on business that summer, but they still planned to marry as soon as they could the following year." She paused once again, this time to glance at her cousin, who stared at her sister's portrait with a blank expression that gave no hint as to his present disposition, until a muscle ticked in his clenched jaw.

Lady Julia sighed. "The wedding was postponed again, however, when Phoebe's betrothed was waylaid by business matters in Canada and couldn't return as planned for another year. Benthower, in the meantime, colluded with his friend and school chum, Lord Abadon, who wanted to marry Phoebe for her substantial dowry. He offered to split her fortune with Benthower if he could convince Phoebe to marry him. Benthower needed the money so desperately that he concocted a phony story about the man Phoebe had planned to marry, telling her that he had thrown her over for someone else and would never be returning to England because he had married this other woman. He then went on to convince her to marry Lord Abadon, telling her that the earl cared for her and would make her happy. That was a lie, of course. Abadon cared for nothing but her money and gave half of it to Benthower after marrying Phoebe."

She glanced at her cousin again. He shifted forward in his chair until his arms rested on the table, but he still stared at the portrait as though he were bored. The muscle twitching in his clenched jaw, however, belied his impassive expression. "Abadon turned out to be a beast. He beat Phoebe regularly when she wouldn't comply with his demands. She endured endless cruelty at his hands, until he finally beat her so viciously she died. Perhaps if she had been able to get away from him as these women have escaped their husbands, she would still be alive. He still lives, of course. And without any consequences because he is a lord and no one would ever charge him with a crime. My brother did call him out, which gave me some sense of justice, and although Benthower's bullet did hit its mark, Abadon's wound was not fatal."

Drake bowed his head at the words "not fatal" but didn't speak. He sat back in his chair after a moment, and when he lifted his head, his stony expression revealed no emotion. Lady Julia, meanwhile, paused a moment to drink her wine. "That was three years ago. She died a few months before my husband and I returned home in 1814. I never got to say goodbye to her, but I let women take refuge at Lexington House in honor of her the following year, after Niles died. Cassandra then set up her haven in Essex last year. We have helped over two hundred women escape their situations and start over. They have survived because they are no longer being threatened and beaten by their tormentors."

No one spoke. Most likely, because they couldn't. Minutes passed before the hush was lifted.

Caroline clutched her hand to her chest. "I'm in awe, Lady Julia. Truly in awe of you and your sister and your mission. It must have taken immeasurable strength and courage to go against the law and the Church to set up your refuges for victims of marital violence." She turned toward him then. "Well, Charles, what do you have to say now? Do you still believe Lady Julia and her sister are wrong to take these women in?"

Duly humbled—and humiliated—Charles felt as though he had been struck in the gut with the realization of what an arse he had been. Shamed over his previous remarks, he could only stare in sympathy at Lady Julia for several seconds as he silently upbraided himself. "I am sorry, Lady Julia. Deeply sorry. For your loss and for my judgment of you and your sister without all the facts. I understand now why you do what you do, and I approve of it. Wholeheartedly. How very magnanimous of you both. I admire the two of you greatly."

No one spoke then, and during the interminable pause, he was struck with the idea that he should try to help these women in some way. He hesitated a moment, trying to muster the nerve to propose his suggestion. "Lady Julia, would you introduce me to the women staying at your house? I would like to offer them my support, and I would like to see if they have any interest in Sunday services. Perhaps I could even ride out there each Sunday to perform the services so that they wouldn't have to leave their sanctuary."

She shook her head no. "Absolutely not, Mr. Rodman. There is no way. It's simply out of the question. The women are skittish about visitors, especially men, even if you are a pastor. They're also afraid of word somehow getting back to their husbands about where they are. They're afraid of being discovered and of their husbands coming for them."

"I promise to be discreet. I will not tell a soul about the women or their plight."

"Nor will I," said Caroline.

Lady Julia huffed, her mouth turning downward into a frown. She obviously did not like the idea.

"Please, Lady Julia. It is my duty as God's minister to everyone in this parish to at least offer them my support and comfort. If they do not want to accept it, I will understand and abide by their wishes."

She did not respond. Instead, she crossed her arms over her chest once more and kept her eyes focused on the portrait of her sister.

Mr. Drake finally broke the silence. "You never know, Julia. Some of the ladies might welcome the vicar's support. You could at least ask them."

She gave her cousin a hostile sidelong glance and then sighed. "Oh, very well. I guess it can't hurt to send them a note to ask them whether or not they are interested in having Sunday services performed at Lexington House. If they are interested and agreeable . . .," she paused a moment before continuing, ". . . then I guess I could introduce you to them."

"Thank you, Lady Julia." He hesitated, not sure he should push his luck by asking her to do anything more. Though her expression was still leery, he decided to be bold. "Would you be able to send them that note sometime this week?"

She shrugged. "I suppose."

"Perfect. Please let me know their decision. Perhaps I could make it out there next Sunday if they are amenable to that."

"I suppose that would be . . . fine. I *suppose*."

"Very good."

She nodded as she shifted in her chair but offered no other comment.

Mr. Drake lightened the mood with the suggestion of dessert. "And perhaps after we're done eating, you could amuse our guests by reading the Tarot, Julia."

"The Tarot? What is that?" asked Caroline.

"It's a deck of cards used for forecasting the future. Julia does uncanny readings with them. She and my other cousins learned to interpret the Tarot from our grandmother who was gifted at interpreting the cards. It's always great fun, and always very . . . revealing."

Lady Julia arched a brow at Drake. "Oh, Arthur, you know I haven't done a reading in a very long time. I'm not sure I remember how."

"Oh, rubbish. You'll remember the moment you look at the cards. It'll come back to you just like that." He snapped his fingers. "Now, do it."

"Why don't *you* do a reading, if you're so anxious for one, Arthur? Grandmamma also taught you the cards, and you're quite as gifted as she was."

"I don't have my deck with me."

Lady Julia shrugged. "Use mine then."

"You know I don't like to use anyone's cards but my own. Now, come on, Julia. Please. Let's see what's waiting on the horizon for everyone. Just for fun. It won't take long."

"I don't know, Mr. Drake," said Charles. "I don't think I want my future read. I'm not sure I want to know it."

"Oh, Charles, you are never any fun. Where's your sense of adventure? I, for one, would love to have Lady Julia do a Tarot reading for me."

"Perhaps some other time, Caroline. We really must be going soon, before it gets too late."

"Well, then, I propose another idea. Lady Julia and Mr. Drake, won't you join Charles and me for dinner at the vicarage on Friday? We would love to have you, and Lady Julia can bring her cards and do readings for us all. And perhaps by then you'll know whether the ladies at Lexington House would tolerate a visit from Charles."

"Really, Caroline? *'Tolerate'* a visit from me?"

"Yes. 'Tolerate.' I myself can barely tolerate you at times."

"You do realize you aren't *required* to stay with me, right? You are welcome to go home and interfere with your own family's affairs any time you'd like. I won't mind. Truly."

His sister dismissed him with a wave of her hand.

Drake chuckled. "Lady Woodfield, Julia and I would be happy to have dinner with you at the vicarage this

Friday, wouldn't we, Julia?"

She flashed her cousin a dubious frown. "I don't know, Arthur. We shouldn't intrude on Mr. Rodman and Lady Woodfield while they are trying to settle in at the vicarage."

"Nonsense. We will not accept no for an answer. Isn't that so, Charles?"

"Now, Caroline, if Lady Julia doesn't wish to visit us—"

"Oh, shush, Charles. They are coming. There's nothing more to discuss."

He knew better than to argue with his sister because he knew he would not win.

CHAPTER 5

Two of Wands: Discovery, new ideas, coopera-
tion, partnership, planning, progress . . .

FIVE DAYS LATER, JULIA TOOK a calming breath as she stood next to Arthur on the vicarage door-step wishing she were anywhere but here. It was not the prospect of dining with Lady Woodfield that trou-bled her so much. It was the prospect of seeing Mr. Rodman again that agitated her, especially after their miserable discussion of her beliefs and their silent but heated interaction over the *Kama Sutra* last Sunday. She didn't like Mr. Rodman. Not really. There was no denying he was attractive and that he had the poten-tial to affect her like no other man ever had. Still, he was an arse. Not only did he disparage her beliefs and practices but also he had condemned her for keeping wives from their husbands by offering them refuge in her home. True, he might have said he approved of the shelters after hearing the story of Phoebe, but when it came down to it, he was a man. And she had no doubt that, as a man, he would side with other men, the law, and the Church over a woman's fate, if ever asked to do so.

She tamped down her anxiety at seeing him again as the housekeeper and the aroma of roasting goose greeted them at the door. The smells from the kitchen soothed her nerves for a moment, but her distress rose again when the housekeeper led Arthur and her into the drawing room. She tried not to look at Mr. Rodman but failed miserably when he stood and bowed to her. His blue eyes locked with hers, robbing her of her breath and scuttling her brain. A hint of his own discomposure seemed to cloud his face when their gazes met, but he quickly recovered himself, and a staid reserve settled over him.

Lady Woodfield heralded their arrival with raptures. "Welcome, welcome, Lady Julia and Mr. Drake! I can't tell you how wonderful it is to see you both. We've certainly been looking forward to this evening. Haven't we, Charles?" Her smile indicated her sincerity, but Mr. Rodman's silence and sober expression gave Julia the impression that he had not been looking forward to the visit at all. "Lady Julia, may I say that your dress is lovely. Doesn't she look lovely, Charles?"

A warm blush crept up Julia's neck all the way to her hairline as Mr. Rodman turned to inspect her.

"Mmm." Though his response was hardly resounding, his eyes remained on her for several heartbeats as if he were appraising her appearance. And though his gaze unsettled her nerves, he left her with the impression that he liked what he saw.

"Won't you have a seat?" His sister pointed to two chairs. Arthur, to Julia's everlasting annoyance, ignored the chairs and sat beside Lady Woodfield on the settee, leaving Julia and Mr. Rodman to sit next to one another in the chairs. He seemed to take his seat with some reservation, but once he did, he turned his attention to his sister, who began a tête-à-tête with Arthur about the weather.

Julia shifted in her chair, uncomfortable with the silence that fell like lead between her and the vicar. He did not look at her or try to engage her in conversation. Instead, he rested his head on his hand as though he were thoroughly bored and only tolerated this evening because he had no choice. Julia studied him for a moment as he focused his vision on the carpet beneath his feet. What was he thinking underneath that indifferent façade? She was tempted to ask him, but he would not even glance her way, making it difficult to engage him in conversation.

Several more minutes passed in which the only two people talking were Arthur and Lady Woodfield. Their conversation now centered primarily on the recent opening of Waterloo Bridge in London, and they prattled on until finally, the housekeeper announced that dinner was ready. As everyone stood, Arthur gallantly offered his arm to Lady Woodfield and escorted her to the dining room, leaving Julia alone with Mr. Rodman. They regarded each other for an uncomfortable moment before he offered her his arm.

She took it with reluctance, much too aware of how close he was. As she touched his arm, the intensity of the contact startled her, and without warning, everything about the man overwhelmed her—his breath, his scent, his masculinity, his very presence. She could barely breathe as she followed his lead into the dining room. And when his shoulder brushed against hers as he assisted her into her chair, she thought she would faint. After he finally took his own seat at the table, she reached for her wine glass and took a fortifying sip.

"Goodness, Lady Julia. You're flushed. Are you unwell?" said Lady Woodfield.

"No, no. I am fine, thank you. Just a little overheated perhaps." She took another gulp of her drink and glanced at Mr. Rodman for his reaction.

Their eyes met again, and his lids lowered ever so slightly. His arousal was unmistakable and sent a tremor of hunger through her belly and below. She inhaled sharply as she set her glass on the table and forced herself to look away.

"And you, Charles? You look a little unsettled yourself. Are you quite alright?"

"Quite." He kept his gaze locked on her. Though she couldn't see it, she could sense it, and it unnerved her. "I'm probably just a little overheated myself." His voice rumbled low around her, as though the words were meant only for her. They caressed her skin almost sensually.

She dared not glance at him again. She might very well expire if she did.

Dinner passed uncomfortably, and as had happened in the drawing room, Arthur and Lady Woodfield were the only ones who spoke—during the entire meal. Julia tried to follow their conversation as they talked and laughed, but her attention—her whole awareness—was focused only on the man who sat to her left at the head of the table. She didn't look at him. Well, not too many times, at least. But when she did glance his way, she shivered with the realization that he always seemed to be looking at her, as though he were studying her, as though he never looked away. His constant scrutiny affected her, and if she were honest with herself, it excited her more than it alarmed her. In a couple of instances, when their eyes met, she still detected that same arousal she had seen in his gaze moments ago.

Her whole reaction to him was entirely stupid, of course. Even if he were attracted to her and she wildly attracted to him, nothing could ever come of it. She was his patroness, for one thing. She didn't like him, for another. Then there was the fact that he was an arrogant holy man who thought he knew everything there was to know about the spiritual world. And in the back of her mind was that thing Benthower had told her about the vicar's late wife, how she had cuckolded Mr. Rodman. Julia could not ignore the irony of that situation. And though the late Mrs. Rodman might not have borne her husband another man's child, as Julia had done with her husband, it was still a brutal paradox, complex enough to thwart any romantic notions she might develop for him. It would be forever impossible for her to get close to him, for he would shun her if he ever found out the truth, and he would revile her if he ever discovered her real nature.

Nevertheless, as preposterous as it was, she could not deny that he affected her in ways no man ever had. Niles had never left her breathless. He had never made her feel like a woman, much less a woman alive. Not even Renesh had stirred the passion that Mr. Rodman awakened in her with just his gaze. And his touch! Even a simple, accidental caress of his fingers or the brush of his arm was enough to ignite her like a spark to kindling. What would happen if he embraced her? Or kissed her? She would probably combust.

Stupid, stupid. *Stu*-pid. She must put this stupid train of thought out of her mind. It was pointless to dwell on her reaction to Mr. Rodman. Nothing could ever come of it.

For the rest of the meal, then, she focused her attention on Arthur and Lady Woodfield. Their conversation was lively and entertaining, and thankfully, diverting. She didn't join in, but she did listen and laugh. More importantly, she thought no more about the vicar.

Well, at least not until everyone adjourned to the drawing room after dinner. She became too aware of him once more when Arthur and Lady Woodfield chose to sit in the only available chairs, forcing her to sit next to Mr. Rodman on the settee this time. As before, everything about him overwhelmed her—his nearness, the heat emanating off him, his sigh—of resignation, was it? That he had to sit beside her, perhaps? She couldn't be sure why he had sighed. The only thing she was sure of was that, as he sat next to her, his scent of bergamot and cedar wood surrounded her like a cloak, and his very presence stoked her like a furnace.

Mr. Rodman cleared his throat, startling her back to the moment. "I almost forgot to ask, Lady Julia, were you able to write to the ladies at Lexington House about me visiting them to conduct Sunday services?"

That would be his only interest, of course, but she kept herself from rolling her eyes. "Yes, I did."

An awkward silence fell over the room when she didn't elaborate.

"And?" he asked.

She supposed she couldn't remain intentionally vague forever. "And . . . they appreciated your offer . . ."

"But they don't want me to visit."

Softened by his disappointment, she sighed. She didn't really want him visiting Lexington House, but she couldn't lie to him. "On the contrary, actually. They very much want you to visit them and perform church services on Sundays since they are unable to venture far from the home themselves." The look of childlike joy in his expression amused her. How easily the man was pleased.

"That is wonderful. I shall visit them this Sunday, then, after church here in town."

"I will need to accompany you out there, of course, to introduce you to the women myself."

"If you insist."

"And I do."

"Should I meet you there?"

"No, I think not. They haven't met you yet, and they might become agitated if you show up unannounced without an introduction. You should come out to the hunting box first. We'll both ride out in my gig so that we arrive at Lexington House together."

"Shall I meet you at the hunting box at one o'clock then?"

"If you insist."

"Oh, I do." He smiled so charmingly then that it scuttled her wits.

Lady Woodfield clapped her hands together. "Now that that is settled, it's time for some fun. Lady Julia, did you bring your Tarot cards?"

Arthur chuckled. "She nearly forgot them, but I reminded her to grab them just before we left."

That was not true. She had not nearly forgotten the cards. She had intentionally left them behind—until Arthur reminded her to fetch them. Rather than argue about it, she had rolled her eyes and retrieved the cards with considerable reluctance. Reading the Tarot for someone was an intimate act. Julia didn't mind so much doing readings for close friends or relatives, but doing them for new acquaintances, like Lady Woodfield and Mr. Rodman, was often awkward for both the querent and herself. She often became uncomfortably aware of the person's emotions—and sometimes, their thoughts—when she interpreted the cards. More significantly, the cards tended to probe intensely personal topics. Secrets could be revealed. Secrets unknown even to the querent.

Despite her reservations, she bent down and picked up her reticule where she had stowed her cards. She hoped, at least, that Mr. Rodman would decline a reading. She didn't want to read his fortune. She feared she would learn more about him than she wanted to know. And she was quite certain she already knew enough.

She reached into her beaded bag and grasped the oversized cards. Their corners were stuck in the fabric of her reticule, so she had to yank them out with considerable force. As she did so, the miniature portrait of Camille that she had received from Kitty three weeks ago—and now carried with her at all times—flew out as well. The portrait sailed through the air, bounced off the table in front of the settee, and landed on the floor at Lady Woodfield's feet.

Naturally. Because, of course, Lady Woodfield would not be able to ignore it.

Indeed, the woman reached down and picked up the picture. "Oh my, who is this lovely little girl?"

Though Julia caught Arthur's alarmed gaze, she remained calm. "That is Camille. She is the daughter of a dear friend I met in Calcutta." The statement wasn't entirely a lie. However, it wasn't the entire truth either.

"Why, she's adorable. Look, Charles. Isn't this the cutest child you've ever seen?"

Mr. Rodman took the portrait that his sister handed him. He scrutinized it thoroughly, which struck Julia as odd, given that he had to have seen it already when he found it in the hotel lobby.

"Well, Charles? Don't you think she's adorable?"

"Indeed."

Julia caught his expression as he attempted to hand her the miniature. It was a mixture of curiosity and wariness, as though he both wondered who the child was and speculated who she might be. Before Julia could take the picture from him, however, Lady Woodfield leaned forward and snatched it from his hand.

"What did you say her name was?"

"Camille."

"And her family is still in Calcutta, I take it?"

"No, actually. Her father is dead."

"And her mother?"

Julia hesitated. How should she answer that question? "Unfortunately, she is not there either." Well, at least that was not untrue.

"But she is not dead."

"No," Julia almost whispered the reply.

Lady Woodfield's smile gave way to a sympathetic frown. "How very sad. Who is taking care of her now?"

Julia took a deep breath to calm herself. "Right now, she is being cared for by some friends of mine—and her parents'. That is to say, they are her parents' friends as well as mine, but I intend to return to Calcutta to take care of her myself. Just as soon as I am able to raise the money for the trip."

Lady Woodfield cocked her head to the side in apparent curiosity. "Why are you returning to take care of the girl?"

"It is my duty to Camille to take care of her. I am the child's . . . er . . . um . . . god . . . mother." Now, that was a complete fabrication, of course.

Mr. Rodman scoffed outright. "You? A godmother?"

Lady Woodfield gasped. "Charles! Shame on you. How dare you disparage Lady Julia's role as the girl's godmother?"

Mr. Rodman merely raised a brow.

Julia shifted on the settee. "Mr. Rodman is right to question it, I suppose. He knows very well that I am not the most devout Christian."

"If you could call yourself a Christian at all."

Julia didn't miss the implication of his comment—or its surliness, but she did not reply.

His sister scolded him, however. "Charles, really. How rude. Lady Julia is a paragon. She's the very definition of Christian virtue with her charity and devotion to the unfortunate ladies at Lexington House." Lady Woodfield turned back to Julia. "Will you be returning to England with Camille?"

"No. I think not. It would be too frightening for her to leave her homeland, I believe. She is accustomed to Calcutta, so I'm going to move there permanently to be with her."

"Oh, my. What will become of Lexington House?"

"I'm afraid it will have to close, which I regret more than anything, but I will need to sell the estate for funds to return to India and settle permanently in Calcutta."

"Goodness. Do the ladies know?"

"Yes, I have told them that I need to sell, but I also promised them that I would not turn them out, not until I can find them another refuge. I will not put Lexington House on the market until all the women living there are settled safely elsewhere. The only problem I have, however, is that I will need to raise money to build or buy them a new refuge before selling Lexington House."

"Oh, dear. That is quite a problem." Lady Woodfield tapped her chin for a moment, as though she were turning the issue over in her mind. Then she sat upright with zealous enthusiasm. "I want to help you, Lady Julia, in any way I can. I will help you raise funds for a new place for the ladies living at Lexington House."

"You are very kind, Lady Woodfield, but I could never accept your offer."

"Nonsense, my dear. I am only happy to do it—as a Christian and as a friend. I will canvass all the ladies of London society for their assistance. I happen to know that most of my friends could donate some—if not all—of their pin money and not be any worse off for it."

"I'm afraid my sister Cassandra and I have already appealed to the ladies of the *ton* for their assistance. To no avail. We hardly raised a farthing."

"Oh, they'll listen to me. I don't know if you've noticed, but I can be very persuasive when I try. Plus, I'm sure Charles will help also. Won't you, Charles?"

Mr. Rodman did a double take and sat forward as his eyebrows shot up his forehead. "How do you expect me to help, Caroline?" Then, as though he realized how awful his question made him sound, he sat back and schooled his features. "That is, of course, I would be more than happy to assist, if I only knew how."

"Don't be obtuse, Charles. You can apply to your friends for donations, obviously. All those men you know from Eton and Oxford should be able to help. And our brothers and cousins also. They're all such dissipated rogues that if they gave just a tenth of the money they spend on gambling and horses to the cause, we would have enough money to build two new homes." Lady Woodfield paused a moment and then snapped her fingers as though she'd hit upon an idea. "Oh! I know! We could even host a country party at Woodfield Manor after the Season. We'll invite all your friends and my friends. And Woodfield's associates, of course."

"And then what, Caroline? We can't just solicit guests for donations for something that is supposed to be secret and that might very well be illegal, can we?"

"I don't think we need to keep the *cause* a secret. We don't want to reveal the location of the new home, for obvious reasons, but I think we can tell folks what we're raising money for. They'll understand Lady Julia's mission. I'm sure they'll even sympathize. And, if they're not comfortable donating because they don't believe in the cause or because they feel it is illegal, well, we shan't harass them. No matter how awful they are, we'll leave them alone."

Mr. Rodman seemed to think on his sister's suggestion for a moment, and then he nodded. "Oh, alright. I suppose it might work."

Julia interrupted them both at that point. "Please. Though I appreciate you both for your kind intentions, I couldn't possibly impose on you for help. It's too much to ask."

"Nonsense. We won't hear another word of protest. Will we, Charles?"

"No, of course not."

"Excellent. I'll start the guest list tomorrow."

Arthur cleared his throat. "If I may make a suggestion, Lady Woodfield, there's no need for you to host a party when I will already be having one at my estate in August. You and Mr. Rodman must come, of course. And I would be happy to invite anyone you think might be willing to donate to the cause, if you'll just give me your list of names."

Lady Woodfield clapped her palms together. "That would be wonderful. It's settled then. We'll raise funds at your house party in August, Mr. Drake."

Arthur beamed. "Now that that's settled, let's have Julia do some Tarot readings. You go first, Lady Wood-field."

CHAPTER 6

Judgment, reversed: Denial, self-doubt, sudden insight, unpleasant revelation, awakening, stark conviction, harsh verdict, reflection . . .

CHARLES PAID LITTLE OR NO attention to his sister's Tarot reading. He was far too engrossed in watching the woman interpreting the cards. She sat beside him on the settee, within arm's reach, and it was all he could do not to reach out and touch her smooth skin just so he could have contact with her. Quite simply, Lady Julia undid him. He had hoped that the unwelcome and inappropriate desire for her that had tormented him at the hunting box last Sunday had been nothing more than a fluke, a temporary lapse—a product of the moment and of his having been without a woman for so long and not of any genuine regard or interest in her.

He knew he was in trouble, however, the moment she walked into the drawing room tonight, for the desire was real. In an instant, she ignited a slow burn that only intensified throughout her visit. Her copper hair, her cinnamon eyes, her jasmine scent—they all conspired against his logic and good sense to create a longing so powerful that it had nearly consumed him by the time dinner was over.

Not good, Rodman. Not at all good.

There were too many reasons why an involvement with her was not only a bad idea, it was absolutely absurd. More than that, it was ludicrous. It could never work between them. Try as he might, though, he could not extricate himself from the fearsome hold she had on him. It was too strong for him to break free, and he was too weak to even try. Part of the reason he couldn't turn off the flame—or at least turn it down—was that he sensed something similar burning in her. Her eyes gave it away. They reflected the barely banked embers of her own desire smoldering within her whenever she looked at him.

His sister's voice cut through the haze in his brain as she snapped her fingers at him. "Charles? Did you hear me?"

What? He had been so consumed with thoughts of Lady Julia that had not been paying any attention to what was happening around him.

"I said it's your turn now. You need to shuffle the cards."

He looked down at the cards in his hand, perplexed as to how they had gotten there. "I don't know, Caroline. I don't really want my future read." He tried to give the deck to her.

"And why not?" She would not take it and pushed it back toward him.

"Because God will reveal His plan for me in His own good time." He did not miss an eye roll from both her and Lady Julia.

"Oh, Charles, where is your sense of fun? Let Lady Julia do a reading for you."

Drake chimed in then. "The reading doesn't have to be about your future, Mr. Rodman. Julia could do a reading of your past. It will give you amazing insight into past events. You'll see things anew with remarkable clarity."

Lady Julia reached out for the cards still in his hand. "Now, Arthur, don't push Mr. Rodman into doing something he doesn't wish to do. If he doesn't want to have a reading, the last thing we should do is pressure him."

Insight into the past, eh? With remarkable clarity? Huh. Intriguing. He kept the cards, and as he weighed them in his hand, he also weighed the pros against the cons of having a reading done. Curiosity sparred with caution. Did he really want to know more about the past than he already knew? Or should he leave it alone and just forget about it? Had he not moved on? Why dredge it all up again, after all? Besides, what more could the cards reveal that he didn't already know? Yet . . .

"Very well." Curiosity prevailed.

Caroline clapped. "Excellent! I can't wait."

Ignoring his sister's jubilation, he grasped the oversized cards with both hands and began shuffling them.

Lady Julia cleared her throat. "Concentrate on your questions as you shuffle the cards, Mr. Rodman. It will infuse them with the essence of your inquiry."

So many questions, mostly about his wife and his

best friend, swarmed his mind. They buzzed around him like bees to a hive. Why? Why had Eleanor betrayed him? What had he done to drive her away? Had she been looking for something that she didn't find in him? If so, what was that something? What had been missing between them? And why Dunham? Why had she turned to his erstwhile boyhood friend, the earl, of all people, to fill that void? Was she acting out in anger toward Charles? Or had she loved the earl? And what of Dunham's disloyalty? What had been his motive in taking what wasn't his? Why had he turned against Charles in the one way he knew would hurt him most?

"Charles?" Caroline's voice broke through his concentration. "Hello there, Charles, you're in a fog. Can you hear me? Are you quite done with the cards? I'm sure you've shuffled them enough. Hasn't he, Lady Julia?"

"Only he can know whether he has or not. But when you do feel like you've shuffled them enough, set them down on the table."

He shuffled once more and then he laid the deck on the table.

"Now, Charles, you need to cut the deck into three piles with your left hand. And then put them back together again with the last pile on top the first."

Confused, he scrunched his brows together as he regarded his sister. First of all, why was *she* giving him directions? And second, why cut the cards with his left hand?

Caroline laughed. "I know what you're thinking, Charles. You're thinking it's strange to cut them with your left hand, but you do it because your entire left side is more receptive to messages from the Universe."

"That's absurd."

"No, it's true! Isn't that what you told me, Lady Julia?"

The woman nodded. "At least, that's what my grandmother always said."

He shrugged and cut the cards as instructed and then gathered them into one pile again, the last atop the first.

Lady Julia picked up the deck and began rifling through the cards, as if she were searching for something.

Once more, Caroline answered for Lady Julia when he knitted his brows. "She's looking for the Significator. That's the card that represents you in the reading."

He nodded as he suppressed an eye roll at his sister's newfound "proficiency" with the Tarot. She'd had one reading, and suddenly, she was an expert. Meanwhile, Lady Julia pulled out a card depicting a man sitting on a throne holding a tall, thick truncheon upright next to him.

He nodded toward the card. "What's that?"

"That is the King of Wands. He represents you."

"Oh? How so? Why him?"

"Like you, he has fair hair and light eyes. He has strong ethics and strict morals and is very focused on his goals. The only thing about the King of Wands that doesn't fit with you is . . . oh, how do I say it?" She paused as she laughed a little. "Well, let me put it this way: the only thing about the King of Wands that doesn't quite fit with you is that he is a man of fiery passions."

He raised his brows. "And I am not?"

She smirked at him. "I don't know. Are you?"

Such a question. He dismissed it as rhetorical until she laid the king on the table and locked eyes with him. Boldly. And as he studied her expression, he sensed an invitation. A dare. A challenge for him to answer her about whether he was a man of fiery passions. He nearly succumbed to the temptation to show her just how fiery his passions could be.

Restraint, Charles. Hold yourself in check.

He sobered, as temperance, his lifelong, rational, and calming friend, curbed his urge to kiss the question right off her lips.

How long they stared at each other he couldn't say, but Caroline broke the spell. "Do the reading, Lady Julia! I'm so curious as to what the cards will say that I can barely contain myself."

Without speaking, Lady Julia turned over the first card and placed it on top the King of Wands, or the Significator. Wasn't that what Caroline had called the card representing him?

Lady Julia eyed the upside-down image of a woman and then looked back to him. "Queen of Coins, reversed."

"What does that mean?"

She tapped the card. "She is a sad woman with dark hair and dark eyes, entangled in emotions and desires so dark that she can't comprehend them. She is not cold and calculating, but she can inflict pain, not out of malice, but out of insecurity and confusion about what is real."

Caroline gesticulated wildly at the card. "Eleanor! It's Eleanor. I know it's Eleanor. No doubt about it, Charles. It's Eleanor."

"Thank you, Caroline." His scowl silenced her. Hopefully, she would be too intimidated to reveal anything more.

Lady Julia turned over the second card and placed it across the first. "King of Coins, reversed. A dark man with dark eyes and dark inclinations. His appetites run dark, and he can't—or won't—rein them in. He is petty and vindictive and not to be trusted."

"Oh! Oh! I know who it is. I know who it is. It's—"

He glared at his sister once more before she could utter her next word. "Never. Mind. Caroline." When she closed her mouth, he returned his gaze to the cards, satisfied that he had contained her near-outburst. "Please continue, Lady Julia."

She drew a third card and placed it beneath the other two.

Charles stiffened. "You don't need to tell me what that is."

Caroline gasped as her hands flew to her cheeks. "Heavens, is that . . . the Devil?"

"Indeed, Lady Woodfield. But one shouldn't think of the Devil as representing evil necessarily. It more closely represents the lure of the physical world and its fleshly delights. It cautions about being drawn to carnal pleasures and becoming entrapped in their snare."

"Oh my goodness, I'm getting chills, Lady Julia.

Chills! It's uncanny, I tell you. That's exactly what happened to *them*. Isn't it, Charles? They were trapped together in carnal—"

Charles held up his hand to silence his sister once more.

Lady Julia drew a fourth card depicting a man and a woman locked in a tender embrace and placed it upside down behind the queen and the king. "The Lovers. Reversed."

He shook his head at its obvious meaning. "No need to explain that card, Lady Julia. Again, I believe I understand."

His sister huffed. "Well, I'm not sure I do. Not completely, anyway. What does it mean, Lady Julia?"

She hesitated a moment and took a deep breath before speaking. "The Lovers, obviously, can represent a romantic couple. However, reversed liked this, it most likely signifies an unhappy couple, a mismatched pair that probably had problems from the very beginning of their relationship. They were never meant to be together, especially not when one of them only had feelings for another from the very start."

Stunned, Charles could barely process Lady Julia's words. A couple, one of whom only had feelings for another? From the very start? It could only be him and Eleanor. Without a doubt, he had loved her. He had loved her more than he thought possible, almost from the moment he met her, and he had thought she returned his love—until the day she told him otherwise. Before he could stop his mind from exhuming painful recollections, the torrid scene he had witnessed that day flashed across his memory.

Lady Julia turned over another card, interrupting the unpleasant recollection, thankfully. The card depicted three swords piercing a single heart, and she placed it above the king and queen.

"Three of Swords. Heartache. Rupture. Betrayal. Separation. A lover's triangle, I think. One that separated two friends and destroyed three hearts."

Charles was reeling now. Even Caroline was rendered temporarily speechless, which was no small feat in his opinion.

"Two men involved with the same woman, one of them in love with her, the other only toying with her. I sense from the cards that she loved only one of them, the wrong one, the one she couldn't have, the one who didn't return her love."

His jaw dropped at the eerie but accurate picture of the past the cards were painting. They were also disinterring emotions he thought he had buried six years ago. Pain, anger, jealousy, resentment, hatred all jousted for his attention as the Tarot reading managed to disentomb long-repressed memories.

Lady Julia distracted him by drawing another card. She placed this one in front of the king and queen.

"Two of Cups, reversed. Falsehoods. Disharmony. I see a lifelong friendship turned upside down with the realization that it was never genuine, at least not for one of the parties. I see a grudge, a rivalry that one of the friends held for the other from the beginning. Jealousy and resentment eventually turned this one-sided competition into a campaign for revenge against the friend and resulted in the irreparable breach of the friendship."

Truly astounded now, Charles could only gape at the unsettling revelation. It was no secret that toward the end of their acquaintance, Dunham did not like him. He despised him, in fact. But had Dunham *never* liked him—even from the start? Was that not what Lady Julia had just implied? They'd been chums since their days together at Eton. Everything they did, they did as a pair. Sure, Dunham had always teased Charles—almost relentlessly—and even mocked him on occasion, but all the jokes at Charles's expense and all the taunts made to harass him had just been in good fun, hadn't they? So what if Dunham's jibes had stung him fairly often and even wounded him on occasion? Surely, he hadn't *meant* them, and Charles had tried not to take them too seriously. The earl was his friend, after all. Why would he have done anything to hurt him?

Thinking back on it, however, there had been times during their friendship when Dunham had seemed angry and resentful toward Charles for things beyond his control, such as his appearance, his intelligence, and his family's vast fortune. Dunham seemed to hold a deep-seated animosity toward him. Though the earl had seemed bitter at times, Charles had always downplayed the hostility Dunham directed at him, certain that he had imagined acrimony where there was none. In light of Lady Julia's reading tonight, however, Charles began to suspect that perhaps Dunham had never liked him and that anything he'd ever done to help him had, in reality, been an elaborate ruse set up to hurt him and make him suffer later. Perhaps Dunham had even appointed him to the living tied to his family's estate just so he could seduce his wife. Had he played Eleanor false by encouraging feelings he never shared with her just to inflict pain on Charles?

Once again, that torrid scene from before flashed across his mind. Through the hazy, amorphous veil of time, he saw Dunham with Eleanor together and heard the sounds they made. Their laughter taunted him anew, conjuring the old and familiar anger and humiliation, until he could bear it no more. He put his hands over his ears to stifle the sound. "Enough. That's enough. I don't want to hear anything more."

But Lady Julia had already turned up another card. She paused before she spoke, however, as she eyed him warily. "Do you want to know what it means?"

Did he? And yet, could he actually walk away without knowing it all? "Just tell me which card it is."

"It's Judgment. Reversed."

"Meaning?"

"A conviction has been handed down by the offended party on those who wronged him. The judgment is harsh, unforgiving, and without mercy, and only leads to further pain and suffering for all involved."

He tried to remain stoic, to display no emotion, but unsure of how much pain his expression revealed, he covered his face with his hands to hide the shame he still felt every time he recalled how harsh he had been in his judgment of both Dunham and Eleanor. But especially of Eleanor. He had called her a whore, wanton, depraved, no better than the biblical Jezebel after finding out about her and his friend. He had sent her away to her family and later heard that she was pregnant, possibly—no, probably—with Dunham's child.

She had called him to her after she had the child, a stillborn baby girl. He had gone—reluctantly—but he had gone to see her one last time. She lay in her bed wasted and pale, so frail she was likely dying, and when she asked him—begged him—for his forgiveness, when he should have held her and comforted her and let the anger go, he just stood above her, seething with rage and suffering in agony as he told her to go to hell. He, a holy man, entrusted by God to show mercy to sinners and accept their repentance, had told the woman he loved most in the world to burn in perdition for all eternity.

Not long after, she died, and with her, a part of him also perished.

And now, here he sat, a broken man. Despite his new life, his new mission, his new start, he was as damaged and lost as he had been the day he found out about her and his friend.

The ride back to the hunting box was silent at first. Julia couldn't speak. She could barely think. She had been so troubled by the reading she had done for Mr. Rodman that she now sat in guilty silence as Arthur controlled the reins. She could not erase from her mind the look of sheer torment and unadulterated pain on the vicar's face as she explained each card. He seemed truly astounded by the revelations. She should have been more sensitive to his distress, less harsh with her interpretations. She should have softened the meanings of the cards

There was no doubt in her mind that the reading had everything to do with the circumstances surrounding his wife's affair with another man. She had almost seen the events unfold before her as she stared at the cards. It was that way with her many times. Sometimes, even she couldn't prevent the images on the cards from showing her in stark detail the events as they had happened in the past or were going to happen in the future.

Even though she had heard from Benthower of Mr. Rodman's wife's affair, she had not quite imagined the tragedy enveloping it. She had not known the other man was his friend. Such betrayal. His devastation was so palpable that she could *feel* it herself. She could feel almost as intensely as he did what he had suffered over the infidelity of the two people he loved most. And when the cards further revealed that his wife had never loved him and that his friend had never liked him, he had been shattered almost to pieces. She had felt him break. She was only sorry that she had been the one to bring the depth of their disloyalty to his awareness.

Still, although her heart broke for Mr. Rodman and all the pain he had endured, something troubled her about his reaction to his wife's adultery, something that was revealed by the last card in the reading: Judgment, reversed. Unless she had misread the card, she had glimpsed the harshness with which he judged his wife. She felt his rage as he condemned her without mercy for her sins, just as the vicar in India had condemned

Julia for hers.

This saddened but did not surprise her. Not really. After all, when she had asked him the day she met him whether he were a judgmental man, he had not denied being one. She had not, however, imagined the severity of his judgment. As she studied the Judgment card reversed, she had felt his loathing and hostility as he sentenced the pitiful woman to eternal damnation.

Now, as she rode home with Arthur in quiet contemplation of the evening, she couldn't keep herself from wondering what Mr. Rodman would think and how he would react if he ever found out about Julia's past.

"Dinner was nice." Arthur broke through her thoughts, but she wasn't entirely sure what he meant with his observation.

"What do you mean?"

He shrugged. "Just that. Dinner was nice."

She gave him a sidelong glance. He didn't appear to be joking, but still, she wasn't certain what he meant by his comment. She decided not to press him to explain further. "Yes, it was nice. I suppose."

"I was impressed when Lady Woodfield and Mr. Rodman offered to help you raise funds for a new home for the women staying at Lexington House."

"I was, too. And thank *you*, Arthur, for offering to let them do their fundraising at your upcoming house party."

"Think nothing of it. In fact, I only wish I had thought of it myself. For Phoebe's sake."

"Of course." She glanced over at him, expecting

him to say more about Phoebe, perhaps, but several moments passed without further conversation.

Arthur finally broke the silence by changing the subject. "I must say, Julia, your Tarot readings were remarkable this evening. As they always are."

She shrugged but said nothing, and though neither of them spoke again for several more minutes, she sensed a question hanging on his tongue. "Go ahead. Just say it."

"Do you think . . . I mean, is it outrageous to assume from Mr. Rodman's reading that his wife had an affair with his friend?"

She rolled her eyes. "Come now, Arthur. Don't be coy. You know as well as I do that it was blatantly obvious from the reading that his wife had cuckolded him with his friend."

"Weren't you a little shocked, though, in all honesty?"

"Not really. I've known for while that his wife had an affair."

"Who told you that?"

"Benthower. He didn't tell me the affair was with Mr. Rodman's friend, however."

Again, a hush fell between them, and again, she sensed a question burning his tongue. "Go ahead, Arthur. Say it."

"Do you find it . . . I don't know . . . ironic?" he whispered.

"*Ironic?* It's horrifying in its irony." She peered down at the road as the gig rolled over it, and then she sighed with relief. "I am only thankful that he—and his sister—will never find out what happened with Niles, Renesh, and me. It would be far too humiliating to have them know the truth about my situation, it being so similar to his."

"Julia, you cannot equate one with the other."

"You're right, of course. My sins were far, far worse than those of Mr. Rodman's wife. I became pregnant with my lover's child. At least Mr. Rodman didn't have to endure that pain on top of his wife's infidelity."

"No, no, that's not what I mean. I mean that you can't equate the situations because, for one thing, Mr. Rodman is not a bad person, whereas Niles was a monster."

She sighed again, not in relief, but in agreement. "Be that as it may, it doesn't excuse the fact that I broke my marriage vows to him with the one man in India he considered his friend—the only person there trying to help him. Essentially, I did the same thing with Niles's friend as Mr. Rodman's wife had done with his. It was worse, in fact, if you consider I conceived a child with Nile's friend."

Arthur scoffed. "I *suppose* you could put it that way, if you wanted to be absolutely literal about it."

"Well, no matter what else, you must admit, that I'm a horrible person for having had an adulterous affair—and worse, having had a child as a result."

"You act like that's the worst thing someone could ever do. You are not now, nor were you ever—nor could you *ever be*—a horrible person."

"You only say that because you like me."

"I say it because I love you, Julia." He paused a moment. "Plus, you aren't the only person ever to have had an adulterous affair."

"*You* never have."

"You don't know that."

She gasped. "What are you saying, Arthur? Surely, you've never been with a married women, have you?"

He shrugged. "That's a subject for another evening, perhaps. For now, I want you to stop tormenting yourself about what happened in the past. It's pointless, especially when you consider that whatever you did, you did because your husband drove you to it with the way he treated you. He was a horrible person."

"Even so, did you see how upset Mr. Rodman appeared after the Tarot reading this evening? I *felt* his distress, Arthur. I *felt* his pain. I can't even imagine how devastated he must have been when he first found out about the affair. And it makes me wonder."

"About what?"

"How much did I hurt Niles?"

"Please." Arthur waved his hand in dismissal. "I mean, certainly, you could torture yourself with guilt over how much it might have hurt Niles to find out about your affair with his friend, but he's not worth the salt in your tears. In the end, the affair probably didn't even hurt him emotionally. Damage his pride? Yes, of course. He was an arrogant arse, and it hurt his pride. Never mind how much he hurt you every time—and there were many, *many* times—he broke the vows he made to you."

She didn't miss his sarcasm. "True, but doing a wrong in response to another wrong never makes it right."

"Humph. That sounds pretty bloody Christian. However, I don't know that I agree with you—at least not all the time. Sometimes, it's bloody satisfying to see the person who kicked you in the gut get disemboweled."

"My God, Arthur. That's unbelievably dark."

"Perhaps, but I can't help it. When I think how Niles treated you—or how Abadon treated Phoebe—I become enraged. Your husband was a fiend and a murderer, just like Abadon. At least the Fates gave *your* husband his just desserts, unlike Phoebe's. How can you not be at least a little glad the man got what he deserved in the end?"

"I know, Arthur. I know. To this day, I'm still angry over what he did to me. It's all I can do not to let my hatred and rage consume me."

"Like mine has consumed me, you mean?" He laughed, but only with bitterness.

She grasped his hand and squeezed it. "You will see justice in one form or another someday, dear cousin. I just know it."

He smiled wistfully as he patted her hand. "You're sweet to say that, but I'll believe it only when I do see it."

Just before noon on Sunday three days later, Julia sat at the dining table watching Arthur as he made out the guest list for his upcoming party in August. According to her cousin, the list, so far, consisted of the wealthiest persons of his acquaintance in the kingdom. Some were noblemen; some were commoners; but either way, these people could afford to part with at least a few quid for a good cause. Whether or not they would, was another question altogether.

Arthur set his quill down and stretched his fingers. Then he removed his spectacles and rubbed his eyes. "Will you read the list back to me, Julia? Everything is a blur to me now."

She picked up the piece of vellum with his barely legible chicken scratch on it and read the names aloud as best as she could decipher them. There were Lord and Lady This and Sir What's-it and Lady That, as well as Mr. and Mrs. Who-the-hell-ever and even a couple of Dukes and Duchesses of Wherever-the-hell.

"How many is that, dear?"

She tallied the names. "I count twenty couples and a few singles."

"I would imagine that Lady Woodfield and Mr. Rodman might have another twenty or so couples to invite, which would make around eighty people total."

"That's quite a crowd, Arthur."

"I think it's manageable. Don't you?"

She shrugged. "It's your house."

He waved away her concerns with a flourish of his hand. "It will be fine. Is that everyone?"

"Well . . . not *everyone*."

"Who's missing?"

She hesitated, weighing in her mind whether or not to mention the missing earl. He was something of a reprobate, and she wasn't certain she could stomach his presence. However, he *was* vastly wealthy, perhaps even the richest man she knew. "Lord Dunham."

Again, Arthur waved his hand in dismissal. "Oh, him. I purposefully left him off. I didn't think you'd want him there after the way he depleted Niles's fortune by seizing all his liquid assets—"

"You mean, *my* fortune."

"Yes, I'm sorry. Of course, I mean *your* fortune. The only money Niles ever had was money he got from your dowry. But why would you want to invite Dunham? Especially after he ruined your husband. I didn't think you'd ever want to see the man again."

"While I do detest him and would sooner drink pigswill than be in his company, you must admit he's one of the wealthiest men in Britain."

Arthur arched a brow as he frowned. "Yes, never mind that he came by most of his fortune smuggling opium."

She nodded. "I realize he's not the most stellar human being, but I'm thinking it couldn't hurt to send him an invitation. He'll likely turn it down, but if he does show up, at least I'll get to see his wife Rebecca again. I always liked her, and despite what happened between our husbands, I always considered her a friend. And perhaps, if we ply the earl with the right amount of liquor, we could convince him to contribute something."

"And, if we get him drunk enough, perhaps we could even get him to sign a voucher pledging a few thousand pounds, at the very least."

"I like it. I like it a lot. I'll add his name."

Julia's maid Burton peeked her head around the doorjamb at that moment. "Begging your pardon, my lady, but Mr. Rodman is here. I've shown him to the parlor."

What? Why was . . . Oh, yes. Of course. *Drat.* She had forgotten. Mr. Rodman had planned to come today so they could both visit Lexington House and he could perform church services for the ladies. He would be early, of course. Julia suppressed an eye roll as she rose from the table and thanked Burton.

As she strode to the parlor with Arthur beside her, she steeled herself against seeing the vicar again. She still wasn't fully recovered from the effects of the Tarot card reading she had done for him the other night. Plus, he just unnerved her anyway, and she wasn't sure how to make herself immune to his presence. He affected her too much with his aquamarine eyes and his penetrating gaze. He was far too attractive, too virile, and she was far too vulnerable to his charms. Well, perhaps *charms* was taking it a little far. The man could be so irksome at times, after all. But there was something about him, something she couldn't quite put a finger on, that made her a little daft whenever he was around.

And today, as she entered the parlor, her reaction to him was no different than the last time she had seen him. He stood and bowed and she went weak in the knees. And in the brain. Definitely, weak in the brain. Must he be so damned magnificent?

She acknowledged him with a curt nod, while Arthur returned his bow.

"Lady Julia, it is good to see you again."

"Likewise, I'm sure, Mr. Rodman." Could he hear the sarcasm in her tone?

"I hope you don't mind that I came out a little early, my lady. It looks like rain, and I was thinking perhaps we should set out as soon as possible for Lexington House."

"No, no, of course not. It's wise that we go early in case there's a storm, but I'll need to have the stable groom ready the gig so we can leave as soon as possible. If you'll excuse me, I won't be but a minute." Happy to leave Mr. Rodman with Arthur, Julia turned to go.

Arthur stepped forward. "Let me speak to the groom, Julia. You stay here and chat with Mr. Rodman."

Oh, good lord, she really didn't want to do *that*—to be by herself with the vicar, but Arthur insisted once more and left her no choice as he rushed out of the room. And just like that, she and Mr. Rodman stood alone in the suddenly tiny parlor. His presence filled the room and overwhelmed her in an instant, and she had to take a seat to steady her nerves. He followed suit, sitting in the chair next to hers by the mantle.

They sat in silence—for how long, she didn't know. It could have been twenty seconds or twenty years. Their mutual discomfort was palpable, until finally, he cleared his throat and made an observation about how nice the weather had been. Though she found his comment odd, especially given that he had told her not ten minutes ago that it was likely to rain, she shrugged and agreed. He adjusted his cravat, looked down at the floor, and began tapping his foot.

Now it was her turn to say something, she supposed. She looked around the room for a topic—something, anything to talk about. Her eyes landed on the *Kama Sutra*, which she noticed still sitting on the bookcase where they had left it last Sunday. Recalling the heat generated between them as they looked at a particular picture in the book last week, she let out a nervous little giggle. His reaction to that did not help. He snapped his head up and regarded her with such a comical look of confusion that she laughed even more. After recovering herself, she asked him whether he had read any good books lately. He smiled and replied that he had not. Then, as if he thought his statement needed more clarification, he went on to say that he had not read anything lately because most of his books were still crated at the vicarage. She nodded in understanding. And so, for ten more minutes, they lobbed silly, awkward comments back and forth to each other in an attempt to avoid a clumsy silence.

Finally—thankfully—Arthur returned. "The gig is ready."

Julia breathed a sigh of relief—and then immediately gulped air again in abject fear. Although they were leaving the vexing atmosphere of the parlor, they would now be thrust into the even more uncomfortable—and close—confines of the gig.

Arthur assisted her up into the gig, while Mr. Rodman strode to his horse and retrieved two satchels, one larger than the other. When he returned to the gig, he opened the smaller one and removed a folded piece of paper, which he handed to Arthur. "Here is the list of guests that Caroline and I made up for your party, Mr. Drake."

"Ah. Very good. Julia and I just finished our own list before you arrived. We'll show it to you if there's an opportunity when you return."

The vicar nodded and then climbed aboard the gig with both his bags.

"We should be home for dinner, Arthur," said Julia.

"Take care. The sky does look rather ominous. You two should just stay at Lexington House if it's raining when you're done."

"No need to worry. We will be fine." She waved goodbye, and as she set the gig in motion with a slap of the reins, she gulped air once more at the realization that she was alone with the vicar. Again.

CHAPTER 7

Two of Cups: Connection, partnership, beneficial relationship, mutual respect, mutual attraction . . .

ONCE AGAIN, SILENCE. MR. RODMAN tugged at his cravat and stared straight ahead, tapping his foot in obvious agitation as he had done in the parlor. The bench atop the gig was not very long, forcing Julia to sit closer to him than was comfortable. As a consequence, their knees touched, and she felt every movement of his leg as his foot hit the running board.

To distract herself from the pleasant, though inappropriate, shiver contact with his knee sent through her body, she racked her brain for a topic of conversation. The weather? No, no, that was stupid. He'd already mentioned it back in the parlor. *Think, think.* How about the latest *on dits* from the scandal sheets in London? Probably not a good idea. His being such a prude, he likely did not follow those papers or engage in idle gossip. Needlework? She scoffed at the idea—in her head. No, of course not. He wouldn't know a *thing* about needlework—or most of her other pastimes, like watercolors or tatting lace. She would have mentioned reading, the only one of her pastimes in which he might share an interest, except for the fact that she'd already brought it up back at the hunting box. Ah! The hunting box. Hunting!

"Do you hunt, Mr. Rodman?"

"No."

And that was as much as he said on the matter. This would be a longish fifty minutes.

So . . . food? He ate, didn't he? She'd seen him do it recently at dinner on two different occasions.

"I shouldn't say that I don't hunt. It's just that I haven't done it in years."

As much as she wished he would expound on that, he said no more.

So . . . food. "Do you—"

"I like rocks."

What? To eat? *No, no, of course not, you ninny. You haven't yet asked him what his favorite dish is for him to give an answer, much less an answer like rocks.*

"What I meant to say is that I enjoy them." He glanced at her for a second and then snatched his gaze away. "Rocks, that is."

"I see." She wanted more than anything to say something clever, but . . . rocks?

"Forgive me. I'm afraid I'm not being very clear. *Collecting* them. As a *hobby. Collecting rocks.* That is to say, I enjoy *collecting rocks* as a hobby. It's unusual, I realize. Rock collecting, I mean, but I enjoy it." He tugged at his cravat again. "That's why I said it. I mean, I thought you were going to ask me what I liked to do, so I said that I like rocks."

His charming discomposure made her smile. "No need to apologize or explain. I like sea shells. I have a whole collection of them stowed away at Lexington House."

He nodded, still staring straight ahead. "Perhaps you could show them to me."

"Yes. Perhaps."

Another. Awkward. Silence.

He moved slightly, bumping into one of the satchels he had brought with him and causing something to clank inside. He reached down to right that bag while settling the other one more closely to his legs.

"What's in your bags, Mr. Rodman?"

"Oh, this?" He lifted the larger bag. "I brought along a few things to perform the service at Lexington House this afternoon."

"And the other bag?"

"This one?" His amicable tone changed to one of annoyance as he kicked the bag ever so slightly, and though he didn't look at her, she caught him rolling his eyes. "Caroline packed me a few provisions before I left. She insisted that I bring along some cheese and wine in case we got hungry or thirsty."

She smiled when his cheeks turned the palest pink. "That was very thoughtful of your sister."

"Well, that's Caroline for you. Always intruding in the kindest of ways."

Julia laughed a little at his remark. "Nevertheless, she has a good heart. I'm sure she only has your best interest in mind."

"I, on the other hand, am sure she does not, but I can't seem to get her to leave." He paused. "I'm open to ideas, however, if you have any."

She laughed out loud, and their eyes met for a second of mutual amusement at his comment. Then, as the second turned into several seconds and the seconds into a moment, the atmosphere between them warmed uncomfortably. Something stirred beneath his hooded gaze, and she had to tear her own eyes away before they revealed the unwanted desire he had just ignited within her. "I'm afraid I don't. Have any ideas, that is. How long does she plan to stay?"

From the corner of her eye, she caught him rolling his eyes once more. "Until she sees me married again."

"Well, there's your answer then. Marry someone. She'll have no choice but to leave you alone."

He flashed her a sidelong glare. "But then I'd have a wife."

She shrugged. "I said it was an answer. Not a perfect answer perhaps, but still an answer."

"I'm hoping a child might lure her away."

"A child? Whose? Hers?"

"No, not hers. Her two sons are both nearly grown and tucked safely away at school—to their great fortune."

She laughed once again, and he laughed with her for a moment. "No, what I was thinking was that one of our brothers is soon to be a new father. I'm hoping that when the child is born, Caroline will leave at once for the north to direct *his* affairs."

She giggled. "You make me laugh. However, I like

your sister."

"And I like rocks."

Julia smiled. She liked his sense of humor. It was both droll and endearing. More importantly, the iceberg between them seemed to have melted just a little. Though several minutes passed in silence once again, the silence was not so awkward this time. Mr. Rodman even relaxed enough to stop tapping his foot. His leg, however, remained uncomfortably close to her own.

"How much farther to Lexington House?" he asked.

"Not far at all. It's just around the bend."

As they rounded the curve in the road, Lexington House loomed into view, and Julia experienced the usual revulsion she felt on seeing the expansive building. She might have loved the house under other circumstances, but since it was her late husband's pride and joy, it never failed to evoke his memory— and with it, an urge to retch. A large pond in front of the house reflected the Palladian style mansion in its placid surface. With two wings, thirty-seven bedrooms, and extensive gardens in the back, Lexington House represented the obscene wealth of its first occupant, the first Earl of Lexington, who had commissioned the building around sixty-five years ago in anticipation of siring a long line of Lexingtons. The entire estate reverted to the Crown, however, when there failed to be a second earl.

Uninterested in resurrecting the Earldom of Lexington, the Crown had sold the property to Julia's husband Niles shortly after their marriage in 1807. The extravagant purchase had incensed Julia for the money it wasted, and she had argued against it because it required most of her vast dowry. Though she considered that money hers, it became his, of course, when she became his wife and lost her status as a person. Her marriage left her powerless to stop him from buying the property, especially with his father pressuring him into the acquisition so that Niles could establish an estate for himself and his survivors—something the elder Lacey had been unable to do in his lifetime with the modest fortune he had made as a shipping merchant. So, while Lexington House was the perfect property for the legacy Niles's father envisioned, it became a symbol of the autonomy—and money—Julia had forfeited in marriage.

And now, it was also a symbol of everything standing between her and her goal of returning to Calcutta to be with Camille. Fortunately for her, though, she would be able to sell it when the time came because Niles had been unable to entangle the estate in an entailment. Thanks to the terms Benthower had imposed on the marriage settlements, Niles did not even own the property. Julia did, but only because the duke had required all property purchased with money from her dowry be hers at law and held in trust for her throughout their marriage. It would have become Niles's, had he survived her, but because he passed before her, the property was hers to do with as she pleased. In retrospect, the marriage settlements were one of the few decent things Benthower had ever done for her.

She glanced over at Mr. Rodman as the gig came

to a stop in the drive. He stared at the structure, his mouth agape. "What a building."

"Haven't you seen it before? When Benthower brought you here to meet with me because he thought I was living here?"

"It was dark when we arrived, so I didn't get a good look at it. It's enormous. You should receive a nice price for the house when you sell it."

"I hope so. I hope it will fetch me enough to return to India and settle there for the rest of my life."

He turned to study her for a moment. "Do you really intend to go to India for the rest of your life?"

"Yes. I must. I must return to care for Camille now that her father is dead and her mother is . . . well, not around."

He regarded her once more, this time with a curious expression. "Couldn't you return to England with the child rather than stay in India?"

She shook her head no. "I think not. It would be a terrible idea."

"Why?"

She sighed. "For one thing, it would be too huge a shock for Camille to leave the only home she has ever known and try to acclimate to England. Plus, I fear she would never fit in. She would never be accepted. Society would shun her."

He drew his brows together. "Why would she be shunned?"

She peered down at her hands folded in her lap. "She just . . . would."

He reached for her chin and tipped her head up

toward him. "Tell me why."

Still, she kept her eyes lowered. "Really, Mr. Rodman. You've seen her picture. She's very dark. Surely, you must realize she's . . . not English."

"So?"

"Well, that's not *entirely* true. I mean, she *is* English. Half English. But she is also Indian. Her father was Indian, and her mother was English." She paused a moment to let that sink in.

"I still don't understand."

"She. Is. Of. Mixed. Race." She couldn't help the annoyance in her tone, but either he was being intentionally obtuse or he was mocking her.

"Forgive me, Lady Julia, but I'm not comprehending. Are you saying you couldn't bring her to England because she is of mixed race?"

She raised her eyes to meet his—to see if his question were sincere. She studied him for a good while. Though he appeared puzzled, his gaze was steady and unaffected. His genuineness stunned her, and she swiped at a tear that fell from her lashes. "Yes. That is what I'm saying. Society would never accept a girl of mixed-race parentage." She pulled her chin from his grasp and looked away.

"Anyone who would shun a child for her mixed race can go to blazes."

Shocked, she turned back toward him and stared, unable to speak. Was he serious?

He hardened his jaw. "I mean it. Racial bigotry is never acceptable, and ostracizing someone, especially a child, for their race is not only abhorrent—it's intolerable."

Tears fell freely now. She was in rare form—crying essentially. He withdrew a handkerchief from his pocket and offered it to her. She took it gratefully and dried her eyes. "Thank you, Mr. Rodman. Pardon my tears, but your words surprise me. I'm very touched, but you are too kind. Very few people would not be offended by her mixed race. You are very rare."

"No need to apologize, my lady." He paused for a moment, as though he were considering his next words. "And I'm not so very rare. Bring her home. To England. I'm sure there are many who would not only accept her, they would embrace her for who she is. She will be fine."

Despite her efforts to control her tears, a sob escaped her. She had never allowed herself to consider the possibility of bringing Camille to England, certain the world would scorn and reject her. And yet, here was this man—this man she had, up until this point, not really even liked—condemning racial bigotry and telling her to bring the girl home. She gathered her composure and sniffled as she wound the handkerchief around her fingers. "You are very considerate, but I think not. It's just not a good idea."

A drop of rain splashed her cheek as they continued to sit in the gig. He wiped it away with his thumb, unaware of the tremor his touch evoked throughout her body. "Just promise me you'll at least think about it, Lady Julia. It doesn't seem right for you to leave here forever and live half a world away from your family. England is your home. Lexington House is your home."

"Thank you." She shrugged. "Perhaps I shall think about it."

"Good. Plus, a huge advantage of returning to England is that you wouldn't need to sell Lexington House to raise money to settle in India forever. All you would need is money for the voyage to and from India, and I'm sure we could come up with that very easily. It wouldn't take us long at all."

We? Us? What could he mean? Was he offering his help in raising funds for her voyage to India? She could see his and his sister's offer to help her raise funds for a new home for the women. That was a good cause. But helping her with something as personal as paying for her journey back to India was too much. Perhaps it had been just a slip of the tongue. In any case, she chose not to read too much into it and didn't press him on it. "That's true, I guess. If I didn't have to sell Lexington House, then the ladies could stay here for as long as they needed to. I wouldn't have to come up with funds to buy or build them a new home."

"No, that's not what I meant. Lexington House is yours. It's where you belong. All I'm saying is that you wouldn't have to sell it if you didn't intend to settle in India forever. You should keep it for *you* and live there yourself with the girl."

"But what about the ladies? Where would they live?"

"The ladies should have their *own* home, of course, one dedicated to the specific purpose of sheltering them and caring for their needs. I still plan on raising funds for a new home for them at Mr. Drake's party, just as we had discussed at dinner on Friday."

"About that, Mr. Rodman . . ." She hesitated and turned away from him.

"Yes?"

"It's not necessary for you and your sister to help raise funds for the new home at Arthur's party in August. Or ever, for that matter. I don't want you—or her—to feel obligated to help, especially you. I know she more or less forced you to agree to raise money along with her, and I don't want you to feel duty-bound to help us with *her* offer. It puts too much of a burden on you."

"It's no burden, my lady. None at all. I am happy to do what I can to help your cause, especially after what you told Caroline and me happened to your sister."

She peered up at him then with new respect. "I don't know what to say, Mr. Rodman. You are too noble. I don't know how I shall ever repay you."

"Repayment isn't necessary." He smiled, knocking all sense out of her brain. "You will, however, have to start coming to church."

What? Shocked by his comment, she snapped her head around in a double-take, staring at him in abject astonishment, her eyes wide and her mouth open. Had he just commanded her to attend church? How dare he? She attempted to formulate a scathing reply, but she was so taken aback that she was stunned into silence. She could only sit there gaping at him, unable to move. Even the raindrops that fell harder now couldn't persuade her to budge.

He smiled once again, but this was not his usual warm smile, the one that weakened her knees and annihilated rational thought. This smile was impish. On top of it, he winked. Totally out of character for him, he actually winked an eye at her, the naughty man. "I'm only kidding, of course. I shan't force you to attend church in return for my help. The only thing I ask is that you at least think about coming back to England with the little girl. I hate the thought of you moving away forever." His mouth twitched into a mischievous moue, somewhere between a smile and a smirk. And as he smirked or smiled or whatever it was, he also swept his eyes over her entire person. His gaze, though almost improper, was the most sensual thing he could have done at the moment, and it jolted her heart into a strange rhythm, leaving her unable to speak. "We should go inside now. We don't want to get wet."

He grabbed the larger of his bags and jumped down from the gig, and as he came around to her side, her breath hitched. And when he took her hand to help her down, her heart did a funny—and frightening—little flip. And not just from the physical desire that his gaze had ignited, but from some new and unfamiliar sentiment that his words—and his touch—kindled in her.

Bad, Julia. Bad. Bad. Bad.

I like rocks.
Brilliant, Rodman. Simply. Brilliant.
Could he have been any more witless? Any less articulate? He shook his head. Clearly, she flustered

him. Like no other woman ever had. To be perfectly truthful, he had been lucky to be able to speak at all, much less coherently, as he sat beside her. He had been so overcome by her jasmine scent and the feel of her leg against his that he had lost all focus. Even now, as he walked beside her to the front door of her imposing home, his mind wandered to the disbelief that had shown in her cinnamon eyes when he told her she should bring the mixed-race child to England. He also thought he had detected some other emotion in her expression, one he hadn't seen before. Gratitude, perhaps? Or possibly even admiration? Whatever it was, it produced a funny little tremor in his gut.

They reached the door, leaving him no more time to dwell on just what he had seen in her eyes. He gathered his senses as a footman bowed in greeting before letting them inside. His mind was instantly distracted when he entered the hall and saw the interior décor for the first time in full daylight. It was vast and magnificent, with oak-paneled wainscoting and a parquet floor. He couldn't help a sharp inhalation. A gasp, essentially. Two great marble pillars on either side of a grand staircase reached to a ceiling frescoed in motifs of classical Greece. Naked nymphs played along a stream, while satyrs chased after them in ribald abandon. "It's incredible, Lady Julia."

"Thank you, Mr. Rodman." She shrugged indifferently. "I suppose if you're not nauseated by the ostentation, Lexington House might take your breath away."

He smiled as he removed his hat, which a footman took from him.

A petite, middle-aged woman approached them and dipped into a curtsy. Her mobcap bobbed as she stood. "Good afternoon, milady. It's such a pleasure to see you."

"Thank you, Mrs. Thompson. This is Mr. Rodman, the new vicar in South Kindale. I don't know whether or not you've made his acquaintance yet. Mr. Rodman, this is Mrs. Thompson, our very capable and devoted housekeeper."

"I've not had the pleasure, Mr. Rodman. I don't get to town much these days, I'm afraid, not with all that's going on here at Lexington House. It's nice to meet you, however."

He bowed to her. "Thank you, and may I say the same."

"Shall I have some tea and refreshments brought into the drawing room for you, ma'am?"

"That would be wonderful. And please notify Mrs. Nash that we would like to speak with her."

"Very good, ma'am." Mrs. Thompson bobbed another curtsy and left them alone in the grand entrance.

Lady Julia motioned for him to follow her to the left down a hall off the entryway, and as he strode behind her to the second room on the right, he watched the twitch of her skirts with something much too much like pleasure, and his mind returned to their interaction in the gig just before it began raining. He shouldn't have teased her as he'd done about having to attend church in return for his help, and he most certainly should not have winked at her. In all his years alive and as a bachelor, he'd never done anything so bold as to wink at a woman. It bordered on indiscretion, and why he had done it with her baffled him, except to say that she brought out something in him, a playfulness he hadn't even been aware he possessed before. Even more shocking, he learned he was actually capable of flirting with a woman.

Shortly after they reached the drawing room, a reedy, stern-looking woman with graying hair that peeked out from under her cap entered just behind them. "Good afternoon." She did not even smile accidentally.

"Mrs. Nash, how good it is to see you." Lady Julia made introductions between Mrs. Nash and himself. "Mrs. Nash is the headmistress here at the house. She looks after the women and makes sure all their needs are tended to, as well as performing all the administrative duties of the home."

He bowed once again. "I'm very pleased to meet you, Mrs. Nash."

Her face remained stoic as she gave him an abbreviated curtsy. "Likewise, I'm sure."

Lady Julia invited everyone to sit, and Mrs. Thompson returned with a cart full of cakes, biscuits, tarts, and tea, which she began serving.

Lady Julia accepted a teacup from the housekeeper before turning to the headmistress. "How is everything going here at Lexington House, Mrs. Nash?"

"Things proceed apace. We've had several new arrivals in the past few weeks, mostly from London. They came to us in fairly rough shape, bruised and battered, but we've nursed them back to health, and they're getting along pretty well now."

"Is there any indication that their husbands know where they are?"

"None so far. I believe the house is a well-guarded secret. We go pretty much undetected."

Charles cleared his throat. "Tell me, Mrs. Nash, how long do the women typically stay here?"

The headmistress sipped her tea and set the cup back on its saucer. "It depends on each woman's unique situation. Sometimes it's a week; sometimes it's several months. Those with more difficult obstacles facing them stay longer. Mrs. Sweeney, for instance, has been here eight months now. She came to us from London after her husband beat her mercilessly when he found out she was with child. She probably won't be able to leave us for several more months, not until after her confinement at the very earliest. She will then need assistance with her newborn babe for a while, I am sure."

"I see. And what happens to the women after they leave?"

"We've been able to help most of them get set up in new situations in various places here in England and sometimes even abroad. One went all the way to Northumberland to become a housekeeper at an inn there, and another went to Southampton and caught a ship to America. We scour the newspapers daily for ads for suitable employment and help train the women for various jobs where we can. We also give them references, and Lady Julia, God bless her, has the kindest heart. No one leaves here empty-handed. Not only does she provide them shelter here in her own home but also she gives each woman money out of her own pocket to help them start out."

Stirred by his patroness's largesse, he turned to commend her, but she would not look up from the floor, obviously uneasy with the praise Mrs. Nash had just given her. "Well, I must say that I'm impressed with all the good work you and Lady Julia do in helping these women begin anew."

Mrs. Nash sighed heavily. "Yes, well, unfortunately, we can't seem to help them all. Despite our best efforts to free them from the endless threat of violence they face at home, some women choose to return to their husbands rather than go out into the world alone."

"I didn't realize that. Do the situations with their husbands ever improve once they're together again?"

She shook her head. "I would like to think so, but sadly, that is rarely the case. A few women have gone home only to be beaten more severely once they return. Some of those come back to us, and the others? I'm not really sure what happens to them."

He was shaken into silence, unable to think of what to say. While he tried to absorb all that Mrs. Nash had just said, he only half-listened to her and Lady Julia discuss more mundane topics now, like maintenance repairs and operations of the home. He was more distracted by the realization that Lady Julia was an amazing woman.

She, a duke's daughter, a duke's sister, a society woman who could probably live wherever she wished, have whatever luxury she wanted, whatever trifle her heart desired, instead chose to live in a modest hunting box while she let the most unfortunate women in the kingdom take refuge in her mansion. She gave them food, shelter, training, and money—her own money—so that they might start anew. More than that, she gave them kindness and offered them hope. He had never met anyone like her. Certainly, no woman—make that no *one*—among his lofty connections with the *ton* had ever shown such compassion and magnanimity as her.

In addition to all that was the fact that she was driven by her kind soul to rescue a vulnerable and defenseless child living in a foreign country, an orphan essentially whose one parent was dead and the other missing. It was inspiring that she would leave the comfort of her cozy home in England and return to the hostile, unforgiving Indian climate, perhaps for good, to raise this forlorn little girl whom she was sure society would reject if she brought her back home.

She astounded him.

She humbled him.

There was no one else like her in the world.

And now, he had a problem. He had fought his fierce attraction to her since he met her, thinking it was only a product of his baser instincts, but now, knowing her for the remarkable human being she was, he felt for the first time that his attraction to her was more than just lust generated by her physical attributes. He was attracted to her essence, her being, her spirit. Even now, as he watched her sitting without pretense in her chair, he was powerless to unhitch himself from the unrelenting grip she had on his soul.

She drew his attention back to the moment when

she set her cup and saucer on the table in front of her. "Mrs. Nash, perhaps now would be a good time to gather the ladies into the chapel so that Mr. Rodman can perform church services for them today."

The headmistress smiled briefly as she rose from her chair. "Yes, of course. They're eager to have private services here at Lexington House. They have been looking forward to the vicar's visit since you wrote them about it last week. I'll go and let them know you'll both be waiting for them in the chapel."

Lady Julia then turned to him and caught him staring at her. "Is something the matter, Mr. Rodman?"

Only this: why did the one woman in the kingdom—the one who undid him like no one else ever had—have to be the one woman he couldn't have? Why did it have to be her, his patroness, an apostate, a heretic, for that matter? And someone who might very well be leaving the continent soon—for good? "No, nothing is the matter."

She laughed. "Oh, well, please forgive me. It's just that you were looking at me with such a grave expression, I thought something was wrong."

Oh, something was wrong, alright. Very wrong. And he didn't know what to do about it.

She quirked her head at him when he said nothing. Still, she smiled, lighting up the whole, dreary world. "Shall we go to the chapel then, Mr. Rodman?"

He nodded, still saying nothing, afraid that if he opened his mouth, something stupid would come out.

She stood and strode toward the door, and as he rose from his own chair, he did what he could to turn his attention from her to his purpose for being at Lexington House in the first place. He was there to offer spiritual comfort and support to the ladies living here. To that end, he rehearsed in his mind the sermon he had written earlier in the week and delivered just this morning at St. Blaise's. As he silently recited the oration in his head, he followed her out of the drawing room, back down the hallway a short distance toward the grand entry, and then past the grand staircase to another hallway at the back of the house to the right.

As they turned down the back corridor, they passed a conservatory on the left that housed all sorts of ornamental plants, along with a couple of citrus trees. As she led him farther down the hallway, she opened each door along the corridor to show him what lay inside the room. They looked inside the enormous library and the well-appointed study next to it.

She then led him to the room beyond the study, and as she opened the door to the room, she cautioned him to hold his breath. He didn't heed her warning soon enough and nearly choked on the fumes of turpentine and linseed oil when he stepped into the room.

"I apologize, Mr. Rodman. This is the art room. The ladies paint with oils as much as watercolors, and there's always a strong odor of the oil paints and paint thinner."

"I see what you mean." He coughed and spewed as he choked on his answer. "Perhaps they should open the windows to air it out once in a while."

"I think the maids do, often, but they may have closed the windows today because of the rain outside."

He nodded as he covered his mouth and followed her back into the hallway. She showed him another drawing room beyond the art room and then the music room at the end of the corridor, before leading him across the hall into a vast gallery that seemed to stretch the length of the house. They cut through the gallery to get to another corridor, which led them to a door at the end of the west wing that opened to an airy, vaulted walkway outside the house.

Astounded at the sheer size of the building, he shook his head as they stepped through the door. "Lexington House is huge."

"That is an understatement, Mr. Rodman. We should've driven the gig around to this side of the house. We'd have made better time. Or, at the very least, we should've brought along the other bag, the one with your sister's provisions, for our long journey."

He threw his head back and laughed, and when she giggled along with him, her laughter scuttled his brain, obliterating most of his good sense. He could barely recall where they were going or why, as he followed her down the walkway past several ivy-covered arches to the chapel doors. She opened one of the doors and led him into the poorly lit narthex, and when they proceeded into the nave, the enormity of the sacred space astonished him. This was no small chapel. It was more a good-sized church, and he marveled at the craftsmanship of the stained-glass windows running down the outside aisles and the ornate carvings at the ends of the oaken pews.

They approached the crossing in front of the chancel and stopped when a door at the east end of the transept opened, allowing residents of Lexington House to enter from yet another part of the building. Around forty women and a dozen children, in his estimation, filed into the chapel and settled into the pews. Lady Julia greeted each individual with a nod and a smile, and they all curtsied to her in return.

After everyone was seated, Charles followed Lady Julia up the steps to the chancel where she stood at the lectern to address them. "Good afternoon, everyone. Thank you all for coming. As you might recall, I sent a note to Mrs. Nash last week asking her to let you know that the new vicar in town had offered to come out to Lexington House to perform church services if any of you were interested. She wrote me back to let me know that everyone she had spoken to was in favor of such an arrangement. So, I told the vicar I would bring him here today to meet you." She turned to him with her arm outstretched toward him. "I'd like to introduce you all to Mr. Charles Rodman, the new vicar of St. Blaise's Parish."

The ladies smiled, and a gentle murmur filled the chapel as he stepped forward and stood beside her at the lectern. "Thank you, Lady Julia. I'm most obliged to you for setting up today's meeting." He turned his attention to the crowd of women and children sitting in the pews. "And I am truly honored to meet all of you."

"I'll just leave you to it then, Mr. Rodman." And with that, Lady Julia smiled and stepped back down to the aisle giving him no chance to ask her where she would go or what she would do while he performed the service.

She spoke to some of the women here and there as she moved farther up the aisle. And as he watched her walk away, he supposed it didn't really matter where she went or what she did while they were apart, but the strangest sense of loss settled over him as he stood there alone, as though the rapport they had established between them since leaving the hunting box earlier had been just a figment of his imagination and would vanish once she was gone. Regretting that whatever it was they had shared this afternoon was over, he continued watching her wistfully, expecting her to leave when she reached the narthex, but as she neared the back of the nave, she caught him off guard by turning into the last pew and sitting as though she were going to stay for the service.

Nonplussed by her unexpected presence, he could only stare at her. She settled back into the pew and smiled at him. She even gave him a small wave. Unable to do anything else, he returned the gesture as his pulse began to race and his palms to sweat. Perspiration formed on his brow and trickled beneath his cravat. Suddenly, like a newly minted curate performing his first service, he was terrified that he would make a fool of himself in front of her and God and everyone. But mostly, in front of her.

A hush fell over the congregation, and he attempted to gather both his wits and his courage. He tore his gaze away from hers and decided it best not to look at her during the rite. Instead, he would keep his eyes fixed on the podium in front of him. He leaned down to retrieve his bag and rummaged through it for the items he had brought for the ritual. He took out a Bible and the *Book of Common Prayer* and donned his vestments. And then he took a deep breath and welcomed the women and children to the service and tried not to look up at Lady Julia. And thus began the longest hour of his life.

CHAPTER 8

Five of Wands: Conflict, differing opinions, disagreements, clash of tempers and personalities, breakdown of communications . . .

JULIA TRIED TO SUPPRESS A smile but couldn't quite manage it. Mr. Rodman appeared so flustered as he stood on the altar and performed the service that it was all she could do not to laugh out loud. He hadn't expected her to stay. That much was obvious, but she hadn't imagined how rattled he would be by her presence. He seemed so disconcerted that she almost got up and left just so he could relax. His reaction was really quite endearing, and she found herself smiling again.

Something had changed between them since they left the hunting box earlier this afternoon. Despite the rancor that had defined their acquaintance from the beginning, they had seemed almost like friends today as they had talked and laughed together. He had seemed genuinely concerned about her and her circumstances when he had offered her such kind advice regarding Camille and India and Lexington House. He had even joked with her, something she didn't think him capable of doing. Her face warmed as she recalled how affronted she had been by his demand that she attend church services, only to have him tell her that he was kidding—and then wink at her, of all things.

And now, as the minutes ticked by and she could once again think beyond his aquamarine eyes, she had a hard time remembering why she hadn't liked the man in the first place. He wasn't the insufferable holy man caught up in his sanctimonious service to God that she had initially thought him to be. Oh, he was staid and reserved and maybe a little *too* pious, to be sure, but he possessed a surprising sense of humor. And whereas before she had thought him to be driven only by devotion to pretentious religious twaddle, she had come to appreciate that he had a more unpretentious—almost charming—human side to him.

She realized—and not for the first time today—that she *liked* Mr. Rodman. And worse, she was attracted to him. And worse than that, she was changing her habits because she liked Mr. Rodman and was attracted to him. It was much easier to ignore one's attraction to a man one did not like, but when one found a man both attractive and agreeable, one might find oneself doing strange things, things one would never do, like attending church services when one had vowed never, not in a million years, to return to the Church of England. Yet, here she was, sitting in the chapel at Lexington House listening to him perform the standard Anglican service—and all because she found him both attractive and kind. Purely on a whim, she had turned into the last pew and sat down because she didn't want to leave him. She decided to stay for the service because she had wanted to please him, to make him happy. And also, she had to admit, because it afforded her the opportunity to observe him, to look at him, to admire him.

And now, as she sat there watching him, she shook her head at the absurdity of the situation. He was a vicar of the Church of England. She was his patroness. He considered her a heretic. She *was* a heretic. Moreover, she was moving to India. Permanently. These were only a few reasons why a romantic involvement between the two of them was impossible. But the biggest argument against it was the fact that he had been so hurt by his wife's infidelity that he never wanted to involve himself with another woman—especially, she would wager, a woman who had cuckolded her own husband and borne him another man's child.

She should put an end to this stupidity right now. Even though it would be rude beyond all measure, she should get up and leave and not look back. That's what she should do. Yes, yes, no doubt about it, she needed to stand up now and walk out of the chapel and forget about Mr. Rodman and his charms. Now. Any time would be good. She should just do it. It would be easy enough to do. *Just get up and leave, Julia.*

She would. She would leave. She would go—just as soon as he finished his sermon. It would be far too impolite to walk out while he was speaking. She would wait just a few more minutes and leave when he was done.

Moments passed, and when he closed his eyes and

raised his arms to pray over the congregation, she saw the perfect opportunity to get up and leave. He wasn't even looking. No one was. She would have no better chance to go than now. So, why wasn't she able to move? Her spirit was willing—only too willing—but alas, as was frequently the case with her, her flesh was weak—only too weak. She could not break free of the hold he had on her.

In any case, it didn't matter anymore. He had lowered his arms, ending the service. It was over now, and she had stayed for the whole thing. She sighed as she stood and began walking toward the altar, intent on fetching Mr. Rodman so that they could depart from Lexington House and return to the hunting box. She stopped halfway down the aisle, however, as a swarm of appreciative women besieged and surrounded him. Not wanting to get jostled about by his throng of new devotees, Julia stood back while they thanked him for his time, complimented him on the message in his sermon, and asked him to return next week.

As she watched him accept their flattery with modesty and decorum, she was struck once again by how much her perception of Mr. Rodman had changed since she met him a few weeks ago. Here she was, admiring him now for how warm and kind he was toward the women as he talked with them. He wasn't the arrogant, self-righteous know-it-all she had originally judged him to be. Of course, none of these women provoked him. They did not shock or exasperate him like she had done the day he visited her at the hunting box and questioned her about her beliefs. Still, his attention and concern for the ladies sounded empathetic and sincere, not hollow and contrived. She couldn't help but be impressed.

The women around him began to disperse, and those who remained turned their attention to other conversations, ignoring her and Mr. Rodman. Essentially, they were alone together again. Neither of them spoke at first, as he put the items he had brought for the service away in his bag.

When he was done, he turned to her and settled his hands on his hips. "You stayed."

She nodded and shrugged, brushing it off as nothing. "I guess I did."

He cocked his head to the side and regarded her through narrowed eyes, as though he were trying to solve a puzzle. "Why?"

She turned aside from him, not wanting to meet his too-intense gaze. "I really had nowhere else to go."

"Ah." He removed his vestments and returned them and his books to his satchel.

She supposed she ought to remark about the ceremony he had just performed or at least compliment him on his sermon, but she was afraid if she opened her mouth, she would gush and sound like a besotted fool. So, she changed the subject. "I think we should head back to the hunting box right away."

"Do you? Wouldn't you like to show me the gardens?" He paused a moment to buckle his bag so that it was securely closed. "Or your shell collection?"

She laughed when he mentioned the shells. "I have no idea where they are."

"One of the ladies told me just now about a folly hidden at the back of the gardens, surrounded by hawthorn and holly trees. It sounded interesting. Won't you at least show me that?"

"Aren't you concerned about your sister? I fear she'll worry if you're not back at a reasonable hour."

He laughed and hoisted his bag over his shoulder by its strap. "You are not wrong there, but I don't think a few minutes in the garden would hurt."

She nodded and smiled. "The 'folly,' as the ladies call it, is quite enchanting, although it's really more of a temple than anything else. I had it built at the back of the garden when I returned home from India. I used to take refuge back there from my troubles—before I moved out of Lexington House. I would meditate out there." She shrugged once again. "I suppose I could show it to you."

"Very good."

They turned to head out of the chapel when Mrs. Sweeney, the pregnant woman Mrs. Nash had mentioned earlier in the drawing room, approached them. "Mr. Rodman?" She waddled as she walked, her petite frame adjusting to the growing babe in her belly.

He turned his gaze to the lady. "Yes?"

Julia stepped in to introduce them. "Oh, Mrs. Sweeney, it's so good to see you. I hope you have been well. You know who Mr. Rodman is, of course, but Mr. Rodman, I'd like to introduce you to Mrs. Sweeney. She came to us from London several months ago."

Mrs. Sweeney gave as good a curtsy as she could manage in her condition. "I just wanted to thank you personally, Mr. Rodman, for coming out to Lexington House to do the service."

He bowed and smiled. "It was my pleasure. Thank you for attending."

"I normally wouldn't." She fiddled with the ends of her shawl as though she were nervous. "Attend, that is. I'm Roman Catholic, you see, but I wanted to say some prayers today—for my baby. And . . . perhaps get a blessing." A forlorn sadness crossed the woman's features.

"Of course, Mrs. Sweeney. May God bless both you and your babe." He made the sign of the cross over her abdomen.

"Thank you," she whispered. "Thank you so much, Mr. Rodman. And you, too, Lady Julia." She appeared to be near tears as she turned to go.

"Is everything alright, Mrs. Sweeney?" asked Julia.

Though the woman nodded, she seemed to swallow a sob. "Yes, yes, everything is fine."

"Then what's the matter?"

The woman shrugged and stared at her feet. "I'm not sure, really. I–I guess I'm just frightened about what will happen to me and my babe. As I get nearer to my confinement, I just worry about how it will go."

Julia approached her and took her in her arms. She embraced the woman for several seconds and then leaned back with her hands still on her shoulders. "Don't worry, Mrs. Sweeney. It will all work out. There's no need to be afraid. Your baby will be born nice and healthy, and you will both stay here until we can find some suitable arrangement for you."

The woman swiped away a few tears from her cheeks. "Thank you, Lady Julia. You are truly too generous. I don't deserve your kindness."

Julia hugged her once again. "Of course, you do. Now, don't cry. Everything will be fine."

Mr. Rodman cleared his throat. "Yes, Mrs. Sweeney. I want to assure you that God loves you and your child very much. He will watch over you both and keep you safe. You have nothing to fear if you have faith in His love and goodness."

Though the woman nodded, her expression remained dubious as she wiped away a few more tears. "I will try to have faith. Thank you. Thank you both."

Mrs. Sweeney turned and shuffled away from them. The pain and fear etched in her face, however, haunted Julia for several moments after she was gone. Clearly, the woman was scared about her impending labor. Yet, there was something more troubling her, something deeper. Her expression revealed some other emotion that was upsetting her, something even worse than pain and fear, but Julia couldn't quite read it. Though she wanted more than anything to help the woman with what disturbed her, she didn't want to press her for an explanation of what was wrong in front of Mr. Rodman.

"Poor woman." He interrupted her thoughts with speculation of his own. "She seems so sad. So hopeless."

"I thought the same thing."

"I wonder what is really troubling her." He paused a moment as if deep in thought. "She's the one Mrs. Nash mentioned earlier, isn't she? The one whose husband beat her after finding out she was with child, correct?"

Julia nodded. "Yes. He kicked her in the abdomen."

He shook his head in obvious horror. "Monster."

He said nothing else and began moving toward the narthex. Julia followed him, also saying nothing more. She sensed, though, that he was still as unsettled over Mrs. Sweeney as she was.

They reached the narthex and exited the chapel via its heavy oaken door, traveling back to the house through the covered walkway. Once inside, neither said much of anything as she led him down another long hallway, pointing out the breakfast room and the dining room, as well as a sitting room and a salon as they passed them on their way back to the grand entry. Once there, she veered right and walked by the grand staircase until they reached the conservatory again. She turned left and led him down a short corridor in the east wing to the set of massive oaken doors opening to the ballroom.

"Extraordinary."

His sense of awe amused her. The room was extraordinary, she supposed, even in it is current state as a storage room. "We're storing furniture from other rooms in the house so that we can accommodate as many women as possible. That's why you see all the dust covers."

He nodded, and she led him through the maze of covered pieces of furniture to one of the many French doors that opened onto a terrace outside the ballroom. They exited through one set of doors and crossed the terrace to a stone path, still wet from the rain not long ago. He followed her down the meandering path away from the house toward the gardens into a lush bloom of flowers, shrubs, and trees. Finally, as they passed through some hawthorn and holly trees, the folly came into view.

He gasped audibly when he saw it. "Unbelievable."

She laughed at his reaction to the ornate structure. Designed to look like the Hindu temples Julia had visited in India, it bore no resemblance whatsoever to Lexington House—or anything in traditional English architecture. He gazed in open astonishment at the detailed carvings of Hindu deities adorning the outer walls before she led him up the stone steps into its interior. He strode to the center of the room and then rotated in a circle to take in the entire chamber.

While he wandered the room taking in what could be seen of the walls in the dim light, Julia managed to light a few candles hanging from sconces on the walls. Once lit, the candles' flames leapt into action, causing the deities carved in stone to dance along the walls. He gasped once again as he regarded the brightly painted images of the Hindu pantheon as they cavorted around the room. She let him admire the scenes while she sat on a low stone bench that projected from the walls of the pavilion.

He spread his arms open wide. "It—it's . . . I'm speechless, Lady Julia. It's magnificent."

"It is. It was always my favorite place to go."

"I can see why."

"It always transports me to another time and place."

"To India?"

She nodded.

"Where did you get those cushions over there on the floor?"

Ah. The cushions. "I had them made special for me in London with fabrics from my saris that I brought back from India."

"They're lovely—very brightly colored. Why are they here? What do you do with them?"

"I sit on them. They make it more comfortable to sit on the floor."

He arched a brow as he continued to eye them. "And you sit on them to meditate, I take it?"

"Yes. As I said before, I used to come here to meditate—at least once a day and sometimes more when I lived here at Lexington House."

He gave her a slight nod. "Hmm. I see."

She sensed disapproval in his tone and his expression, but she didn't ask him what bothered him. She could guess what it was and why.

"And you pray to that Hindu god of yours while you meditate here?" Again, he gave the impression that he did not approve.

"Yes."

He strolled around the chamber examining the brightly painted figures carved into the walls. "Is he here? Your Indian god?"

"Yes, of course. Lord Ganesh. He's the elephant-headed god over there. By the altar." She remained seated on the bench but pointed to the wall opposite from where he stood.

He snapped his head toward her and arched a brow in what she sensed was disapproval. "Altar?"

"Mmm-hmm." She probably shouldn't have mentioned the altar.

"A 'pagan' altar?"

She shrugged.

He narrowed his eyes. "And what do you do with your pagan altar?"

"It's where I burn incense and place offerings to the deities."

He nodded as he strode to the image of Lord Ganesh near the altar and scrutinized both the god and the table for a moment. Then he moved on to the next figure carved into the wall and the next, inspecting them all. "And these other figures carved in the walls? Are they other Hindu gods?"

"And goddesses. The Hindus worship the female side of the Divine as much as the male."

He scoffed—almost inaudibly. Still, the sound was unmistakable, and when she heard it, the mood between them changed at once. She caught his eye as he cast her a sidelong, derisive glance. Ah, there he was, the Mr. Rodman she knew, once again mocking what he didn't know or couldn't comprehend and resembling the superior Christian she'd thought him to be the day she met him.

"Not a fan of the feminine side of the Universe, Mr. Rodman?"

He kept his gaze fixed, ironically, on the image of Shakti on the wall in front of him as he crossed his arms over his chest. "Humph. I wouldn't say I'm not a fan . . . exactly."

"But you just don't see the need to worship the feminine Divine along with her masculine consort?" Like him, she folded her arms across her chest. "Or, I bet I know what it is. You don't see anything at all divine about the feminine aspect of nature. Women are property, not to be revered for their intellect or their abilities or their devotion to their families. Though they sacrifice themselves for the happiness of their husbands and children, you see nothing deific, much less goddess-like, about them in their roles as mothers, daughters, sisters, and wives, especially in this patriarchal society where men rule and women have no power."

Again, he shot her a sidelong glance. He said nothing, however.

"That's it, isn't it? You don't see anything holy or sacred about women, do you?"

"You put words in my mouth, Lady Julia."

"Do I, Mr. Rodman? Or is it more likely that I see the truth of the matter? You, along with every other typical man in this world, think women are wicked and profane, not to be trusted and certainly, not to be worshipped. We are sinful, evil, and corrupt, right?"

"Don't forget weak."

Outraged at his statement, she shot up off the bench and stomped over to him, her hands balled into fists. "*Weak?!*"

He turned to look at her then, and the anger in his eyes made her take a step back. "Yes. Weak. All women are weak. They're dissipated creatures who crave carnal pleasures over spiritual piety. They're always caving in to their baser instincts and causing trouble for the entire world. All of mankind suffers for their waywardness."

She tried not to gape, but she couldn't help it. "All of *mankind?* How so?"

"May I remind you of Eve? If it weren't for Eve's weakness against the serpent's temptation, mankind wouldn't have been kicked out of the Garden."

She nearly hit him. That she didn't was a testament to her restraint. And though she dearly wanted to slug him, she realized she could clobber him all she wanted—on the head even—and she still wouldn't get anything through his thick skull. "You couldn't be more wrong. Women. Are. Strong. They are the strongest *creatures* in nature."

He scoffed once again, blatantly this time. "I'd love to hear why you think that."

She stepped closer to him, closer than was comfortable. She looked up into his face, and her head nearly touched his chin as she captured and held his gaze. "May *I* remind *you* of Mary? The mother of God? Co-redemptrix at the crucifixion of her Son?"

"Co-*what?*"

"Redemptrix. That's right. She redeemed humanity with her suffering every bit as much as her Son did the day He was murdered. She died for humanity right along with Him. It had to have killed a part of her soul to bear witness to her Son's torture and His hanging on the cross. Talk about *strength.* Surviving that alone must have taken herculean fortitude, but on top of it, she then had to watch Him die—a slow, excruciating death. She sacrificed her Son as much as God the Father did, and the agony she suffered watching it qualifies her as co-redemptrix of humanity."

He threw his arms in the air, while his jaw dropped and his eyes shot open wide in blatant shock. "That— that's the most outrageous thing I think I have *ever* heard anyone say. I-I-I don't even know how to respond." He scrubbed his hands down his face. "I've said it before, and I'll say it again. You, madam, are an inveterate heretic."

"Oh, really?"

He nodded.

She dismissed him with a wave of her hand. "Do you want to know what your problem is?"

"I don't have a problem."

"Oh, yes, you most certainly do. You, sir, are an unmitigated, chauvinistic male arse."

"*Arse?*"

"You heard me. *Arse.* You are an arse."

He had never been so infuriated by a woman in his life. Or more flummoxed. And never more aroused. He didn't know whether to rant at her or kiss her. In the end, he scrubbed his hands down his face, as he'd done a moment ago, in unqualified exasperation. Then he turned and walked away from her, afraid that if he remained in front of her, he would take her in his arms and it would all be over. Or perhaps it would just be the beginning. He didn't know. All he did know was that he needed to get away from her and her heretical nonsense.

And her jasmine scent. And her copper hair. And those cinnamon eyes whose beguiling depths could seduce a saint as they reflected the temple's candlelight in a provocative spiral dance.

Get a hold of yourself, Rodman.

He nearly laughed out loud when he recalled that earlier just this morning, he had given serious consideration to the idea of ignoring all reason and courting her romantically, especially after the amusing repartee and laughter they had shared up until a few minutes ago. At the moment, however, as he stood there in her temple, all thought of pursuing an amorous relationship with her perished without hope of resuscitation. He turned back to her. "Perhaps we should go, Lady Julia."

"Yes. Perhaps that would be wise." She spoke through her teeth and then huffed as she stalked away from him toward the entry of the pavilion and then out into the garden.

Though he followed, he remained behind her, maintaining a good distance between them as they traipsed back through the garden to the ballroom and then traversed their way back through her vast house and outside to the gig that stood waiting for them in the drive. He attempted to help her up into the gig, but she wouldn't have it. Instead, she asked a groomsman who was just finishing feeding and watering the horse to assist her.

To say the ride back toward the hunting box was uncomfortable would be to understate it by a hundred-fold. The air between them virtually crackled with hostility. He kept his arms folded across his chest and his vision focused on the scenery to his right. He could still see her, however, from the corner of his eye. She held on tight to the reins and kept her gaze trained on the lane ahead. When their knees inadvertently knocked together after they hit a bump in the road, she jerked hers away from his as though he had branded her.

This would be a longish fifty minutes.

He settled back into his side of the bench, still keeping his arms crossed and his eyes fixed to his right. They rode like that in painful silence for some time. How long it was, he couldn't tell.

And then, he felt the first drop. He ignored it until the second one hit him and then a third. When a fourth drop landed on his face, he thought they might have an issue. Now a fifth pelted him and then a sixth, followed by a seventh. Still, he remained hopeful that it was nothing more than a light summer shower. Only when the number of drops multiplied to infinity and lightning shot across the darkened sky did he know they had a problem. Thunder cracked overhead, and a ridiculous amount of water fell from the clouds, as though the heavens had opened up and the angels had thrown a bucket of water over the earth. They were getting drenched as the rain fell in torrents. If it kept up like this, they would be soaked through to the skin unless they found shelter.

"Lady Julia?" he called over the roar of the storm.

"I know, I know."

Though he waited for her to say more, she remained silent as she turned the gig down a narrow gravel lane. The rain continued to hammer them as she slapped the reins on the horse, forcing the animal into a trot. At last, he saw her apparent destination when a tall, crumbling stone tower, the keep of an ancient castle, rose out of the mists generated by the rain. She drove the gig across a rickety wooden bridge above a dry moat and into the ruins of an arched gatehouse. She pulled the horse to a halt under the barbican's brick arch supported by two intact sandstone columns.

When the vehicle came to a stop, he gathered his bags and jumped down from his side of the bench and then rounded the gig to help her down as well, and this time, she took his hand and accepted his assistance. After securing the gig, she worked quickly to unhitch the horse. The animal seemed reluctant to leave the shelter of the gatehouse but would have plenty of room to roam the grassy inner courtyard once the rain died down later. Lady Julia, meanwhile, motioned for Charles to follow her as she dashed through the downpour across the yard to a portion of the castle keep that still provided cover.

They entered what appeared to be an old kitchen. The remains of giant stone hearth, where ancient pots and kettles would no doubt have once hung over an open fire, stood on one end of the chamber. He approached the hearth and glanced around for any materials they might use to build a fire. A pile of old, dried leaves sat in a corner near the fireplace. He also spotted countless twigs and branches scattered across the stone floor tiles that must have blown in on the wind.

He set the smaller of his bags, the one Caroline had packed with provisions for him, on the floor and began unbuckling the other bag that he had slung by its straps across his chest. He reached into the open satchel and pulled out the candles and candlesticks he had packed for the church service as well as the flints he had brought along to light them. He gathered the branches, twigs, and dried leaves and laid them in the center of the hearth, setting aside a small pile of debris for the kindling. Before lighting the kindling, he looked up into the chimney to make sure it would allow smoke from the fire to escape. He found mostly open air above the back of the hearth. The chimney proper had long ago disintegrated, and what remained of it would pose no problem with venting the smoke.

He crouched in front of the hearth and began striking the flints to spark the kindling. When the kindling began smoking, he laid it atop the other materials to get them burning too. Finally, after a few minutes, he had a fairly decent fire going, and it began to warm the air in front of the hearth. He stood and looked around for Lady Julia. She sat across the room huddled on the floor with her arms wrapped around her bent knees and her forehead resting on her arms. Even with her shawl draped about her like a blanket, she shivered.

He strode over to her and squatted beside her and tapped her shoulder gently to get her attention. She raised her head and regarded him with a look of caution.

"Come. Sit by the fire." He stood and held out his

hand to help her stand.

She took it, but with reluctance, he could tell. Still, she rose from the floor and followed him to the hearth. Her dress was wet, but to his relief, it was not soaked, despite the deluge they had just ridden through. Even so, as she sat and began warming her hands near the glowing fire, she continued to shiver while her teeth chattered. He removed his coat and then his waistcoat and placed them both snugly around her shoulders. Though she said nothing, she nodded, which he took as a gesture of gratitude.

The storm, meanwhile, still howled outside with the wind driving the torrential rain against the stone ruins as thunder cracked and rumbled over them every now and again.

He sat beside her, though not too close, and opened the smaller bag with the provisions Caroline had insisted he bring along. *Humph.* It appeared that he would actually have to thank his sister for her consideration and foresight when he got home. She had outdone herself with the items she had packed. He pulled out not one, but two bottles of red wine, a loaf of bread, a block of cheese, several slices of ham, a half-dozen hardboiled eggs, some biscuits, a bunch of grapes, and a few apples. He also found napkins, a knife for the bread and cheese, and two pewter goblets for the wine, along with pewter plates for the food. How long had she anticipated he would be gone? She had stocked enough to sustain him for days. He would have rolled his eyes at the excess except that he was by now parched and starving—and grateful.

He uncorked one of the wine bottles and poured the liquid into the two goblets. He also sliced up the bread and cheese and peeled a couple of eggs. When he was done with those tasks, he put some bread, ham, cheese, and an egg on a plate and handed it to Lady Julia along with a napkin. He then gave her a goblet of wine. Again, she nodded in apparent appreciation as she took them but said nothing.

They sat and ate and drank in silence, the crackling of the fire providing the only accompaniment to the tension between them. He watched her as she stared at the flames. Her expression gave no hint as to what she was thinking, but he would have bet she wished she were anywhere but here—and with anyone other than him. Strangely, at the moment, he did not feel the same way about her.

Though he was still shaken over their argument and stung that she had called him an arse, and though he couldn't understand, much less tolerate, her religious beliefs, he couldn't stay mad at Lady Julia. He supposed that had something to do with her jasmine scent, copper hair, and cinnamon eyes. He also couldn't remain angry with her when he admired her so much for her generosity and charity toward the women of Lexington House. But there was something else going on here. He had to admit even to himself that the woman challenged his intellect and his beliefs with her own, and she wasn't afraid to disagree with him or to disapprove of his views. Nor did she make any attempt to school her sentiments behind the polite, prim, and proper demeanor of the typical English noblewoman.

She was fierce. She was passionate. She was fiery and intense. She was like no other woman he had ever met.

And suddenly, just like that, he was under her spell once again. Moreover, the idea of pursuing her romantically, a proposition he had declared dead a half hour ago, revived. It had really never died, he supposed; it had only lain dormant for a while, kindled into life now by her mere presence and bursting into flame once again like a smoldering ember in a banked fire.

"I'm sorry."

What? Had she just said something? He was so caught up in his own thoughts that he hadn't paid much attention to anything around him. He turned to her, confused. "I'm sorry?"

"You're sorry?"

"No. Well, that's not what I mean. I meant I'm sorry I didn't hear what you said."

"Oh, I'm sorry. I said I'm sorry."

"Sorry for what?"

"For calling you an arse."

He smiled, but she couldn't have seen it because her gaze was fixed on the floor. "Don't worry too much about it."

With her finger, she traced a circle in the dust covering the floor tiles. "Still, it was rude and unladylike and—and just plain mean." She looked up at him then, her eyes glistening. "And I'm truly sorry."

"Thank you, Lady Julia. I accept your apology. I did, however, provoke you."

She nodded. "That is true. You did. However, I should have had control over my emotions. I'm far too quick-tempered and outspoken for my own good. And opinionated." She shook her head. "So *very* opinionated. My father used to say so. My husband used to say so, and my brother still says so every so often. And what's worse, my opinions spark my temper, and anger gets the best of me. I need to rein in my tendency to rage at things that bother me."

"Well, for what it's worth, I admire your passion and your honest opinions. It's refreshing."

She scoffed. "I've been accused of many things before, but never of being refreshing."

He chuckled. "Well, whatever you are, you are unique, and that's something."

She laughed and turned her attention once more to the floor.

He untied his cravat and unwound it from his neck. "I'm sorry, too."

She didn't look up. "Oh?"

"Yes. I'm sorry I called women weak. I shouldn't have said it, but please know that I didn't really mean it and I certainly don't believe it. Women are strong. I know they are. They have to be to survive the world's expectations of them."

"Hmm." She studied him through a sidelong glance. "I can't tell if that's what you really think or if it's just some pretty speech you came up with to restore my good opinion of you."

"You had a good opinion of me?"

"Yes. For at least a moment or two today."

"I'm honored. I hope someday I can keep your good opinion for more than a moment or two. At the very least."

She laughed. "So, why did you say women are weak if you didn't mean it?"

He shook his head. "I don't know. I guess I let my own temper get the better of me. I think I said it because . . . what I mean to say is . . . I—" He shrugged midsentence and then turned to her. "I said it, I think, because something you said about women and their devotion to their families and husbands provoked me. Please don't ask me why. It regards an upsetting incident from the past." *Eleanor—and how she betrayed me with Dunham.* He shook his head to clear unsettling thoughts of his dead wife and his dead friendship from his mind. "I still haven't come to terms with it. It still has a firm grip on me, and I can't seem to move beyond it. Any attempt to explain the situation would only make others look bad—and wouldn't flatter me too much either."

"Very well. I won't ask you to explain. And though it will be hard, I will also try not to let what you said bother me any longer."

He exhaled loudly. "How about this? How about we put the whole scene behind us and never speak of it again."

"I'm agreeable to that."

"Good." Neither of them said anything else for a while as they both stared quietly at the fire.

She continued tracing figures on the floor for a while and then released a heavy sigh. "Do you think we'll be here for long?"

"Tired of my company already?"

She laughed. "No, no, that's not it. It's just that I don't want Arthur or your sister to worry about us if we're not able to make it home tonight. Look at it out there. The rain isn't letting up, there's still lightning, and it's nearly dark. I don't think we can make it back tonight, not even to the hunting box, much less for you to get back to town."

"Well, I'm not worried. And neither should you be, and you especially shouldn't worry about my sister worrying about me. Whether she acknowledges it or not, I'm a big boy now, perfectly capable of taking care of myself." He paused a moment. "Although—and I hate to admit this aloud and do so with great reluctance—I do have to say that her provisions came in handy, since it does appear we may be stuck here. For a while, at least."

"It was nice to have them with us. I will have to write her a note to thank her."

"Please don't."

She shrugged. "Well, I suppose I don't have to write her, but I will certainly thank her in person when I see her at the public assembly rooms for my birthday on Friday."

"No, no, please don't thank her at all. It will only encourage her to do more . . . things . . . for me. And I don't want her doing even *one* thing, much less *more* things, for me."

She laughed again. "Well, I really ought to say something."

"I think not. Or at the very least, I wish you wouldn't thank her. I'd rather you tell her that she looks like she could benefit from the waters at Bath. And then give her directions."

She threw her head back this time when she laughed. "I shall do no such thing."

"Pity." He moved to put a few more twigs on the fire and then returned to sit beside her, offering her more wine. She smiled as she accepted a refill.

CHAPTER 9

Eight of Wands: The arrows of love; the beginnings of a romance; rush of excitement, swift action, moving forward at great speed . . .

THEY BOTH STARED AT THE fire for some time without saying anything. What Lady Julia was thinking, Charles hadn't a clue, but his mind was lost in thoughts of her, of her fiery spirit, her kind heart, her willingness to help the women at Lexington House, her integrity, her beauty, and her sharp wit. And as he pondered these things, he burned to know how she might react to the suggestion of a liaison between them. A romantic liaison. Would she hesitate? Would she allow him to court her? Would she even consider it? Or would she recoil in horror at the very notion?

On more than one occasion, he thought he had seen something in her eyes that hinted at an attraction on her part. Something seemed to smolder in her gaze when she looked at him sometimes. He recalled the day when they had stared together at the erotic picture in that *Kama* whatever-it-was book. Something had certainly sparked between them that afternoon. Then there had been the moment she had touched his arm when he had escorted her to the dining room the night she and her cousin came for dinner at the vicarage. Again, something had burned between them then. He hadn't been able to think straight throughout the meal. And today, while they were together at Lexington House, he'd have sworn he sensed a desire in her nearly as strong as his own—before their argument, at least. But perhaps he only saw what he wanted to see.

As he regarded her now, her soft features and copper hair glowing in the firelight, he imagined a kiss, their first kiss. How would her lips feel pressed against his? Would they part for him, allowing him to explore her mouth with his tongue? How would she react to his caress, to his touch? Would she touch him back? And if he pulled her close, would she melt into him and press her body so tightly to his that he could feel her breasts against his chest and she could feel his erection against her abdomen?

Alright, that's enough.

He should never have gone down this train of thought, not with the way she made him feel.

Get a hold of yourself, Rodman, before you do some foolish thing you'll only end up regretting.

She rose to her feet at that moment, snapping him out of his inappropriate and dangerous fantasy. She stretched her body and then gave him back his jacket and waistcoat.

"Where are you going?"

"I thought I would go to that corner over there and meditate for a while. Unless, of course, it would bother you."

He chuckled. "I think you would do it anyway, even if it did bother me."

She smiled. "You're probably right, but I hope you wouldn't think I would do it to bother you *intentionally*."

He shook his head. "No, I wouldn't think that."

Saying nothing more, she walked over to a corner near the hearth and cleared a space on the floor by kicking some debris out of the way with her foot. Then she removed her slippers and hiked her dress up to her knees, revealing her stocking-clad legs and the garters that held them up. She could have no idea how much that aroused him, even more than his imagination had done. Though he should've been ashamed of his reaction to her exposed legs, he couldn't look away. Transfixed by everything about her, he watched her settle herself onto the floor, and once seated, cross her legs one over the other so that each of her stockinged feet rested on one of her knees. He cringed at how uncomfortable the position must be.

She covered her legs with her shawl and sat with her back ramrod straight by the wall. Then she positioned her hands palms up on her knees in an odd configuration, touching each thumb to a forefinger and leaving the other fingers outstretched. She closed her eyes and inhaled deeply through her nose. She held her breath a moment before letting it out slowly, exhaling through her mouth.

"Why do you sit like that?" The question was out of his mouth before he could stop himself from disturbing her.

Her eyes shot open. "Like what?"

"With your feet up on your knees."

"You mean in the lotus position?"

He shrugged. "I guess."

"It's a yoga position that most easily facilitates meditation for me. It also destroys all disease as it calms the body and brain and awakens the kundalini."

"Kundalini?"

She smiled as she closed her eyes. "I will tell you about kundalini another time perhaps." She adjusted her legs and arranged her hands again in that peculiar pose atop her knees. Then she began breathing in once more and continued for a few moments.

"Why do you rest your hands atop your knees in that strange position?"

She opened her eyes again. "You mean in the Gyan mudra?"

"Uh, I guess. I have no idea what those words even mean."

"A mudra is a positioning of the hands to align with sacred purpose. The Gyan mudra symbolizes the unity of fire and air, as well as the unity of the individual consciousness with the universal."

Again, she closed her eyes and inhaled deeply, holding her breath before releasing it slowly through her mouth. She repeated this breathing ritual several times before she began uttering strange words in a foreign tongue, just as she had done the first day he met her.

He watched her for several seconds as she repeated the words over and over. "Why do you do that?"

She opened her eyes once again, and this time, she

rolled them. "Do what?"

"I don't know. Breathe that way, I guess, and say those words."

She sighed. "Breathing in and out with intention helps me empty my mind of random thoughts. And the words I chant are called a mantra. It's a type of prayer, as I think I've told you before."

"Ah, yes. I recall now." He chuckled briefly. "You mentioned it the day I visited you to find out why you missed my first service at St. Blaise's."

She arched a brow in apparent irritation as she nodded and then closed her eyes yet again as she began her intentional breathing.

"Is it hard?"

Her eyes shot open as they had done before. "Mr. Rodman. *Please.* Are you trying to interrupt me so that I cannot meditate?"

"No, no. That was not my intention at all. I-I just wondered if meditating was difficult, what with all the things you have to do before you even begin."

She huffed. "No. It is not difficult. At least, not usually. I will admit that it is rather challenging with someone continually asking you questions as you try to settle your body and clear your mind—like right now—but otherwise, it isn't hard to do." She paused a moment, and then her eyes lit as if she had hit upon an idea. "In fact, would you like to try it? Maybe I could meditate more easily if you did it along with me."

"I don't think so. I could never pray to a Hindu god."

"You don't need to pray to a Hindu deity. Any god

will do."

"*Any* God? You're straddling that blasphemy-heresy line again."

She laughed when he waggled his finger at her in a teasing manner. Then she sobered her expression. "All gods—including the Christian God—emanate from the one Source of everything in the Universe."

"I've heard you say that before. You'll have to forgive me, however, if I have trouble adjusting my Christian beliefs to your Eastern ones."

"Yes, I don't suppose Christian beliefs are as accepting of other faiths as Hindu beliefs. One can be a Christian Hindu but not a Hindu Christian. Now, do you want to meditate or not? Because if not, I'd like to close my eyes and do so myself."

He peered down at the floor as he thought about the idea for a moment but rejected her suggestion in the end. Meditation was not for him. When he looked up again and saw the hope and anticipation in her expression, however, he wavered a moment. She appeared almost childlike in her eagerness to have him join her and show him how to meditate. Still, he couldn't do it. He couldn't bring himself to embrace such a foreign religious practice, one that would feel like a betrayal of his own religious beliefs and of God. "Thank you for the offer, Lady Julia, but I believe I'll pass this time. It's just too heathen a ritual for me."

Her disappointment was obvious, as was her lack of astonishment. She shrugged and nodded. "Well, there's always next time, isn't there?" She narrowed her eyes at him before closing them once again to meditate, but he did not miss her subtle dig. She did not believe his decision to pass on it this time in any way meant there would be a next time.

He watched her like that, chanting her rhythmic mantra in the lotus position with her hands poised in the Gyan mudra, for what seemed like eternity. And as he continued to observe her for a while, he wondered where she went when she became so immersed in meditation as she appeared to be now. Clearly, she was no longer in this world. She was unaware of her surroundings, lost in some chamber of her mind, he supposed. Yet, she was not asleep. What must it be like to be still conscious but oblivious to the outer world?

The soft refrain of her mantra coupled with the rain outside and the gentle rumblings of thunder somewhere in the distance lulled him into his own sense of peace. He would fall asleep sitting here on the floor if he let himself. Instead, he rose with as little sound as he could manage and made his way with as little noise as possible to a wall on the other side of the room. He lay down with his back against the wall and closed his eyes.

He must have drifted off, at least for a little while, for he didn't open his eyes again until movement across the room roused him. The first traces of dawn gently illuminated the chamber in grayscale as it chased away the darkness, while a figure moved slowly about the room scrutinizing the floor, occasionally bending down to scatter dried leaves and other debris from the stone tiles as though searching for something.

"Lady Julia, is that you?"

The figure spun around with a hand to her heart. "Goodness, Mr. Rodman. You startled me." She came into clearer view as she moved closer.

He sat up and stretched his arms above his head to loosen them after sleeping on them all night. "I'm very sorry. It's just that I couldn't quite make you out in the dim light. Is it morning already?"

She nodded. "Just barely."

Shocked that he had been oblivious to his surroundings for what must have been hours, he shook his head. "How long was I asleep?"

"For some time now. I meditated for over an hour. When I opened my eyes, I saw you lying there asleep on the floor. I got up myself and moved nearer to the hearth to lie down and keep warm. I fell asleep sometime around midnight, I would say, and you were still sleeping." She returned to inspecting the stone tiles, scooting leaves and dirt about with her foot.

"Are you looking for something?"

She nodded once again as she stopped and turned in a circle, scanning the floor. "My necklace." She touched her throat as if to confirm something was missing. "I've lost my necklace."

He got to his feet then and brushed the dust off his clothes while smoothing the wrinkles out of his pants. He stretched his back and legs to work out the tightness in his muscles from lying on the floor. "What's that you're wearing? Isn't that a necklace?" He pointed to her neck.

She fingered the heart-shaped locket at her throat, the same locket that had fallen from her parcel onto the floor at the inn, the one that he had picked up and handed to her the first day they met. "Yes, but I was also wearing another one—one my grandmother gave me. It's very dear to me, and I can't believe I've lost it."

The distress in her voice undid him, and he began searching the floor for the necklace himself. "It has to be around here somewhere. I'm sure we will find it. What does it look like?"

She shrugged. "It's hard to describe. It's . . . a carving. In sardonyx. Depicting one of the Tarot cards."

"Which one?" He kept his eyes focused on the floor and continued to scour the tiles for a necklace as he waited for her to answer. She said nothing, and figuring she hadn't heard his question, he raised his head to find her across the room carefully searching the floor around her feet. "Which Tarot card does it depict, Lady Julia?"

She shrugged and mumbled something indistinct.

"I'm sorry. I couldn't hear you. Which card did you say?"

She turned back to him then and rolled her eyes before speaking. "The Lovers."

"The what?"

She huffed in apparent irritation. "The Lovers." She turned her attention back to the floor. "It's Grandmamma's favorite card, alright?"

He arched a brow at her tone. "Alright." He paused for a second. "Why that card? What's so special about it?"

She raised her arms and let them flop to her sides as though he were trying her patience. "I don't know.

I guess because it represents the sacred love between two people, and she believes love is the greatest force in the Universe. Do you have a problem with that?"

He chuckled at her level of pique. "No, of course not. I didn't mean to upset you. But can you describe the card to me so I know what the necklace looks like?"

"You already know what it looks like. You saw it. Remember?"

He shook his head. "I never saw your necklace."

"Well, I've always worn it, so I'd say you've never *noticed* it. But you have seen The Lovers Tarot card."

"Ha. When?"

She turned away again and began toeing through small piles of dried leaves here and there. "Friday night. At the vicarage. When I did your Tarot reading. The Lovers came up as the fourth card. It was upside down. Or reversed, as it's called."

"Oh."

"Do you recall it?"

He recalled it, alright. How could he not? It was a man and a woman obviously in love with one another holding each other tenderly. "The couple in the tight embrace."

She nodded.

"And it was upside down in my reading because it represented me and my wife and our failed relationship." She didn't nod this time. Nor did she say anything. But then, she didn't have to. "Well, at least now I know what I'm looking for."

She turned and continued shuffling her slippers

through piles of leaves, while he searched the corner where she meditated last night. "So, when did your grandmother give you this necklace of The Lovers?"

"On the night of my debut. She gave each of us girls—my sisters and me—a sardonyx cameo carving of The Lovers when we debuted so that it would guide us each to our true love."

He stood, dumbfounded, unable to respond. How could a woman as intelligent and sensible as Lady Julia believe in such drivel?

She turned to him and laughed when she saw his expression. It must have revealed his skepticism. "I bet you think that's superstitious nonsense."

He raised a brow. "Well, I'd be lying if I said I didn't. How could a silly necklace ever lead anyone to their true love? Has it ever guided you to *your* true love?"

She pursed her lips and rolled her eyes before she peered down at the floor. "Well, no. Not yet, anyway. But Grandmamma assured me I will meet him one day. On the night of my debut, she told me I would find a man like the King of Wands. Not right away, perhaps, but someday."

He shook his head in disbelief. "King of what?"

She laughed once again. "You don't believe in anything, do you, Mr. Rodman? King of Wands. It's a Tarot card that is supposed to represent my true love. The man Grandmamma believed I would find. She also told me I may not know him for who he is right away, but when I finally do recognize him, I'll see it was him all along."

"And he'll be like the King of Wands?"

"Yes. He'll be a man with light hair and eyes and strong ethics and morals."

"And fiery passions."

She glanced over at him as she laughed. "Yes, exactly. How did you know?"

"From the Tarot reading you did for me the other night. You said the King of Wands is a man with fair hair and light eyes with strong ethics and strict morals who's very focused on his goals. Like me, you said. In fact, you used him to represent me in the reading. What did you call him? The significant one?"

Her mouth fell open just a little, almost as if his question astonished her. She regarded him for a moment through narrowed eyelids before responding. "The Significator . . ." Her voice trailed off, and then she swallowed—or rather, gulped essentially, as though something dreadful had just occurred to her.

"Quite right. The Significator. You said I resemble the King of Wands. Except for the fiery passions." He chuckled.

She did not laugh with him and, in fact, said nothing. Instead, she nodded once, while her brows scrunched together and her cinnamon eyes widened almost imperceptibly. She seemed to study him with guarded wariness for a few seconds, and if he weren't mistaken, a newfound discomfort, like something troubled her.

"Which I do not seem to possess."

She tilted her head to the side in apparent confusion at his last comment but remained silent.

"Fiery passions. You seemed to doubt my ability to . . . become . . ." Though the word he was trying to think of was on the tip of his tongue, he couldn't quite articulate it, so he motioned to her with his hand to encourage her to help him out. "Oh, what's the term? You know—"

"Aroused?"

He shrugged but nodded. It was not the expression he would have used, perhaps, conjuring as it did something carnal, but he supposed that aroused was essentially the word he was looking for. "You think me incapable of becoming . . . aroused, correct?"

She both nodded and shook her head at the same time as she backed away toward the hearth. Silently, she reached down for her shawl that still lay on the floor where she had apparently left it last night. "We should be going."

"What about your necklace?"

"It'll probably turn up somewhere, I'm sure. Let's go. I don't want Arthur to worry about us." She lifted the wrap, and when she shook it out, something flew out from the middle and hit the stone tiles with a ping.

He walked toward the hearth, and they both looked to the floor. She took a step back, and as her shadow shifted, the sunlight that had begun to filter through the cracks in the stones of the ruins glinted off something metallic that lay coiled in front of him. He bent and picked up a delicate gold chain and unwound it to find an oval medallion about the size of a sovereign coin attached to it. It was a cameo carved in an orange stone—sardonyx, no doubt.

"This must be your necklace." He held out his palm to show her the cameo, and as she stepped closer to inspect it, her jasmine scent wafted around him while sparks of gold glittered in her coppery hair. She touched the image gently, almost reverently, her face in awe. And as she caressed it with her finger, she also caressed his skin. Inadvertently, of course, with no intention whatsoever, and yet, her touch was enough to stoke the embers of that uncomfortable desire that constantly smoldered within him when she was around. In a matter of seconds, the embers sparked into a blaze, and he nearly reached for her.

She looked up at him then, her cinnamon eyes meeting his. "Thank you." She scooped the necklace from his hand with her fingers and shook her head as if to clear it before turning to go.

"Wait." He should just let her go. He needed to clear his own thoughts, or he would do something crazy, like pull her into his arms.

She hesitated a moment before turning back to him but said nothing.

"Don't you want to put it on before we leave?"

She shrugged slightly but then nodded as she lifted the chain to eye level so that she could unhook the ends that were still clasped together. He watched her trembling fingers fumble with the catch for several seconds.

"Here." He stepped forward and took the necklace gently from her and unfastened the ends. "Turn around." She turned away from him, and he encircled her neck with the two ends of the chain and then affixed the clasp to the hook. After the two ends were secured to one another, he set the chain gently against her neck. And as his fingers skimmed over her skin, sparks of desire once again roared into flames within him. "There you go." He dropped the chain as though it burned him and took a step back from her before he did something mad, like taste the nape of her neck with his tongue.

She turned around and touched her fingers to both the heart locket just below her throat and the cameo that now hung a little lower against her décolletage. "Thank you, Mr. Rodman."

When he heard her whispered response, his gaze fell to her lips, and desire coiled through his body as he imagined how they would feel beneath his. Warm and pliant, no doubt. Eager and willing, maybe. Greedy with insatiable need? He hoped. "You're most wel-come."

She didn't move, and he? He couldn't move. He remained rooted to the stone floor as her lovely face entranced him. He was too aware of how close they stood to one another for rational thought. It would take no effort whatsoever for him to lean down and kiss her luscious lips. Something flickered in her eyes as they stared at each other, and he could sense the moment she felt the same pull as he did. Something primal, something hot flashed between them, and as he reached up to stroke her cheek with the backs of his fingers, he determined right then he would do it. He parted his lips slightly and bent down subtly. He was inches away from contact, but he wavered just one second too long as he debated with himself whether to touch her lips lightly with his own or give in to the powerful urge to crush his mouth and body against hers.

Oh, no. *No, no, no.* Whatever was happening was not good. She needed to do something—fast. So she took two steps back and abruptly spun around to get away from him. "We need to go. Now."

When his fingers had grazed the back of her neck as he was fastening the necklace, his touch had scorched her skin and lit a fire within her so intense she thought her hair would ignite. Worse, when she turned around to thank him, she froze, spellbound by his gaze, realizing that if she didn't do something to tamp down the desire that his aquamarine eyes, his bergamot scent, and his very presence had enflamed within her, she would do something entirely inappropriate, like reach out and launch herself into his arms.

He is not the King of Wands. He is not the King of Wands. He is not the King of Wands.

He had been about to kiss her. That much was certain. Even had she not seen the unmistakable incendiary spark of desire burning in his eyes, she had sensed the moment he had made his decision to do it when he caressed her cheek. And when she had recognized the subtle lowering of his head and the slight parting of his lips as further indication of his intention, her heart pounded as she anticipated the moment their lips would meet. He was going to kiss her, and lord, how she had wanted him to do it.

He is NOT the King of Wands.

She had wanted him to pull her close and release

all the power and hunger and lust and passion that raged within her, but—she couldn't let him do it. She couldn't let him kiss her, for if he had but touched her, he would have unleashed that *thing* within her that threatened to break free every time she desired a man. That force, that—that longing, that wicked and wanton unnaturally passionate creature that lay inside her just waiting for the right—or wrong—moment to burst forth and reveal her true nature.

He is not the King of Wands.

She did not possess the kind of chaste inhibitions of some women, of those who could just lie there passively and accept a partner's kiss or embrace with no emotion. Her passion was shameless, immodest, unrestrained, and once let loose, it led her to cast aside her moral compass and abandon all propriety in order to satiate her physical desire. It had disgusted her husband to the point that he rarely touched her. He considered her too much of a harlot, a jade, a strumpet to be attracted to her, and he had called her every one of those things at one time or another. She was not the prim and proper English wife who could contain her urges and quash her libido and simply lie there like a respectable lady while he took his satisfaction. Her inability to behave with modesty and decorum in the bedchamber revolted him. In his view, only whores acted the way she did, so he spurned her most of the time, choosing instead to bed—in blatant hypocrisy— the very whores and dissipated women he chastised her for being because at least the carnal impulses of a paid escort weren't unnatural.

His infidelity had hurt her, had torn her apart, but there was nothing she could do about it when she couldn't stop herself from becoming a raging inferno in his arms. And when Renesh had come into her life, which he had done, ironically, to heal her husband, he had shown respect and reverence—and most of all—appreciation for her fiery nature. When he had offered her not only the slightest morsel of reciprocated passion but also had returned it with full force, she had lost all good sense and taken him to her bed.

She couldn't let that happen with Mr. Rodman. He was not the King of Wands. She couldn't lose herself to him in that way and allow him to see the tempest that was her true nature. He wasn't the King of Wands, after all. He already thought her strange. What would he think if he kissed her and her passion erupted like a volcano? He would think she was positively perverse, the worst woman alive—weak, like Eve, a slave to her baser instincts. So she had done the only respectable thing there was to do in the moment. She had spun away from him to break the spell between them, for she had no doubt that if she'd allowed him to kiss her, she would have ended up on the floor with him, her skirt tangled around her waist and her legs tangled around his hips urging him to pump harder as he pounded her with his cock—as if he were the King of Wands.

Such an image. She fanned her face when her vagina clenched at the mere thought of him inside her, and then she laughed at herself out loud, for she had no doubt that if the very staid and proper Mr. Rodman knew her thoughts, he would be horrified beyond all measure. Moreover, he could never ever be encouraged to let go his inhibitions and take her on the cold, stone floor, much less pound her with anything but words of disdain and derision, never mind his cock.

"What's so funny, Lady Julia?"

She sobered at once. "Nothing. Let's go."

"Go where?"

"Home, of course. It's time I got back to the hunting box and you to the vicarage."

"Of course." Though he seemed surprised—and a little confused—by her abrupt decision to leave, he nevertheless sensed her urgency and hurried to gather his things.

She had to leave—and now. *He is not the King of Wands.* She had to do something—anything—to get away from him. *He is not the King of Wands.* Unfortunately, he followed close behind her as she practically sprinted across the grassy courtyard toward the gig. When they arrived, she refused to let him assist her up to the bench, fearing that his touch would only further enflame the need within her.

He, meanwhile, tended to the horse, harnessing it to the carriage before jumping up into the gig himself. He sat close beside her, uncomfortably close, so close she couldn't think rationally. Still, she managed to guide the horse and gig back to the main road. When a blessed silence settled between them, she hoped perhaps the swaying of the gig and the damp, dewy petrichor of an early morning following a thunderstorm would distract her mind from imagining the two of them together, entwined in a lover's embrace. It was no use, however. His presence next to her merely taunted her, while the feel of his thigh next to her own tortured her already aroused senses, sending warmth, wetness, and quivers to the most intimate flesh in her body. Her torment only increased as she fantasized about all the delicious and decadent things she would do to his body, if he let her, and the different positions they could try from the *Kama Sutra*.

Stop it, you ninny. Now. Do you want to end up straddling his lap seeking release when you can no longer control your urges? Because that's where you're headed if you continue with these wicked thoughts.

That inner voice chastising her now was the same inner voice that had warned her about Renesh. She hadn't listened to it then, obviously, but she was doing her level best to listen now. She imagined anything—and everything—she could think of to banish thoughts of Mr. Rodman from her mind. Puppies. Kittens. Rainbows. Anything at all chaste and pure. The English Channel at sunrise. The peaks of the Lake District at sunset. Stonehenge enveloped in a thick mist. Anything beautiful and awe-inspiring. Prinny. Parliament. The Corn Laws. Anything dull and boring enough to put her to sleep. Her upcoming birthday party. Arthur's house party. The party she would have when she returned to India. Anything to distract her mind from *him*.

He is not the King of Wands.

When that was not enough, she took to silently reciting Chaucer, Shakespeare, even parts of the Bible—the *Bible*, for the love of God—she had been forced to memorize when she was younger to clear her mind of him. Finally, finally, *finally*, she freed her mind from thoughts of him—and all the sensual things they could do to one another—and returned it to some semblance of sanity.

He chose that moment to clear his throat, and she made the mistake of glancing over at him once more. *Fool.* When they made eye contact, she was once again lost. Flustered by his handsome face, with its overnight growth of whiskers, she stared at him for longer than was proper.

He is not the King of Wands.

Neither said anything, but then, neither had to. The desire between them was like kerosene, needing only a small spark to make it burn. Worse, when he attempted a smile, she found herself in grave danger of succumbing to temptation and throwing herself at him. She scowled and turned away from him abruptly—rudely, even, making the already uncomfortable atmosphere in the gig tense and awkward. Out of the corner of her eye, she caught him turning on the bench to face forward rather than continue looking at her. She also caught his wounded expression, and though it troubled her, she didn't trust herself to say anything to comfort him.

"Is something wrong, Lady Julia?"

"Wrong?" *Good lord, no.* She laughed. Nervously. *Nothing's wrong. You are not the King of Wands.* "Why would you think that?" Another laugh bubbled out of her—inconveniently.

"I don't know. It's just that . . . I don't know." He

huffed. "Have I done something to upset you?"

Again, she erupted in nervous laughter. "Upset me? No, no, of course not. Why would you think that?" *And you are not the King of Wands, just so you know.*

"It's just that you've seemed bothered by something since we left the ruins, and I wonder if it's because of me—of something I did. Or something I was about to do . . . perhaps."

Oh lord, he was referring to the near kiss. She laughed—guffawed really—even more stupidly now out of sheer apprehension, snorting in the end. She did not wish to get into a discussion of their mutual attraction and desire for one another, or God forbid, that other thing going through her mind. *He is not the King of Wands.* So she waved away his concern as though it were inconsequential and silly. "Good heavens, no, Mr. Rodman. Don't mind me. I am just preoccupied with . . . something else altogether." *You are not the King of Wands.* "And please don't worry. It's certainly nothing to do with you—" *(You.)* "—in—" *(Are.)* "—any—" *(Not.)* "—way—" *(The. King. Of. Wands.)* . . . *(In. Any. Way.)* "—at all. Do you understand that?" She was nearly shouting at him now. "Whatsoever. It's another matter entirely. Do you hear me?"

"Alright, yes, I hear you. Quite clearly, in fact." He paused for a moment. "But what is it then, if you don't mind my asking?"

"It's nothing." She laughed and then shook her head to reassert how silly his concern was. "Nothing at all."

He narrowed his lids and eyed her with obvious skepticism.

"Alright. Fine. Perhaps I have a small . . . headache."

"And that's what's been bothering you since we left?"

She shrugged. "Yes?" *Certainly not the fact that you resemble the King of Wands, if that's what you're thinking.*

"Are you sure it had nothing to do with me? With us? With something—I don't know—*between* us?"

"Between *us*?" His questions were hitting too close to the truth.

He nodded.

"Between you and me?" Again, she laughed like a ninny. "There's nothing between us." She clucked her tongue for emphasis. *Good lord, sir, when will you get it through your thick skull that you are not the King of Wands?*

He said nothing more for several glorious minutes, and she breathed a sigh of relief that she had finally been able to terminate any further discussion of there being "something" between them because there was no way, no how, no possibility that he was the King of Wands.

"Lady Julia?"

Oh, my lord, sir. Exasperated that he wouldn't just drop the subject—and accept the fact that he was not the King of Wands—she shot him a fuming glare. "What?"

"Whether you think so or not, something happened—or almost happened—between us at the ruins, and I think we need to discuss it, or it will always remain out there between us."

Humph. Why? Do you seriously think you are the King of Wands? She attempted to trivialize his persistent concern by laughing at it once more. Unfortunately, her anxious laughter sounded more like hysterical cackling. "I have no idea what you're talking about." *You are not the King of Wands, sir!*

"I think you do."

"No, really. I don't. Oh, look! Look! Here we are. Yes, indeed, we are here." At last, and thank God. She was never more relieved to see the hunting box than she was at this moment as she turned the gig up the little lane leading to its front porch.

Arthur rushed out the door to greet them, effectively ending their conversation.

"Arthur! I'm so glad to see you."

"And I can't tell you how good it is to see the both of you." Thankfully, he came around to Julia's side of the gig to help her down so that she didn't have to accept Mr. Rodman's assistance.

"I hope you weren't worried about us, Arthur."

"I wasn't. Well, alright, perhaps I was a little at first, but then I figured with the storms blowing all yesterday afternoon and evening that you had stayed the night at Lexington House."

"Actually, we didn't stay there. We left just before the worst of the storms hit and ended up having to take refuge in the medieval castle ruins between here and Lexington House when the deluge struck."

"That must have been dreadful. Were you able to find a dry spot in the ruins to escape the storm?"

Julia nodded. "And Mr. Rodman even managed to build a fire to keep us warm." *But that doesn't make him the King of Wands.*

"You both must be starving. Why don't you both come inside for some breakfast?"

Mr. Rodman smiled broadly. "That sounds—"

"I think not, Arthur." Julia cringed a little as the vicar's eyebrows rose in response to her rude interruption, but there was nothing she could do for it. He was not the King of Wands. "We had plenty to eat because Lady Woodfield sent along some food and wine for our little trip. Fortunately. So, of course, we're not hungry. And while I'm sure Mr. Rodman appreciates the offer, he probably wants to get home as soon as possible so that his sister doesn't worry overmuch about him. She is probably pacing the vicarage with great apprehension as we speak, wondering where he is and whether to send out a search party."

The man scoffed—audibly. "I don't think she is as apprehensive about me as you are."

She cackled. "I have absolutely no idea what you are talking about." *And I absolutely do not think you are the King of Wands, so there.*

"While you have said that before, I think you do. Moreover, I think you know very well we have much to discuss."

She harrumphed. *Who did he think he was? The King of Wands?* "Truly, I am at a loss, and I have to say that I'm quite tired after our long journey of yesterday and today." She yawned then to make her point obvious.

He tipped his hat to her. "Very well, Lady Julia. I will take my leave now. I want to thank you for taking me out to Lexington House yesterday."

"It was nothing."

"No, it was something. It was something very special, in fact. And I would be remiss if I didn't also tell you I enjoyed our time together." His sensual smile smoldered once again with that desire between them.

Good lord. Will you stop acting like the King of Wands? "Likewise, I'm sure." She attempted to feign boredom but could barely form the words for the pounding of her heart.

"Farewell then." He bowed and turned toward the stable to fetch his horse. "Oh, Lady Julia?" He snapped his fingers as he swiveled back toward her. "I almost forgot. I'll see you on Friday. We can talk more then."

She scoffed. "On Friday? Whatever for?"

"Don't tell me you've forgotten about your birthday?" He flashed her a wicked smile.

Julia gulped. *Stop that. You are not the King of Wands.* "Of course not."

"Good." He turned toward the stable once again, but not before casting her another shameless smile as he glanced back over his shoulder. Then, he had the audacity to *wink* at her as he had done yesterday, throwing her heart into an erratic cadence. "Talk to you then."

Heat rushed to her face—and to far more private places in her body, but not because he was the King of Wands.

Arthur waved to Mr. Rodman as he rode away on his horse a few minutes later. Then he turned to Julia. "Do you mind telling me what that was all about?"

"Really, Arthur. I have no idea what you mean." *Are you implying he is the King of Wands?*

He raised a skeptical brow. "I think you do."

"And I think I have a headache and need to lie down."

She ignored his smirk as she spun away from him and raced into the house toward her room to avoid an uncomfortable discussion. And as she flopped back on her bed and stared at the ceiling, she finally confronted the awful, alarming, dreadful, and entirely horrifying possibility that she had been rejecting all day. Though she could hardly accept it, she could no longer deny it. She was pretty sure Mr. Rodman was the King of Wands.

CHAPTER 10

The Devil: Earthly cravings, raw desire, temptation, giving in to baser instincts, gratification of physical senses . . .

FOR THE NEXT FOUR DAYS, Arthur needled Julia for the details about her visit to Lexington House and her night at the ruins with Mr. Rodman. After countless attempts at evasion, she finally managed to get her cousin to accept an abridged version of the story. She left out many of the details, for the simple fact that she was too confused herself about what had happened between her and Mr. Rodman. She didn't want to try to explain to Arthur her mixed up emotions about the vicar when she didn't understand them herself. On the one hand, he annoyed every fiber of her being with his insulting views on women and his aggravating opinions on religion. And yet, on the other hand, he astounded her with his kindness toward the women of Lexington House. And his suggestion that she not sell her home and instead, return to live in England with Camille despite her mixed race, had thoroughly stunned her and forever warmed a soft, tender spot for him in her heart.

And then, of course, there was the nearly uncontrollable desire for him that burned inside her whenever he was around. She couldn't even describe to herself in rational terms how Mr. Rodman made her feel, much less hope to give anyone else a clear picture of the passion his mere presence ignited within her. Since their near kiss at the ruins, she had tried to sort out why the man affected her as he did. He was just a man after all, and one she hadn't even liked at first. Yet, he was also like fire on a cold night, and she was a shivering, naked creature who couldn't get close enough to capture his warmth. Despite that, she had done everything in her power to resist him for fear of driving him away. Once released, the intensity of her all-consuming passion would no doubt terrify him and send him running for shelter out of shock and disgust. Yet, she didn't know that she could resist any further temptation if he offered it.

For that reason, she dreaded her birthday celebration tonight. He would be there, and without question, he would want to discuss their near kiss at the ruins and what it implied about their desire for each other and how it might open the door to new possibilities—frightening, disturbing, horrible possibilities—possibilities for a relationship between them. How could she hope to quash the desire to leap at the chance to be with him when it was all she could think about? And what if he tried to kiss her again tonight? Or, worse—succeeded? She shuddered. She couldn't even entertain the thought of what might happen then.

The hour for reckoning was upon her, however. She

would be on her way to South Kindale with Arthur in just a few minutes. She could've used another fortnight at the very least to purge herself of the far too improper thoughts she had been entertaining of the vicar since their near kiss, but there was nothing for it now. For better or worse, she would see him soon.

After helping her into the gig, Arthur jumped aboard himself and took the reins as he settled beside her. Meanwhile, her stomach clenched. Whether in anticipation or dread of what was to come, she wasn't sure. As the vehicle lurched forward, she folded her gloved hands in her lap and squeezed them tightly together to prevent them from shaking.

"Are you nervous, Julia?"

"Nervous?" She laughed at the question. "Of course not. Why would I be nervous?" She laughed again for good measure as she shook her head. "I mean, do I look nervous?"

"You're tapping your foot faster than a humming-bird flaps its wings. In fact, your entire leg is shaking."

She looked down at her leg and realized he spoke the truth. She had been so preoccupied with thoughts of Mr. Rodman that she had been unaware that any part of her was moving, much less that her leg was bobbing up and down like a cork in a turbulent sea. "I-I suppose I am a little nervous," she confessed.

"Would it have anything to do with him?"

"Him? Who's him?"

"Mr. Rodman."

"Mr. Rodman!" She laughed again, trying her best to convey incredulity. And just for good measure, she waved her hand at Arthur to dismiss his comment. "That's preposterous."

He merely turned to her with a raised brow.

"Oh, alright. Yes. I'm nervous about seeing Mr. Rodman again."

"Why?"

"Must we discuss it?"

Arthur shrugged. "It might help dissipate some of your nervous energy to talk about what's bothering you."

She harrumphed, but only because she knew he was right. "It's just that he . . . unsettles me."

"Unsettles you? From the way you're bobbing your leg, I'd say he positively terrifies you."

"Humph. That's a bit of an exaggeration."

"Is it? Or does the man scare you so much that you can't contain your fear—or stop your leg from shaking?"

"You're so melodramatic, Arthur. He doesn't terrify me. Much. Alright, perhaps he does terrify me. A little, but only because he has this strange ability to unnerve me so much that I behave like a cake brain whenever he looks at me a certain way."

"I've noticed the way he looks at you. I'd be nervous, too."

"What?! Now, why would you go and say a thing like that? You're only making it worse." She paused a moment. "And what do you mean? Why would it make you nervous, too?"

"If anyone looked at me with the raw desire that shows in his eyes when he looks at you, I'd be petrified they'd have me for dinner—and that I would be their willing victim. I might even throw myself on a plate, salt myself, and offer them a lick—you know, just so they could taste me."

She sighed. "You've pretty much captured it, Arthur. It's so awful. And what's worse, I'm afraid I feel that same desire for him."

He threw his back and laughed. "Afraid? Why? You should both hop on that hay cart and enjoy the ride."

"It's not that simple."

"I've never seen anything less complicated. He wants you. You want him. Good lord, where's the obstacle?"

She rolled her eyes. "*The* obstacle? Really, Arthur. Sometimes you're so obtuse that I wonder how you graduated Oxford. Let me list the *obstacles* for you. One, he's a vicar. I hate vicars. Two, his wife cuckolded him. I cuckolded my husband. Three, he's here in England. I'm moving to India—to be with my lover's child. Four, he considers me a heretic. I'm so heretical they would burn me at the stake if this were fourteenth century France. I could go on and on with the reasons I should have nothing to do with Mr. Rodman, but I think you get the point."

"The only thing I've gotten so far is a list of excuses for you to avoid the one man who could be everything to you. If he's as besotted with you as you are with him, there are no obstacles. Love conquers all."

"You know we are not talking love here. At best, we're talking mutual esteem. At worst, we're talking about unbridled lust."

"Mutual esteem and unbridled lust are wonderful things. They're a place to begin at least. Love has the potential to develop more easily when you start with those two things."

"So does pain, Arthur. And hurt and betrayal and suffering and animosity and disgust and eventually, loathing."

"No one could ever loathe you, Julia."

"Niles did."

Arthur huffed. "You know the green scum that grows on stagnant ponds in summer?"

She nodded.

"Niles wasn't fit to lick that. He wasn't fit to lick the bottoms of your feet. He wasn't fit to lick the stain on the carpet left by the cockroach you squashed after walking through a field of manure in the filthy boots you wore to cover the bottoms of your feet after you dipped them in a pond full of green scum—in the middle of July."

She bent her head and smiled. "You're too kind, Arthur. And I adore you."

"And I, you."

Feeling better, she relaxed her leg, unclenched her hands, and exhaled a long breath. It had worked. His suggestion to talk about what was bothering her about Mr. Rodman had released some of the anxiety she had kept bottled up since their near kiss at the ruins.

That anxiety returned with a vengeance, however, the instant she walked into the assembly hall and locked eyes with him from across the room. All sound, all scenery, all movement vanished, and it was just the two of them alone. As she stared at him, a gamut of emotions rushed over his features. She saw heat, lust, and desire at first, which ignited her own, followed by vulnerability and uncertainty, which touched her heart. The determination and resolution she witnessed next intimidated her, but all fear dissipated when he smiled and she sensed his heartfelt joy at seeing her. She also sensed something more in that smile, something far too frightening to even contemplate, as he began making his way through the crowd. The intensity of that something more disconcerted her to the point that she had to break eye contact with him and take a deep breath in a desperate attempt to regain her equilibrium before he reached her.

From out of nowhere, it seemed, one of her sisters hugged her, and suddenly, she was surrounded by the rest of her family. Only when she looked about her did she realize that it was probably not all of a sudden that everyone was there. More likely, they had all gathered 'round her trying to catch her attention while she stood there oblivious to everything except Mr. Rodman. Her heart pounded as he finally drew nearer, but she was unable to greet him properly for all the people separating them. He smiled once again, though, causing something to flutter low in her belly while her knees went weak. Then Lady Woodfield pushed her way past everyone—including her own brother—and accosted Julia in raptures. Mr. Rodman's expression soured at once, as he rolled his eyes and scowled at his sister.

"Happy Birthday, Lady Julia! Oh, how happy I am to see you once again! It seems like eons since we were last together."

It had been a mere week, but Julia didn't point that out. She didn't have the chance, for Lady Woodfield began gushing once again. "And, oh my, may I say how handsome you look this evening? Doesn't she, Charles? Isn't she stunning? Charles? Charles? Where are you, Charles? Where is he?" The baroness turned to glance around for him. She spotted him several feet away and waved him over with her hand. "What are you doing all the way over there? Do come closer and say hello to Lady Julia."

Julia wanted to laugh when his eyes glazed over with annoyance as they always did when his sister spoke to him—or when she spoke at all, really; yet he managed to nod sedately as he followed her orders and made his way through the host of bodies between them. At last, he stood in front of Julia, close enough that she caught his scent of bergamot and cedar wood. As she stood breathless waiting for him to say something, he took her gloved hand in his, sending a shiver throughout her entire body, and then he laid a kiss on her knuckles. Oh, how she wished it were her bare skin. "Happy Birthday, Lady Julia. You look lovely this evening."

"Indeed she does! That scarlet dress is gorgeous on you. I adore it. The silk is exquisite. And the lace! Where did you get it? From London when you were there recently? Yes, yes, of course, of course. What a daft question. Where else would you get such lace? And oh, Mr. Drake! I didn't notice you there. I can't tell you how happy I am to see you again as well."

Lady Woodfield's energy waned just enough to

allow Julia a moment to catch her breath before she began introducing Mr. Rodman and his sister to the members of her family who'd gathered nearby. At first, she worried that Lady Woodfield might overwhelm everyone with her enthusiasm, but the baroness managed to subdue her usual ebullience and greeted Julia's siblings with poise and grace.

Following introductions, most of the group dispersed for other amusements, leaving Julia alone with Mr. Rodman. With no one between them, he moved closer, and her heart hammered so violently, she could hear it beating in her ears. If he didn't hear its clamor, it was only because the room was too noisy.

He caressed her with his gaze. "Care to dance?"

Too intimidated by the heat in his eyes, she couldn't speak. She could only nod.

He held out his arm, and she placed her hand atop it. He then led her to the dance floor where they took their place among the other dancers waiting for a waltz to begin. As the first strains of music filled the room and they began to move as a couple, neither spoke, but then, neither had to. Their eyes locked in a mutual exchange of desire that spoke volumes. Unable to withstand the intensity of his gaze any longer, she broke their silence with an attempt at distraction—anything to avoid discussing the attraction between them. "Your sister seems in good spirits."

He leveled a dry look at her. "More likely, she's *had* some good spirits."

"Now, Mr. Rodman, that's not very kind. Besides, I didn't get the impression that she'd had anything at all to drink."

"Yes, I suppose you're right. She's just always that way, which makes me wish I had some good spirits whenever I am around her. She is in rare form tonight, though. I'm only thankful she didn't topple you when she rushed to greet you."

"She's a delight. I like her more and more every time I see her."

"And I like her more and more every time I don't."

She smacked his shoulder with her folded fan.

He flinched. "Ow. That hurt, I'll have you know."

"It's no less than you deserve for your remarks about your sister. She's a gem. She's very kindhearted, always very concerned about everyone around her."

"Well, I will give you that. She is very concerned about others—you especially, in fact."

She laughed. "Me? Why me?"

He shrugged. "Perhaps I shouldn't say anything, but she was very concerned about you after our outing to Lexington House last Sunday. I'm surprised she didn't say something to you about it, or worse, ask you anything about the night we were stranded at the ruins. She's pestered me relentlessly since then with questions about what happened that night. She nags me constantly for details about our time together."

Stricken with dread, Julia's eyes shot open wide. "Whatever for?"

He lifted a corner of his mouth in a wry smile as he leaned in to whisper to her. "She's concerned for your reputation."

"What! That's ridiculous. Why would she be concerned about my reputation?"

"She's worried I might have tried to compromise you while we were alone. She's even gone so far as to accuse me of doing just that, especially because I haven't denied it." A wicked gleam shone in his eyes.

Julia's mouth fell agape. "But that's absurd. You're a vicar."

He shrugged. "That may be true, but I am also a man. And the more I ignore her questions and refuse to answer her, the more suspicious she gets that something is not right. She has even gone so far as to suggest I marry you as soon as possible to avoid scandal should it ever become public knowledge that we spent the night alone together at the ruins. She's afraid that if anyone finds out about it, they will assume something improper most definitely happened between us that night."

Julia huffed. "Why, that's ludicrous. Nothing whatsoever happened between you and me. In any way. At all. Nothing. Not a thing."

He leaned in closer than before. "Nothing?"

Unsettled by his nearness and the heat it produced in inappropriate parts of her anatomy, she composed herself and leaned away from him lest she give into the temptation to throw herself against him. She focused her gaze over his shoulder rather than look into his eyes. "Of course. Nothing happened. And you must tell her that."

Though she couldn't see his face directly, she caught his smile out of the corner of her eye. It was a smile of apology, not humor. "You know I can't do that."

"Why ever not?"

"Because it would be a lie, and as a man of the cloth, I try to avoid lying whenever possible."

Alarmed beyond words, she ruminated for a moment on what his statement implied. "How could you possibly consider it a lie? We didn't do anything."

"Didn't we, Julia?" He used her given name without the honorific, and at that moment, as her heart pounded in her chest, she realized that whatever their relationship had been before, it had just crossed a line into something else. "Didn't we almost kiss? Didn't we want to, in our hearts at least?" He eyed her through narrowed lids. "Did I not see desire in your eyes— equal to mine?"

His question dumbfounded her, and worse, he continued to gaze at her with such intensity that she couldn't think clearly enough to answer him.

He cocked his head to one side as though he were trying to glean an answer from her expression. "Did I misread the heat in your eyes? Was I wrong about what you wanted?"

Still unable to form words, she said nothing.

"Because I know without question what I wanted in that moment." He paused as though he were waiting for her to respond, but still, she remained silent. He chuckled, his voice low and seductive. "Wouldn't you like to know what that was?"

She shook her head no.

He shrugged. "I'll tell you anyway. I wanted more than anything in the world to take you in my arms, Julia, and kiss you senseless. And much more. So. Much.

More."

Her belly plunged at the meaning of his words, as though the bottom of her world had just fallen out from beneath her. Once again, he paused, as though waiting for a response. And once again, she found herself unable to speak for the sound of the pulse pounding inside her head.

"And you want to know something else, Julia?"

No. Absolutely not. She did not want to know another thing. She did not want to discuss this topic any longer and only hoped her silence conveyed her wishes.

He continued anyway, with no encouragement from her. "Though I wasn't entirely sure what you were feeling in the moment, I think you wanted me to kiss you. In fact, I think you wanted to kiss me back, didn't you?"

"That's not true." Her mouth was so dry and her tongue so thick that she could only rasp the words in a whisper. He said nothing, and she wasn't entirely sure he had heard her. She opened her mouth to repeat the words, but he shook his head, stopping her from saying anything else.

"Do not dissemble on me, Julia. I know what I saw in your eyes. You wanted me as much as I wanted you."

"That is most definitely not true, sir." The words came out clearly now and firmly, too, and suddenly there was no air in the assembly room, and the dance-floor was hot as Hades. Breathless and too warm, she had to get away from him—and fast—or he was going to discuss the thing between them.

She broke free of him and stepped back, scanning the room for the nearest exit. She left him standing on the dancefloor in obvious dismay, as she dashed for a door across the assembly hall. When she reached it, she struggled with the doorknob, unable to make it function. Worried that he was right behind her, she twisted and turned the knob in a frantic attempt to escape. At last, the thing worked, and she threw the door open and rushed through it to find herself standing in a dimly lit corridor. She hesitated a moment, letting her eyes adjust to the low light while deciding whether to go right or left. When she could finally make out the scenery around her, she turned to her right and fled toward another door at the end of the hallway.

She flung that door open and charged through it, letting it slam shut behind her. She stepped outside onto a secluded stone terrace that overlooked a small stream running behind the building. She rushed to an iron guardrail meant to prevent one from falling off the terrace into the stream and grasped the railing with both hands as she inhaled deeply. She tried to catch her breath and compose herself, while the sound of the bubbling brook and chirping night creatures offered a soothing alternative to the clamoring thoughts in her head.

She did not want to talk to Mr. Rodman and confront what they most needed to discuss: their mutual attraction. She stood motionless for a moment letting her heartrate and her breathing calm down while she leaned over the railing and inhaled the night air.

Then she heard it—the unmistakable creak of metal

hinges as the door behind her opened and then closed once more, followed by footsteps on the cobblestones. His, no doubt.

The footsteps got closer until the scents of bergamot and cedar wood enveloped her. "Julia?"

She stood upright, frozen in terror, her eyes closed as his warm breath caressed the nape of her neck. Dare she turn? What would she find? She ventured a glance over her shoulder. He wasn't even looking at her. Instead, he appeared perfectly harmless as he stared up at the night sky. Her tension eased when she realized that perhaps he was merely studying the constellations and that he had not come out here to continue their previous discussion. She even laughed at herself a little for thinking he posed a threat. His mind seemed a million miles away, not occupied with thoughts of her. Convinced she was in no danger of succumbing to him after all, she turned.

She was wrong.

Oh, so wrong. He dropped his gaze to meet hers, and her heart slammed into her rib cage when that panoply of emotions she had witnessed earlier flashed across his face.

"What are you doing out here, Mr. Rodman?"

"Isn't it obvious?"

With caution, she shook her head no.

"I'm admiring the moon, of course. And the stars. They're lovely tonight, don't you think?"

She swallowed and nodded. "You shouldn't be here . . . with me."

He chuckled a little. "Oh? And why's that?"

"What will everyone think after seeing me run from the dancehall and you following me out here? Won't there be . . . talk?"

"I believe the better question is why do you care?"

"Decorum, of course. And decency. And propriety. Your sister certainly would not approve."

He flashed her a wicked smile. "Never fear. My sister will never know. Neither will anyone else. I was discreet. No one will ever suspect I followed you out here, and they'll certainly never know that anything improper happened between us."

She stared at him a brief moment, unsettled by his bravado, and then scooted to her left to put a few feet between them. "I'm a little alarmed, Mr. Rodman. You said no one will ever *know* anything improper happened between us. You did not say there will *be* nothing improper between us."

"And I meant what I didn't say." His dangerous smile left no doubt as to his meaning, and though she was disquieted by the implication, she couldn't make herself move out of his way as he stepped toward her, closing the distance between them.

She swallowed. "Why *did* you follow me out here, Mr. Rodman?" Her voice came out a whisper because that's all the sound she could produce with no air in her lungs.

He caressed her cheek with the backs of his fingers as he had done that morning at the ruins. "Call me Charles. And I think you know."

"I have no idea." Again, her voice was a whisper.

He chuckled. "As I said before, do not dissemble.

There's something between us, and you know it. It's been there since we met. You're aware of it, I'm sure, and I know I am. We've both been fighting it, however. Or I have at least, and I think you have, too. Why we have fought it, I'm not sure. Fear, perhaps, but I followed you out here to tell you—to show you—that we shouldn't fight it any longer."

Scared witless, she turned her back to him and faced the stream once more. "I disagree."

"Why, Julia? Why do you disagree?" He stepped closer to her and toyed with a few strands of hair that had fallen out of her coif.

She closed her eyes and inhaled deeply. "It would be foolish to give in to what's between us when there are so many reasons not to do it."

"Name one."

"I'm a heretic. You're a vicar."

He chuckled. "Name another."

"I despise clergymen. And, once again, you are a vicar."

He began stroking the back of her neck and the slope of her shoulders, sending shivers along her spine. "Name one more."

If he continued his ministrations to her neck and shoulders, she wouldn't be able to name the letters of the alphabet. "I'll be moving to India soon. Forever. Why start something that only has to end?"

He stepped even closer, so close now that the fabric of their clothes rustled together. "It doesn't have to end." His breath caressed her ear when he whispered those words into it. "Anything else?"

She moaned, despite attempts to refrain from making any sounds. "There are so many more reasons not to become involved with one another that I can't even begin to name them all."

"I have yet to hear any good ones. The reasons you've given so far aren't difficult to resolve. What else could possibly stand between us?"

You wouldn't want to know. "Obstacles and things."

"What obstacle, what thing could be so bad that we shouldn't explore what's going on between us?"

"I can't begin to explain it. All I know is that I don't want to hurt you, and I don't want to get hurt myself."

"How would either of us get hurt by trying to understand what's between us?"

"It's *misunderstanding* what's between us that worries me."

He leaned in so close that his body touched hers as he caressed the bare skin of her back above her dress with his hands. "I think there can be no misunderstanding. I want you, Julia, and I think you want me." Now he was kissing the shell of her ear, nipping at it gently and then soothing the nips with soft kisses.

"You have no idea what you're about to unleash if you continue."

He chuckled low once again, but said nothing as he bit the nape of her neck and gently licked it with his tongue.

"You play with fire, sir."

"Let it burn, Julia. Let me be your King of Wands."

She turned to face him then and stared into his gaze for several heartbeats. "Don't say I didn't warn you."

"Warning noted." He encircled her waist with his arms and pulled her against him. And as their bodies met, their mouths collided. She threw her arms around his shoulders and caressed the hair at the nape of his neck, evoking a low groan from his throat as they devoured one another.

And as their kiss deepened, as their tongues parried for dominance, as one of his hands slid down her back and groped her bottom while the other reached up between them and caressed her breast, she mentally rebuked herself for giving in to her desire, for letting *this* happen. *No! Stop this, you fool.*

The voice screeching in her head, the one telling her no, was no match for the pulse aching between her legs, urging her onward. She ran a hand down his back, feeling his solid muscles contract beneath her caress. He moaned and pulled her closer until his knee was between her thighs, urging them to part and putting pressure at the apex. *End it, Julia! You can't continue this insanity.* Again, that shrieking voice of wisdom and experience faded into background noise as he kneaded her breast. She threw her head back at the sheer pleasure, exposing her neck to his licks and kisses. *Stop it! Get a hold of yourself at once.*

She was helpless, however, as he nipped the skin at her throat with his teeth, but when he squeezed her hardened nipple until it ached, she was absolutely lost to all reason and began rubbing herself against the solid leg situated between her thighs to relieve some of the tortuous pleasure rising there. *Oh, bloody hell, no! Stop that before you do something you'll truly regret.* That voice in her head, the one pleading with her to come to her senses and end this lunacy, was merely a whisper now. A faint echo of sanity that had no hope of discouraging her from taking her pleasure in whatever way she could, especially not when so much emotion comingled with the sensuality coursing through her body.

She whimpered now as she rode his leg, and abandoning any sense she had left, she reached down between them and felt for his erection. She found it straining against the placket of his pants and ran a finger down its rigid length to tease him. He broke from their kiss the moment she touched him. Encouraged by his low, throaty groan, she grasped and stroked his member through his pants until it jumped against her hand and his eyes glazed over. She toyed with the tip through the fabric covering it, as he gazed down at her through hooded eyes and released another deep moan.

She reached her mouth up to his and licked his lips, nipping them once or twice and then kissing them tenderly, but as he rocked his pelvis against her hand and she continued squeezing and stroking him through his pants, their kiss turned hungry, ravenous. And as she stroked him again and again, imagining the pleasure his long thickness would give her as he slid into her, she realized through her haze that they were nearly past the point of no return. Already, she was lost to any sense of decorum or propriety. Forget decency. She needed him. Now. Right now, and she nearly sank to the ground, pulling him down with her. She'd be there even now, her skirts up, her thighs spread, him inside her, except that she heard something—something vague calling to her.

She ignored the annoying little drone in her ear and continued to kiss him and stroke him and ride his thigh. And then, somehow, there it was again. Through the deafening roar of emotions crashing through her head, she heard a voice. Her own, perhaps? And then it was clearer. The faint sound of reason, the little voice that she usually ignored when lost to passion, broke through her fog of pleasure. *Stop.* It was a whisper, almost inaudible, but she heard it. *Stop.* She heard it again, a little louder this time. *Stop yourself, Julia. Before it's too late.*

Still kissing him, still in a fog, she hardly noticed as he backed her against the nearest wall and tugged at her skirt and petticoat, raising them up her leg with one hand. Meanwhile, he fumbled with the buttons on the placket of his pants with his other hand. And after he released himself from his bindings, he grasped her wrist, tore off her glove, and brought her bare hand down to touch his naked shaft. When she felt his hot, bare skin in her palm, that bothersome voice of reason cautioned her again. This time, as the voice admonished her, the fog dispersed just a little, and reality intruded ever so slightly. This—whatever they had been doing—was moving to another level—one too dangerous to continue. She had to stop it. Now. Or she would not be able to stop it. Ever.

Yet, she couldn't bring herself to stop, not when his moans encouraged her to stroke him harder and his kisses lulled her back into her fog of pleasure. Once more, as the warning voice faded, she lost herself to sensation and desire. Only when he raised her skirts a little higher and caressed the back of her naked bottom did the spell end. She went rigid with awareness, and her eyes shot open as if she'd just woken from a too-intense dream.

CHAPTER II

Ace of Cups, reversed: Blocked emotions,
repressed desires, pain, loss, emptiness . . .

H E SENSED THE CHANGE IN her demeanor the
instant he touched her bare bottom. He broke
their kiss at once and peered down at her hooded eyes.
Still in his own haze of pleasure, he shook his head,
struggling to clear it, but had difficulty making sense of
the situation. Only when she stroked him once more
did awareness slam him in the gut. Shock, alarm, and
most of all, shame overwhelmed him when he looked
down between them and saw her bare hand circling
his naked cock. He pulled away from her abruptly, letting go of her petticoat and skirt so that they fell to
the ground. Distressed beyond all measure, he ran his
fingers through his hair before turning away from her
to close his placket.

After he righted himself, he turned back to her,
realizing he still held her glove in one hand. Embarrassed, he held it out to her, and she took it from him
with an awkward smile. "Forgive me, Julia. I–I'm truly
sorry. I–I didn't mean to let things get so out of hand."

She gave him a lopsided smile. "No apology necessary, sir. It was I who let things go too far."

Horrified that she would blame herself, he dropped his head to his chest in remorse and then lifted his eyes to hers once more. "No, no, absolutely not. I will not let you put any guilt on yourself for this . . . this . . ." He couldn't bring himself to name what "this" was, so he merely moved his hand back and forth between them, hoping she'd take his meaning. "It was my fault entirely. I-I don't know what came over me. Truly, I don't. I've behaved abominably—like an animal." He shook his head as he ran his fingers through his hair once again. He backed farther away from her when she reached out to caress his cheek in an obvious attempt to comfort him. "I don't know what to say for myself. I'm at a loss for words."

"Please don't worry yourself so much about it. I, too, got lost in the moment."

He shook his head again. "I only hope you can find it in your heart to forgive me."

"There's nothing to forgive, Charles. We both simply got carried away."

"I don't even understand how I could've let myself compromise you so badly. It was appalling. Indecent. Beyond the pale."

She laughed a little and stepped forward to tease him with a brief poke to the chest. "Isn't that what you wanted? What about everything you said before—about wanting to be improper with me? Was that all bravado?"

Still ashamed and embarrassed by his behavior, he did not laugh along with her. "I meant to kiss you,

Julia. Not rut with you. I let things get completely out of hand."

She laughed again as she waved away his concern. "I'd hardly say we rutted."

"And I would say we were headed in that direction. I don't know what would have happened had you not stopped us."

"You give me too much credit. I wouldn't say I stopped us necessarily."

"But at least you reacted with alarm when I . . . when I—"

"Touched my bottom?"

He closed his eyes and swiped his hands down his face. "Please don't remind me."

"Oh, Charles." She shrugged. "You're being much too severe with yourself."

"Not severe enough, I would say. I took complete advantage of you, and again, I apologize profusely. I should never have let it happen, not before we're married by any means."

She eyed him through narrowed lids, apparently alarmed by what he'd just said. "What do you mean, not before we're married?"

"Just that. We're going to marry, of course, and after that, we can give in to our physical desires as much as we want, as we did tonight, but not before. We'll set an early wedding date. We could even start the banns this Sunday and be married within the month."

She folded her arms across her chest and laughed out loud as if to dismiss the idea. "You are joking, are you not? You do not truly mean for us to marry."

"Of course, I do. We have to now. It's the only thing we can do."

"Whatever for?"

"I think it should be obvious, Julia. I've compromised you. I must marry you. Moreover, there's no doubt whatsoever that we're attracted to one another. I want you as much as you want me. We clearly suit each other on nearly every other level. We just need to make our union legal in the eyes of the law and God."

She laughed again, this time with all her heart. "Your humor is priceless, Charles." She sobered when he did not laugh along with her. "Oh, my lord. You are serious, aren't you?"

Of *course,* he was serious. What did she think he would do but marry her? It was the only decent and proper solution for having used her so badly just now.

"I'm sorry, Charles. I truly am, but that's out of the question. I can't marry you."

His mouth fell agape at her refusal. "Why not?"

"I'll be moving to India, for one."

"As I've told you before, there's no need for you to move to India forever to take care of your godchild. We'll go get her after we're married and bring her back to England to live with us."

"Even if I would consider bringing her back to England, I would never consider marrying you. You know how much I loathe the institution of marriage, and I know you do as well. It's simply out of the question."

"I know what I've said about marriage in the past, but that was before. My views have changed." He reached out to her, but she backed away before he could touch her. "Please, Julia, we could be so good together as husband and wife."

She strode to the iron railing, turning back to face him, her head tilted in obvious puzzlement. "How could your views of marriage possibly have changed in so little time?"

He followed her to the railing and grasped her hand this time without giving her a chance to pull back. "Because of you, Julia. I want you, and I think you want me."

She didn't nod, but neither did she deny it.

"Marriage is the only logical choice, if we want to be together."

She pulled her hand from his. "I don't see why."

Shocked by her comment, he reared back and stared at her for a moment. "You are aware, are you not, that we can't be together—not intimately, at least—until we're married."

"I don't know, Charles. Marriage would only complicate everything. Especially our relationship. Let's just keep things simple. We don't have to marry to be together."

He frowned. "Do you know what you're suggesting?"

"Yes." She shrugged and then explained in no uncertain terms what she meant. "A liaison. A tryst. An arrangement."

Stunned by her candid nonchalance, he couldn't prevent himself from gaping. He exhaled a long breath before being able to say anything. "Are you saying we should be intimate without the benefit of marriage?"

She seemed to sense his outrage now because she folded her arms tightly across her chest as though she were uncertain of herself. "I don't see why not."

He threw his hands in the air in thorough disbelief. How could she be so obtuse? "Because it's fornication. And I'm a vicar. And it's a sin."

"Oh, Charles, you're much too proper. Half of England is in an arrangement of some sort without the benefit of marriage."

He raised his brows when it occurred to him that perhaps she wasn't obtuse. Perhaps she was something else entirely. Perhaps she was . . . unchaste. "I don't understand, Julia. You shock me. You were the one who seemed against us acting on our attraction in the first place. And now you're suggesting an 'arrangement'?"

She shrugged once again. "I really don't know what I'm suggesting. I'm just saying that others have arrangements outside marriage."

"Well, not I. I would never do such a despicable thing."

"Then that makes it difficult for us to be together because I will never marry again. I detest marriage. Having tasted freedom since my husband died, I much prefer it to wifely servitude. But just because I don't ever want to marry again doesn't mean you and I can't enjoy something pleasurable with each other, especially if we're discreet."

He couldn't fathom what he was hearing, and when realization struck him, he shook his head in disbelief—and horror. He stepped back from her, and as he stared at her, it was as if he were seeing her for the first time.

"You're just like her."

"Who?"

"My wife. She was a trollop in the worst way. I can't believe you would turn out to be like her."

"You think me a trollop?"

He shrugged. "I don't know what to think. Would you have let me have my way with you just now, had I not stopped myself?"

Again, she didn't nod, but she also didn't deny it.

"Tell me this, Julia. Exactly how many men have you been with since you became a widow?"

"Exactly? None." She paused a moment before continuing, "Of your business."

"Spoken like a genuine trollop."

"First a heretic. Now a trollop. What else would you call me, Charles?"

Still reeling from her brazen suggestion of an affair, he threw his hands in the air. "I don't know, Julia. I might call you an aberration."

"An aberration."

"Yes. You are certainly like no other woman I've ever met."

"Except your wife. The trollop."

He crossed his arms over his chest now. "I don't know. I–I think you might be worse than her, actually. I think she regretted her sins in the end. She had a moral compass of some sort, even if it didn't always guide her as it should have done. But you? I sense no morality in you whatsoever."

"I see." Her calmness surprised him, and truth be told, scared him somewhat. "Amoral now, am I?" She paced toward the door leading into the building and then turned abruptly to stab him with an icy glare. "Well, call me what you will, but I would rather be an aberrant, amoral, heretical trollop than a servile, albeit virtuous woman who willingly marries a man and gives up her freedom just to have a little sex."

He didn't know what to say to that. He just didn't.

"Furthermore, I think you are an uptight, judgmental, overly pious prig who most likely drove your wife into the arms of another man."

This time, her words struck him in the heart. Astonished by her venom, he couldn't reply. He could only stare at her in utter pain and shock.

"Stunned you speechless, have I? Well, good. Allow me to continue. I wouldn't marry any man, but least of all you, now that you have shown yourself for what you truly are—a judgmental arse. In fact, now that we've squelched the desire—or whatever it was—between us, I'm certain I would never like to see you again. Don't ever come out to the hunting box again, and I will avoid town at all costs. You may tell your sister whatever tale flatters you the most, but please make sure she knows that I despise you and never want to breathe the same air as you, much less look at you again. And whatever you do, stay away from Arthur's party. I most certainly don't want to run into you there, so you are not to come. There's no need for you to be there anyway, since you are under no obligation to raise funds for a new home for the women at Lexington House. I *suppose* you may continue to perform church services for them. I wouldn't want to deprive them of whatever comfort they get from you, but I will not be there when you are there. In fact, you are not to be at Lexington House at any other time than Sunday afternoons.

"With diligence and good luck, we'll never be within five feet of each other, much less have to see each other, again. Ever. Certainly not before I leave for India. And once I am gone, you may admire yourself for your restraint and piety while you spend the rest of your days rusticating in this quaint little town as the arrogant, sanctimonious holy man you are. I, on the other hand, will take my aberrant, heretical, amoral, trollop self to somewhere vastly more interesting. Have I made myself clear?"

Quite, and though he knew the question was rhetorical and required no response, he nodded anyway.

"Good. Adieu, Mr. Rodman. Have a pleasant life."

The door slammed behind her as she disappeared into the building.

As he stood in mild shock, wondering exactly how things had gone from glorious to abysmal between them in so short a time, several thoughts raced through his mind. She wanted to leave? Good. Let her go. She never wanted to see him again? Fine. So be it. There was just one problem. Somewhere between the time she had knocked him over at the Queen's Cross Inn and just now when she had let the terrace door slam behind her, he had fallen in love with that outspoken, aberrant, heretical trollop.

Nearly a fortnight passed, but true to her word, she did not come to town. Nor was she at Lexington House the past two Sundays when he performed services for the women living there, but then, he hadn't expected her to be there. Not really. No, he was quite aware that if he wanted to see her again, he would have to go to her. Afraid she might injure him—or worse— if he showed up at the hunting box, he did not venture out there, however. What would have been the point, anyway? To try to make things right? To try to discuss things more rationally with her? To try to convince her that they should marry? To try to tell her he loved her? Of them all, that would have been the hardest thing to say, for she didn't just hate him. She loathed him, and there was no way to get beyond that. So, he'd stayed in town these last few days, at the vicarage mostly, sequestered in his study, trying to take his mind off her with his books and rocks.

Looking through his rock collection had been a mistake. It reminded him of their trip to Lexington House the day he blurted out to her that he liked rocks. Forget books. They failed to provide much of a distraction. Nor did the daily newssheet. He tried diverting his thoughts with a stroll through the garden or a walk through town, but nothing helped. Nothing could keep his mind off her, not when all he saw were cinnamon eyes filled with desire as he broke their kiss.

She was the most passionate woman he'd ever met. Eleanor had never been so passionate—not with him at least. With Dunham perhaps, but that was another story. Julia, however? Every time he thought about the scene between them on the terrace behind the assembly hall, he became hard as stone. She had ignited his passion that night like no one else had ever done, releasing something primal and overpowering in him. He had never been so out of control of his carnal urges before that night, and after almost two weeks of perseverating on how he could have lost all self-restraint as he did, he finally figured out the reason. It was her. It was Julia. It was how she had reacted to him with a desire that rivaled his own. It was the way she had returned his kisses and caresses with equal fervor and abandon. She had lost control right along with him. She had wanted him every bit as much as he wanted her, and that was a heady aphrodisiac.

He truly might have taken her against the brick wall or on the stone terrace floor, had she not reacted with hesitation when he touched her bare bottom. And from that moment until now, he had wondered, speculated, fantasized about how it would have felt to sink himself into her. These thoughts only served to torture him, however, because as much as he wanted her, he couldn't go against all he believed and give into the temptation to be with her without marrying her first. And she would never have him as a husband. Not now. Not in a million years from now.

His ruminations were interrupted by his housekeeper, who peeked into his study to tell him that dinner was ready. He rose from his desk with very little enthusiasm for food and walked down the hallway and into the dining room with no desire at all for company.

"Oh, there you are, Charles. Where have you been?

I've been looking everywhere for you."

In no mood for chatter, especially not his sister's, he turned abruptly to leave rather than answer her question.

"Charles! Where on earth are you going? I asked you a question. Now, please get back in here at once. Dinner is served, and I need to talk to you."

Resigned to his fate, he turned back toward the table, determined to eat quickly and be done with it. She was already seated in her usual spot, so he picked up the dinner service meant for him, which was situated next to hers, and carried the items to a space at the far side of the table. He set everything down and then took a fortifying sip of wine before taking his chair.

"Charles, really. Why are you all the way at the end of the table?"

"I prefer the scenery here."

"Don't be rude. I can't talk to you with you on the other side of dining room."

That was precisely the idea, but she picked up her own plate, silverware, napkin, and wineglass, and carried everything to a spot right next to his. "Now . . ." She paused, evidently waiting for him to help her with her chair. When he did not move, she harrumphed and pulled the chair out herself and sat down. "Now, as I was about to remind you, we leave for Mr. Drake's party in a few days, and I wanted to talk to you about what we'll need to bring along with us. His country house is less than a day's ride from here, so we won't need to stay anywhere overnight, but I was thinking that perhaps—"

"We're not going."

She stared at him as though he had sprouted a second head. "I beg your pardon?"

"We are not going to Drake's party."

"What! Why ever not?"

"It's just best that we stay away."

"But—but—I don't understand. Why?"

He rolled his eyes and huffed. He had been dreading this conversation for the very fact that he would have to give her some sort of explanation, so he had avoided it. He supposed he had to tell her something now, though. Perhaps honesty was the best approach. "Lady Julia prefers not to see me."

She cocked her head to the side as if he had spoken in a foreign tongue.

"Ever again. She never wants to see me again."

She closed her eyes and shook her head in apparent confusion. "Why? What did you do?"

He leaned back in his chair and scrubbed his hands down his face. "Please don't ask."

She gasped as she put her hand to her heart. "Charles, please don't tell me you did something to offend Lady Julia."

Obviously, he couldn't give his sister the sordid details of what really happened between him and Julia, but he didn't like to lie to anyone. Even her. So, he went along with her mostly accurate explanation. "Yes, you could say that. I offended her. Deeply."

"How? What in the name of all that is holy did you do?"

"It's not so much what I did."

She narrowed her eyes at him. "Did you *say* something then?"

"It's complicated. Too complicated to explain, but trust me when I say that she wants nothing more to do with me."

She frowned. "So, we're really not going to the party?"

He shook his head no.

She raised her hands in obvious frustration. "When were you going to tell me this?"

"I just did."

She rolled her eyes and brooded a moment. "What about raising money for a new home for the ladies staying at Lexington House? Who will do that for Lady Julia if you're not there?"

He shrugged in defeat. "I don't really know. Perhaps Drake will solicit his guests for donations, but she made it very clear that she doesn't want me at the party—even to raise funds."

Caroline crossed her arms over her chest in obvious annoyance. "Humph. I have no idea what you said to her to make her despise you so much, but it must have been dreadful."

He agreed with her but said nothing.

She protruded her lower lip in a pout as she uncrossed her arms and then re-crossed them over her chest in the opposite configuration. "Oh, I'm so disappointed. It promised to be such fun. Plus, I don't know what to do with the dresses I ordered from the local seamstress especially for the party. Of course, I have nowhere else to wear them with the Season being over."

"Perhaps you can wear them next Season."

"Don't be gauche, Charles."

He rolled his eyes at her and served himself some roasted duck and boiled potatoes. He offered some to her as well.

She waved them away with her hand. "I couldn't possibly eat now. My appetite is ruined. And just how will I ever get word to Woodfield in time to tell him not to go to Drake's estate for the party? He was going to meet me there, and I was going to return home with him after the party rather than come back here with you. I thought you had things well enough in hand that I no longer needed to be here with you, but . . . it looks like I'll just have to stay put for a while."

Now *his* appetite was ruined. "Woodfield could always come here to get you. Soon. In fact, when you send him word not to go to Drake's, why don't you tell him to come here to fetch you instead?"

"Well, I can't now, Charles. I can't possibly leave you now, not with so much unpleasantness between you and Lady Julia. I must stay, of course, until I can see you two reconciled and help her raise funds for a new home for the women at Lexington House."

"Really, Caroline, I see no reason why—"

His housekeeper's sudden appearance in the doorway stopped him from finishing his sentence. Standing beside her was one of the footmen he recognized from Lexington House. "Forgive my interruption, Mr. Rodman, but Mr. Winslow here says it's urgent he speak to you."

Winslow bowed. "I'm sorry to intrude, Mr. Rodman, but there's something of a crisis happening at Lexington House."

Charles rose at once. "What's happened?"

"It's Mrs. Sweeney, sir. She went into labor late last night, but something's not right. She still hasn't delivered her babe, and the midwife says there's nothing more she can do, so she had Mrs. Thompson send me to town to fetch Mr. Norton, the surgeon. He's waiting out front in the carriage right now. Mrs. Thompson also sent me to get you because Mrs. Sweeney has asked for a priest. Mrs. Thompson is fairly sure she meant a Catholic priest, but we don't know of one in the area. Will you come?"

Without losing a second, Charles ran from the dining room to his study to get his bag. After bidding Caroline goodnight, he boarded the carriage in front of the vicarage and took a seat on the bench across from Mr. Norton. As the carriage sped toward Lexington House, he stared out the window. The sun was setting in the west, and as purple twilight filled the sky, he wondered if Julia knew about Mrs. Sweeney. Or if she had any idea that he was headed toward Lexington House right now in what he assumed was actually her carriage to tend to the poor woman.

He had about an hour to contemplate the question before he had his answer, and as he walked into the grand entrance of Lexington House, it was apparent that no, Julia had not known he was coming and was as surprised to see him as he was to see her, judging from the look of shock on her face. She said nothing to him, but as the shock faded, her face reflected another emotion altogether: contempt. Utter and complete.

Clearly, she had just arrived herself, for she was still handing her spencer off to a footman.

The surgeon stepped forward and bowed to her. "Lady Julia, how good it is to see you again. I only wish it were under more pleasant circumstances."

"May I say the same, Mr. Norton? The situation is most unfortunate. And unwelcome."

Though she spoke to the surgeon, her eyes were locked with Charles's. He did not miss the meaning in her comment or in her icy glare. Only when the housekeeper called her name did she turn her gaze from him to the second floor landing above.

"Thank goodness you're all finally here!" Mrs. Thompson's agitation was apparent in both her pained expression and the way she wrung her hands together. "Hurry, everyone! Please come upstairs at once. Mrs. Sweeney is not doing well."

Julia rushed up the staircase with the surgeon beside her, while Charles kept his distance behind them out of respect for her feelings. The two of them were forced closer to one another, however, as the housekeeper corralled all three of them through the doorway of Mrs. Sweeney's chamber. His arm accidentally bumped against Julia's as they walked over the threshold together. She glared down at the point of contact and then up at him. Intense hostility roiled off her for a moment, and then she jerked her arm away from him and bolted toward Mrs. Sweeney's bedside. The woman lay on her back with a sheet covering her lower torso and legs.

He did not approach the bed immediately, waiting at the back of the room instead for Mrs. Sweeney to call for him. A couple of candles on the bedside stand illuminated the room but not well enough so he could see anything in detail. He could see enough, however, to alarm him. Most of Mrs. Sweeney's hair had fallen out of its coif and was plastered to her head and around her cheeks with sweat. Her face was pale and waxen, and her expression was dull and vacant, as though she'd had all she could take and had surrendered to her fate. She hardly responded when Julia greeted her with sympathy and clutched her hand in reassurance.

Mrs. Thompson pulled a chair over to the bed, and Julia sat upon it, still holding Mrs. Sweeny's hand. Seconds later, Mrs. Sweeney began whimpering, and then her face contorted in anguish as though something excruciating had gripped her body.

The housekeeper's hands flew to her cheeks in obvious distress at Mrs. Sweeney's pain. "Is it another contraction, Mrs. Bell?"

"It is," replied a thin woman wearing a white pinafore and mobcap who stood near the end of the bed attending Mrs. Sweeney. She lifted the sheet covering the woman and placed a hand on her rounded belly.

Mr. Norton stepped over to the bed, beside the woman in the pinafore, while Charles turned away to ensure Mrs. Sweeney's privacy. "Did the babe move with the contraction, Mrs. Bell?"

"No, sir. The babe hasn't moved an inch this last hour. And I'm afraid Mrs. Sweeney is too weak to push anymore."

"I'll get the forceps." He went to his bag and opened it. As he rummaged through its contents, metal instruments clanked together.

"Be brave, Mrs. Sweeney." Though Julia's calming voice was low, it carried across the room with a note of apprehension.

Mrs. Sweeney's weary voice echoed off the walls. "Must . . . speak to the priest first."

Charles turned then. While Mrs. Bell and Mr. Norton conferred with each other in whispers at the end of the bed, Mrs. Thompson leaned over Mrs. Sweeney and patted her right hand. "We weren't able to find a Catholic priest, Mrs. Sweeney, but Mr. Rodman has come."

Mrs. Sweeney closed her eyes and nodded. "Please send him here."

Mrs. Thompson motioned him forward. She stood back as Charles approached the bed opposite where Julia still sat holding tightly to Mrs. Sweeney's left hand. She would not meet his eyes. Instead, she remained focused on the patient as Charles grasped the woman's right hand. "How may I be of assistance, Mrs. Sweeney?"

The woman, however, was unable to answer him and began whimpering as another contraction apparently seized her. Her whimpering crescendoed into a scream, and she gripped his hand so hard he momentarily lost feeling in it. After the contraction subsided, Mrs. Sweeney closed her eyes and lay quiet.

Had she passed out from the pain? "Mrs. Sweeney?"

She opened her eyes and swallowed hard. "Can you hear my confession and absolve me of my sins, Mr. Rodman?" Her voice was a ragged whisper.

He clasped her hand tighter. "Yes."

"And can you give me the Eucharist?"

"Yes."

She swallowed once more. "Are you able to perform Last Rites on me and my babe in case we . . . don't make it?"

He wasn't certain he heard her last three words correctly, but he nodded and squeezed her hand once again to comfort her. "Yes, of course."

Julia let go of Mrs. Sweeney's left hand and patted the woman's arm. "I'll just leave you alone with Mr. Rodman."

"No, Lady Julia—please stay." Mrs. Sweeney's voice was a rasp by now. "It will comfort me to have you here with me when I tell Mr. Rodman what I must confess."

Julia then glanced up at him, her expression unsure. He nodded. She returned her focus to Mrs. Sweeney and took her hand once more. "If it will make you feel better."

Mrs. Sweeney pulled her right hand out of Charles's grasp and made the sign of the cross. She closed her eyes for a moment as yet another contraction overtook her body. After it passed, she reopened her eyes, and a few tears fell from her lashes. She looked up to the ceiling as she whispered, "Forgive me, Father, for I have sinned. It has been eleven months since my last confession. I accuse myself of the following sins:

I have spoken harshly to different people on several occasions. I have lied many, many times, and . . ." Her voice trailed off as she took a deep breath. "And . . . I was unfaithful to my husband on two occasions that I have not yet confessed to a priest." Her lips trembled as more tears fell from her lashes. "When my husband found out I was with child after my affair, he kicked me in the stomach because he was sure the babe was not his." Her voice broke off again for a moment. "In truth, I don't know whose baby I am carrying, whether it's my husband's or the other man's."

Charles didn't blink. He couldn't even move for several seconds because he was trying to make sense of what he'd just heard. Had she just confessed to adultery? He tried to keep his composure and maintain a stoic expression, but inside, he was reeling. He kept calm but said nothing, not sure what to say to the woman.

Then he remembered what he had told Eleanor when she asked him for forgiveness as she lay on her deathbed. *Go to hell.* He closed his eyes now in shame as he recalled his words to his dying wife.

"Mr. Rodman?" He opened his eyes again at the sound of Mrs. Sweeney's raspy voice. When he said nothing, she broke down and cried. "My current circumstances are God's wrath, aren't they?" He still didn't know what to say, and when he didn't reply to her, she broke into a hysterical sob. "What am I to do? I am surely going to die and go to hell."

"Please calm yourself, Mrs. Sweeney," Julia whispered to soothe her. She stroked the woman's brow, obviously trying to ease her despair.

He couldn't bring himself to meet Julia's gaze, but he felt her eyes upon him, watching his reaction, gauging his emotions, perhaps even sensing his inner turmoil, but most of all he felt her imploring him to answer the suffering woman. Though his voice wavered, he said as he made the sign of the cross over her, "Your sins are absolved, Mrs. Sweeney."

Mrs. Sweeney sniffled and wiped her eyes with the sheet covering her. "Do you mean it, Mr. Rodman? I will not go to hell if I die tonight?"

Without emotion and certainly without reassurance, he nodded as he whispered. "No. You will not go to hell. Jesus redeemed all lost souls with His death on the cross. His Father will welcome you to Heaven when it is your time."

Mrs. Sweeney breathed easier now. "May I say the Act of Contrition now?"

He nodded and listened as she recited the prayer. When she finished, she promised to say fifteen decades of the Rosary as her penance and then asked him to give her Last Rites and the Eucharist. He opened the bag he'd brought with him and pulled out two vials, one full of anointing oil and the other of holy water, and proceeded to give Mrs. Sweeney the sacrament of Extreme Unction. He also gave her a piece of the Communion bread he had blessed at one of his recent church services.

When the religious rites were completed, Mr. Norton stepped forward and asked Mrs. Bell to help him move the patient to the end of the bed so that he could work on her more easily with the forceps. As the surgeon and the midwife helped Mrs. Sweeney slide into position, the poor woman began sobbing again, even worse than before, and Charles sensed it was more out of fear than any pain she was suffering.

Julia once again tried to calm her with a soothing voice. "What's the matter, Mrs. Sweeney? Are you in pain?"

She whimpered as she shook her head. "No, no," she whispered. "I fear for my babe. What will become of it if I should die? The parish will not take in a Catholic orphan. Where will it go?" She put her fist in her mouth in an apparent effort to stifle her sobs.

Julia clutched the woman's hand tightly to her heart. "There, there, now, Mrs. Sweeney, everything will be alright. Nothing is going to happen to you. You will be fine, but if—God forbid—the unthinkable should happen, I will make sure nothing happens to your baby. I will take care of him or her myself, if necessary."

Tears swam in Mrs. Sweeney's eyes. "You will?"

Julia nodded as she once again squeezed the woman's hand. "Yes."

"As will I."

Julia raised her head and gaped at him in obvious shock, while Mrs. Sweeney's features softened in clear relief and gratitude. "Thank you, Mr. Rodman, and thank you, too, Lady Julia." She grasped Charles's hand and held it to Julia's, so that neither of them had a choice but touch each other. "You are both too kind."

For the second time since the evening's ordeal began, Charles locked eyes with Julia as they clasped their hands together over Mrs. Sweeney's to comfort her. The two of them stared at one another for a half-second. Or perhaps it was an eternity. In either case, his heart swelled with love for this woman.

"We must do this now. There is no more time." The urgency in Mr. Norton's voice broke the spell between them.

Charles stepped away from the bed to allow privacy for the procedure, but Julia remained holding Mrs. Sweeney's hand. When Mrs. Sweeney groaned in discomfort, he had to escape for some air. He opened the door and rushed into the hallway. Not long after, he heard an infant's robust cry. He opened the door to confirm what he heard.

"You have a healthy and very large baby boy, Mrs. Sweeney."

"Congratulations, Mrs. Sweeney!" Julia stood and let go of her hand while the midwife rested the child on Mrs. Sweeney's abdomen as she tended to the babe.

Charles caught Julia's eye when she stepped away from the bed. They stared at one another again for a few seconds, and then she went to the window, opened the sash a bit, and breathed deep. He closed the chamber door and returned to the hallway, taking another deep breath himself.

CHAPTER 12

Nine of Swords: Nightmares, isolation, reliving old traumas, focusing on things from the past, anxiety, inner turmoil . . .

CHARLES TOSSED AND TURNED BUT couldn't find a position comfortable enough to allow for sleep. Perhaps it was the foreign bed. It had been late after Mrs. Sweeney had given birth, and when it was all over, Charles had dreaded the long, tiresome ride back to the vicarage. He was standing in the entryway a half hour ago along with the surgeon and midwife, waiting for the carriage to take them back to South Kindale, when Julia entered the hall. Concerned that they were all leaving when they were so obviously exhausted, she had insisted that Mr. Norton and Mrs. Bell stay the night in a couple of unused rooms upstairs rather than head out. Though she didn't specifically include Charles in the invitation—and perhaps even omitted him on purpose—her housekeeper had had the good grace to show him to a chamber of his own.

Now, as he lay wide awake in the strange bed, he ruminated about the events of the evening. He tried to calm his unsettled mind, but it would not be at peace.

It raced with a thousand disjointed images, some from earlier that evening and others from earlier in his life. He saw Mrs. Sweeney, as she lay in her bed a while ago in excruciating pain, seeking forgiveness of her sins and asking him if she would go to hell for them. He hadn't known what to say to her at the time because all he could think about was Eleanor, his wife, and his response to her in nearly the same circumstances. Eleanor had lain in her bed, dying from the heart-wrenching loss of a child and the life-threatening loss of blood, asking him to forgive her for hurting him, and his response had been to condemn her to hell, as though she deserved an eternity of punishment for all that she had put him through.

Julia was right. He was a judgmental arse.

Still, as he had witnessed Mrs. Sweeney's ordeal and heard her heartfelt plea for forgiveness after confessing her sins, he could not prevent himself from reliving the pain of Eleanor's infidelity. He thought he had laid that pain in the ground next to her corpse, but Mrs. Sweeney's circumstances had disinterred it, and its desiccated remains splattered him once again with grief. Unresolved grief. And though the woman's suffering distressed him, all he could think about in that moment was her husband and the agony the man must have endured when he realized his wife had cheated on him. Unable to take it any longer, Charles closed his eyes and tried to banish thoughts of betrayal and the feelings they conjured. Although he drifted in and out of consciousness, his mind would not allow him the sweet liberation of oblivion. Though restless sleep finally settled upon him, it only carried him into a memory . . .

He sighed in relief as he stepped up to the door of the vicarage following a long afternoon of visiting parishioners. His mind was on one thing, and one thing alone: Mrs. Knight's mouth-watering roast chicken for dinner. It surely had to be ready for him and Eleanor by now. Hardly able to wait, he attempted to open the door, but when he turned the doorknob, he found it locked. Odd. Even odder, when he knocked, no one answered. Where was his housekeeper? Had Eleanor given her the day off? And where exactly was his wife? He shook his head and shrugged as he searched his coat pocket for his key. Upon opening the door, however, something felt strange, peculiar almost—as if nothing were right and everything were wrong.

Eleanor did not greet him when he came home as she typically did, and this unsettled him. Perhaps she was in the garden behind the house tending to her flowers. He shrugged again, dismissing his unease, as he set his hat on a table in the entryway. Then he heard it. A man's voice followed by a woman's laughter. The man laughed as well then, and everything went quiet once more. Except for . . . the faint, rhythmic creaking noises coming from somewhere inside the house and the sound of something banging against a wall. And was he mistaken, or did he also hear muffled moans and groans beneath the creaking and the banging?

He looked in the drawing room, but it was empty, as was the dining room and Eleanor's sitting room. His study was likewise vacant, but as he made his way down the corridor toward the bedrooms, the noises grew louder and louder until he reached the door to the chamber he shared with Eleanor and heard the sounds much more clearly now, not muffled as before. He also heard a conversation above the creaking and the banging and the moans and groans.

"You like that?" It was a man's voice, an oddly familiar man's voice. "Do you like when I pound you senseless, Ellie?"

Charles's gut clenched at the low, feminine groan in reply.

"You have to say it, Ellie. Tell me how it feels."

"Good. It feels so . . . good . . ."

"Does my cock feel better than his?"

"Yessssss . . ." Her voice trailed off into a sibilant hiss.

"That's what I want to hear, sweet." Neither spoke for a moment until the man chuckled softly. "You want it harder, Ellie?"

"Oh, yes, my lord . . . harder . . . I need it harder."

The man chuckled once again, but this time his laughter was low and sinister. "Here you go, sweet. Just for you."

Whatever he had been doing before, he was doing it harder now, as evidenced by the sounds coming from the room as they crescendoed into a raucous chorus of creaking and banging and moaning and groaning so loud, Charles thought it might bring down the house.

"Louder, Ellie. Scream for me. Let me know how it feels."

The woman moaned until she was screaming, but without a doubt, pleasure and not pain, provoked her cries. Who was she? Who was this woman? It couldn't be Eleanor, could it? It couldn't possibly be the sweet, demure woman he loved with all his heart. Eleanor would never say such things or behave like that. At least she never had with him in the last eight years. And exactly who was with her? Who was that man? His voice was familiar, but surely it wasn't the man Charles was thinking of, was it?

"That's it, Ellie. That's it. Come for me, sweet. Tell me how much you want it."

"I want it . . . so bad. I need it. It feels so . . . good."

Charles could no longer take it. He had to see for himself what was happening. He had to verify with his eyes what he heard with his ears.

He opened the door.

Both of them were naked on the bed. Dunham was on his knees, his back to the door, while Eleanor was on all fours in front of him as he took her from behind. Though Charles couldn't see the whole of what was happening between them, he saw enough. What he couldn't see, he heard, and those sounds confirmed plenty. The wet, slick slapping of their bodies together left no doubt in his mind that his best friend's cock was even now sliding in and out of his wife's body, and her soft, urgent moans left no doubt that she liked it. The bed boards creaked under their movement, while his thrusts drove the headboard into the wall behind the bed.

"Eleanor?" It was Charles's voice, but why he called to her would forever baffle him.

She turned her head to look over her shoulder and gasped. Still maintaining the rhythm of his thrusts, Dunham turned his head, too, but he didn't gasp or show any other signs of shock. Instead, he laughed. It was a cruel, jeering chortle, without a doubt meant to mock Charles.

"Excellent timing, Rodman. I'm almost through tupping your whore of a wife."

"Whore?" Eleanor shrieked as she looked back at Dunham. She seemed more upset at what the earl had just called

her than the fact that her husband had just caught her in flagrant adultery.

"What else would you call yourself, darling? You like it, though, don't you? You like it long and hard and rough, like a Covent Garden strumpet." He slapped her bottom as he threw his head back and laughed again, this time at her. He continued pumping into her.

She gaped at him in obvious confusion as tears filled her eyes. "I don't understand. How can you say those things? I thought you loved me."

"Love you?" He snorted and then threw his head back in derisive laughter once more. "No, my sweet. I like tupping you maybe. But love you?" He laughed again, more cruelly this time. "Hardly. You revolt me. I only seduced you, if you could call it seduction, in the first place because Rodman seemed to like you, and I wanted to spoil his fun before he married you. Fortunately, you've thrown yourself at me since we met, so getting you to lift your skirts was shamefully easy. I kept tupping you after you were married because I have to admit that I enjoy watching you turn into such a wanton tart whenever . . ." He paused as he thrust twice more into her and then grunted like the pig he was when he reached his own climax. He recovered after several seconds and withdrew from her. ". . . I'm inside you. But I don't love you. In fact, you make me ill. And now that your husband has finally found out about us, I won't be back."

Eleanor began sobbing as she collapsed to the bed and buried her face in a pillow.

Dunham jumped off the bed and bent down to retrieve a pair of trousers lying on the floor. "She's all yours, Rodman. Have at her while she's still good and slick."

Rage coursed through Charles's veins. Unable to control himself any longer, he lurched at his one-time friend, as the urge to commit murder overwhelmed him. He fisted his hand and smashed it with all the force he had in him into Dunham's nose. The reprobate stumbled backwards a few feet as blood began flowing from his nostrils over his lips and down his chin.

Despite his injuries, Dunham laughed at him. "This is the thanks I get after all I've done for you—and your wife? I gave you a living in this parish, and I gave her a good time whenever I could."

"Rot in hell, you bloody bastard." Charles leapt for his old friend once more, but the man sidestepped the assault.

Dunham grabbed his other clothes and his shoes off the floor and strode swiftly toward the door. "See you in church," he sneered. With those as his final words, he disappeared through the door, taunting Charles with his laughter. It echoed down the hall and then faded away into nothing.

Charles's rage abated into sorrow and then into pure, unadulterated pain as he stood in the room, alone with Eleanor now, and glanced over to the bed where she still lay prone and sobbing.

"Eleanor?"

She lifted her head and wiped her eyes and nose on her pillow case. She looked over her shoulder at him but said nothing.

"Why? I don't understand. Why would you do this? And with Dunham, of all people."

She shrugged. "I love him." Another sob escaped her at her admission.

"I-I thought you loved me."

She sniffled as she shook her head. "No, Charles, no. I don't love you. I've never loved you. I have no feelings for you whatsoever."

Tortured by her words, he lifted his arms in bewilderment. "Why did you marry me then?"

"I had to. It was my only choice." She laughed through her sobs. "It turned out to be all for naught in the end because I lost the baby. I really needn't have married you at all."

"The baby?"

She nodded. "Dunham wouldn't marry me. He promised he would before he seduced me, but then he married Rebecca instead, for her much larger dowry, I suppose. I had to accept your offer when I discovered I was with child. I was devastated when I miscarried his babe."

Her confession crushed him. She returned to sobbing into the pillow, while he backed out of the room. He put everything he'd just heard and witnessed—the entire scene—into a little box and buried it deep in his brain where he would never find it again. Oh, the pain would surely remain for a long time to come, but he quashed any remembrance of the scene of his best friend tupping his wife. He also tamped down the ache in his heart from learning she had never loved him . . .

No, no, no, no.

Charles bolted upright in the bed. Had the sound of a door closing somewhere down the hall woken him? Or had his own screams awoken him? He attempted to breathe but couldn't pull air into his lungs as images from his disturbing dream faded into the ether. It had been so real, so vivid and visceral, that he'd found himself back in the bedroom of the old vicarage watching the both of them again until he could no longer take it. He had to shake himself awake to get out of it.

He struggled for a moment trying to figure out why he was reliving the agony of his wife's infidelity with his best friend.

Then he recalled Mrs. Sweeney. He had been distressed by her miserable ordeal and had likened it to Eleanor's. And though he felt a deep sorrow for Mrs. Sweeney, he also felt a strange sympathy for her husband who must have been devastated by his wife's adultery and the fact that she might possibly have been carrying another man's child. Outraged—and probably hurt—the man had kicked her in the abdomen. The attack was brutal, barbaric, and unforgivable, and that she hadn't lost her child as a result was a miracle.

Although Charles condemned the man for taking his pain out on his wife by kicking her mercilessly, he froze with the realization that he had done essentially the same thing to Eleanor. He had not literally assaulted her perhaps, but hadn't he figuratively kicked her in the gut when he threw her out to live with her parents, while he escaped to London after finding out about her affair with Dunham? He had abandoned her as much as Dunham had, and worse, he'd sent her away when she most needed someone to care for her. And although he could acknowledge that his actions had been harsh and that he was perhaps a heartless arse, he couldn't let go of the pain she had caused him. He still could not, after all this time, forgive her for marrying him out of desperation and then betraying him with another man, least of all his best friend.

He could no longer lie there reliving the misery he thought he'd buried deep in his soul long ago. It turned out the grave holding his painful memories had not been very deep at all. It had been shallow, and the memories interred in it had always lurked just beneath the surface of his current reality, just waiting for the right word, the right sound, the right image, the right situation to resurrect it.

He donned an old, worn banyan the housekeeper had given him to use for the night. He wrapped it around him and tied the belt tightly to cover his smallclothes. He shook his head at the irony that the robe probably belonged to Julia's late husband, but he couldn't help that. All he could do in this moment was to focus on forgetting the pain. He had to breathe some fresh air. He had to get out of the room, out of the house, if necessary, and most of all, out of his head. He needed to do something to dispel the raw memories of his deceased wife and his former friend in bed together. The crushing recollection that she had never loved him, had never wanted to be with him, had never desired him, and worse, that she had loved his former friend and married Charles only when the man jilted her, tormented him. He needed to escape.

Om.
Still so much turmoil.
Om.
Still so much anguish.
Om.

Julia shook her hands and released a breath and then tried the mantra again.

Om.

It was no use.

She couldn't dispel all the pain, the memories, or the sorrow of her ordeal in India that had resurfaced as she witnessed Mrs. Sweeney's suffering earlier tonight. It was Calcutta all over again, and she couldn't escape it. She couldn't stop reliving the nightmare over and over again in her head. She couldn't soothe or clear her mind, not even with meditation and a simple mantra in the refuge of her temple.

She closed her eyes once again.

Om.

Current reality slipped away, and she couldn't prevent herself from slipping back to Calcutta three years ago . . .

Such pain. Such excruciating pain.

Om.

Not even meditation would allow her to rise above the pain. Nothing helped. Each contraction was worse than the last, and now they were coming closer and closer together and lasting longer and longer.

Her belly burned with the latest one. It gripped her midsection so tightly, squeezing it like a vise, that she was left with the desire to bear down and push.

"Must . . . push." She forced the words through gritted teeth.

"No! It's not time yet," the British midwife said. "You'll

tear. You're not opened up enough."

Delirious, Julia lay back on her pillow as the contraction subsided. Her jaw slackened, aching from clenching it so hard. She licked her lips with her parched tongue. She wanted water, but more than anything else, she wanted Renesh. He would know how to soothe her. He would guide her through this. But she couldn't have the man she loved with her when her husband was just outside the door.

She closed her eyes and tried to recall the things Renesh had taught her about quieting her mind, body, and soul. She breathed deep and imagined a quiet garden hidden from the outside world. She sat near a pond watching lotuses floating placidly on the water. Above her, birds softly sang in the fronds of a palm tree.

She envisioned Renesh at her side, holding her hand and wiping her brow. His presence comforted her as he whispered sweet endearments and words of encouragement in her ear. She imagined her ordeal was over and she was holding her baby in her arms. Her peace lasted but a moment, shattered by the beginning of a new contraction and the recollection that the baby might actually be Renesh's. How would she explain to Niles that the baby he had so looked forward to having was not his, but another man's? An Indian man's. His doctor's, his friend's.

Reality intruded. Renesh disappeared from beside her, and the garden evaporated into the ether. This spasm in her abdomen was worse than any she had yet experienced, but for two more hours, she was not allowed to push. Then, finally, the midwife told her to bear down with all her might. As Julia did so, a burning sensation tormented her, and the babe moved but an inch.

Forever seemed to pass before she felt the child slip from her womb, and then a wee cry pierced the heavy atmosphere of the room, sending Julia into euphoria. Her baby was here.

"It's a girl." The midwife held the infant up for Julia to see. Then she worked diligently to cut the child's cord and tie it off. Afterward, she swaddled the infant and placed her in Julia's arms.

Tears slid down Julia's cheeks as she gazed at her daughter in adoration. The miracle of her existence filled her with wonder and an all-consuming love.

"Camille," she whispered. She looked into the infant's large, black eyes, and so much love filled her heart that it almost hurt. She traced a finger through the girl's black hair, while a tiny brown hand clasped another of her fingers.

Then the realization hit her.

Oh dear lord. It was unmistakable. This baby, this lovely child, was Renesh's. She could in no way pass for Niles's, not when he had such a fair complexion and light hair.

Real terror struck when she heard a knock on her chamber door. Niles.

Her husband walked into the room without making any sound and strode over to the bed. He smiled. Grinned, actually. His excitement was palpable, as was his happiness. He had wanted a baby for so long, but Julia had not conceived in the five years since they'd been married—until April of last year, a few months after she'd begun her affair with Renesh. She had never thought that her inability to conceive with Niles was a result of his infertility. She had always assumed it was her own. Consequently, she and Renesh had done nothing to avoid conception.

"What shall we call her?" he whispered.

"*Camille. After my father's mother.*"

"*Camille Lacey. It's beautiful.*" He reached down to stroke the babe's cheek. "*May I hold her?*"

Julia froze, her heart pounding. She couldn't keep the child he thought was his from him forever, yet she did not want him to see the baby too closely today. Another day, perhaps. "*She's sleeping. Let's not disturb her.*" She clutched the infant more tightly to her chest.

"*Did you see her eyes? Has she opened them at all yet? What color are they?*"

"*All babies' eyes are dark at birth,*" said the midwife. "*It's only after a few months that they take on their natural color. Same with their hair.*" Bless the woman for sensing Julia's discomfort and her fear.

Niles brows knitted together in obvious confusion. "*But her hair is black.*" He stroked Camille's cheek again. "*And why is her skin so dark?*"

"*That happens, too.*" The midwife approached the bed, almost like a sentinel, perhaps sensing trouble. "*Some babies are born yellow . . . or dark. It goes away after a few days.*"

"*Let me hold her, Julia.*" It was a command this time, not a request. "*I want to see her more closely.*"

"*No, Niles. She's sleeping.*" Julia kept her voice to a whisper, partly to prevent the baby from awakening and partly out of fear.

Without warning, Niles reached down and grabbed the child from Julia's arms. The babe opened her eyes as he brought her closer to him to scrutinize her. Julia's gut clenched when he peered into the girl's black irises, knowing how dark they were. He then ran his fingers through the black hair covering the girl's head. There was so much of it for such a tiny *infant. He touched her little hand, and it gripped his finger in response. He shook off the baby's hand and opened her blanket to inspect the skin on her belly.*

His eyes darted from the baby to Julia. He fixed her with a terrifying glare. Saying nothing, he shoved the child into the arms of the midwife whose frightened eyes were brimming with tears. "Get that thing out of my sight. I don't care what you do with it. Drown it, if you must."

"No!" Julia shrieked. "My baby! Give me back my baby! Camille!" But her cries were useless.

"You will never see that abomination again." The infant began wailing as Niles turned to the midwife who had crouched in a corner holding her. "Leave, if you know what's good for you . . . and it."

The midwife stood.

"No!" Julia cried even louder this time, and the midwife backed into the corner again with Camille, while Niles stalked to the bed. "Whose child is that?"

Sobs racked Julia's body, but she refused to answer him.

"Who's the father, Julia? Name the bloody bastard." His voice was low, calculating, and above all else, menacing.

She wept quietly but made no other sound.

He seized her neck. "Tell me who it is, Julia, or so help me, I will kill you."

Her hand flew to her throat, but she couldn't dislodge her husband's fingers. He gripped her neck too tightly. She gasped for air but only gagged as his stranglehold tightened.

She was able to gulp some air a few seconds later when he let go. He put his face right up to hers so that their noses touched briefly as he snarled through his teeth, "Whose. Baby. Is. That?"

"I . . . I don't . . ."

"Do NOT say you don't know, Julia." He roared the words now. "Whose is it?"

She closed her eyes and willed him to go away. She opened them abruptly when the back of his hand hit her cheek. He slapped her again when she would not answer, and he clutched her throat once more when she tried to rise from the bed. She wanted Camille.

This time he strangled her with all his might. Her lungs burned, and the room spun until everything went black.

He must have let go, for a few minutes later, she regained consciousness. Julia lay there delirious for a moment while he paced the room in obvious agitation. She somehow managed to regain her senses and escape the bed. She ran for Camille, blood seeping down her legs.

In two steps, Niles was at the midwife and seized the baby from her arms. Julia tried to grab the child, but her husband threw her back against the wall. Then he placed a hand at the baby's throat. "Tell me, Julia. Or so help me, I will kill this child with my bare hands." His voice conveyed a viciousness she had never heard before.

Frightened for Camille's life, Julia called out, "Renesh!"

Niles's eyes opened wide in obvious incredulity. "Sengupta? My doctor?" He paused as though he were trying to process her answer. "My friend?"

"Yes." Sobbing, Julia reached for Camille, but Niles moved too quickly and once again placed her in the midwife's arms. He then punched Julia in the gut for good measure. She doubled over and reeled backward, while he opened the chamber door and thrust the midwife out of the room.

"Camille!" Julia screamed. "Bring her back!"

Niles scowled at the woman. "Take her away from here. Anywhere. Just get her out of my sight." He turned to Julia after growling the words.

"Take her to Renesh Sengupta!" Julia's scream faded along with the midwife's footsteps as she disappeared down the hallway. She could only pray the other woman had heard her. She ran for the shelter of the bed once more as Niles stalked toward her, but she could not escape him or his violence. When he reached her, he thrashed her until her body was as bruised as her soul.

Days later, she lay in bed mourning the loss of her child as her body tried to heal itself from the birth and the beating afterwards. She had sunk into deep melancholy since Niles had thrust the infant into the arms of the terrified midwife and banished them both. She had hoped for word from Renesh about Camille but heard nothing about either of them. As her milk came in and then dried up, her post-partum anguish increased to the point that she did not know what she would do or how she would go on. Her heart grieved over Camille, while her conscience rebuked her incessantly for her adultery and betrayal of Niles.

Finally, after several more days in deep distress, she sought out the only succor she could imagine was available. She dragged her weary body out of bed and washed and dressed. She then asked her maid to fetch Mr. Harding, the Anglican vicar who served the English personnel of the East India Company in Calcutta, hoping that if she confessed her sins to him, he would ease the guilt and pain she had suffered because of her misdeeds and the loss of Camille. She prayed that he would comfort her with assurances of God's love and forgiveness despite her sins.

Mr. Harding was a wretched person and a worse cler-gyman. He sat in her sitting room in the bungalow Niles owned and seemed to listen to her story with compassion and concern, but it was only a pretense of sympathy. After Julia confessed her sins to him and admitted to having had an adulterous affair with her husband's doctor and giving birth to the man's baby, Mr. Harding rose out of his chair and crossed to hers.

He stood before her and screamed the word "harlot" as a vein twitched in his temple. "Madam, not only are you a sinner, you are an adulterous whore, and I can hardly stand the sight of you. You should fear the wrath of God, for it has only begun to be visited upon you. There is no forgiveness for your transgressions. They are far too horrid for redemption and offend the Lord far too much for Him to absolve you. You ought to suffer from now until your death for the sins you have committed. And then, you will surely burn in hell." After he spat the words at her, he stormed out of the room in all his righteous indignation, leaving her shocked and in tears.

Astounded by his cruelty and his merciless censure, she ended all affiliation with the Church of England and stopped attending Sunday services. She pined for her child and her lover, and although she did not see Camille again, she even-tually learned of her daughter's fate after she sneaked a letter to Renesh, who wrote back to tell her that Camille was fine and living with him and that she was being cared for by a wet nurse he had hired.

Shortly after that, Niles forced a grieving Julia to return to England with him. She longed more than anything to see Camille once again—one last time—before they sailed, so she tried to sneak out of the bungalow. Niles caught her before she could leave, however, and after beating her senseless for attempting to escape, he laughed as he told her with cruel and twisted delight that she would never see her lover or their child again because they were both dead. Both Renesh Sengupta, the only man she had ever truly loved, and their daughter Camille were gone. Forever . . .

A rustling sound near the temple door disrupted her wretched memories. She opened her eyes.

Oh. *Him.*

CHAPTER 13

The Lovers: Soul-searing connection, sacred bond, harmony, passion, love . . .

HE LOOKED AWFUL—PATHETIC, REALLY—BUT SHE held her tongue as she watched him from the vantage point of her cushions near Lord Ganesh and the altar. His eyes seemed hollow and his cheeks gaunt in the shadows cast by the soft light of the candles flickering in the temple. His hair was disheveled, and he wore no shoes. He stood in the doorway scowling at her with his shoulders rolled forward and his arms crossed over his chest defensively, as though he expected her to begin ranting at him at any second.

She remained silent, certain she was scowling back at him, puzzled by the robe he was wearing. Was that Niles's banyan? She didn't ask. She couldn't bring herself to question him whatsoever, not when his expression revealed so much pain. They stared at one another without saying anything for several interminable seconds.

"I apologize. I didn't mean to intrude." His voice was low and raspy, and he turned to go when she said nothing.

"What are you doing here?"

He turned back to her and shrugged, keeping his arms crossed over his chest. "Don't know." He peered down at the floor and then back up at her. "I was looking for refuge, I suppose."

She didn't invite him in, but he didn't turn to leave this time. Instead, he stood there in pitiable form, as though he were lost and all alone. She didn't have the heart to tell him to go.

After several seconds, he uncrossed his arms and then crossed them over his chest again in the opposite direction. "Why are you here?"

She raised a brow. "The same."

He nodded and stood for several more minutes in apparent hesitation. Finally, he turned toward the door. "I should go."

"Charles?" He glanced over his shoulder back at her. "Wait." She wasn't sure what to say next. She didn't want to know what was troubling him. She didn't want to sympathize with him in any way, shape, or form. She was still stung by the hurtful comments he made to her the night of her birthday. Yet, he appeared so wretched that she couldn't let him leave. "You look like you could use a friend."

He didn't respond as he peered down at the floor again.

"What's the matter?"

He uncrossed his arms and scrubbed his hands down his face. "I don't want to burden you."

"It's no burden." That wasn't entirely a lie, but while it was no burden to have him there, his presence was

still bothersome. Against all good judgment, she scooted to her right to make room for him on the cushions.
She patted the vacant spot next to her. "Come. Sit."

He shuffled his bare feet across the floor with obvious reservation and sat with even more reluctance.
"Were you meditating?"

She nodded. "Or trying to, at least. My mind is a
jumble for some reason this evening."

He nodded in return. "It's not a night for clear
thought."

"No, it is not."

Though he said nothing more, his previous statement attested to his state of mind. She studied his forlorn expression, searching for clues as to why he was so
morose. Something troubled him, obviously, but what
it was, she couldn't guess. Neither said anything for a
while, but somehow, the silence was comforting. It was
for her at least, so she let it be.

Minutes passed, and then he exhaled a heavy breath.
"Did you ever . . ." His voice trailed off, and he said
nothing more for another minute. "Have you ever had
your heart ripped out of your chest—while it was still
beating?"

Inside, she reeled at the question, but she tried not
to reveal how much it actually affected her. "Yes."

"What did you do . . . for the pain?"

"Meditate."

He nodded and smacked his forehead as though her
answer were obvious. "Of course. Silly question."

"Not silly at all."

He stared forward, but again, he said nothing.

Several more minutes passed without words, and she was tempted to let that be the end of their conversation. His obvious melancholy touched her though, so she couldn't just say nothing. "Would you like to discuss it?"

He shook his head no.

"Perhaps it would help if you talked about it. Who ripped your heart out, Charles?"

He remained brooding and silent for a while, and then he sighed as he closed his eyes and bent his head forward. "Never mind. What would help most is to laugh." He turned to her then and stared at her with grave intensity. "Tell me something funny."

She smiled in an attempt to lighten his mood while also trying to think of something remotely amusing to tell him. He stared at her until finally, after several moments, she cleared her throat. "You know my brother?"

He nodded, while his gaze remained fixed on her face.

"Of course, you do, but I don't know if you know that he was not always the kind-hearted soul he is now."

He arched a brow.

"That's sarcasm, in case you were wondering."

"Ah."

"In any case, Benthower was even more horrid in his youth than he is now—if that's possible. He was a terrible prankster when we were all younger and would laugh at us and our misfortunes. Us, being my sisters and me. He used to tease us without mercy. He knew all our weaknesses and fears. With Phoebe, it was spiders, so he would put spiders where she'd least expect to find them, like in her empty teacup. With Cassandra, it was mice, so he would slip them down her back or let them scurry loose around her room. With me, it was snakes, and whenever he would capture them, he'd hide them under my covers. Well, with Bess, it was frogs and toads."

He quirked his head to the side. "Bess? Who's Bess?"

"My next youngest sister, before Violet."

"Was she at your birthday party? I don't recall meeting her."

She sighed. It still hurt to talk about Bess, as much as it hurt to talk about Phoebe. "Bess is no longer with us."

His eyes shot open wide, but he said nothing.

"It's a long, tragic story, but basically, she ran away the night before she was to be married to an old reprobate thirty years her senior. Benthower had arranged the marriage with the understanding that the horrible man could marry Bess if he split her fifty-thousand-pound dowry with our brother after they were married. All our matches were made in Benthower's best interest, in case you didn't realize."

"Even yours?"

She rolled her eyes. "Oh, yes. Even mine." She paused a moment to straighten her legs and wiggle her toes. "At any rate, the night before her impending wedding, Bess ran away from home. The authorities found her spencer and bonnet floating in the Serpentine the next morning. Most people assume she drowned that night. I held out hope for many years that she did not drown and was, in fact, still alive because her body was never recovered, but in all honesty, I now believe she is gone. We don't know whether she fell in the Serpentine or jumped intentionally. And of course, there are worse theories out there. Some of the authorities have speculated that she might have been accosted by footpads in Hyde Park, and whether they abducted her or killed her, all they left of her were coat and hat, which they threw into the river."

He leaned back and touched her shoulder in a gesture of overt sympathy. "I'm so very sorry, Julia. It must be torture not knowing what happened to her."

She nodded. "It is, and I'm sorry to have depressed you with such a sad tale when you asked for a funny one. What I actually wanted to tell you was how Bess got revenge on Benthower one time—with my help, of course."

He smiled for the first time since appearing in the temple. "Of course."

"She and I were playing with our dolls in the garden behind Benthower Castle where we grew up when, suddenly, she let out a blood-curdling scream. I looked over to see her staring wide-eyed at a toad that had landed on her skirt. Benthower and some of his obnoxious friends were playing lawn tennis nearby, and of course, he sprinted over to us at the sound of her scream. When he saw Bess sitting there scared spitless with a toad on her pinafore, he laughed like it was the funniest thing he'd ever seen. Then, he picked the toad up and held it up to her lips for her to kiss. She squealed before jumping up and running away, and he chased after her with the toad until he finally caught up to her. He held her hostage until she finally kissed the creature. I tried to comfort her as best as I could after he and his abominable friends—and the toad, of course—had left us alone. She cried for a while, and then I helped her plot how to get back at our brother. We were going to get him where it would hurt him most."

Charles gave her a bemused smile but remained silent.

"Back then, Benthower prided himself on his thick head of hair. He wore it long in those days and tied back in a queue. The night of the toad incident, Bess and I made sure that everyone in the castle was asleep, especially him. We found a pair of scissors in our mother's sewing basket and sneaked into his room late that night to cut his hair. I let her snip his tail off and then showed her how to chop off chunks of his remaining locks. Fortunately, he was a sound sleeper and didn't wake up while she worked. He didn't even move. When we left him, there was hair all over his pillow and sheets, and he had tufts of hair sticking up willy-nilly all over his head. She took his tail as a trophy, and to this day, I don't know what she ever did with it. At any rate, he woke the whole house up with his scream the next morning when he realized what had happened to him."

Charles laughed out loud. "You did not cut the mighty duke's hair while he slept."

"Oh, yes. Yes, we did. Or should I say, Bess cut his hair after I showed her how. Anyway, he accused her right away of butchering his hair in retaliation for the toad prank and went to our mother insisting that she punish Bess on his behalf. Mama had no sympathy for him whatsoever and told him it was exactly what he deserved for teasing a poor girl half his age. Benthower never suspected me, and neither Bess nor I ever confessed, but we did take great delight in how infuriated he was. He looked so hideous with his hair chopped up in different lengths that he had to shave his head entirely and wear a wig for several months. It was at least a year before his hair was long enough to wear in a queue again."

"I find it hard to believe that you had a hand in any of this."

"Is that sarcasm, Mr. Rodman?"

"It is." He laughed once again, and she laughed right along with him.

"Can't you just picture it? The powerful and invincible Duke of Benthower begging our mother for justice against a little girl as he stood blustering with his hair hacked up like a barbarian's?"

He chortled once again, shaking his head.

She shook her head, also, and then sighed. "To this day, I still take pleasure when I recall his level of outrage."

Charles threw his head back and laughed even more roundly as he clapped his hands. She laughed, too, and as their laughter turned to unadulterated snorts and giggles, they both fell backwards onto the cushions so that they lay next to one another staring up at the ceiling.

Finally, their guffaws died down into infrequent,

shortened snickers as they both tried to catch a breath. He sighed after a while and patted her hand. "Thank you, Julia. I needed that."

She grasped his hand and squeezed it in reassurance. "You're welcome, Charles. It's good to laugh like that now and then." She released him and turned on her side to face him, propping her head against her hand and regarding his profile for several moments as he continued to stare at the ceiling. She reached over and swept a lock of his hair away from his brow. "Now, would you like to tell me what's troubling you so?"

He closed his eyes for a few seconds, and when he opened them again, he rolled on his side to face her. "No." He gazed at her for what seemed like an eternity before reaching out to stroke her cheek. "I'd just like to forget. Forget every last thing."

Her heart beat erratically from the emotions flickering through his eyes. Need and want. Fear and hope. She couldn't tell where one emotion ended and the next began. The only thing she could tell for certain was that, in the subtle flicker of candlelight, something had changed between them. Profoundly changed. Desire coiled in and around them like a vine and settled low in her belly. Heat blossomed over her, quashing her ability to think straight as he bent his head and touched his lips to hers. She closed her eyes to everything but the feel of his mouth on hers, in a kiss so different from their first that it astonished in comparison. This was not the wild and savage connection they had shared behind the assembly rooms. Yet, there was passion in its tenderness, and hunger in the languorous fusion of their tongues.

His hand settled on her hip as he pulled her closer to him, and his rigid arousal against her belly sent a tremor through her core. He slipped his hand beneath her wrapper and caressed an unhurried path up her body over the fabric of her shift, and when he found her breast, he softly brushed the backs of his fingers across it until she ached with pleasure. He turned his palm to her breast and gently squeezed it when her nipple hardened. She moaned, low and deep, and he slid his lips from hers, trailing kisses and warmth along her jaw and down her throat.

As she reveled in his attention, she stroked her hand over his back up to his shoulder and ran her fingers through the hair at the nape of his neck. He moaned then, and encouraged by the sound of his arousal, she slid her hand to the front of the banyan he wore and unfixed the tie at his waist. She slipped her fingers beneath the opening of the robe and caressed the hairs on his chest, while he shrugged the robe over his shoulders giving her freedom to run her hands all over his bare torso. His body was beautiful and hard, his muscles like chiseled marble. He smelled all at once spicy and earthy, bergamot mingled with cedar wood.

She worshipped him with her mouth and hands, unable to stop herself from trailing kisses along his jaw and down his throat as she continued stroking her hand over his shoulders and chest. She found a nipple and toyed with it, eliciting a deep groan from his throat. He returned his lips to hers, and as their kiss deepened, his hand drifted down her back and settled on her hip. From there, it stroked lower over her bottom and squeezed her through her shift, sending ripples of pleasure through her core. He reached his hand down to the bottom of her gown and hiked it up her thighs and over her belly, breaking their kiss just long enough to pull the garment up and over her head until she lay naked beside him.

His eyes raked her nude form up and down with obvious appreciation, and when he looked up at her, his gaze smoldered with a primal hunger no man had ever shown for her before. Moisture trickled from her core, and more ripples of pleasure cascaded through her when he bent his head to a hardened nipple and sucked it between his teeth.

And as he kissed and caressed her body, she lost herself in the connection between them, never forgetting that this was Charles, a man who could infuriate her in an instant and soothe her the next. One minute, he provoked her like no one else ever could, and the next, he enchanted her as no one had ever done. He was the one man she never wanted to see again, and yet, the only man she ever wanted to be with again. She loathed him for his rigid views on religion and morality and his tendency to judge people when he didn't fully comprehend their circumstances. Yet, he possessed a good nature and a wry sense of humor. He was also kind and gentle to those suffering and in need, and he did not tolerate racial bigotry or condone a husband's right to discipline his wife through physical violence. For these and other reasons, she loved him.

Her hand stilled over his heart with the realization

that she loved him. Thunderstruck, she didn't breathe for an eternity. She simply lay there astonished as she marveled at the beating of his heart beneath her palm, barely mindful of his hand sliding from her breast to the apex of her thighs, barely cognizant that he was stroking his fingers through her damp curls. She gasped with full awareness, though, when his fingers found the sensitive flesh hidden between her legs. He parted her folds, stroking and probing until she thought she would die from the pleasure. She was nearly delirious when he dipped his fingers into her sheath and spread the moisture there all around her labia. She rotated her hips against his hand as he slid a finger in and out of her, well aware that she wouldn't last much longer if he continued. The intensity built until she couldn't withstand it. She needed him inside her. Now.

She reached her hand down to his smallclothes and ripped apart the strings holding them together. She slid her hand inside and ran it down his long, thick member, squeezing and stroking it until he moaned. His hand flew to hers and stopped her from pumping his shaft. He shifted until he was atop her, while she spread her legs and rubbed herself against him until her exposed wet flesh made contact with his stony length. She stilled at the sensation of his naked flesh against hers, anticipating how glorious it would feel inside her, and then began undulating her hips so that her wetness coated him once again. Her breath quickened when he joined her this time, gliding himself against her folds until the head of his staff met her opening. He thrust his hips gently, almost imperceptibly, breaching her entry where he paused for a moment, as though debating whether or not to go any further. Finally, he began sliding into her, and she gasped once again as he stretched her walls in a long, slow introduction. He settled himself deep inside her, and while she lay motionless, savoring the sense of fullness he gave her with their physical joining, she couldn't help but marvel at the sense of fullness in her heart for this man.

He broke from their kiss after he was fully seated within her and gazed down at her lovely face. Though her eyes were closed, her mouth was open in what he could only interpret as awe. He hoped it was awe, in any case, because he felt it, too, the wonder in the connection of their hearts and bodies. Thankfully, she remained still beneath him so that he could revel in the sensation of being inside her at last. Though he had imagined it many times, reality far exceeded his fantasies. Her channel was tight and hot and so drenched in moisture from her obvious arousal that he marveled at how responsive she was to his touch and his caresses. To him. He had not known a woman could react to him with such passion until he met her.

He watched her expression as he began moving ever so subtly within her. Though her eyes remained closed, she threw her head back and groaned with obvious pleasure. Inspired by her response, he rocked his hips against hers more demonstrably as he found her sensitive bud with his fingers. She moaned loudly when he applied pressure to it. He took her mouth in a commanding kiss and started moving his cock in and out of her with more force. He kept up the pressure on her swollen pearl as he increased the frequency and intensity of his penetration until he was pounding into her taut, moist passage and she was undulating fiercely beneath him, matching him thrust for thrust. He nearly lost himself inside her when she cried out his name as her flesh contracted around his and shuddered in orgasm. His own climax was imminent, and he thrust a few more times before pulling out of her sheath and spilling on her belly.

Sated and spent, he remained atop her while he dragged ragged breaths into his lungs. She panted along with him, obviously breathless from her exertion, and when their breathing slowed, he peered down at her and regarded her expression. Her half-open eyes and her slackened jaw attested to her satisfaction. She raised her lashes and returned his gaze with heady acknowledgement of what they had just shared. He bent his head and brushed his lips over hers and then rolled off her onto his back. Unable to speak, unable to think, he closed his eyes and lay next to her in stupefied serenity, unable to express the love that swelled for her in his chest as he circled her shoulders with his arm and she snuggled her body next to his.

He opened his eyes to the sound of birds chirping outside the temple. He lifted his head and looked around him. How long had he slept? Several hours apparently, if the muted light of the dawn breaking outside the temple were any indication. His already semi-hard cock stirred when he saw Julia beside him, her body entwined with his in a lovers' coil. Her copper hair tumbled everywhere as her head lay upon his chest. She had draped her arm across his abdomen and bent her leg over his thigh so that he could feel the heat emanating from her intimate flesh.

She moved closer to him, and his cock hardened to stone as her damp curls brushed his hip. She was still wet from their lovemaking last night, and the scent of their passion lingered in the air between them. She raised her head when he shifted beside her and regarded him with confusion at first. Then her befuddlement dissolved into a dreamy smile as realization appeared to dawn her.

"Good morning." Her voice, still raspy from sleep, aroused him even more.

"Morning, love."

She peered down at their entangled bodies and smiled back up at him as she stroked her hand over his hard shaft. "Is this for me?"

He groaned. "You and only you."

She laughed a little as she stretched her body next to his, rubbing her warm, moist flesh against him before she climbed atop him and straddled his hips. She glided her wet lips over his shaft for a moment and then ground herself against him until he thought he would spill right then. Without words or encouragement from him, she raised her hips and grasped his cock until its tip met her entrance. She closed her eyes and sank slowly down on him, and when she had his length fully inside her, she rocked her hips and ground herself against him once again before she began riding him. She picked up her pace until she was sliding up and down his shaft in a frenzied rhythm. He couldn't move, but then, he didn't have to, as she took her pleasure from him. He could only lie there and wallow in sensation as her tight passage swallowed him over and over again. At last, her head fell back, and her channel clenched around him in violent spasms.

Her movements slowed as her climax subsided, and she opened her eyes and gazed at him through heavy lids. He grasped her hips and held her to him as he flipped her to her back. Then he drove into her with powerful thrusts until the tension in his testicles was unbearable and the rush of his impending orgasm overcame him. She cried out his name in another release that left him with barely the ability to control himself. He pulled out of her just in time for his semen to shoot over her belly.

Winded and panting, he collapsed onto her and buried his face in her neck as he recovered. Sticky and sweaty, they clung to each other for what seemed like eternity, and as he lay atop her, his heart beating so close to hers, he contemplated the experience they had just shared. It had been more than a physical joining. Certainly he had taken pleasure with her body, but their lovemaking had transcended a mere carnal act. It had been a joining of their spirits as well as bodies, and the depth of his feelings for her staggered him. There was no going back to how it had been between them before last night. He wanted her—he needed her—

with him forever.

After his breathing calmed and his heartbeat returned to normal, he nuzzled his lips against her ear. "Marry me, Julia. We have to make this legal, if we're going to keep doing it."

He found a loose strand of her hair and wound it around his finger as he waited for her to say something, but she didn't answer him right away. Of course, he hadn't really expected her to respond. Besides, he knew what she would say if she said anything at all. She would say no. She had her reasons, he supposed, but all the same, the idea that she could walk away from him after their connection last night and this morning stung him. He let go of her hair in painful awareness of all she did not feel. The thought that she did not return the powerful love he felt for her wounded him more than a cudgel to the heart.

He didn't ask her again. In fact, he couldn't ask her again and risk the absolute agony a verbal rejection would give him. Better to be done with it and just go. So he took her non-answer as her answer and said nothing more as he rose on his knees and elbows to leave.

"Alright."

Stunned, he peered down at her to determine if he had heard her correctly, and if so, to see whether or not she were serious. She didn't smile. She just reached up and stroked his cheek.

He remained above her on his hands and knees. "I beg your pardon?"

"I said alright. I'll marry you."

He toppled to his side and lay next to her with his head propped on his hand. "But I don't understand."

"What's to understand, Charles? I said I would marry you."

"With no argument? No list of a thousand reasons why we can't?"

She wrapped her arms around him and snuggled her head to his chest. "No, no argument. No thousand reasons not to."

"Please, Julia, don't joke. It's hurtful, and it isn't funny. If you're toying with me, I beg you to stop. I'm utterly serious in my proposal to you. I want to marry you, and if you don't feel the same, you should just say so at once."

She clung to him more tightly. "I'm not joking. I would never do anything so cruel as to joke with you about marrying you. I want to marry you."

Truly astounded, he said, "Why?" It was the first thing that entered his mind.

She pulled back from him then and looked up at his face. "Does there need to be a reason?"

"Yes."

"Isn't it obvious? I love you, Charles. I love you, and I want to spend the rest of my days with you."

Her profession of love flabbergasted him as much as it overjoyed him. He could only stare at her in complete shock. "I don't know what to say."

Was that a tear shimmering on her lashes? He wanted to comfort her and brush the tear away, but she lowered her gaze too quickly and rested her head against his chest once more. "I understand." Her voice wavered as she sniffled. She recovered her composure, however, and steadied her voice. "Please don't feel you have to say anything. You want to marry me out of duty now that we've been intimate. Nothing more. And I hope you know I don't expect anything more from you."

"Is that what you think? That I want to marry you only because we've been intimate and I feel somehow obliged to marry you now?"

She shrugged and remained silent without looking up at him.

"Julia," he said. "Look at me." When she didn't raise her head, he reached down and lifted her chin. "I want to marry you because I love you. I love you more than I have ever loved anyone in my life."

Tears—more tears—brimmed along her lashes. "You do?"

"Yes, my love, I do." With his thumb, he swiped away a tear that had fallen to her cheek. "Although, I do have to admit that a tiny part of me wants to marry you just so Caroline will leave me alone."

She smacked his shoulder playfully. "Be nice to your sister. She's a good person."

"That may be, but I will not be sad to see her return to Woodfield Manor. She will be overjoyed when she finds out I'm finally to be married and truly ecstatic when she learns it's to you."

She sat up on her knees. "When are you going to tell her?"

He sat up as well. "The moment I see her next, after which I'll help her pack."

She laughed as she shook her head.

"You think I'm joking."

"You do realize that she'll most likely want to stay on until the actual wedding."

He frowned. "Then we must marry soon as soon as possible. I'll start the reading of the banns at this Sunday's service. Then we can be married in less than a month. Does that sound agreeable to you?"

"Yes, but I can't be there because I'll be leaving for Arthur's house tomorrow to help him prepare for the guests arriving on Monday."

"You don't have to be present for the banns to be read."

"Then I suppose there's no reason you can't start reading them. Will you and your sister travel to Arthur's estate on Monday for the party then?"

He eyed her with circumspection. "Are you sure you want me there?"

She stood and threw on her shift and wrapper. "Well, of course. Why wouldn't I want you there?"

He stood as well and tied the strings to his small-clothes and donned the banyan he'd worn last night. "You were fairly clear that you didn't want me there when you told me not to come on the night of your birthday party."

"Oh, Charles, that was when I was angry with you for being so judgmental. Please forget every mean thing I said to you at my birthday celebration."

"I shall. But only if you can find it in your heart to forgive all the hurtful things I said to you that night. I was a judgmental arse."

"I forgive you. We both said things we didn't mean in the heat of the moment."

He drew her into an embrace and kissed the top of her head. "This is a new beginning for us, Julia. And after we're married, we'll sail to Calcutta to get Camille."

She frowned as she pulled away from him. "It all sounds so wonderful."

"Then why don't you look happy?"

"It's just that, well, it's almost too perfect, you know? I just don't want anything to ruin our plans."

"Never fear, my love. Everything will all work out fine." He stroked her cheek to reassure her and then kissed her for good measure.

CHAPTER 14

*Five of Cups: Loss, grief, regret, disappoint-
ment, despair . . .*

JULIA CLOSED HER EYES AND tried to relax in
the warm, jasmine-scented water of the tub, but
she couldn't stop her agitated mind from whirling
from one apprehensive thought to the next. Between
reliving every last wonderful moment of the time she
and Charles had spent making love in the temple last
night and contemplating all the changes that would be
occurring in her life in the next few weeks, she could
barely find peace. She had a thousand things to do to
prepare for her impending wedding and trip to India
and virtually no time to accomplish them.

Complicating everything, of course, was Arthur's
party in the middle of it all. She had to return to the
hunting box later today and pack so that she could
leave for Arthur's tomorrow to help him prepare for
the party. Then, while she was at the party, she would
have virtually no time to rest with all the festivities he
had planned for his guests, much less to plan for the
wedding. That meant that after the party, she would
need to hurry home to South Kindale for a couple

of days to make arrangements for the ceremony and the wedding breakfast. Then, she would need to rush to London right away after that to have her seamstress make a new dress for the wedding and other new outfits for the long voyage to India.

And finally, she would need to book a passage to India for Charles and herself.

She could hardly believe that she would be seeing Camille again in a few months or that she would be bringing the child back to England to live with her and Charles. She also could hardly believe that she would be marrying again in less than a month or that she was marrying him, of all people. Her heart fluttered with joy when she thought of spending the rest of her life with him and her daughter.

It also trembled with fear. She needed to tell Charles the truth about Camille, but she dreaded revealing all her shameful secrets to him. How would he react to the fact that she'd had an adulterous affair with her husband's doctor and friend, or that she had conceived a child as a result of that illicit relationship? Would he still want to marry her, knowing just how much she was like his deceased wife—or that she was, in fact, worse? His wife, at least, had not borne a child from her affair. Would he judge her even more harshly than he seemed to judge his wife, knowing that Julia had given birth to her lover's child while still married to her husband? Could he even still love her, or would he be so revolted by her affair that he would no longer want to be around her?

His potential disgust frightened her. Her only comforting thought was that he had been kind to Mrs. Sweeney last night. He had not berated her for her adulterous affair or the possibility that her child was not her husband's. He had even assured her that God would forgive her sins and not condemn her to hell. His compassion for the poor woman had been a consolation to Julia. Even so, she couldn't be sure he would react to her story with the same consideration.

That didn't mean she shouldn't tell him. No, in fact, she needed to confess everything to Charles before they married. She should've told him the whole sordid story before she accepted his proposal. She had debated telling him everything for a couple of moments after he'd asked her to marry him, but she couldn't bring herself to do it, not when it would've ruined the idyllic atmosphere in the temple this morning. She had been so intoxicated with pleasure and love after the connection of their bodies and hearts that she hadn't had the wherewithal to break the spell. It was important, however, that she tell him everything now, in the event that he could not accept her past sins and wanted to break off the engagement. The sooner she told him, the better.

The bathwater had grown cold, so she climbed out of the tub. As she reached for her towel, she determined that she would find him right away and tell him everything. She could only hope that he would not judge her too severely. Perhaps he would even be able to listen to her side of the story with sympathy and take into account all that she had been going through at the time with Niles's animosity toward her and his own infidelity. Perhaps he could even understand her need to take refuge in another man's arms when her husband had treated her so heartlessly. She prayed, at least, that he might acknowledge that she had acted out of misery and despair. All the same, though, she dreaded telling him.

She rang for Burton, and after the maid styled her hair and assisted her with her clothes, Julia left her room to find him. She didn't have to go very far or search very hard. As she neared Mrs. Sweeney's room, the woman's door opened quietly, and Charles stepped out of the room behind the housekeeper and the midwife.

Julia met them at the doorway, and forgetting her unease for a moment, she peeked into the room and caught a glimpse of the babe sleeping in his cradle, while his mother lay on her bed quietly slumbering. She backed out of the doorway and whispered, "They look so peaceful."

Mrs. Thompson nodded as she closed the door with a gentle click. "Finally. It took a while, though. Mrs. Bell first had to show Mrs. Sweeney how to nurse her son. Then, after the poor woman ate some breakfast herself, she was so exhausted that she fell asleep the instant her head touched the pillow." The housekeeper motioned for the others to follow her as she headed toward the stairs. "You should all come down to breakfast now, while the food is still warm."

Both the midwife and Charles fell in line behind her, but Julia froze as her gut clenched. It was now or never. "Thank you, Mrs. Thompson, but I need to have a word with Mr. Rodman first. Why don't you show Mrs. Bell to the breakfast room? We'll be down shortly."

Both ladies nodded, and each bobbed a curtsy before proceeding down the hall.

Charles, meanwhile, turned and regarded her with a sensual smile that warmed all the wrong places in her body. "What is it, Julia?"

She fidgeted with her fingers as her composure faltered. After a few seconds, she took a deep, calming breath. "I-I need to talk to you. In private."

"Very well." He smiled wickedly as he grasped her hand and pulled her along behind him to a door farther down the hall. After checking both ends of the corridor to his right and his left, he opened the door and led her into a bedchamber, the one he had used last night, no doubt. He shut the door behind him and turned to her. His eyes smoldered with hunger and need, making her knees tremble, as he guided her to the bed and backed her against the post. He wrapped his arms around her and bent his head to brush his mouth against hers. The kiss intensified when he used his tongue to coax her lips apart. He moaned when she opened for him and met his tongue with her own. This was not going well—or at least not how she had intended it to go.

She was nearly helpless to stop him as he continued to plunder her mouth. Desire overwhelmed her when he began stroking her body with his hands, but somehow, in the riot of sensation and pleasure that overcame her, she marshalled the ability to tear her mouth from his before things got too out of hand. "Wait, Charles. I need to tell you something."

He began trailing kisses along her jaw and down her neck, pausing briefly when she didn't speak. "Go on. I'm listening."

She tried to find the right words as his hand found her breast and managed to squeeze it through the barrier of her garments. "It's very difficult to think with you doing that."

He stopped a moment and raised his head to look at her. "Very well. What is it?"

"I . . . I don't know where to begin."

He said nothing but continued toying with her breast as he lowered his lips back to her neck. And though she tried to keep her wits about her, she squirmed under his touch. "You're not making this easy, Charles."

He ceased kissing her and lifted his head to look into her eyes once again. "I'm sorry, but now that I know you're mine, I can't think of anything but making love to you." He caressed her cheek when she didn't reply. "What do you need to tell me?"

She bit the corner of her lip as he gazed at her. Telling him was going to be even harder than she imagined, especially when his love for her shone in his aquamarine eyes.

"Go ahead. You can tell me, Julia. What is it?"

"It's about Camille."

"What about her?"

Julia couldn't bear the tenderness in his expression, so she turned her back to him. "I wasn't really truthful to you about my relationship to her."

"What do you mean?"

She exhaled. "I-I am not really her godmother." She glanced over her shoulder when he laughed. "What's so funny?"

He sobered and squeezed her arm. "Forgive me. I shouldn't laugh, but I have to tell you that I never really believed you were the girl's godmother."

"Humph." She turned to face away from him again. "Very funny."

"I am sorry for making light of it, Julia, but what does it matter if you're not really her godmother? It doesn't change anything, does it?"

Her heart pounded as she searched for the right words. "I—"

"You still care for her, don't you? And you still want to bring her home to England, I assume?"

"Yes, yes, of course, of course. It's not that. It's just that . . . well, it's so complicated." She trailed off, afraid to reveal the truth and possibly face his censure.

He said nothing for a few moments while he caressed her back. "I think I know what it is."

She swallowed hard and whispered, "You do?" Could he have guessed the truth?

"Yes, and I want you to know that it won't matter."

Scarcely able to believe that he could overlook her past, she turned to face him with incredulity and joy. "Really? Do you mean that?"

"Of course. Society might not welcome her at first, but we will love her and support her and shield her from anything hurtful. We won't let them bother us, and we won't let them upset Camille. In time, I'm sure, everyone will realize how wonderful she is and accept her for the lovely, precious little girl she is."

"Oh, Charles." Julia released one sob, and then they all flowed out of her. He was too good. He was too kind, even if he had no idea what she had really wanted to tell him.

She continued crying as he wrapped his arm around her and cradled her head against his shoulder. "Shush, now. Don't cry. Everything will be fine."

She shook her head as she swallowed hard once again and stifled her tears. "No, Charles, you don't understand. Camille is my—"

Several loud raps on the door startled her before she could say more.

He shushed her with his finger. "Don't move." He then strode to the door and opened it a crack. "Yes?"

"Oh, Mr. Rodman!" Mrs. Thompson's frantic voice carried into the room from the doorway. "Thank goodness I've found you. I'm trying to locate Lady Julia. I've looked everywhere but can't find her anywhere. I thought maybe you might know where she is since the last time I saw her was with you. Do you know where she could be?"

"I might have an idea of where she is. Is something the matter?"

"Yes, it's dreadful! Lady Julia's sister, Lady Kingspointe, has just arrived with another lady—Lady Something-or-other—who needs our help. I didn't catch her name, but she's a countess, I believe, and she has come here seeking shelter with her children. She escaped from her husband who assaulted her three days ago, and Lady Kingspointe said she's in rough shape. Mr. Norton will be examining her once she's settled in a room. In the meantime, if you see Lady Julia, please send her downstairs as soon as possible."

"Of course."

"Thank you, Mr. Rodman."

Charles closed the door and turned back to Julia.

Alarmed by the agitation in her housekeeper's voice, she rushed to the door and reached for the knob. "I've got to get downstairs."

"Wait. Let me check the hallway." He peeked his head around the doorjamb. "It looks clear, but let me go out first to make sure. Wait a couple of minutes before you leave, and then meet me down the hall at the top of the grand staircase."

She nodded. As she waited the requisite time, she paced his room, unsettled at the prospect of hiding a countess at the sanctuary. Lexington House had never given refuge to a noblewoman before. The implications were enormous, for if her lord husband discovered his wife missing, it would be nothing for him to track her down with any means available to him, including hiring his own investigators to locate her. And if a peer ever found out about the shelter, it could jeopardize the entire mission and all the ladies staying there.

Who was she, this countess? Julia couldn't speculate as to her identity, but it could very well be that she knew the poor woman. As distressing as it was, the nobility were not above domestic disputes, and noblemen were certainly not above disciplining their wives with physical violence. Phoebe had been the victim of one such nobleman's wrath. She had died as a result of the Earl of Abadon's brutality.

Julia could no longer stand the uncertainty. She had to find out who this woman was, so she opened the bedroom door and ran to the stairs where Charles stood waiting for her. He smiled as she approached, and then they both descended the stairs leading to the grand entryway on the main floor.

The entire household was in commotion. Four footmen rushed through the front door carrying a couple pieces of luggage and a large trunk, while a few maids scurried in from the kitchen with pails of water. Mrs. Thompson directed the staff to take everything upstairs and await further instructions. She also asked Mr. Norton to wait upstairs so he could examine the newly arrived countess after she was settled.

Julia barely had time to catch her breath before her sister Cassandra appeared at the front door with a woman clutching her arm for support. The lady was bent over as though she were in pain, and she hobbled into the entrance hall favoring her right leg. Three young children, a wary boy and two frightened little girls, followed the woman into the house. One girl, the smaller of the two, sucked her thumb as she clutched a doll in her arms, while the boy clenched a blanket to his body. All three of them clung to the hem of the woman's cloak with their free hands. Her large-brimmed bonnet obscured her face, so her identity remained a mystery.

Julia hurried over to her sister. "What's going on,

Cassandra?"

Cassandra's strained features relaxed into relief. "Oh, Julia, thank God you're here. I was afraid I'd need to send a footman to fetch you from the hunting box."

"Why? What has happened? And who is our guest?"

The mystery woman raised her head, and Julia gasped. Her face was beaten and bruised, and her right eye was swollen shut. It was also various shades of purple fading into various shades of green. Her nose, also a deep shade of purple, deviated to the left, while her distended lower lip bore a nasty cut. She cradled her left arm in a sling next to her torso, and though she was hardly recognizable, Julia knew her in an instant.

"Rebecca?"

Shocked when Charles said the woman's name in unison with her, Julia snapped her attention to him. His eyes also shot open in apparent surprise that they had both said the woman's name together. They stared at one another for several seconds in confusion and only turned their attention back to the woman when she inhaled sharply and then grimaced in pain.

"Charles? Is that you?" Panic crossed her battered features as her left eye shot open in obvious fear, while the swelling in the right one prevented it from opening.

"Yes, Rebecca. It's me."

"Oh, no! I don't understand. What are you doing here? Did Dunham send you after me? I thought we'd be safe here in Hampshire. Does he know I am here?" Still slightly bent, she cried out in pain as she attempted to stand up straight.

Charles stepped closer to her and gently touched her hand. "Shh, shh. No, no, he didn't send me here." His soothing voice seemed to calm her for a moment.

"Then what are you doing here?"

"I have taken a living not far from here in South Kindle, and I am only here at Lexington House because I was tending to one of the residents here last night. She was in distress and needed a clergyman."

Rebecca clutched Charles's arm with her right hand. "Don't let him find me, Charles. Please don't let him find me." She began weeping softly.

"Don't upset yourself, Rebecca. He won't find you." He softly patted her uninjured arm before touching her bruised cheek. "Did he do this to you?" The edge in his voice seemed to startle Rebecca, while it sent a chill down Julia's spine.

Rebecca nodded through her pain and tears.

"Tell me what happened. And where are you hurting?"

She winced as she drew in breath. "He had been drinking heavily Sunday night and threatened me with a knife when I wouldn't submit to his demands. He can be so rough when he's drunk. I ran to get away from him but turned my ankle so badly that he was able to catch up to me. He socked me several times in the face, as you can see."

She touched her lip with her free hand. "Then he grabbed me by my left arm so hard and spun me around so violently that he sprained my wrist and dislocated my shoulder. When I tried to break free, he trapped me against him and held the blade against my throat, saying he would kill me if I didn't let him have what was rightfully his. I begged him to let me go, but he only laughed like a maniac. And when I struggled to get away once more, he threw me to the floor and . . . h-he—" She was unable to speak as a sob escaped her throat.

More sobs broke free before she was able to continue through her tears. "He had his way with me. After it was over, he got up and kicked me in the ribs." She cried softly for a moment more and then wiped her eyes with a handkerchief. "I was in such pain the following day and afraid for my life that my maid helped me escape Dover to find a sanctuary for women she'd heard about. She wasn't sure where it was located, but on the advice of her friend, we sought out Lady Kingspointe in London. The marchioness suggested coming here to Hampshire, thinking Dunham wouldn't know to look for me here so far away from Kent, so she hired a post chaise to take us all here. Do you think he will find me, Charles? I fear he'll kill me, and then what will become of the children?"

Once again, he comforted her with his calming voice. "Don't worry, Rebecca. He does not know you are here."

Julia reached out and touched the countess gently on her right arm to offer her reassurance. "You are safe here, Rebecca. We'll have you settled in no time so the surgeon can look at your injuries." Julia then asked Mrs. Thompson to direct the maids to prepare her own suite of rooms in the southwest wing where Rebecca and her children would have more privacy and much more space, with two sitting rooms, a breakfast parlor, and a dressing room all to themselves. She summoned two footmen to assist the countess up the stairs.

Cassandra stepped forward and hugged Julia. "Thank you for everything. I'll be upstairs helping Lady Dunham and her children get situated."

After the others left, Julia stood alone with Charles in the vast entry hall. She turned to find him clenching his fists in agitation as his eyes darted about the hallway as though he were looking for something.

"What's the matter, Charles?"

He closed his eyes. "Air. I need air. And whiskey. I think I need whiskey."

"Let's go to the study. There's whiskey there and a doorway to the terrace out back."

He nodded his head shakily as he followed her out of the entry hall down the back corridor into a room on the left. She strode to a sideboard near a large desk and poured him four fingers of whiskey from a decanter on the cabinet. He looked like he needed at least that much, if not more. She handed him the glass and watched as he downed half of it in one gulp, took a breath, and then downed the rest of it in another gulp. He wiped his mouth dry with his coat sleeve and handed the glass back to her.

"More. Please."

Clearly, Rebecca's situation had unsettled him.

She moved back to the credenza and poured him more whiskey and then returned to him with the drink. "What is it, Charles? What's the matter?"

He sipped the liquid this time as he stared off into

space. A while passed without him saying anything, and Julia didn't know whether to prompt him for an answer or let him tell her in his own good time.

Finally, after several minutes of silence, he downed the rest of the whiskey and set the glass on a nearby table. "Air. I need air."

She motioned for him to follow her through the door that led to the terrace overlooking the gardens in the back. She said nothing as he walked to the end of the terrace and clutched the railing with both hands and peered down at the ground. She still didn't know whether to intrude with a comment or a question, so she remained silent.

He looked up after a while but faced away from her. He inhaled deeply and then exhaled loudly. "Do you remember when you asked me last night who ripped my still-beating heart out of my chest?"

She nodded even though he couldn't see it. He remained silent as he continued to stare ahead. Then it dawned on her whom he must mean, and her eyes shot open wide, though he still couldn't see her. "Rebecca?"

He shook his head and scoffed with laughter. "No, not Rebecca. Her cousin. Eleanor. My *wife*." He growled the last word.

So that's how he knew the countess. "I see." She didn't coax him any further, sensing that he needed to tell the story at his own pace and in his own way.

"You're aware she betrayed me, I'm sure."

She nodded, but again, he couldn't see her gesture so she spoke as well. "Yes."

"Who told you? Caroline?"

"No. My brother."

He let go of the railing and turned around, his brows knit in obvious confusion. "What? How did he know about it?"

"From your brother, I believe."

"That figures. And I suppose Pruitt told him all the disgusting details."

"I don't think so, actually. I believe he told Benthower only enough to acquaint him with your situation."

He looked away at nothing in the distance. "Still, that's enough."

She didn't answer. She didn't know what to say.

"Did your brother also tell you who her lover was?"

"No. I don't believe he knew that much."

Several seconds passed without him speaking. Though Julia didn't press him for more information, she had a pretty good idea of who his wife's lover had been.

He folded his arms and focused his gaze down at the boards of the terrace. "It was my best friend. My *very* best friend. In the world. He had offered me a living shortly after Eleanor and I married, and I believe he did that so that he could continue his affair with her. They were lovers before she married me." He paused, perhaps for effect.

Staggered, Julia could find no words. How could she say anything about his wife's infidelity with his friend when she had been unfaithful to her husband—with her husband's friend?

"She married me only because she was pregnant

with my friend's child and he wouldn't marry her. He married her cousin instead."

She remained silent, too stunned and distressed to say anything.

"You know who I'm talking about, don't you?"

"Dunham?"

He nodded. "Yes. Dunham. He seduced Eleanor before she and I married, and then he married her cousin Rebecca. I'm not sure whether he loved Rebecca or not. I am sure he married her to improve his fortune. He did a lot of things to improve his fortune, now that I think on it. Of course, I had no idea of his affair with my wife or that she had been pregnant at our wedding. She miscarried shortly after we married and never told me about it. Until later, that is." He laughed acerbically. "And then, she only told me about it after I found them together, in my own home and in my own bed. I suppose she figured at that point she might as well confess it all since she was caught." Again, he laughed. Bitterly. And then he gazed up at the balcony overlooking the terrace. "But that's not what ripped my heart out. Her infidelity destroyed me alright, but do you know want to know what really ripped my heart out?"

She wasn't sure she did want to know, but felt compelled to nod as she moved toward him. "What was it?"

"Her confession—which she made, again only after I caught them together—that she didn't love me and never had loved me. She loved him and had always loved only him. My best friend." He shook his head and laughed again. His laughter died into a bleak sigh.

"I was *such* a fool. Such an idiot. I loved her with all my heart and thought she returned my feelings. But to tell you the truth, now I don't know if she ever even *liked* me." His lower lip trembled, and Julia's heart broke for him. She reached out and touched his shoulder to comfort him. "I loved her, and she never loved me. That's what ripped my heart out. While her infidelity devastated me, the fact that she never loved me is what utterly eviscerated me." His breath hitched, and his voice wavered. "She told me she had no feelings for me, whatsoever."

He put the palms of his hands to his eyes, no doubt to try to stop his tears, but they fell anyway as he released a pent-up sob. "I sent her away after that. To her parents. She died six months later, after giving birth to a stillborn baby girl. Dunham's, most likely. She sent for me near the end and told me how sorry she was. She asked me to forgive her, and I told her to go to hell."

His head fell to his chest as he cried. Julia took him in her arms and held him. She rocked him a little and let him weep. She kissed his hair and stroked his back to soothe him, as he settled his head on her shoulder. She shushed his cries softly until he finally broke from her embrace and stood up straight again.

He sucked in a breath and stifled his emotion. "I'm so sorry for breaking down like that."

"Don't apologize, Charles."

"I should never have burdened you with my story. Please, forgive me."

"Shush. There's not a thing to forgive. I'm grateful

you felt comfortable enough to confide in me. And I'm glad you told me. It helps me understand you and your viewpoints better."

He laughed, this time ironically. "Yes. I suppose the story sheds some light on why I'm such a judgmental arse—as someone once called me."

She smiled and stroked his cheek tenderly. "Whoever told you that you were a judgmental arse was also a judgmental arse."

"No. You were right, Julia. I am—or at least, I have been—a judgmental arse. It was so hard for me to give Mrs. Sweeney absolution last night. I'm sure you noticed my hesitation."

She hadn't at the time, but when she thought back on it, she did recall his voice wavering. She didn't tell him so now, though.

"It was hard for me to hear her confession because it brought everything with Eleanor back to the surface. I had repressed most of what happened and forgotten much of the pain until Mrs. Sweeney's ordeal brought it all back last night, in fact. I had suppressed all memory of finding Eleanor with my best friend."

Julia said nothing as she took his hand in hers and squeezed it to comfort him.

"I had buried her confession of never loving me so deep in my mind and my heart that I had nearly forgotten about it. Until last night, anyway. I was so disturbed after I left Mrs. Sweeney that I had trouble sleeping. And then, when I finally did fall asleep, the whole scenario of finding Dunham and Eleanor together played out in a dream—a nightmare, really. The memories came flooding back to me when I woke up after the dream, and I had to get out of the room and the house. That's how I ended up at the temple."

She squeezed his hand again, and this time, he squeezed hers back. "I'm so glad you did."

"Do you know what's ironic? Or weird, at least?"

Humph. Did *he* know what was ironic? Or *weird*, at least?

"Do you remember the Tarot card reading you did for me after we all had dinner that night at the vicarage?"

She nodded.

"When I think back on that reading and how astonishingly accurate it was regarding my situation with Eleanor, I get chills."

"The Tarot can be astonishing in its revelations."

"It's downright eerie. You saw the triangle involving me, my wife, and my best friend with such clarity. I was—and still am—amazed."

She smiled, but only with sadness.

"Did you know at the time that you were seeing what had happened with my wife and her lover?"

She shrugged but nodded again. "I had an inkling. The cards showed me the story of a love triangle, and I had a feeling it involved you, your wife, and another man, given what Benthower had told me before. However, I didn't want to tell you everything I knew while I was doing the reading because I didn't want to make you uncomfortable or embarrass you in front of your sister and Arthur."

He regarded her for a moment before reaching out

to stroke her cheek. "You're so good, Julia. So kind. So compassionate. So trustworthy and faithful. You would never do what Eleanor did to the man you love, and I am so lucky to be that man. I can hardly wait until we are married." He kissed her briefly and then took her in his arms.

Julia's heart clenched as guilt gnawed at it. More than anything else at that moment, she wanted to confess everything about her infidelity with Renesh, but how could she after his comments? She did not know how she could ever tell him that she had betrayed her husband in the same manner as his wife had betrayed him.

There was one thing she did know, however. She could not marry him now. Not with knowing how devastated he had been over his wife's infidelity. Not when she couldn't keep her own infidelity from coming to light after they brought Camille back to England. He would eventually find out that Camille was her daughter because Julia wanted the girl to know the truth. Which meant telling him the truth also. She did not want to make her daughter keep the shameful secret of Julia's affair. He would know—sooner or later—that Julia had conceived the child during an adulterous liaison with her husband's friend, just as Charles's wife had conceived a child in an affair with his. He had once said she was no better than his wife. And now, she agreed.

The realization tormented her as she broke from their embrace. "I must go inside now, Charles. I must see to Rebecca."

He inclined his head toward her in obvious confusion. "How do you know her, by the way?"

"I met her, and we became friends a couple of years after I got married, when her husband formed a business partnership with mine. Lord Dunham approached Niles about investing the funds he'd gained by marrying me—my dowry funds, essentially—in a shipping venture in Calcutta. Dunham was a shareholder in the East India Company at the time, and still might be, for all I know. He needed money to start a shipping company to smuggle opium into China for the Company, and he pounced on Niles after hearing about his new-found wealth—and his father's shipping connections.

"Running opium to China turned out to be an insanely lucrative venture for the both of them. Dunham sent Niles to India to oversee shipping operations and to make sure their ship captains weren't skimming any profits for themselves. Three years ago, however, Niles abandoned his post, leaving Calcutta suddenly and returning to England. We left Calcutta so abruptly that Niles didn't have the chance to hire someone to replace him."

"Why did he leave so suddenly?"

Julia reached for the nearby railing to steady herself and turned her gaze away from him to the temple in the distance. "Because of me."

"He left because you wanted to leave?"

She shook her head no. "He left because I wanted to *stay*."

"Ah." He said nothing more for a few seconds, perhaps expecting her to elaborate. When she didn't, he nudged her shoulder gently. "Why did you want to stay?"

"Because of Camille. I wanted to remain in India to take care of her." She didn't want to give him any of the other sordid details, not here, not now, so she returned to the previous topic. "Anyway, with no one left there to run day-to-day operations, matters deteriorated quickly in the Calcutta office. It was chaos, as I understand it. Their opium shipments continued but only sporadically and inefficiently and finally dwindled to nothing. Worse, profits declined drastically without Niles's oversight when the captains began pocketing most of the smuggling proceeds. The partnership lost vast sums of money as a result. Dunham recouped most of his losses when Niles returned to England by seizing every liquid asset he had, leaving him ruined. I had nothing left but Lexington House after he died."

"I am sorry Dunham caused you misery. Fortunately, we never have to think of him again. After we're married, we'll head to Calcutta and get Camille, and then we'll return home." When she didn't smile at first, he chucked her gently on the chin with his knuckles. "And live happily ever after, of course."

She did smile then, but it was a wistful smile, full of melancholy and regret, rather than a cheerful smile filled with joy and hope. She had to break off their engagement, but she didn't have the courage to do so right now. And most probably, she would never find the courage to end it with him in person. She couldn't bear to witness the crushing pain of rejection in his features.

She decided she would write to him instead. Tonight, when she was back at the hunting box, she would compose a letter and have it delivered to him at the vicarage tomorrow, after she left for Arthur's house. She would tell him not to come to Arthur's party next week, of course, but she didn't know yet how she would break it to him that it was over between them or explain her change of heart in a way that wouldn't hurt him. She would just have to make him see that they were all wrong for each other and always had been. She would have to make him see that he was better off without her and that he should begin his life anew and search for someone else—for the perfect woman, one who could be his perfect match and perfect mate. And, she would wish him well—the very best that life had to offer because that was what he deserved after everything he had endured.

CHAPTER 15

*King of Coins, reversed: Wealthy, corrupt, and
debauched man who uses his power to frighten
and intimidate others . . .*

CHARLES HUMMED A TUNE AS he entered
the dining room at the vicarage the next morning with new hope in his heart and vigor in his step.
He filled his plate with bacon, eggs, and toast from
the sideboard and even kissed his sister on her cheek
before taking his seat.

"My goodness, sir, but I don't believe we've met.
I'm Baroness Woodfield. I'm here visiting my brother.
And you are?"

Even his sister's droll attempt at humor could not
darken his spirits. "Ha, ha. Witty as always, Caroline."

She smirked as she sipped her tea. "It's just that I
don't believe I've seen you this chipper in six years.
And certainly not since I've been here, in any case. To
what do I owe thanks for your good mood?"

"Not what, but whom."

She raised her brows in obvious surprise. "Alright
then. To whom do I owe thanks for your good mood?"

"Julia."

She blinked twice. "You mean *Lady* Julia?"

"The very same."

"I take it you saw her then at Lexington House when you were there yesterday and the night before?"

He nodded as he chewed his toast.

"Well? Don't leave me in the dark. Tell me what happened. Did she forgive you for what you said to her at her birthday celebration?"

"Better. She's agreed to marry me."

He would always remember with delight the look of absolute astonishment on his sister's face. And he would always relish with satisfaction the fact that he'd been able to render her utterly speechless for more than a minute. "Well? Aren't you going to congratulate me, Caroline?"

"Oh, Charles!" She jumped from her chair and ran to his to embrace him. She hugged him around his shoulders as she squealed with glee. "I am so happy! This is better than even I had hoped for you! When? When is the wedding? We have so much to do, so much to plan for!"

"We are to be married within the month."

She gasped. "But that is not enough time! We'll never be able to pull everything together for the ceremony and the wedding breakfast."

"Nevertheless, reading of the banns will begin on Sunday and then continue for two more Sundays. We could be married as soon as we like after the third reading."

She clutched her hands to her chest in complete

surprise. "But—but what about wedding clothes and a trousseau for Lady Julia? What about making arrangements for the families to stay here in South Kindale to attend the wedding? Will everyone fit at the inn?"

"Don't fret. I'm sure all the details can be worked out in a short amount of time."

"But why the rush? I won't even get to see Lady Julia to begin helping her plan things for another week, what with her being gone to her cousin's party."

"We want to marry as soon as possible so that we can head to India to get her goddaughter Camille, although I have to tell you that she confessed to me that she is not actually the child's godmother, which I had figured from the beginning, but it makes no difference. At any rate, don't worry about planning for the wedding. You'll be able to talk to Julia next week at Drake's house. We're going to the party after all."

More raptures. More glee. She laughed. She clapped. She sang. She even danced around the table. "We're going? We actually get to go?"

He nodded.

"I'm going to start packing right away."

"But you haven't even finished your breakfast. Besides, it's only Friday, and we don't leave until Monday."

"Still, I am much too excited to sit back down and eat. I must make myself busy, or I will burst from the jubilation."

"Then, by all means, please go pack your things."

"I can't tell you how happy I am, Charles. You're marrying Lady Julia! And we get to go to Mr. Drake's party! It's all so wonderful. I hope you are happy as well." She hugged him once more before rushing out of the room.

He rolled his eyes as he sipped his coffee. He was happy. Yes, indeed, he was happy.

Two minutes later, his housekeeper popped her head through the door. "You have a message, Mr. Rodman. One of Lady Julia's footmen just delivered a note from her."

He held his hand out for the folded, sealed paper, and took it from Mrs. Haskins before she left the room. He broke the seal impatiently, anxious to find out why Julia had written to him rather than stopping by to tell him something, especially if it was important. He recalled, however, that she had probably headed out from the hunting box for Drake's house first thing this morning and did not have a chance to stop by South Kindale to say goodbye.

My Dearest Charles,

It is with a heavy heart that I am writing to tell you that I cannot marry you after all and that I must break our engagement. You don't know how difficult this is for me to do, but I have to end what's between us as soon as possible because I believe we are not meant to be together. We never really suited each other to begin with, and I'm afraid we never will in the end. Though I love you with all my heart, I am not the person you think I am. If the truth were ever revealed, not only would you be hurt once again but also you would be disgusted by my past. Besides, I am far too outspoken and unorthodox in my beliefs and practices to be a good companion for someone like you. You need a gentle, biddable soul who will help and support you in your ministry. I only hope that you find her soon. You have so much goodness and love to offer her that, whoever she is, she will be the luckiest woman alive to have you.

As for me, I am going back to India—forever. I am going to raise funds to buy or build another shelter for the ladies at Lexington House and then sell the estate so I can settle in Calcutta with Camille. It is best for everyone if she and I remain in India, so I will not return to England with her.

Please do not come to Arthur's party next week. For one thing, Dunham will be there most likely. I didn't tell you he might be there when we talked yesterday because I did not want to upset you further by mentioning him. He is a vile, despicable beast, and Arthur and I only invited him because he is one of the wealthiest men in the kingdom and we thought perhaps we could solicit a donation for the shelter from him. That is out of the question now, of course. Nor will we be able to solicit donations from any of the guests at the party, lest Dunham find out that his wife is staying at Lexington House with their children. I will worry about raising funds for the new home later, when I return to South Kindale after the party.

Also, I'm asking you to please stay away from the party because I couldn't bear to see you again. It would be too painful to even be near you. Please do not seek me out before I leave for India. It would hurt too much.

I wish you only the very best in the future, Charles. You deserve every happiness you can find and more. You deserve a wonderful woman, one who will not break your heart again. May you find her soon and live the life you were born to live. Even though we must part, I hope you know that I will always love you and that you will always hold a special place in my heart. Please understand that I am doing this now only because I don't want to hurt you in the future.

   With deepest regrets,
   Julia

He crumpled the paper in his fist. This was unacceptable. How could she break things off between them? And in a letter, no less? His first instinct was to bolt for the door, saddle his horse, and chase after her. He could not summon the strength to rise from the table, however, so he remained in his chair contemplating his next move as he un-creased the note and reread it.

No, damnation. This wasn't possible. She could not be breaking it off with him. He could not and would not accept it. He could never live without Julia, and he would never let her go. He had to find her and make her see that not only were they meant for each other but also they were destined to be together—forever. He had never before felt the soul-searing love and the scorching passion that she inspired. What he felt for Eleanor paled to a school-boy crush in comparison to what burned inside him for Julia. He would go to the ends of the earth for her, if necessary. He would die for her, if required. Nothing she could say, nothing she could do could ever change his mind or his heart. Not in a million years.

Three days later, he sat across from his sister in a modest carriage that he had hired to take them to Drake's estate roughly forty miles northwest of South Kindale in Somerset. They had left town at the crack of dawn, and now, nearly eight hours later, he stared out the window, brooding about how to approach Julia to discuss their situation when he reached Drake's house.

"You're very quiet, Charles." Caroline had no clue that Julia had uninvited him—and thus, her—to the party once again. She also wasn't aware that Julia had broken off the engagement. He hadn't said anything to her about it yet because he was certain he could change Julia's mind, and the less he had to explain to his sister, the better. "You haven't said a word since we left South Kindale."

That was true, and not just because he was lost in thought. He couldn't have gotten a syllable in edgewise had he wanted to, not with Caroline's nonstop prattle. She had been carrying on a conversation—or delivering a soliloquy, more like it—since they rolled away from the vicarage. "I have a lot on my mind."

"I'm sure you do, but I've asked you twice now when we should hold the wedding so that I can discuss it with Lady Julia when we arrive. I have so many arrangements to make, and I need her opinion."

"Caroline, a couple of things. 'We'—that is Julia and I—will decide the best date for the wedding without your help. And as to arrangements, *she* will make them herself and perhaps ask you for *your* opinion, but *you* are not the one planning the wedding."

"Humph." She shifted on her bench as she grumbled. "That may be, but she will need help, I assure you, and I just want her to know that I am willing to assist her in any way I can."

"And I thank you, Caroline. As I'm sure Julia will also. I am merely telling you, however, that you should not grab the reins with this wedding, as you do everything else."

"Well!" She folded her arms as she harrumphed again. "I only try to help, Charles."

"And it's not that I am ungrateful. It's just that Julia should make plans as she sees fit. And please, whatever you do, do not accost her with questions about the wedding the moment we arrive."

She rolled her eyes in reply and then turned to stare out the window. She didn't speak for five blessed minutes until the carriage turned up a lane and a large house came into view. "Oh, my! Look at it, Charles. It's so grand!"

Grand was an understatement. Drake's home was extravagant in its proportions, and its magnificent façade loomed ahead as they rounded a horseshoe-shaped drive bordered on either side by enormous oak trees. Their carriage pulled behind several others that had apparently also just arrived, while a crew of footmen and grooms scurried about the grounds assisting guests out of the vehicles and into the house with their belongings.

He worried for a moment that their arrival would create a quandary for everyone, given that Julia had told him not to come. He feared that neither his nor

Caroline's name would be on the guest list and that they would have no rooms reserved for them. He breathed a sigh of relief, however, when the head footman directed a couple of other footmen to show them to chambers on the third floor. Perhaps Julia had neglected to tell Drake to remove their names from the list of guests. Whatever the case, he was just thankful they had rooms.

They climbed the stairs to the third floor, and Caroline followed a footman and maid to her room near the staircase, while another footman led Charles to a room farther down the corridor. As he walked down the passage toward his room, he would've sworn he smelled a hint of myrrh in the air. Could Julia be near? Wishful thinking, probably. The scent became stronger and stronger, however, the closer he got to his room. Finally, the footman stopped at the next-to-last door in the hallway. He let Charles in and set his luggage on the floor.

"Thank you, my good man." Charles handed the footman a coin but stopped him before he left. "Can you tell me where the scent of myrrh is coming from?"

"Next door, gov'nor." He pointed to an inner door along the wall that divided his room from the one next to it.

"You mean, through *that* door?"

The servant nodded.

"I see. Can you tell me whose room that is?"

"Lady Julia Lacey's. But I don't believe she's there at the moment. I saw her on the back lawn with the other guests not long before I showed you up here."

"Where's that?"

The footman pointed to the window. "You can see it from your room."

"Very good." And very interesting. Was it just good luck that his room was next to Julia's and that they shared an adjoining door, or had Drake placed him there on purpose? If so, he would have to thank the man.

When he was alone, Charles stepped to the window. He scanned the numerous guests milling about the expansive back lawn for a familiar face. Some people were playing various games, while others sat in chairs sipping tea. He had difficulty picking Julia out of the women in the crowd because most of them wore bonnets that obscured their features. Three ladies playing lawn bowls together caught his eye, and when one of them threw her head back and laughed, he knew in an instant he had found her.

He debated whether to head down to the back lawn now or wait until later to accost her. He didn't wish to upset her in public, and he didn't want to discuss their relationship with an audience. Plus, he really didn't even know what he was going to say to her. He hoped he could maintain his composure and remain calm and pleasant, but he couldn't trust himself not to fly into a rant the moment he saw her. He decided, therefore, that it was best to put off their inevitable meeting and the possible argument that would follow until later—much later. Perhaps even after dinner.

A knock on his door startled him from his thoughts. He strode to the door and was mildly irritated to find

Caroline on the other side.

"Well? Aren't you coming, Charles? Everyone's on the back lawn, and I want to see Lady Julia at once."

He placed his hands on his hips in frustration. "Caroline, what did I tell you about pestering Julia at this party about the wedding?"

She scoffed. "Well, I am not going to pester her about the wedding. I merely want to say hello and let her know we have arrived."

"That can wait until later."

"It most certainly cannot." She turned and headed for the stairs without waiting for him. "Are you coming or not?"

He threw his hands up in exasperation, but hoping to prevent a scene when she found Julia and learned the wedding was off, he followed her to the main floor where a footman directed her through a drawing room that exited to the back lawn. He didn't catch up to her until she reached the lawn and paused to scan the crowd. "Caroline, please. Don't overwhelm Julia with your usual enthusiasm."

He was too late, however. His sister had already spotted her quarry and was now madly waving her hand to get her attention. "Lady Julia! Lady Julia! There you are! I'm so excited to see you once again!"

The astonishment on Julia's face was complete and absolute. "Lady Woodfield?"

If Caroline sensed any confusion from Julia, she ignored it. Meanwhile, he could only stand by and cringe as his sister wrapped his erstwhile fiancée in a constrictive hug. "Oh, Charles told me the happy news, and you must call me Caroline now that we are going to be sisters. And may I call you Julia?"

Julia's bewilderment changed instantly to alarm as her brows shot up her forehead. "What happy news?"

Caroline chortled. "You are such a sketch, Julia. What happy news? As if you didn't know. The happy news about you and Charles, of course. I just want you to know that I am at your service in helping you plan everything. Have you thought about a date though? Charles told me not to ask, but I can't help myself. He said the two of you intended to marry within the month. If so, I'm concerned. That seems a bit ambitious. However, if you are set on an August wedding, then so be it. We will make it happen. I don't know how, but we'll work out the details together."

Again, Charles could only stand back and watch with mild horror the frenzy of excitement and jubilation Caroline's news inspired in Julia's sisters. He took pity on her as she was assailed with hugs and kisses amid shrieks of joy and disbelief.

When the commotion finally subsided, Caroline covered her mouth with her hand. "Oh, dear, Julia. Please tell me I didn't ruin any surprises. I just assumed you'd have told your whole family by now."

"Well . . . I—"

"We thought we would announce the engagement at tonight's party," he interrupted her to rescue her from an awkward explanation.

Caroline clucked her tongue in obvious irritation. "Well, I wish you would've have told me that, Charles."

"Me, too." Julia scowled at him with unmistakable

hostility.

His cravat suddenly too tight, he tugged at it as he stepped closer to her. "I think Julia and I should have a word. Why don't you and her sisters get some refreshments, Caroline?"

"Oh, very well. But why don't you two also set a date?"

He glowered at his sister, but she had already turned and walked away with Lady Kingspointe and Lady Violet. He returned his attention to Julia who still regarded him with extreme displeasure.

"Didn't you get my letter?"

"Yes, but I can explain."

She crossed her arms over her chest. "Then what are you doing here, Charles?"

"We need to talk."

"What's there to talk about? I thought I was abundantly clear. I can't marry you, and I asked you not to come to the party because . . . I-I didn't want to see you again. Yet, you ignored my wishes."

"Yes, but only because they are not my wishes, Julia. I love you, and I want to marry you."

She raised her arms in obvious frustration. "Why are you making this so difficult? Why won't you just accept that you and I are not suited to one another?"

"Because we are suited. You are the love of my life, Julia, and I see no valid reason for us not to marry."

"You don't understand, Charles. I would only end up disappointing you if we married, and the last thing I want to do is to hurt you."

"How could you possibly hurt me? Or disappointment me?"

She scoffed and rolled her eyes heavenward. "You simply have no idea. But please believe me when I say we do not belong together. You're a vicar, for one thing, and I am still a raging heretic. I don't know that I'll ever be able to reconcile with the Church. How would it look to your parishioners if your own wife refused to attend services?"

"We will address those issues later. After we return from India with Camille."

"No. Things have changed, Charles. I am going to Calcutta—forever. I will not return to England with her."

"Why not? I don't understand. What has changed since—" He lowered his voice. "What has changed between us since we made love in the temple?"

"Quite a lot, actually." She turned away from him and began pacing the lawn in front of him. "I accepted your proposal too hastily. I did not think the situation through until after I returned to the hunting box. And when I thought about it long and hard, I realized that I-I am just not the woman for you. Now, will you please leave me alone? If you must stay at the party, please keep a respectful distance between us." She started to go.

"That will be hard to do with our rooms adjacent to one another."

She stopped in her tracks and swirled around to face him. "What!"

"It's true. Evidently, your cousin assigned us rooms next to each other. We even have an adjoining door."

"This is outrageous. I am going to murder Arthur Drake right this minute. I need to find another room." She turned away from him once again, and as she started toward the house, she called a warning over her shoulder. "Stay away, Charles. Everything between us is over. There's nothing more to say."

As he watched her stalk off in a huff, ostensibly to kill her cousin, he vowed that he would change her mind. He would make her see reason. He would convince her that they belonged together no matter what. Whatever it took, he would show her that they were meant for each other, and somehow, he would prove it to her. He returned to his room more determined than ever to make her his wife.

Julia's heart would not be still. It would not stop the riotous beating it began when she saw Charles on the lawn. He had come for her. Despite her wishes, despite her orders to stay away, he had followed her here to Drake Manor, and she loved him all the more for it. Yet, it changed nothing. They still could never be together. Once he found out who Camille truly was, he would realize that not only had Julia committed the very same sin as his wife but also like her, she had borne her husband another man's child. It was unforgivable, and he would revile her for it when he discovered the truth.

She didn't find Arthur until just before dinner. She sensed he had been hiding from her all day—with the help of his staff—because every time she thought she had him pinned down to a certain room, he managed to have just left the room the moment she entered. That was the story from the servants, at least. She had him cornered now, however. He couldn't escape the drawing while he waited with his guests for dinner to be announced. Using stealth as her weapon, she approached him from behind as he stood conversing with an elderly couple. She tapped his shoulder to get his attention and nearly laughed as he winced when he turned and caught her expression. He even backed away from her as she crossed her arms in vexation.

"I need a new room."

"I take it Rodman showed up after all, then?"

"You know he did." She narrowed her eyes at him. "But what I don't understand is how you knew he would."

"Simple, really. A man in love would walk through fire to be with the one he cherishes."

"That's rubbish, and you know it. However, he is here, and I require another room."

"I haven't any others. The house is filled to the rafters."

"I can't stay in a room next to his, Arthur. It is far too convenient, and he is much too tempting. I know myself well enough to realize that given the opportunity, I will always behave badly. And I can never be with him again."

"Fine, then. You may have my room, and I will take yours."

"That's ridiculous. I can't put you out of your room."

"I see no other solution, unless you wish to sleep

in the stables."

"Drat and damnation, Arthur." She stomped her foot and crossed her arms once again in frustration. "You're a conniving schemer, and I don't appreciate your efforts to play Cupid here."

He flashed her an irksome, self-satisfied smile. "You'll thank me someday."

She threw her arms up in frustrated defeat and moved to a secluded spot near the mantle to brood.

At least she had managed to avoid Charles since earlier. Though he stood across from her in the drawing room now, he kept his distance. She caught him glancing her way often but only because she could not prevent herself from glancing at him more than she should. Therefore, their eyes met frequently, leaving her disoriented and breathless. For now, she did her best to calm her nerves, taking a deep breath and a long sip of champagne.

"Well, well, well. Mrs. Lacey? How good it is to see you after all this time."

She jumped at the ominous voice behind her and twirled around to see the Earl of Dunham looming over her. He bowed and took her gloved hand in his, and she nearly retched when he kissed it. Too shaky to offer him even a brief curtsy, she acknowledged him with a nod. "Lord Dunham. I did not realize you were here."

"I just arrived actually. And right in time for dinner, it appears. How long has it been, my dear?"

Not long enough. "At least two years, I'm sure."

"Of course. Not since Niles went to his great reward. Pity he died so young. But that only means you are free now." He leaned in and lowered his voice. "Not that you weren't *free* before his death, from what I've heard." He leered at her with unsettling indecency as he swirled his drink.

Stunned speechless by his lurid insinuation, she could only stare at him in horror. Just what had he heard? And from whom?

"May I say you look very lovely tonight? Life must be agreeing with you."

"Thank you." Though she whispered the obligatory reply to his compliment, she shivered at the nauseating smirk of approval on his face as his eyes raked her up and down. She stepped back but couldn't put any distance between them when he stepped closer to her.

He sipped from his flute of champagne. "Dreary little party, isn't it? I had hoped for some interesting guests and some of the more, shall we say, *diverting* amusements one sees at house parties these days."

"I'm sorry if you find it dull, Lord Dunham. However, Arthur invited some of the most interesting people in the kingdom, and he has put together all sorts of entertainment for the week ahead."

He leaned in close and lowered his eyes to her bosom as he lowered his voice. "The only person I might find remotely interesting here is you. I'm sure you could entertain me all week long."

"Dunham."

They both turned. Charles stood coolly swirling the champagne in his glass. She wanted to throw her arms around him in gratitude for deflecting the earl's smarmy attention away from her.

Dunham's jaw dropped, and his eyes popped open wide. "Rodman? Is that you?"

Charles remained silent as he merely sipped his champagne.

The earl displayed no further emotion as he shuttered his features. "Fancy meeting you here. I have to say, I never thought to see you again."

Charles flicked a piece of lint from his coat with delightful sangfroid. "It is such a small world. Isn't it?"

"Tiny, it would seem." Dunham directed attention to Julia with a flourish of his hand. "Tell me, have you met the enchanting Mrs. Lacey? May I introduce the two of you?"

A muscle tensed in Charles's jaw, the only indication that the earl was affecting him. "We've met, actually."

"Really? How? Do tell."

"Lady Julia is my patroness."

Dunham's brows rose in obvious surprise. "Indeed? Mrs. Lacey gave you a living, did she?" He chuckled darkly and then sipped his drink.

Charles nodded but said nothing as he narrowed his eyes at the man beside him.

"Outstanding. Tell me, has she bestowed any other favors on you?"

Julia blanched at the question. Had Dunham meant to imply something lurid again, or was she reading into it?

Charles remained unmoved by the earl or his inquiry. "I'm not sure I understand what you mean."

Dunham snickered. "Oh, nothing really. Just curious about what all Mrs. Lacey has done for you. She is known for her generosity. She's always ready to do a chap a favor."

This time, she had no doubt that he meant to suggest something lewd, and not for the first time, she wondered how much Dunham knew of her past. Surely, Niles wouldn't have told him all the coarse details of her adulterous affair with his doctor and her resulting pregnancy, would he? Surely, he would have kept the particulars of her scandalous behavior secret, if only to avoid his own embarrassment and the ridicule of others—Dunham's mockery especially. But could the earl have found out some other way? And if he knew of her shame, would he be so bold as to reveal it here? In public? In front of Charles?

She needed to separate the two of them just in case, before he exposed her disgrace. Perhaps Charles would eventually find out about her illicit affair, but she couldn't let that happen here and now. She couldn't bear to see the look of horror and disgust on his face when he realized she was no better than his wife. Sweat trickled down her back as she tried to think of something—anything—to divert the conversation.

Charles cleared his throat as though he sensed her discomfort. The same muscle from before ticked in his jaw, exposing his own disquiet. "I don't see Rebecca. Is she not here with you?"

The air surrounding them chilled ten degrees as Dunham's gaze turned dark. "No, she is not here with me, in fact."

"Oh? Is she at home then?"

Dunham's jaw clenched as he shifted his weight from one foot to the other. "That's exactly where she is."

"She is not ill, I hope."

"Not in the least."

"Still, it's odd she didn't accompany you here. She used to enjoy parties like this, as I recall."

The earl lifted his glass to his lips with a tremoring hand and slurped his champagne, as though he were on edge and couldn't get enough of the alcohol to lessen his discomposure. "She preferred to stay home this time. She likes parties but not so much the traveling."

"And you felt comfortable leaving your wife home alone to attend this party without her?"

Dunham shrugged, but his attempt at nonchalance failed when he pulled at his cravat. "Comfortable enough. She didn't want to come, but I thought it important that I be here, so I came without her."

"Interesting." Charles paused a moment. He swirled what was left of the champagne in his glass and then downed it in a long gulp. "I'm curious, though. Why did you feel it was so important for you to be here?"

Julia sensed he was toying with his former friend. She also sensed that he was enjoying it.

Dunham's eyes darted about the room in apprehension, as though he were searching for an exit. Even so, he remained rooted to his position between Charles and Julia. "I came here, in fact, because I heard through various gossips that this was more than just a party for fun and games."

"Indeed? Tell us what you heard. I'm dying to know."

The earl leveled his gaze at Charles, giving the impression that he was searching for any indication of insincerity in his countenance. "I heard it was a fundraiser, and I thought I might contribute."

"A fundraiser? For what venture?"

"You haven't heard?"

Charles shook his head.

"It's not a profitable venture, as such. It's more of a charity. Apparently, there's some sort of refuge for women whose husbands beat them. There's a house where they keep these women from their husbands." Dunham cleared his throat. "That is, the house keeps these women *safe* from their husbands' brutality. It's terribly noble and all that . . . stuff. At any rate, as I've heard it, Drake is attempting to raise funds for another house during his party. I'm here looking to find out more about it and where this house is."

"Don't you know where it is?"

"No. Why? Do you?"

Again, Charles shook his head no. "I was just wondering how come you don't know where the house is located."

"Its location is meant to be a secret, as I understand it. No one knows where it is, and no one is supposed to know. The only ones who do know its location are keeping it undisclosed so the women's husbands can't find them. Nobody I've talked to can tell me where to find it at any rate."

"Fascinating. But tell me, why would you need to

find it?"

"Did I say find it?" The earl smacked his head. "I meant *fund* it. No one can tell me where I should go to donate funds."

"Perhaps you should try Drake. It's his party and fundraiser after all."

"Good advice."

"I have to say I'm surprised, Dunham. I never took you for the type that would give money to a place that keeps wives from their husbands. Does that mean you approve of the mission?"

"Would you?"

"I don't approve of physical brutality as a means of disciplining anyone, so yes, I do approve. As you said before, it's a noble project to protect women from violence."

The earl nodded. "Yes, of course. I agree."

Julia was never more relieved when the butler chose that moment to announce that dinner was served.

CHAPTER 16

Six of Wands, reversed: Unwelcome news, setbacks, frustrated plans, overwhelming challenges, failure, defeat . . .

LATER THAT EVENING, AFTER A sumptuous though uneventful meal, Charles stood on the periphery of the ballroom watching the guests dance. He also watched Julia. She sat in a circle across the room with her sisters and Caroline, and he could only imagine her torment as his sister no doubt commandeered the conversation and turned it into a planning session for the nuptials. Poor Julia. He shook his head and took a sip of his punch.

He had not been seated by her at dinner, so he had not been able to talk to her since their conversation with Dunham. He wanted to get her opinion on everything the earl had said—if she would even allow him to talk to her, that is. She had made it clear earlier that she did not want to see him or speak to him at the party. He intended to ignore her wishes, of course. Well, perhaps not ignore them so much as not heed them. He paused a moment as the horrid thought crossed his mind that he was more like his sister in her willful disregard for others' wishes than he would have liked, but he dismissed the idea as inconsequential. It did not matter. No, the only thing that mattered was getting Julia to reconsider her decision to end their engagement, but he needed to talk to her to do that.

Perhaps he should walk over to her now and ask her to dance. Doing so would not only afford them a chance to talk but also rescue her from her present situation. She could turn him down, he supposed, but she wasn't likely to do so in front of his sister and hers. Even she could see that it would be strange not to dance with her fiancé. And he was almost sure that she had not yet disabused either her sisters or his own of the notion that the two of them were engaged. No, actually, he was completely certain she had not told them. Otherwise, he would even now be enduring Caroline's lamentations.

He set his punch glass down on a nearby ledge and strode across the room to the circle of women. Julia frowned as he bowed. Hmm. This might not go as well as he thought. "Good evening, ladies. It's a pleasure to see you."

"Mr. Rodman," said Lady Kingspointe, "it's nice to see you also."

Caroline patted the marchioness on her shoulder with her folded fan. "Please, Cassandra. Feel free to call him Charles, now that we're all going to be family. You, too, Violet. And of course, he will address you as Cassandra and Violet. Won't you, Charles?"

He tried not to roll his eyes. "Yes, of course. And thank you, Caroline. On task, as always."

"You're welcome, of course. We were just discussing the wedding."

"I had no doubt you were."

His sister arched a brow as her lips formed an amusing moue of annoyance.

To prevent Caroline from saying anything more, Charles stepped over to Julia and smiled as he held out his hand to her. "May I have the honor of the next set?"

Her eyes spoke volumes, and he was certain they said, "No, absolutely not, you self-serving arse. I'd rather dance with a skunk." Yet, she stood and accepted his hand, sending sparks flying up his arm despite her frostiness.

Caroline tapped Julia with her fan. "Don't forget to tell him the plans we've made so far."

"Oh, I'll tell him alright."

Though alarmed by her curt tone, Charles nevertheless led her to the dancefloor where they formed a square with three other couples for the quadrille. As the music began, they danced in silence for several minutes. He was bracing for her to rant at him about the wedding plans, and when she did not, he opened with a topic he knew would surely concern her. "Interesting conversation we had with Dunham earlier, wasn't it?"

Though she said nothing, she nodded. He took that as a good sign. At least she hadn't completely ignored his question, which was a start.

"Do you believe him when he says he doesn't know where the shelter is located?"

"Yes."

"Has your cousin been careful not to divulge where it is to any of the guests?"

"Yes."

Though he was happy that she was at least speaking to him, the lack of detail in her answers bothered him. "Don't you find it interesting that he spoke of only one shelter? As though he did not know there were two?"

"Yes."

"Monosyllables are nice, Julia, but I'd like to know what you think in more detail. Please elaborate."

"Very well." She said nothing else for a few seconds, tempting him to prod her with more questions. Finally, however, she took a deep breath and let him have it. "Your sister is planning our bloody wedding, and I think you are a thoughtless, uncaring, insensitive arse for not telling her we are no longer engaged."

"What does that have to do with Dunham?"

"Not a thing. But you asked me to tell you what I thought, and there it is."

"I meant what you thought about Dunham."

"Moreover, I think it's cruel to leave her in the dark."

"Then why don't you tell her?"

"Because it would disappoint her so, and I haven't the heart. She is so happy and excited for us and has such lovely plans for the ceremony and breakfast that she has even me reconsidering."

"Well then, I don't think I'll tell her."

"You must tell her."

"I think not."

"Charles," she said his name through gritted teeth. "I am not joking here. Tell your sister there will be no wedding."

"And if I don't?"

"Then I will go ahead and marry you just so I can make you miserable."

He laughed, but she did not crack a smile. "Oh, come now, Julia. You couldn't possibly make me miserable. If you married me, you would only make me the happiest of men."

She tilted her head as if he spoke a language foreign to her. "You say that as though it's true. I know differently, however. I'm fairly sure I would only make you miserable." She closed her eyes a second and took another deep breath before continuing. "And I am positively certain that you could never make me happy."

"That's absolute claptrap, and you know it. Do you know what I think, Julia Lacey? I think you're afraid of just how happy I could make you. You're afraid of how happy we could be together. For some reason I can't fathom, you're afraid that if you allow yourself to be happy with me, it will all go bad. You're afraid that something will make me stop loving you, when the truth is . . . there's nothing that could make me stop loving you. Ever. Do you hear me? Nothing."

She scoffed. "So, what should we do about Dunham? Do you think there's a chance he might discover where his wife is?"

"Changing the subject will not change the facts, Julia. I love you and want you to marry me."

"I think if we just remain cool and calm through-out the week, everything will be fine. He'll never sus-pect where his wife is if we don't slip up and reveal it in conversation. I'll make sure Arthur and my sisters remain silent. Will you make sure Caroline doesn't say anything?"

"Yes, of course. I'll tell her to keep quiet."

"Humph. Quite frankly, I'm surprised you'll tell her that when you won't tell her we're not engaged."

He smiled sweetly, but she did not. In fact, if her scowl could've have injured him, he was certain he would have waddled from the dancefloor a eunuch.

Julia slept fitfully all night long and awoke the next morning with a raging headache. Too many things from the previous day had left her unsettled. For one, she was hiding the wife of one of the wealthiest, most influential, not to mention most powerful men in the kingdom at her home, and she couldn't afford to let him find out about that. For another, she was plan-ning a wedding that would never take place with her ersatz fiancé's sister, and she hadn't the heart to tell the woman that they were making preparations for an imaginary event. And finally, she still loved that ersatz fiancé of hers. More than she thought she could ever love anyone again, she loved Charles. Yet, she couldn't marry him, not without telling him the truth about Camille. He deserved to know the whole story, but just how was she supposed to tell him all the sordid details about her past without revolting him?

She pulled the blankets over her head in an effort

to block out not only the morning light filtering in through the curtains but also any hint of reality. She scolded herself for giving in to her desire for Charles a week ago. She should never have done it, not even for just one night. Letting him into her heart had thrown her whole life in chaos, and making love to him had been disastrous, the absolute worst thing she could have done. Why, why, why had she done it? The memory of what they had shared and the thought of what they could have together only made her ache for him all the more.

Startled from her self-recriminations by a knock at the door adjoining their two rooms, she threw back the covers and got out of bed. It had to be Charles, of course, and that vexed her. Even though she had just admitted to herself that she loved him still, she was nevertheless angry with him for letting his sister believe they were engaged. Intent on ranting at him for that and for having the gall not only to disturb her before breakfast but also to presume that she would actually open the door for him, she didn't bother putting on her wrapper and padded to the door wearing only her night rail.

The rant died on her tongue the moment she beheld him. In fact, she momentarily lost the entire faculty of speech. He was divine. He looked and smelled wonderful, having obviously just washed and shaved. He wore a navy, superfine coat, a lighter blue waistcoat, and fawn trousers.

"Good morning." His voice was low and silky, and it worked its way through her blood like an opulent red wine.

Despite the effect he had on her senses, she managed to regain her ability to speak and even recovered a bit of her acerbity. "What do you want?"

He arched a brow as his mouth dipped into a lopsided smile. "I think you'd slap me if I told you."

"I might just slap you anyway for your impertinence in knocking on my door without permission."

"We're in a fiery mood this morning."

"'We' did not sleep well last night."

"We are sorry to hear that."

"'We' still want to know why you knocked."

"We—*I* wanted to know if you'd like to go down for breakfast with me."

"I think not. How would it look if we walked into the dining room together?"

"I think it would look like we are both hungry."

She rolled her eyes. "I am not dressed, as you can see, and getting dressed will take me some time. I need to send for Burton and some hot water. I won't be ready for another hour at least. I suggest you go on downstairs without me."

He pushed the door open a little farther and stepped across the threshold into her room. "I could help you dress."

"I think that's a horrible idea, and I'm sure it would end badly." She began pushing him back to the doorway. "Now, if you please—"

"Julia, wait. What I really came here to do was talk to you about our future—together."

"We have no future—together. Only apart. You

must accept that, Charles. Now, please leave."

"But we could be so good together. So happy."

"No. Now, go." She put both hands against him and pushed on his chest, but he wouldn't budge. She pushed him again, and when he still didn't move, she raised her eyes to his and glared at him. That was a mistake. When she met his gaze, she made the error of falling into his aquamarine eyes. His desire was unmistakable, as was his love, and within seconds, her heart pounded for him, as her knees—and her resolve—buckled under her own desire. She longed for him to take her in his arms. As if reading her thoughts, he did so as he lowered his lips to hers. And, like that, she was lost. *Damn it.*

Two hours and three climaxes later, she lay in her bed, her arms and legs—and heart—as entangled with his as they had ever been. Their passion sated, they both labored for breath. She also labored for clarity as she stared up at the ceiling. *Now what?*

Again, as if reading her thoughts, he caught his breath and said, "Julia, I'm asking you again. Will you marry me? Please? I'm begging you."

Yes. She said the word in her mind and in her heart but couldn't bring herself to say it aloud, not unless she told him the truth about Camille. Yet, she dreaded his reaction. She couldn't bear his disappointment and disgust—or his pain when she revealed to him that she had committed the same transgressions as his wife and bore her husband another man's child. He would probably leave her the moment he realized she had been as faithless and wicked as her.

Then, as she lay there still staring at the ceiling, it occurred to her that perhaps that wasn't the worst thing. Perhaps that's how things had to go. Maybe he needed to hear all the horrible details about her past for things to move forward one way or the other. Who could predict his reaction, after all? Perhaps he loved her enough to be able to move beyond his initial revulsion to a place of acceptance and understanding. She didn't count that as likely, however. No, likely, finding out her secrets would extinguish all desire he had for her, and he would turn tail and run. But she would be no worse off if the relationship ended because he quit it than she was right now. If—when—he ended it, she would simply proceed with her plans to leave England and move to India forever.

She took a long, deep breath when he shifted as though he were going to get up. It was now or never. "Yes. But—"

"What?" She laughed when he did a comical double-take. "Did I hear you correctly? Did you say yes?"

"I said yes, but I need to tell you some—"

"No. No 'buts.' I don't want to hear all the reasons it won't work. Let's not worry about our troubles. Let's just get married. We will confront any problems later."

"But—"

"No, Julia. Stop. I'm not listening. I am serious when I say I do not want to know why it's a bad idea. Now, I am going to get dressed and leave before you can change your mind. I will see you later." He kissed the tip of her nose as he moved off her and rose from the bed.

Very well. She accepted defeat as she closed her eyes and surrendered to his wish to remain ignorant—for now. But eventually, she would tell him the truth.

She rose from the bed herself after he was gone. She rang for Burton to help her with her morning toilette and went downstairs to the dining room afterward, hoping to find something left for breakfast.

Later that afternoon, she ventured out to the back lawn to watch the archery tournament, hoping to sit with Charles. She scanned the crowd for him but did not see him, so she found an empty table under an umbrella and sat down alone to a cup of tea that a footman handed her, along with a couple of biscuits.

It was nearly two, and as she took a sip of tea, a low, gravelly voice rumbled over her left shoulder. "Good afternoon, Mrs. Lacey."

She didn't have to turn to know it was Lord Dunham who stood behind her. He was the only person in her acquaintance who would not address her using her courtesy title. He had never used it, even years ago when Niles had first gone into business with him. He had always called her Mrs. Lacey. She speculated that he did so in part to mock her ranking as a duke's daughter married to a commoner. And also because he didn't like her. The feeling was mutual.

"May I join you?"

No, you may not. Though she thought it, she didn't say it aloud. Instead, she filtered the silent, off-putting reply in her head through the repertoire of socially acceptable responses also in her head. "Yes, of course, you may. I'd be delighted, in fact. Please—do sit." She even added a smile, fake though it was, because, no matter what else, she was still a duke's daughter and a lady, and it was what she had been taught to do back when she was a young girl and everyone referred to her as *Lady* Julia.

He pulled out a chair across from her and made himself comfortable as he smiled at her. His smile was just as insincere as hers, though, with perhaps a touch of sarcasm added. "I'm surprised you're out here all alone."

"And I'm surprised you're not participating in the archery contest. You're missing all the fun."

He arched a brow as he ogled her. "Depends on your definition of fun, I suppose. I prefer having my fun in private without an audience, though I have to admit that I have performed with others watching on more than a few occasions."

He was the most revolting person she knew, but she hid her disgust behind a mask of boredom.

"How about you, my dear? Would you let others watch? I'd certainly pay to see you and Rodman together. Which reminds me, I am very upset that you didn't tell me the whole story last night."

If he made his remarks to rattle her, it worked. The veneer in her mask of indifference cracked a little. "The whole story about what?"

"About your engagement to Rodman, naturally. I saw you dancing with him last night, so I asked around about the two of you and learned you were engaged. I also heard a lot of other interesting information. You'd be surprised what all I found out."

This time, she couldn't hide her agitation. Had he heard something about the shelters?

"For instance, I did not know you aren't currently living at Lexington House. Imagine my surprise when I learned you are living at your dead husband's hunting box."

"Who told you that?"

"Rodman's sister. Now, she's a delight. A little too chatty perhaps, but then she always was that way—even back when Rodman and I were youths. I was talking to her about her brother and you, and I asked her if he planned to move into Lexington House with you after the wedding. She let it slip that you weren't staying at Lexington House. Naturally, I wondered why, but she claimed not to know the reason when I asked her."

Though Julia tried not to react with alarm, she couldn't prevent her mask from fissuring just a little more. Still, she waved her hand casually in an attempt to convey apathy. "In truth, I never liked Lexington House. It's too . . . grandiose, so I moved some things to the hunting box. It's much less pretentious."

"So where will you and Rodman stay after you're married then?"

"At the vicarage in South Kindale, naturally."

"Ah, of course. Pity. Do you plan to sell Lexington House then? It's rather a shame to leave such a large house unoccupied." He regarded her through narrowed eyelids as he shifted forward in his chair. "It *is* unoccupied, isn't it?"

"Servants are still living there."

"Just servants? No one else?"

She shook her head no, as sweat trickled down her back.

He arched a dubious brow. "Really? Because I'm certain it could easily accommodate at least sixty."

He knew. Not the entire story, perhaps, but he knew at least something was going on at Lexington House. And he was now trying to pump her for more information. She remained silent, however, to prevent herself from accidentally providing him any further clues. Still, he flashed her his smarmy smile, giving her the impression that he already comprehended far more than he was letting on, so she tried to change the trajectory of the conversation. "Would you be interested in buying Lexington House, my lord?"

His eyes shot open in authentic surprise. "You *are* selling then?"

"I've been considering it."

"I'm surprised you haven't already sold it actually, given how penniless your husband was after abandoning our partnership in Calcutta before he died." He leaned back in his chair. "Speaking of that, does Rodman . . . *know?*"

She averted her gaze to some archers in the distance so as not to reveal her distress, but her heart missed a beat at the question. "About what?"

"You know. About . . ." He waved his hand in a circle, as though that somehow explained what he meant. "Oh, how do I put it? Calcutta. Does he know what happened in Calcutta?"

She nearly swooned as the blood drained from her head and the ringing in her ears became deafening. Her first instinct was to jump from her chair and run from the lawn to avoid answering his question. Panicking, however, would only give him satisfaction, so she stayed at the table and sipped her tea in a desperate attempt at nonchalance. "I'm not sure I know what you mean."

"Don't you?" Again, he flashed her that slimy, counterfeit smile of his, shaded this time with a hint of malice. When she didn't answer, he leaned in as though he were going to break a confidence. "Does he know Niles died bankrupt after deserting our shipping business in Calcutta three years ago?"

She swallowed hard as she struggled not to tremble. "Yes."

"Hmm. Really? How extraordinary. He knows *everything* then? He knows *why* Niles abandoned everything he had and left India so suddenly?" She did not answer him one way or the other because she couldn't form a rational response. Apparently, he took her silence to mean yes as he scoffed. "Well. That surprises me, I have to say. I find it hard to believe he proposed to you after learning the scandalous details about your situation. Especially given what happened with his own wife. I assume you are aware that he discarded her for the same offense?"

She said nothing once again.

He laughed in obvious mockery. "The hypocrisy is rich. The irony, however, is glorious."

She remained quiet as she contemplated her escape options.

A footman approached the table, interrupting her thoughts. "Excuse me, my lady, but you've an urgent message from Lexington House. It just arrived by special courier." He held out a silver salver with a sealed letter resting on it.

Alarmed, Julia snatched the missive from the tray and broke the seal. She then unfolded the foolscap and scanned its contents.

Dear Lady Julia,

Please forgive my intrusion with this letter, but I'm writing to ask you to return home as soon as possible. Things are in chaos here at Lexington House. The women have been restless and anxious since Lady Dunham's arrival. They are panicked, in fact. They fear that because her husband is so powerful and well-known, he will surely find the shelter and expose it and them to the entire kingdom. They're afraid their husbands will then come after them and force them back home. Some women were even packing and planning to leave a few days ago with no money and nowhere to go, until Lady Dunham said she would leave and take refuge elsewhere so that the other ladies would feel more secure. The problem is that the countess has nowhere to go herself without her husband finding out about it. She can't take shelter with family or friends because he will surely find her. The other women have begun packing once again and are planning to leave soon. Mrs. Sweeney is especially distraught. She says she is leaving on Thursday with her son. She plans to take him to London and place him in the Foundling Hospital for his

safety so she can work the streets. She says she would do any-
thing to avoid having to return home to her husband. I have
tried to dissuade her from her plans, but she won't listen to
me and insists that she must leave. I'm afraid you're the only
one she might heed. Would you be able to leave your party
in the morning and be here by tomorrow evening to talk Mrs.
Sweeney out of going back to London? Thank you.

Your faithful servant,
Harriet Nash

Julia looked up from the letter to see Dunham watching her with disturbing interest. He also eyed the letter with excessive curiosity. Afraid that he might snatch the note from her hands, she folded it and stuffed it safely into her reticule before he could make a move.

"Bad news, Mrs. Lacey? I do hope nothing is the matter at Lexington House." He paused a moment and narrowed his eyes with unmistakable malevolence. "Or with anyone who might be staying there."

Unqualified fear scattered her senses. It was imperative that she leave the table now, but it was also crucial that she not give away her apprehension. She slid her chair back from the table and managed to rise with such tranquility that she surprised even herself. "There's no reason to worry. All is well. Excuse me, my lord." Without a backward glance at Dunham, she turned and strode across the lawn toward the house with as much composure as she could feign.

CHAPTER 17

*The Moon: Mystery, apprehension,
unforeseen peril, threats to loved ones,
impending doom . . .*

JULIA SLAMMED INTO CHARLES AS he rounded
the corner into a hall leading away from the grand
entry in search of her, almost as if he had conjured her
out of the ether. Flushed and breathless, she put her
arms up against him to steady herself as he grabbed her
by the shoulders to prevent her from toppling backward. "In a hurry?"

"Oh, Charles, I'm so sorry. Please excuse me, but
I have to leave." She stepped around him toward the
grands stairs.

He turned and followed her, trying to keep pace.
"Wait, Julia. Where are you going?"

"Home. I have to get to Lexington House as soon
as possible."

"Why? What's going on?"

"I-I don't have time to talk, Charles. I must go." She
said the words over her shoulder as she hurried to the
staircase.

He rushed alongside her until they reached the first step where he grasped her arm to prevent her from going any farther. "Julia, what on earth is wrong?"

She rolled her eyes heavenward and lifted her arms as though she were surrendering in defeat. "What isn't wrong? Everything is just a mess."

"What's a mess? Tell me what's happening."

She removed a folded piece of foolscap from her reticule and held it out to him with a shaky hand. "This arrived for me just now while I was watching the archers out back."

He unfolded the letter and scanned the message, each word more alarming than the last. "I'll go with you."

"No, no. You just stay here. I can handle this on my own."

"There is no way I am letting you go by yourself. Like it or not, I'm coming with you."

"Oh, very well, but we must hurry. We need to pack, and then I must find Arthur to let him know we're leaving. I also need to have my carriage readied."

"You run on upstairs and pack your things while I take care of the rest for you. I'll find your cousin and Caroline and let them both know we're leaving. Then I'll head upstairs and get ready myself."

"Thank you, Charles. You're so good to me."

"Do you happen to know where I might find your cousin—or my sister, for that matter?"

"Try the back lawn. They might both be out there for the archery contest."

"Alright. I won't be long." He turned to go.

"And, Charles?" She stepped closer to him and scanned the grand entrance as if she were searching for eavesdroppers. "Whatever you do, don't let on to Dunham that we're leaving, if you happen to see him. He was sitting with me outside, and I'm certain from comments he made that he knows at least *something* about Lexington House. He might not know everything about the women living there, but he knows enough to be suspicious. He was questioning me and trying to get me to reveal more. Unfortunately, I received the letter from Mrs. Nash while he was with me, so he also knows something is wrong at Lexington House."

"Don't worry. I won't say a thing if I see him."

She smiled and kissed him tenderly on the cheek before disappearing up the stairs. He left the entryway and strode down the corridor toward the drawing room that exited to the back lawn. He reached the drawing room and jumped in surprise when Dunham stepped in front of him, blocking the doorway. The earl's sudden appearance out of nowhere, as though he had been lying in wait close by, alarmed Charles. Had Dunham been watching him? Or even following him?

"Sorry, old friend. Didn't mean to startle you." He smiled with insincerity, as though he were anything but sorry for the ambush.

Charles said nothing. He merely nodded to acknowledge the faux apology and then attempted to sidestep Dunham, but the man wouldn't move out of the way. After several seconds of impasse, Charles leveled his gaze at his former friend and said, "Excuse me, if you will. I'm trying to get out to the back lawn."

"Won't you join me for a toast first?"

"To what?"

Dunham snickered and punched him in the arm with feigned comradery. "To your engagement, naturally. I heard you and the lovely Mrs. Lacey are going to be married, and I'd like to express my felicitations properly."

"Thanks, but I don't have time for a toast right now. And besides, it's hardly necessary."

"Nonsense. What kind of friend would I be if I didn't wish you joy? It'll only take a second. Surely, you have just a second for a brief draught of whiskey."

Charles narrowed his eyes at his ex-chum, skeptical that the man wanted to wish him anything but everlasting misery. He would have declined the drink, except that he didn't want to raise Dunham's suspicions that something was wrong by dashing out to the lawn. "Very well. One drink."

"Good show. Let's see what spirits Drake has in the drawing room, shall we?"

They both stepped through the doorway, and once inside the room, Dunham strode to an array of decanters sitting on a credenza across from the door. "Looks like we've got some brandy, whiskey, sherry, port, and even gin. What's your poison?"

"Whiskey, I suppose."

Dunham nodded and poured two fingers of amber liquid from one of the bottles into a tumbler and handed it to Charles. He then poured himself an equal measure and raised his glass. "To your wedding. May

your marriage be blessed with happiness and good fortune."

Dunham lifted the glass to his lips and tossed the
liquor down his gullet in one gulp. Dubious as to why
his erstwhile friend, a man who had betrayed him long
ago in the worst way, was now drinking to his happiness, Charles lifted his own glass in hesitant salute to
the toast and took a small sip.

"Come on, Rodman. Drink up. It isn't every day a
man gets engaged to a lovely and, shall we say, diverting woman like Mrs. Lacey." He poured himself some
more whiskey and downed it once again in a single
gulp. Then, he poured himself even more. "So, tell me,
what are your plans after the two of you are married?"

Wary of Dunham's motive in asking, Charles took
another sip of his drink as he considered his answer.
Deciding there was no harm in letting the earl know
their plans, he shrugged and said, "We're going to India
right away."

Dunham's eyebrows shot toward his hairline in
overt surprise. "Indeed? Whatever for?"

"Julia has long desired to return to Calcutta. Before
we met, she had planned on moving back there permanently."

The earl shook his head. "Good God, why would
she want to move to a place with such a dreadful climate?"

"There's a young girl back in India she wants to
take care of. Her name is Camille."

Dunham gawped at Charles in apparent and sincere
incredulity and then laughed as though the informa-

tion were vastly humorous. "The girl? She actually told you about the girl?"

Charles tilted his head in confusion at the statement. "Why wouldn't she?" Then he regarded the earl with a sense of unease. "How do you know about the child?"

"I know a lot about the Laceys. Niles Lacey was my business partner, in case you didn't know. He ran our shipping company in Calcutta for a few years." He swirled his glass around and around and watched the liquid circle the bottom. "We made huge profits through our operations—until Lacey abandoned the venture all of a sudden and returned to England with his wife."

"I was aware of that actually. Julia told me everything."

Dunham scoffed. "Indeed? Everything? I'm astonished."

Charles nodded. "Yes, of course she told me everything. I don't know why that would surprise you so much. She and I have no secrets."

The earl grinned with apparent relish, as though the statement amused him. "You're sure about that?"

Charles nodded. "Quite sure."

This time, Dunham smirked with a hint of satisfaction, as though he'd just bested an inferior opponent. "Then you must know about the girl's parents and that she is of mixed race."

"Yes. Julia told me that Camille's mother was English and her father was Indian, but her parentage makes no difference to me in the least."

"I think you'd see it differently if you knew the *whole* story."

Charles gazed at the earl with blatant suspicion. "That *is* the whole story."

Dunham's lips curled into a malicious smile before he laughed with what could only be described as twisted delight. "Mrs. Lacey didn't tell you who the girl's mother is, did she?"

Charles narrowed his eyes and took another sip of his whiskey, leery of what amused Dunham so much. "Of course she told me. The girl's mother was a close friend of hers. As was the child's father. The father is dead, as I understand it."

"And the girl's mother? Did Mrs. Lacey tell you anything else about her? Like where she is these days?"

"No, not really. I don't know if she knows what happened to the woman or has any other information beyond the fact that she is no longer around to take care of her daughter, and Julia feels an obligation to step in and take care of the child herself, on behalf of her friend."

Dunham laughed again, this time with cold-hearted satisfaction. "I think it might surprise you to know what did happen to the girl's mother."

"Why? What happened?"

"She left India with her husband shortly after her daughter was born."

Charles tilted his head in confusion. "I don't understand. I thought her husband was dead."

Dunham smiled suspiciously. "Well, he is now, but he was alive when they left Calcutta together. The child's father, on the other hand, remained in India and died shortly after his lover left with her husband back to England."

Charles cast a cautious, sidelong glance at the earl, trying to make sense of why Dunham was telling him about Camille's parents or how he knew so much about what sounded like a sordid tale. "So, are you saying the girl's parents weren't married?"

Dunham smiled suspiciously as he nodded. "Not to one another."

"How do you know so much about the story?"

Dunham shrugged with nonchalance. "As I said, Lacey was my partner. I wanted to know why he left Calcutta so suddenly, so I asked around, of course. I found out from some associates that he left so abruptly because he was livid with Mrs. Lacey after the girl was born."

Something about the statement made Charles's gut clench. "Why was he so livid with Julia after Camille was born?"

"Because the girl looked nothing like him, and that's when he realized he wasn't her father."

Unable to make any sense of the earl's befuddling narrative, Charles shook his head in utter bewilderment. "I don't understand. Why was Lacey upset with Julia because he was not the girl's father? What did she have to do with it? It's not like she was the girl's mother . . . or . . . anything—" His voice broke off as Dunham's oblique implication began to sink in. "Are you saying . . .?" He shook his head in horror as he finally grasped the stark truth. Dumbfounded, he let the whiskey glass slip from his hand. It fell to the floor and shattered into a thousand pieces. It was the perfect metaphor.

Dunham, meanwhile, laughed darkly as he took another swig of his whiskey. "I think you're beginning to see the picture."

Staggered by the revelation, Charles ran his hands through his hair and then down his face in abject shock. It all made sense now. Horrible, devastating sense. Everything she had ever said about why she couldn't marry him, why they were all wrong for one another, suddenly registered in his mind.

"I have to say, Rodman, you sure know how to pick them. You're two for two now in falling for a shameless lightskirt."

Dunham's insults were no worse than the recriminations Charles hurled at himself. He couldn't have been more humiliated at his own denseness than he was at this moment. It was all so obvious. Why hadn't he been able to put the pieces together until now?

Dunham downed the last of his whiskey and set his empty glass on the credenza. "Well, old friend, I can tell that you're in no mood to talk any longer, so I'll just leave you to yourself." He exited back to the hallway, but not before laughing darkly one last time.

Fool. Idiot. Imbecile.

The rebukes flew through his head for his naïvety in trusting Julia and believing her to be a virtuous woman when she had only ever given him indications of the opposite. From the very beginning of their acquaintance, she had shown him the kind of wanton she was. From the moment she had teased him with the explicit picture in the *Kama Sutra* depicting two people in coitus to her rejection of his marriage offer and her subsequent suggestion of an arrangement between them after their interlude at her birthday celebration, she had shown herself to be a licentious jade, exactly like his wife. It was no surprise then, that like his wife, Julia was also a dissipated adulteress.

And an imposter. In letting him believe she was an honorable, upright woman, she had deceived him. She had also deceived him by not telling him the truth about her daughter, and her deception wounded him deeply. Worse, she had betrayed him by not revealing that she had cuckolded her husband the way Eleanor had cuckolded him. She had been especially heartless in not telling him about her own affair, after he had confided to her about the pain he suffered because of his wife's affair.

He kicked the shards of glass at his feet in rage at his stupidity. He couldn't marry her now. He wouldn't marry her now. She might very well betray him as Eleanor had done—and as she had betrayed her own husband. No, it was over between them. He was too angry at her—and too devastated by the truth—to consider chaining himself to her for eternity. He didn't know if he could even be in the same room with her ever again. No, he was done, and though he would always berate himself for his foolishness in ever trusting her, it was behind him now, and he could take consolation in the fact that he hadn't married her yet.

Finished with packing at last, Julia closed her bag. She needed to find Charles so they could get on the road soon, but he hadn't yet returned to his room to pack his things, as far as she knew. She was about to peek through their adjoining door for the third time in ten minutes to see if he were there, when a knock on the main door to her chamber startled her. Perhaps it was him, though why he wouldn't just enter through their connecting door puzzled her.

She ran to the door and opened it, fully expecting Charles to be standing in the hallway. She was mildly irritated to find a footman instead.

The servant bowed. "Pardon me, milady, but Mr. Drake sent me up here to tell you he would like to speak to you on the back lawn. He says it's urgent."

Julia scrunched her face in confusion. Why would Arthur need to speak to her on the back lawn at all, much less urgently? Hadn't Charles found him yet to explain the situation with Lexington House? Or had something else happened? Apprehension set in as all sorts of dreadful scenarios played out in her imagination. "Did Mr. Drake say why he needed to speak with me?"

"No, ma'am."

"Very well. Thank you." She exited her room, locking the door behind her. Rather than walking all the way down the hall to the main staircase, she headed for the servants' stairs at the end of the corridor nearby. She ran downstairs to the first floor and took a short-cut through the kitchen to the back lawn.

She found Arthur among the archers, preparing for

a tournament he would undoubtedly win, as he was by far and away the most skilled person Julia ever knew to handle a bow and arrow. She strode over to him and waited impatiently for him to notice her, finally tapping his shoulder when he did not. "I'm here, Arthur. What did you need?"

He turned toward her and regarded her with a vacant stare as he rested his bow against his leg. "Hmm?"

She tilted her head to the side in confusion. "What did you want to see me about?"

He shrugged. "Nothing."

"Didn't you send a footman upstairs to fetch me just now?"

He shook his head no.

She huffed in frustration. "Well, this is all very strange, but I don't have time to sort it out. Charles and I have to leave for Lexington House as soon as possible."

"What? You're leaving? Why?"

"Didn't Charles tell you?"

"I haven't seen him all morning."

"You mean he hasn't told you yet about the letter I just received from Mrs. Nash, requesting that I return home as soon as possible because the women are panicking about Rebecca being at Lexington House? Some of them are even threatening to leave though they have nowhere else to go."

"Why would they do that?"

"They're afraid Lord Dunham will come looking for his wife and expose them all. I fear he already suspects something odd is going on at Lexington House as it is, given the questions he asked me just recently. I don't understand why Charles hasn't spoken to you yet, though. He said he would tell you everything and then have my carriage prepared so we could leave. Where could he be?"

"I have no idea, but why is he going with you? Aren't you still upset with him?"

She shook her head. "Not anymore, I guess." She explained how the two of them had reconciled this morning and that she had agreed once again to marry him.

"Congratulations, Julia!" He hugged her tightly. "See? It turned out exactly as I thought it would, and I just know you'll both be happy together."

She shrugged unenthusiastically and peered down at her nails to avoid his gaze. "I'm not so sure we will."

"Why not?"

"Because I haven't told him about Camille yet. I tried to tell him earlier, but he cut me off and wouldn't let me say what I needed to say because he didn't want to hear about anything that could ruin our happiness. And I fear—no, I am certain—that he will end the engagement and disavow me when he finds out the truth."

"Don't say that, Julia. He won't care about anything from the past if he loves you, and trust me, the man does love you."

"Perhaps. But the real question is whether he loves me enough to overlook my having committed the same sin as his wife. He was devastated by her betrayal."

"But *you* haven't betrayed him. How can he be upset about something you did that doesn't even concern him, especially when you acted out of desperation and despair? It's not as though you cuckolded *him*. Besides, it was so long ago. What happened in the past has nothing to do with the present, and I predict he will realize that, even if he's shocked by the truth at first. He loves you, Julia. You'll see, and he won't allow what happened in India to ruin your current happiness or destroy the future you two have together."

She shrugged once again, holding little faith in Arthur's assurances. Still, something he said just now cast a tiny ray of light into the shadows of doubt that had occluded her happy ending with Charles. Her cousin was right. She had done nothing to hurt Charles. While it was true she had betrayed her husband, she had committed no sin against Charles and done nothing injurious to him. All this time, she had been admonishing herself for her past and acting under the assumption that he would be angered and hurt by choices she made long ago, as though he were the wounded party. Perhaps she wasn't giving him enough credit to see for himself that the transgressions she had committed long ago and far away were not against him and did not involve him in the here and now. Perhaps he loved her enough to get beyond his initial shock about what she had done and to accept her mistakes as lessons learned. And maybe, he could even come to understand why she had acted as she had done.

Heartened somewhat, she left Arthur and returned to the house, intent on finding Charles and telling him what he had to know about her past—before they left for Lexington House and before they set out on their future together. She reached his room and tapped lightly on his door a couple of times as she whispered his name to get his attention. Frustrated when he didn't answer right away, she rapped again, a little louder this time. When he still didn't come to door, she twisted the doorknob a few times and found it locked. She banged on the door several more times as she called out his name in a louder voice. Still no answer. Perhaps he hadn't returned to his room yet after their conversation a while ago, but where could he be?

She finally gave up on his door and moved down the hallway to her own. When she went to unlock it, however, the knob turned with no effort. How peculiar. She clearly remembered locking it. Unsure why it was now unsecured, she opened the door slowly and glanced around the doorjamb with caution, gasping in outrage at the condition of her room as she stepped across the threshold.

Her luggage was open and her belongings were strewn everywhere—on the bed, on the floor, on the chair, on the dresser. Who had done this? Then she spotted Dunham standing next to her bed, pawing through her reticule in search of something.

"What the hell are you doing? And how did you get in?"

He chuckled. "A kindly footman let me in after I instructed him to get you out of the room with a fictitious summons from Drake."

"How dare you ransack my room and throw my things around in such chaos."

He pulled a folded piece of foolscap from her reticule and held it up in triumph. "Aha! Found it!" He opened it and scowled as he read it, regarding her with abject contempt when he was through. "It's just as I thought. You *are* hiding delinquent wives at Lexington House, including my own, you witch."

Unable to deny it, Julia swallowed in fear.

He sneered sinisterly. "How lucky is it that I attended this party? I'd never have known otherwise. I hadn't planned on coming, you know, because I thought it strange that Drake had sent me an invitation in the first place. I hardly know him, after all. When I mentioned it to someone at my club in London, he informed me that your cousin was hosting this party and inviting the very richest men in England in order to raise funds for a refuge for women who have deserted their husbands. I was skeptical at first but decided to check it out after Rebecca vanished. Imagine my surprise when someone here at the party told me that you and your sister are operating these refuges. I hardly believed it until I sat with you a while ago and observed how uncomfortable you were when I questioned you about Lexington House. And then when I saw your reaction to this note as you read it, I knew something was going on at your husband's estate. I came up here to find this letter to prove my suspicions, and I was right." He pointed an accusing finger at her. "You've got my wife."

She remained silent. Horrified that he now knew for certain that Rebecca was hiding at Lexington House, she lost her capacity of speech. And what could she have said anyway? She had no way to deny the truth now, not with the letter as proof. He had all he needed to find his wife. He also had all the evidence he required to demonstrate to a magistrate that she was hiding wives from their husbands. He could bring the authorities down on her and close the shelter—for good, forcing the women back to their former wretched lives. As for her? She might very well face prosecution.

After several seconds of standing there in mute panic, she found her voice, shaky though it was. "What are you going to do now, Dunham?"

He threw his head back and laughed maliciously. "Rest assured, my dear, that I'm going to do my very worst." He tossed her reticule to the floor and took a step away from her bed. Something caught his attention as it fell out of the bag onto the carpet. He picked the object up and brought it near his face for closer examination.

Julia gasped once again when she realized he held the miniature portrait of Camille.

He smirked at the picture. "Who do we have here? Is this the misbegotten mongrel then?"

Incensed at the denigrating moniker he used for Camille, Julia stomped over to him and attempted to grab the frame, but he tightened his grasp on it. "Give it to me, you bloody bugger!"

He laughed as they tussled several seconds for the picture, but he did not loosen his grip.

"Let go of it, maggot." She pushed against his torso to leverage her strength but ended up trapped against his chest facing him when he seized her around the waist with his arms. The more she writhed to break free, the tighter he held her.

"Such a feisty wench. I knew you would be, though. I'll bet you're even more of a saucy little spitfire when forced to do something you don't want to do." He bent his head and attempted a kiss.

She shrieked as he struggled to assault her mouth with his. She pushed back at his shoulders and thrashed her head from side to side so violently that his lips couldn't make contact with hers. "Let me go, you filthy swine!"

"Not when I'm enjoying this so much." He pushed her down on the bed and imprisoned her there with his body. "You like to squirm under a good, hard cock, I hear. Let's see how much I can get you to wrestle against mine. I'll wager a crown that I'll have you bucking in ecstasy before it's over."

"Let. Her. Go."

The grim voice startled Dunham enough that he lifted his head and looked toward the source. He did not loosen his hold on her, however, pinning her more firmly than ever to the bed.

Julia glanced up when the stern voice commanded Dunham to release her once more.

The earl snarled. "You do have the most impeccable timing of anyone I've ever known, Rodman. How did you get in?"

"I heard Julia scream, so I came through the adjoining door." Without averting his gaze, he pointed over his shoulder to the door connecting their two rooms.

"Ah, a private door. How nice. Not to mention convenient for nighttime trysts. Or daytime trysts." He barked out a brash laugh. "What say we share her? I'll go first and open her up for you. Then you can have at her. You should have no trouble at all sliding in and out after I'm done. She'll be pretty loose and greasy by then."

"Get the hell off her, Dunham."

"Or what? What will you do? Ha! What can you do? Pray for her?" He laughed malevolently once again.

"You're the one who should start praying, if you don't leave her alone right now."

"That's brilliant! And while I'm down on my knees praying, I'll lift her skirt and have a little lick."

"You no good, bloody bastard." Charles stalked to Dunham and hauled him off Julia. He slammed the earl against the wall and wrapped his hands around the man's neck. Something in him seemed to snap then as he appeared to use every ounce of strength in him to cut off the earl's airway. Julia jumped up and ran toward the two of them when Dunham began choking for breath. Afraid that Charles might actually kill the man in his current temper, she grasped his hands and tried to break his fierce grip while also attempting to insinuate herself between them. "Charles! No! Let go! You'll hang if you kill him!"

"I'll claim benefit of clergy," he said through clenched teeth as he tightened his stranglehold.

"Charles! Stop!" She tugged at his hands. "You know murder is non-clergyable."

Julia's voice seemed to have broken through his

murderous rage, for he let go of the earl abruptly and stepped back.

Dunham bent over, sputtering and coughing, as he gasped for air. Several moments passed before he stood upright and finally caught his breath. He brought his hands to his throat and fingered his skin gingerly, as though he were making certain everything was still intact. "Good God, Rodman." His voice was a raspy wheeze. "Why didn't you just demand pistols at dawn?"

"Because . . ." Charles panted and huffed for air, trying to catch his breath as well. "I couldn't wait that long to kill you."

Julia rushed to him and laid her head against his chest as she hugged him around the waist. "Oh, Charles, thank you. I'm so grateful to you. I don't know what I would have done if you hadn't rescued me when you did, but you shouldn't have strangled Dunham on my account. He's not worth going to the gallows for, and I couldn't bear it if they hanged you. There's no way I could live without you."

He did not return her embrace. In fact, he held his arms out to his sides, away from her, as if he didn't want to touch her. She ignored his apparent rebuff and hugged him more tightly in an effort not only to comfort him but also to reassure herself that he wasn't spurning her affections. After a few seconds of letting her cling to him, however, he settled his hands on her arms and unwrapped them from around his torso. He then disengaged himself and pushed her firmly away from him.

"Charles? What's the matter?" She reached out

to hold him again, but he blocked her arms with his hands, not allowing her to touch him. "I don't understand. What's going on? Why are you being this way?"

He let her arms go as he stepped back. "When were you going to tell me, Julia?"

She eyed him with caution, crossing her arms against her chest to shield her heart from the blow she sensed coming. "About what?"

"Or were you just never going to mention it? Were you going to keep me forever in the dark? Were you going to go through life letting me believe that Camille was not your daughter?"

She closed her eyes for a moment, unable to withstand the unforgiving expression on his face as he glowered at her. When she reopened her eyes, she cringed at his flinty stare. "So you know."

He clenched his jaw and hardened his gaze even more, as he regarded her with blatant revulsion and contempt. He retreated when she stepped toward him.

"Who told you?"

"That may have been me, Mrs. Lacey. I may have let it slip when he and I were talking a bit ago. I do hope you can forgive me." The earl's voice dripped with feigned penitence. "In my defense, though, how was I supposed to know he hadn't a clue about your affair with your husband's doctor? I got the impression from all you told me this afternoon that he knew every sordid detail, like how you seduced the doctor with a filthy little picture book you found at a bazaar and that he later had translated for you."

She cast a sidelong glance at the earl. "Stay out of

this. You know nothing of what happened."

"Oh, don't I?" He laughed. "I know you're a witless slattern who didn't have the good sense to terminate your condition after you found out about it, or not to get with child in the first place when you cuckolded your husband. Thanks to you, I lost a fortune. Lacey wouldn't have abandoned our business had he not had to drag you back to England to keep you away from his doctor's prick and his doctor's get."

"Shut up, Dunham." Charles's voice betrayed no emotion when he spoke to the earl, but his expression conveyed nothing but disgust as he regarded Julia.

"She's such a strumpet, Rodman. You sure you want to marry her?"

Charles shook his head no, and in that moment, the bottom fell out from under her world. He fixed his blue gaze on hers. "No. In fact, I'm sure I don't. The marriage is off."

Her free-fall began with his words. They impaled her heart and pierced her soul and sent her into a dizzying, headlong dive into a fiery pit of despair.

The earl laughed once again. "Good show, old friend. Good show!"

"Get out, Dunham. While you can still walk out."

"Very well. I'll just leave you two lovebirds alone. I'm off to Lexington House anyway to retrieve my wife." He strode to the door but turned back to jeer at them one last time before leaving. "See you in church."

At a loss for words, Julia said nothing after Dunham's departure. Charles remained silent as well, and the awkward silence persisted between them until he turned and strode to the adjoining door without saying a word. Afraid she would never see him again if he walked across the threshold, she ran to the door and placed herself in front of it to block his exit.

"Please move."

"I can't let you leave, Charles. Not until we work this out."

"I have to go."

"Please don't. Can't we at least talk?"

"What's there to say? You should have told me, Julia. Especially when I confided to you how hurt I was after what Eleanor did with Dunham. I shouldn't have had to hear from my wife's lover that my fiancé had a child with her husband's doctor."

"I tried to tell you. Truly, I did. Several times, in fact. But you wouldn't let me. You stopped me whenever I tried to speak. You said you didn't want to hear all the reasons it would never work between us." She stepped closer to him, but he backed away.

"Still, you should have told me."

"I was going to tell you. Really, I was. In fact, I came upstairs just a bit ago because I wanted to tell you everything before we left for Lexington House. I knocked on your door earlier, but you weren't there."

"I was there. I just didn't want to see you."

He turned and walked to the other door, the one that opened to the hallway—the one she was not blocking.

"So it's over then? There's no hope for it? And you're just going to leave without saying anything?"

He nodded but did not turn to face her.

"Fine then. Go." Though her voice was shaky, she did everything in her power not to break down or show emotion. She would not reveal her pain, but she would speak her heart. "I love you, Charles, but I was right about you. You're very judgmental, which is why I didn't tell you about Camille in the first place. I knew this was exactly how you'd react. I had no delusions that you were someone who could accept my error or absolve the mistake. You have cast me off exactly as I knew you would when you learned the truth. The moment you heard I had done to my husband what your wife did to you, you quashed any love you felt for me because you equivocated what I did to Niles with what she did to you. I suppose I understand that, on the one hand, but on the other, I think you're blaming me for the pain you still feel from your wife's betrayal, as though I'm the one who has hurt you. I did not betray you, Charles. I did not cause your pain. I think in ending it between us, you're acting out of fear."

"Damn right I'm afraid." His voice reflected his anger, but when he whirled around toward her, his face reflected his pain. "Only a fool would not be afraid. Look at what you did." He shook his head at her, as his expression transformed into one of disillusionment and then a moment later, repugnance. "Perhaps Dunham was right. Perhaps you are a slattern. You betrayed your husband in the worst way—in precisely the way Eleanor did me. What's to say you wouldn't also betray me like that? I can't get hurt again. I won't survive the pain this time. I loved you, Julia. Heart and soul. I loved you more than I have ever loved anyone in my life. Which is why I can't marry you. I know for certain that if you ever betrayed me the way you did your husband, it would kill me. I can't take that chance."

He turned back toward the door and left without saying goodbye, slamming the door shut on his way out.

Tears fell freely after he was gone. She couldn't contain them or the sobs that racked her body. It was over between them. Well and truly over. And although she had expected nothing else in all honesty, the pain of knowing she would never see him again was greater than she had imagined it would be, while the agony of hearing him say he loved her, in the past tense rather than the present, crushed her. The worst thing, however, was having her fears about him confirmed. She had put off telling him about Camille for fear his judgment would be harsh and that he would end their relationship. And wasn't that what happened when he learned the truth?

She stood motionless for a moment, letting the tears flow. Grief threatened to bring her to her knees, until she shook her head. She stifled her weeping and steeled her sentiments. He couldn't forgive her for her past sins? Well, she could not forgive him for not forgiving her, and she would not let a vicar and his judgments crush her again. She would not let yet another man make her feel unworthy for the choices she had made. She would not get lost in self-reproach and self-pity. She had no time for it right now. She had to get to Lexington House as soon as possible to warn the ladies about Dunham. As she collected her things, she also collected her dignity and her composure and formed a clear resolution in her heart to forget Charles Rodman. He was not worthy of her love.

CHAPTER 18

*Queen of Wands: Intrepid, spirited,
independent woman who confronts her
struggles and fears with strength and
courage . . .*

OUTSIDE HER ROOM, CHARLES LEANED
against the door and closed his eyes in anguish.
Not since the day he had discovered Eleanor with
Dunham had he needed something to dull the pain
so badly. He walked to the grand staircase and headed
down to the same drawing room where his erstwhile
friend had toasted to his engagement not an hour ago.
He would find whiskey there.

Once inside the drawing room, he stepped over to
the credenza and poured himself five fingers of solace.
He swallowed it in two gulps, enduring the burn of
the liquor as it slid down his throat so that he might
enjoy the oblivion it promised on the other side. The
alcohol did not work quickly enough to conquer the
pain, so he took the entire bottle and his glass to a chair
near the French doors overlooking the back lawn. He
would sit there and drink until it didn't hurt any more,
even if it took the rest of the day and the whole night

ahead.

As he slogged through another glassful, he tried to distract himself from his troubles by watching the guests frolicking outside. Unfortunately, complete escape wasn't possible, not when he saw reminders of Julia everywhere. For one thing, he spotted her sisters playing shuttlecock and battledore in one area of the lawn. Then, when he averted his gaze to the refreshments table, his eyes landed on her brother as he stood near it talking with some other men. He then turned his attention to the archery contest on the opposite side of the lawn, but the first person he noticed there was her cousin as he shot an arrow into the bullseye of a target. Could he get no peace?

He watched Drake prepare to take another shot, until a footman interrupted him and handed him something. Charles then scanned another section of lawn, looking for anything else to distract him, only to find Caroline playing lawn bowls with her husband. He cringed as he anticipated the protracted melodrama that would ensue after he told her his engagement to Julia was off.

Without warning, the French doors flew open, interrupting his thoughts. Drake charged into the room wearing a grim expression, stopping abruptly when he noticed Charles. The longer Drake scrutinized him, the deeper his scowl became. Wary of the other man's mood, Charles greeted him with a circumspect nod, which he did not return. The atmosphere in the room grew heavier and heavier when neither of them spoke for a few moments.

Finally, unable to withstand the tension in the air, Charles cleared his throat. "I take it you know the engagement is off."

Drake held up a note and nodded. "Julia did mention it. I rushed inside hoping to say goodbye to her before she leaves for Lexington House."

"Please don't let me stop you then."

Drake nodded once again, brusquely this time, and headed for the hallway. He didn't exit, however. Instead, he stood with his hand on the doorknob as though he were debating his next move. After a moment, he spun around to face Charles. "You know, Rodman, I gave you more credit, but you are a bloody fool. You spurned one of the most beautiful people in the kingdom, both inside and out, because of something that happened years ago. Something that doesn't even concern you. She told me you would abandon her when you found out, but I didn't believe her. She said you wouldn't be able to accept the past, and I told her you would. I told her that you loved her enough not to let something from ancient history destroy your future together. I was wrong, evidently. Very wrong. She once called you a judgmental arse. It turns out she was right."

Charles scoffed under his breath and tried to ignore the jibe. He couldn't refrain from defending himself, however. "You don't understand, Drake. I've already been hurt by one faithless woman. I can't risk getting hurt by another."

"How is it that you would risk getting hurt by Julia?"

"Isn't it obvious? She betrayed her first husband. No doubt he suffered greatly from her infidelity. And she has given me no reason to think she wouldn't also betray her second husband and cause him as much suffering. And I can't be that man. I can't be the one to get hurt again."

"You don't know that she would betray you, yet you're acting as though she already has. You also don't know what a worthless piece of dung her first husband was. You have no idea what she suffered because of him." Fuming now, Drake paused to catch his breath.

"It's immaterial to the fact that she had cuckolded him, and I don't care to hear it." Charles rose from his chair and turned toward the door.

"Sit back down." Drake glowered at him. "You're going to hear it whether you care to or not."

Charles sat, intimidated not only by Drake's tone but also his glare.

"Julia's husband was a debauched pervert. He was so twisted that he made Caligula look like a saint. She lost count of the number of times and the variety of ways he betrayed her outside the marriage bed."

Unsettled by Drake's description of Niles Lacey, Charles shifted in his seat but said nothing.

"He was not only a degenerate but also a monster who berated and belittled her on a daily basis. He mistreated her both mentally and physically, beating her whenever the notion seized him."

Stunned and sickened by this account of Julia's husband, Charles shuddered. She had never mentioned that she had suffered as much cruelty at the hands of her husband as her sister Phoebe or the ladies at Lexington House had with their husbands.

"She was a shell of a person until she met his doctor, Renesh Sengupta. Thank God the man came along when he did. He saved her and helped her survive her torment."

Charles flinched on hearing Julia's lover's name. Though her plight troubled him deeply, he did not want to hear anything about the man who saved her or how he and Julia met, so he raised his hand to silence Drake and stood to leave once again.

"*Sit.* I am not finished."

He settled back into his chair with great reluctance.

"Sengupta helped her overcome her sorrow and distress over her situation with Niles by teaching her yoga and meditation. He also showed her how a real man treats a woman by helping her to see what a lovely human being she is. Who could fault her for falling in love with him after all the pain she endured with her first husband?"

Charles considered the question for a moment, and as he pondered an answer, he could perhaps see how Julia might have turned to someone else for comfort given her situation. Still, the thought of her in love with another man troubled him, and the thought of her in another man's arms tormented him.

"Sengupta fell in love with her, too, I believe. Should they have become lovers?" Drake shrugged. "I don't know, and I don't care. I'm in no position to judge her or anyone in that situation, nor is it my place to pass judgment. All I can tell you is that she finally knew happiness and peace because of him. When she got with child, however, she was distraught for the entire pregnancy, not knowing for sure who the father of her child was. It wasn't until the day Camille was born that it become obvious that Sengupta was indeed her father."

Charles's mind began spinning. He couldn't find his equilibrium now as he tried to sort out his conflicting feelings about Julia's past. The more he heard, the more he comprehended the choices she had made. Right or wrong, they had led her to find a little happiness in a life filled mostly with pain. He was on the verge of sympathizing with her, and this bothered him. He didn't want to feel anything but anger and disgust— and his own pain—over her sins, and yet, as his empathy deepened, his anger, disgust, and pain over what she had done began to ebb away. He sat in silent distress for several moments, unable to reply one way or the other. Finally, when it appeared that Drake might not continue with the tale, Charles cleared his throat and ventured a question. "What did Lacey do when he realized the child was not his?"

Drake shook his head as though the answer disturbed him. "It was horrible. When he realized the babe was not his, Lacey went into a blind rage and grabbed the infant from the midwife and threatened to strangle her if Julia did not reveal the father's identity. Only after Julia told him Sengupta was the father did he release the child and send her away with the midwife. He then brutally punched Julia in the gut for her betrayal."

Charles buried his face in his hands, anguished for what Julia had suffered at the hands of her husband, disgusted as he tried but failed to make sense of the pain the man had inflicted upon her and everyone she loved. He dropped his hands after a moment and lifted his head to find Drake regarding him through narrowed lids, as though he were assessing Charles's reaction for sincerity. "What became of Camille after the midwife took her away?"

"Julia found out sometime later that the old woman had taken the baby to Sengupta and that he cared for her as best as he could. She heard that he tried to enlist his family for help, but they shunned him and the baby. They were members of the Brahmin caste, and since Julia was an Untouchable, so was her daughter. Julia tried to contact Sengupta, hoping they could all escape to somewhere safe, but when Lacey found out about her attempts to reach the other man, he immediately booked passage on the first packet to England and forced Julia to abandon India and all hopes of ever seeing Camille again. He also concocted a story about how Sengupta and her baby both contracted a fever and died just days before they sailed, to discourage Julia from trying to contact him once she was back in England."

"How did she find out that Camille was still alive?"

"A year after her husband died, Julia found a letter hidden among his belongings from one of his East India Company associates in Calcutta accusing Lacey of having had Sengupta poisoned shortly after he and Julia sailed home to England. The letter didn't mention anything about Camille, so Julia didn't know if the girl was truly dead, as Niles had told her before they left, or if she was possibly still alive. She wrote to her friend Kitty, the associate's wife, last October asking about Camille, and heard back just recently—in June, as a matter of fact—that Camille is indeed alive and being cared for by Kitty and her husband."

Overwhelmed by Drake's revelations, Charles sat back in his chair as his head reeled and his sentiments shifted. As the breadth of Julia's suffering became apparent, familiar and uncomfortable emotions flooded his senses. If he weren't careful, feelings that he had wanted to suppress would surface again, and if he lowered all defenses, he would be as vulnerable as ever to being hurt by her again. Still, he couldn't tamp down the emotions breaking through the wall around his heart.

Drake cleared his throat, startling Charles from his thoughts. "I'll go now, Rodman, but before I leave you here to wallow in your self-pity, I want you to think about one last thing: Julia has done nothing to hurt you. Not one thing."

Charles shook his head in confusion. What was the man talking about? How could he possibly know what Charles felt? Julia most certainly had hurt him. She had concealed her past. She had betrayed him by refusing to admit she had committed the same sin as Eleanor. And yet, he couldn't fight the feelings that burned as hot as ever for her.

Still, how could he make things work with Julia after her betrayal? Could he forgive the pain she had caused him? Moreover, could he accept what she had done in her past and, if not condone it, at least move beyond it to try to build a future for the two of them? He wasn't sure he could do any of it, but he was sure he needed to try. "Drake?"

The man regarded him with an arched brow but said nothing.

"Can I borrow a horse?"

"Humph. I wish you would."

Charles ran out of the drawing room and up the stairs to his room. Once inside, he knocked on the door adjoining Julia's room against the odds that she might still be there. Not surprisingly, he received no answer. Still, he opened the door to be sure she wasn't inside and just ignoring him. When he scanned the room and found it empty, he closed the door once again and stepped over to the dresser in his room to retrieve a few items to take with him back to Lexington House.

He slid the top drawer open to pull out a clean shirt and fresh cravat but stopped short when he spotted a piece of paper lying on top of the linen cloths. The paper was folded twice, and when he picked it up, something fell from the folds. He reached for the object as the afternoon light slicing through his curtains glinted off the gold chain. It was Julia's pendant, The Lovers, the one her grandmother had given her for her debut.

He held it to his heart with reverence as he read her note.

My Dearest Charles,

I want you to have this pendant as a symbol of the love I will always hold in my heart for you. It represents the deepest and truest love two people can share. I will always be thankful that it led me to you, if even for a short while. My wish now is that it will also lead you to your true love, the one you are searching for and the one you deserve. Au revoir, mon amour.

Love,

J.

Julia woke with a start when the carriage stopped. She shot up from the bench where she had lain sleeping for some time and scanned the dark interior of the carriage, trying to recall where she was and what she was doing. Her maid Burton lay on the bench opposite hers, still sleeping. Julia shook her head to clear it of the remaining wisps of a dream she couldn't quite remember and parted the curtains covering the window beside her. Though the sky was clear, it was still very dark. The moon had waned to nothing over the past few days, and with no ambient light source to cast away the darkness, she couldn't discern anything through the blackness of the night.

At last, the coachman opened the door, startling her. "What time is it?" Her voice croaked, waking Burton from her slumber.

He withdrew his watch from a side pocket and lifted his lantern to provide illumination. "Nearly midnight, milady."

"Where are we?"

"Lexington House."

She cocked her head to the side, astonished by his answer. "Lexington House? Already? How did we get here so fast?"

"I took a shortcut along the back roads."

She smiled broadly. "Well done, Mr. Curtin." She took his hand with gratitude as he helped her down from the carriage.

She stood on the drive a moment examining the angles of the house as it loomed ahead in the shadows, searching for any sign of disturbance. When they left Arthur's house late this afternoon, she had had very little faith that they could get here before Dunham, but now, as she scanned the house for evidence of activity, she became optimistic that the earl had not been here yet. There were no lights and no movement coming from inside. From the looks of it, everything was peaceful and everyone was at rest. Perhaps they had beaten him here after all. Bewildered as to how that was even possible, she nonetheless began to hope that she still had time to warn Lady Dunham about her husband and take precautions against his imminent arrival.

Mr. Curtin held the lamp high and guided her up the steps to the main door with Burton close behind. A couple of footmen posted inside the dimly lit entry hall bowed to her in greeting.

"Good evening, Harold and Barney. You're the only ones awake, I take it? The rest of the house is abed?"

"Yes, milady."

"Very good. Hopefully, we can keep it that way.

However, it's urgent I speak to Mrs. Thompson and Mrs. Nash to warn them that Lord Dunham will be here shortly. He's on his way as we speak and will surely arrive before dawn. Please wake them and send them to the green parlor as soon as possible, and then rouse the other footmen as well. We may have something of a battle on our hands when the earl arrives."

She then asked her maid to wake Lady Dunham and her children and help them prepare to leave Lexington House. She also instructed her coachman to keep the carriage waiting in front of the house, ready to go at a moment's notice. After the servants dispersed to do their tasks, Julia made her way to the green parlor. She found the tinder box on the mantle and lit a couple of candles around the small room. She began pacing the Aubusson carpet in front of the fireplace as she contemplated the best way to execute the plan taking form in her mind for protecting Rebecca. Evacuating the countess to another location seemed the only logical way to thwart the earl and prevent him from running off with her.

Mrs. Thompson shuffled into the parlor, yawning as she secured her wrapper around her waist. She nodded to acknowledge Julia and then dipped into a lopsided curtsy. "Lady Julia, it's such a surprise to see you back so soon."

"I came as soon as I could after receiving Mrs. Nash's letter about how upset the women have become over Lady Dunham's presence."

"Oh, yes. It's true. The other women are quite beside themselves over it."

Mrs. Nash entered the room with her usual precision and asperity. She gave Julia a crisp nod and curtsied as well. "Lady Julia, I hope my letter didn't upset you. I hadn't expected you to leave your party so quickly."

"I decided to go ahead and set out for home this afternoon after I received your note so that I could get back here to try to convince Mrs. Sweeney not to leave and to help reassure the other women that everything would be alright, but then the situation changed, and it became urgent that I return as soon as possible. Mr. Curtin, bless his heart, took a shortcut along the back roads and drove like mad to get here so quickly."

"Goodness. What happened?"

Julia paused a moment and took a deep breath to steady herself. "Unfortunately, Lord Dunham was also at the party and happened to be sitting with me when your note arrived. He found the letter when he rifled through my things and is now on his way here to get his wife."

Both Mrs. Nash and Mrs. Thompson gasped in obvious horror. "I'm terribly sorry, Lady Julia," said Mrs. Nash. "I hope you can forgive me. I never would have sent the letter had I known Lord Dunham was there."

"Don't fret over it, Mrs. Nash. There's no way you could have known. And besides, I believe he would have found out about Lexington House eventually anyway. He already suspected that either my sister or I might be hiding Lady Dunham, and his only reason for attending the party in the first place was to try to discover where she might be. He'd have sniffed out the truth about his wife, even if he'd never found the letter."

"Still, I'm truly sorry for any trouble it may have added to the situation."

Julia waved away the woman's concerns. "We have much bigger things to worry about at the moment, like getting Lady Dunham and her children out of here before her husband arrives. Burton is helping them prepare to leave as we speak. I will have Mr. Curtin take them to a safe hiding place."

Mrs. Nash nodded. "Where?"

"I'm thinking that they should go to the hunting box for tonight at least. They can stay there temporarily until we can figure out a more secure place to send them."

"What would you like us to do?"

"Mrs. Thompson, would you please prepare a basket of food and other provisions to tide them over at the hunting box until we can move them somewhere else? And Mrs. Nash, would you please get some money out of the household safe to give Lady Dunham for expenses she will have after leaving the hunting box?"

"Yes, ma'am."

Both ladies curtsied and turned to leave the parlor just as Barney burst into the room. His alarm was unmistakable as he paused a moment to catch his breath. "We have a situation, Lady Julia."

Dread sank its icy claws into her very essence, sending shivers rippling through her body as it crawled up her spine. "He's here?"

The footman affirmed his answer with a shaky nod.

She closed her eyes in frustration and distress. They

had been so close. Ten more minutes and they would have succeeded in getting the countess out of here, but all Julia's efforts in racing to Lexington House to warn Rebecca about her husband and trying to help her get away were for naught. He was here, and there was no escaping him now.

And he was making a ruckus. His shouts carried from the grand entrance all the way to the parlor. If he continued his barking, he would wake the whole house.

She strode to the parlor door. "Are the other footmen awake?"

"Yes, milady. I told them to keep him at bay and not let him in the front door."

"Well done." She marched, with more confidence than she felt, out of the parlor and down the hall to the grand entrance. She squeezed through the phalanx of footmen at the door preventing the earl from entering. Finally, she came face to face with him. "What do you want, Dunham?"

"Mrs. Lacey." He sneered as he mocked her name. "I think you know why I've come. Tell your men to stand aside so that I can collect my wife."

"She is not here."

He threw his head back in laughter. "You are such a delight, Mrs. Lacey, but only a simpleton would believe your obvious lies. Now, let me in."

"Your wife is not here, sir. She left even before I arrived, and I don't know where she's gone."

He eyed her through narrowed lids in obvious suspicion. "Then there is no reason not to let me in to have a look around for myself."

"There's no way I'm letting you step foot inside my house." Several angry footmen crowded around her to prevent Dunham from entering.

"No matter. We'll just have to do this the hard way then." He drew a pistol from his coat. "Stand aside, or I'll shoot."

The footmen now stepped between her and the earl, their formidable bodies forming a wall of protection. Though she could no longer see the man over their broad shoulders, she nonetheless stood her ground, refusing to back down. "Put your gun away, Lord Dunham. It's useless with only one shot. You can hurt one of us perhaps, but you will never get past all of us."

Dunham growled. "Very well. But you have not won, Mrs. Lacey. On the contrary. I know my wife is still here. I will be back tomorrow morning with the constabulary and an order from the magistrate to produce her and my children, as well as to cease and desist all activity here at Lexington House. Anyone who stands in my way will be arrested."

He stomped his boots in retreat down the front stairs, and Julia pushed past the footmen blocking her to see him as he jumped up into his carriage. Before closing the door, he turned back toward the house and shouted, "And don't think to sneak her away before I return, Mrs. Lacey. I'm leaving a man stationed here to make sure you don't try to abscond with her in your carriage." He nodded toward a man seated on a horse in the drive and then slammed the door as his carriage trundled off toward South Kindale.

Julia's heart sank. She closed her eyes in somber defeat, hit with the realization that it was truly over now. Without a doubt, the earl would make good on his threats. He would be back in the morning with reinforcements, and he would take his wife away.

Moreover, he would ruin the future for Lexington House. It was as good as over already. No doubt it would be shut down forever and its mission aborted. Once the home and its purpose became known to the world, there would be public outcry—at least from most men—over the perceived objective of the shelter: keeping husbands from their wives. Never mind that its real goal was to keep battered wives safe from their brutal husbands. But men ruled the world, and the husband ruled the household. Married women were chattel with very few rights, their identities subsumed into their husbands' through the doctrine of coverture when they married. Divorce was virtually impossible to obtain, requiring an act of Parliament. Cruelty was the only grounds and was difficult to prove because a man had the absolute right to discipline his wife as he saw fit, backed by his government, society, and church; it was a wife's duty as his virtual property to obey her husband no matter what.

Though she wanted nothing more than to sit down and cry, she gathered what little remained of her fortitude and retreated past the footmen still standing around ready to protect her. She stood in the center of the vast entryway, exhausted and numb, without a clue as to what to do next. She couldn't send Rebecca away in her carriage now, not without the man outside seeing the countess leave and then most likely following her. And there was no other way she could protect her or the other women at Lexington House from the inevitable. The only thing she could do now was wait and watch it happen.

CHAPTER 19

The Tower: Catastrophe, chaos, upheaval,
disruption, destruction, shattered perceptions,
revelations, awakening, enlightenment . . .

AS HE MADE PROGRESS TOWARD Lexington House, Charles berated himself over and over again for being such an unmitigated and judgmental arse in condemning Julia for the past and ending their relationship. He needed to get to her as soon as possible and make things right—if it weren't too late to do that. Would he be able to convince her that he was truly sorry and wanted to make amends? What if she would not forgive him for his stupidity? What could he even say to her to win her back? He had racked his brain for the right words since leaving Somerset. Now, however, weary from the miles of road he had traversed, he could no longer form rational thought. His mental exhaustion and the bone deep aches from eight hours in the saddle had addled his brain to the point that it was producing fantastical images of large scaly beasts crossing the road in front of him. Ignoring the phantasms as best as he could, he trudged onward to Lexington House. It couldn't be too much farther now, could it?

He stopped his horse as he caught sight of a strange orange glow in the distance. What was it? Was it even real, or was this yet another hallucination caused by fatigue? He sat still, watching the luminous mirage and trying to make sense of it, and as he continued to observe it, he could just make out a silver-white haze rising from the orange radiance.

When realization hit him, it sent a shiver down the length of his body. The silver-white haze was smoke, and where there was smoke, there was almost always fire. Moreover, at what had to be a mile in the distance, the orange glow ahead could only mean something enormous was ablaze. But what was burning? What was up ahead that was large enough to produce a fire of such proportions and create that much smoke?

His heart lurched. Lexington House. It could only be Lexington House. Even from a mile away, it was obvious that it was Lexington House that was burning. He sent up a prayer as he kicked his horse into a gallop.

The nearer he got to the house, however, the more alarmed he became. The conflagration backlit the sky above the treetops of the surrounding forest in an eerie glow, and as he turned onto the estate's front drive, the scene ahead filled him with both awe and terror. Fire raged out of control in the southeast corner of the building toward the back of the house where the ballroom was. Worse, it had begun to engulf much of the east wing. Flames lurched from the rear roof toward the sky as both floors of the southeast wing burned out of control.

Dear God. *Julia*. His gut clenched. Was she alright? *Please don't let her be trapped in that inferno.*

As he rounded the drive toward the main entrance, he breathed a little easier when he realized that the building's north-facing front façade appeared to be in less peril than the back of the house, and the west wing in general was nowhere near as bad as the east wing—yet. Still, as he reached the steps at the center of the building leading up to the main doors, he noticed a few flames rising from the roof at the back of the house in the southwest wing.

Heart pounding, he climbed down from his horse and let the animal run free. It took off for the forest as he sprinted toward a group of women, children, and servants gathered on the other side of the driveway. Some of the women and most of the children were crying, while others stood around them in obvious shock. Charles searched the crowd for Julia, but she was nowhere to be found.

He approached Mrs. Thompson and Mrs. Nash who appeared to have just finished counting the throng of residents. "What happened? How did this start?"

The headmistress turned to him and scowled. "Lord Dunham."

The same chill that Charles had experienced earlier ran up his spine once again. "He started the fire?"

She nodded but offered no other information.

"Why? When?"

"He was trying to force his wife out of the house. He stopped here not long after midnight to get her, but Lady Julia told him the countess wasn't here. He didn't believe her, of course. He pulled a gun on her, but she still wouldn't let him in the door or give up his wife. He then made all sorts of threats about coming back in the morning with the authorities to fetch Lady Dunham and to shut Lexington House down. In the end, though, he came back less than an hour ago and decided to burn her out instead."

"How do you know?"

"He as much as admitted it. He's skulking around the premises somewhere waiting for her to come out."

"Dear God, you mean she's still in there? She hasn't come out yet?"

She shook her head no. "Not that I know of. Everyone else is present and accounted for, but I believe she's still inside with her little ones. Lady Julia's in there, too. She had come outside with the rest of us at first but ran back into the house when she realized that Lady Dunham and her children were still in there, possibly trapped."

His heart slammed into his ribs. "Good God. Do you know where in the house they could be?"

Mrs. Nash's face crinkled in distress. "Not for sure, but they might be in the countess's suite. One of the other residents thought that's where they were headed. She said that Lady Dunham and her children were right beside her as they all escaped down the main stairs toward the front door. Lady Dunham's youngest daughter then started screaming about a doll she left behind in their room, and before anyone could stop her, the child broke away from her mother and dashed back up the stairs. Lady Dunham tried to stop her, but with her injured ankle, she couldn't move quickly enough to reach her. As I understand it, she hobbled up the stairs after the girl, and the other two children followed her into the smoke-filled hallway off the second-floor landing. When Lady Julia heard they'd gone back upstairs, she ran into the house to help them. A couple of women tried to stop her, but she wouldn't listen to them and ran inside anyway. That was about twenty minutes ago, but Harold and Barney went in after them not long ago."

"Where is Lady Dunham's room?"

"It's the next-to-last suite of rooms on the left at the end of the south hallway in the second floor west wing."

Without a word, Charles turned and bolted toward the front steps but stopped short when the main doors flew open and two liveried footmen carrying lanterns rushed out of the building to escape the smoke and flames now billowing from the house.

They ran to the lawn and set their lanterns on the grass as they both bent over, panting for air. "It's no use, Mrs. Nash. Fire's broke out in the entryway, and the stairs are engulfed in flames. We'll have to find another route."

"Can you try going through the chapel, Harold? It hasn't been affected by the fire yet."

The man nodded, and without a word, he and Barney picked up their lanterns and trotted toward the west side of the house.

"Wait! I'll go with you." Charles ran toward them, and the three of them dashed across the length of the mansion's northwest façade toward the chapel. They were there in seconds, but as Charles grasped the door-knob leading to the narthex, he froze when he heard his name.

"Rodman!"

He reeled around to see Dunham racing toward him in unadulterated panic. This was not the sneering, cavalier lord who had nearly assaulted Julia in her room just hours before. No, this man was genuinely upset, his eyes wild with undeniable fear as he approached. "Where's Rebecca? I haven't seen her come out. Is she still inside?"

Charles let go of the door and stomped toward Dunham. He grabbed the earl by his lapels and shook him. "Did you do this?"

Dunham laughed, but strangely, it was not his usual snide, sinister laugh. It was a maniacal, deranged laugh, the cackle of a madman. He raised his hands in supplication. "How else was I going to get her to come out? They wouldn't bring her to me, and they wouldn't let me in to get her. I had to do something, didn't I? I couldn't leave without her, could I? She's my wife, for Christ's sake."

Charles released the earl and pushed him away. The pathetic lord began pacing the grass in a chaotic pattern, his hands on his head tearing at his hair. "I had to smoke her out—I had to! It all made sense at the time." He gazed down at the grass as he circled a small patch shaking his head. "I was just trying to create a little smoke."

"How? What did you do?"

Dunham lifted his head, his crazed eyes darting all over the place. "I love her. Don't you see? I-I truly do. I-I'm sorry for all I did, but I couldn't leave without her. I-I only lit a few drapes on fire in a couple of rooms to force her out."

"Which rooms?"

He shrugged and then pounded his head with both his fists. "I-I don't know. It-it's hard to think . . . the ballroom . . . and the library . . . and the music room." He threw his hands in the air and began circling the grass again. "I-I figured she'd have to come out with the smoke, and then I could grab her." He stopped his mad pacing and regarded the smoke billowing off the roof on the other side of the house. "I didn't think it would turn into this. What have I done?" He ran his hands down his face, his stark expression attesting to his remorse.

Dunham's obvious anguish stirred something inside Charles, something resembling sympathy. He didn't want to feel anything but contempt for the man who had betrayed him so thoroughly years ago and who had put his own wife and children and Julia in such extreme peril this evening. And yet, the more he watched the earl descend into madness over what he had just done, the more Charles took pity on him. He strode over to Dunham and grasped his arm, pulling him toward the chapel door. "Come. Follow us. We're going in to get her—and your children, and Julia. You can help us search for them."

The earl wrested his arm from Charles's grip and retreated several paces back, laughing like a maniac.

"Are you mad? We can't go into the burning building. We'll die!"

"We have no choice, Dunham."

The earl shook his head frantically. "No, I can't! I-I . . . I can't do it."

Disgusted—but at the same time saddened—by his onetime friend's cowardice, Charles shook his head at the man he had once loved as a brother. He said nothing, however, and wasted no more time as he turned and rushed back toward the chapel, leaving Dunham behind.

Barney held the door as Charles and the other footman, Harold, entered the narthex. "Did I hear Lord Dunham say he set fire to the drapes in the library and music room?"

Charles nodded as the two footmen exchanged horrified expressions. "Why? What's the matter?"

"We haven't much time," said Barney. "If fire reaches the art room between the library and the music room, it'll blow the place to kingdom come."

"How come?"

"Turpentine. Oil paints. The fumes are always so overbearing in that room, it won't take much to set them off, and Lady Dunham's room is right above it."

The blood in Charles's veins iced over as he recalled the overpowering smell of fumes in the art room the day Julia and he walked by it toward the chapel. "Good God. What'll we do?"

"Let's head to the house through the walkway off the narthex. It'll lead us to the first floor of the northwest wing, which isn't as affected by the fire yet. From there, we can take the servants' stairs to the second floor and then make our way to Lady Dunham's room in the southwest hallway by using the short corridor connecting the north and south hallways."

The three of them crossed to the door that opened to the covered walkway connecting the narthex to the house. Charles held the door for the footmen, and they all ran down the walkway, their boot steps echoing loudly off the stone pavers. Harold opened the door leading into the house, and Charles stepped over the threshold.

"Rodman! Wait!"

He turned back to see who had called his name but couldn't make anyone out through the obfuscating darkness. A shadowy figure tromped along the covered walkway toward them, his identity revealed only when he neared the door. Dunham.

"I'm coming with you."

Stunned, yet heartened that the man had chosen to come after all, Charles stifled his astonishment as he moved aside to let the earl through the door. The man hesitated a moment, doubt and terror flashing across his features, until Charles squeezed his shoulder in reassurance. Dunham took a deep breath and gave a single nod before proceeding past Charles into the murky northwest hallway.

Once all were inside, Harold lifted his lantern. It cast a soft light into the gloomy darkness and revealed wisps of swirling gray smoke in the air. Though fire was not burning anywhere within sight, smoke from flames burning elsewhere on the first floor had infiltrated the atmosphere here in the hallway. Charles's eyes began to sting and water from the acrid vapors, and as he took his first breath of the tainted air, he tried to tamp down his anxiety as it rose to a level he'd never experienced before.

Barney opened the door to the servants' staircase. "Cover your noses, fellas, and follow me. We'll take these stairs up to the second floor and then head halfway down the north hall where there's another corridor on the right that leads to the south hall. It'll lead us right to Lady Dunham's room in the southwest hallway."

The others nodded, pulling their cravats up to cover their noses as they followed Barney up the staircase. The wooden steps creaked in the eerie silence as the men ascended the stairs, guided only by light from the footmen's lanterns.

Once at the top of the stairs, Harold cautioned Barney to touch the doorknob with just his fingertips to check for heat.

Barney nodded before he reached out and tested the metal knob. "It's not hot." He then opened the door and led the others into the second floor hallway, holding his lantern aloft to light their way.

Once again, the muted glow from the lantern revealed smoke swirling in the air. Charles's eyes continued to sting and water, so he kept his nose covered as he followed the others along the corridor. They stopped halfway down and turned right when they reached the passage that connected the north and south hallways in the west wing. Smoke grew heavier now, the nearer they got to the south hall, and Harold gestured for everyone to crouch down to avoid the denser vapors toward the ceiling.

They all bent at the waist and kept their heads low as Harold led them farther until finally, they came to a door in the south hallway. "This is Lady Dunham's suite." He tapped the metal knob with his fingertips to test it for heat before turning it and then opened the door.

Charles followed the others across the threshold, and as he entered the room, he dropped to his knees to avoid the copious smoke swirling at the ceiling. The soft light of the footmen's lanterns revealed dense smoke seeping in through a door cracked open on the far right side of the room. The other men also fell to their knees to avoid the smoky air hovering higher in the room. They had to act quickly. That much was certain, or they would all end up lying on the floor, knocked unconscious by the smoke.

The atmosphere was eerily quiet. Charles lowered his cravat an inch to call out to the women hoping they would be able to hear his voice. "Julia! Rebecca!" He choked on their names, coughing and spluttering so much that he had to cover his nose again.

Following Charles's lead, the other men alternated among themselves lowering their protective neck cloths and calling out for the women as well.

"Rebecca!" Dunham bellowed, his voice remarkably loud and clear. "Rebecca! Tell us where you are."

A hush fell over the men when a muffled feminine voice from behind a door somewhere near the back of the room on the left penetrated the stillness. The door's doors hinges creaked open. "Avery? Is that you?"

The earl began crawling on his belly toward the woman's voice. "Yes! Where are you?"

"Back here. In the sitting room."

Dunham crawled quickly toward the door, while Charles and the two footmen crept along behind him, both managing to drag their lanterns with them. The door opened a little more when they reached it, but only enough to allow the men to scuttle through it. Charles entered last and slammed the door behind him to keep smoke in the main chamber from rushing into the smaller space.

Though the air in the sitting room was acrid, it was nearly free of smoke, allowing the men to breathe more easily. Dunham jumped to his feet and pulled Rebecca into his arms and sobbed into her shoulder. "I thought I'd lost you."

"Papa, Papa!" Three young children rushed to hug the earl and his wife.

The footmen rose also, as did Charles, and while he was touched by Dunham's emotional display of relief, he panicked when he did not see Julia. "Where's Julia? Is she not in here with you?"

The countess pulled away from Dunham's embrace, and without saying anything, pointed to the floor behind her. Charles could make nothing out in the inky darkness until the footmen cast their lanterns toward the area behind Rebecca.

His heart lurched, and he could not process what he saw at first. A figure lay there supine and lifeless. When he finally comprehended who it was, he cried out, "Julia! No!" He rushed to her and dropped to his knees beside her. "Oh, God, Julia! Are you . . .? Is she . . .?"

Rebecca knelt next to him and touched his shoulder. "She is not dead, thank the Lord."

He sobbed with relief as he lifted her up and cradled her in his arms. "What happened to her?"

"I believe she passed out from the smoke when she entered the bedchamber looking for us. After we got trapped in here by the fumes in the bedroom, I thought I heard a woman calling my name out there. I then heard a loud thud, as though she'd fallen, so I cracked the door ajar and saw Julia lying on the carpet. I crawled out toward her and dragged her back here with me. She hasn't woken since."

The weight of the guilt threatened to crush Charles until Harold strode over to him and touched his shoulder. "We don't have much time, Mr. Rodman. We'd best hurry before the fire hits the art room downstairs."

The footman was right. There was no time for recriminations or sentiment. Charles stood and bent to lift Julia up and then settled her limp body over his shoulder like a sack of flour.

Harold, meanwhile, pointed to a different door than the one they'd just come through. "Let's go back to the bedroom through the dressing room over there. That way, we won't have to breathe as much smoke."

Charles nodded and then directed the footmen to carry the two girls as he led the way to the dressing room. Dunham, meanwhile, held onto his son while helping Rebecca hobble through the door. Everyone proceeded quickly through the dressing room to the bedroom and then fled into the south hallway.

From there, Charles rushed ahead of the others into the corridor leading to the north hall. Just as he reached the north hallway where he was supposed to turn left, a deafening explosion from the south hallway rocked the entire house. The force of the blast knocked him into the wall.

What the bloody hell?

That had to have been the art room below. Fire must have finally reached it and detonated the combustible fumes from the open containers of turpentine and oil paints, along with the chemicals themselves, and thrown the entire mix into a violent eruption.

Disoriented, he managed to remain standing while keeping hold of Julia. He then struggled to regain his equilibrium as he pushed away from the wall. Through the ringing in his ears, he caught Rebecca's chilling shriek and spun around to see her leaning against the wall clutching her son as they both stared down in shock at Dunham.

Charles glanced down to see the earl lying face up on the floorboards in the middle of the corridor with a piece of wood protruding from his chest. He guessed that Dunham had turned toward his wife's bedroom at the sound of the blast, and the explosion must have knocked him onto his back as it hurled the wooden stake into his chest. The countess bent over her husband and touched his shoulder, but he did not respond.

"Rebecca!" Charles shouted. "Come along! We must leave. Now!"

She appeared not to comprehend him as she lifted her horror-stricken face. "I can't just leave him here."

Still carrying Julia's slack body, Charles strode to Rebecca and her son. He nudged the boy ahead into the north corridor as he reached for the countess's hand. "We have no choice. We have to get out of here *now.* I'll come back for him after the rest of you are out safely." Though she resisted at first, she finally capitulated and followed him to the north corridor when he pulled her arm.

CHAPTER 20

*King of Wands: Courageous, passionate, honest
man who fights evil, injustice, and oppression
with valor and conviction . . .*

JULIA OPENED HER EYES TO a star-filled sky.
Unsure where she was, she stared for several
moments at the lights twinkling in the black canopy
above, attempting to make sense of her surroundings.
She tried to lift her head to look around, but a raging
megrim made it difficult to do anything but lie still.
From what she could gather, she lay on a carpet of
grass, the cool blades tickling the bare skin on her arms
and at the nape of her neck. Her shawl covered her
midsection, and she drew it up to her chin to warm
herself when a slight breeze circled above her, chilling
her to the bone.

Where was she? Wherever it was, it was quiet and
serene. Had she died and gone to Heaven? No, even in
her current state of confusion, she was certain she was
not dead, for had she died, she would undoubtedly be
surrounded by the hot flames of Hell right now.

Flames. The fire. She took a deep breath as she began to recall the earlier events of the evening, but even

the sweet night air caused her to spew and sputter and gasp as it irritated her inflamed throat and lungs. Everything hurt. It hurt to breathe. It hurt to swallow. Her nose, throat, and lungs burned.

Then she remembered that Lexington House had been on fire last night. Or this night. Or in the wee hours of this morning. Or whenever it had been. Was it over? Had she lost an entire day? Or was it still the same night? And where was everyone else? Was anyone here with her? Had anyone else survived, or had they all perished?

She attempted to lift her pounding head again and raise her shoulders off the ground, but it hurt too much to accomplish anything, so she remained flat on the bed of grass. How had she ended up here, wherever here was? *Think, Julia. Think.* She recalled being outside on the lawn earlier when a woman who had just fled the burning house said that Lady Dunham and her children had all gone back upstairs to retrieve something from their room. On hearing that, Julia then dashed into the house, up the grand staircase, and down the south hallway of the west wing to the countess's room to try to locate them. Although she had had no clear plan for how to help them escape other than leading them back down the main staircase, she rushed into the building because she had to do something.

She wasn't prepared for the smoke or how ill it made her feel when she reached the second floor landing. The world began spinning, and she nearly retched as she turned into the southwest hallway, sputtering and coughing and gasping for air. As a last resort, she covered her nose and mouth with her shawl to protect herself as best as she could from the smoke as she ran down the corridor to the countess's room. Thinking the fumes in the bedroom would be less dense than in the hall, she flung the chamber door open and made the mistake of lowering her shawl to call out for Rebecca as she entered the room, not realizing how thick and noxious the smoke was inside the chamber. It overpowered her as she stepped farther into the room until she could no longer fight it. She fell to the floor as she succumbed.

That was the last thing she could remember. Whatever happened next was a mystery. Confused and fatigued and still unable to discern where she was now, or even imagine how she had gotten there, she closed her eyes and lifted her fingers to rub her temples as she tried to recollect the events *before* the fire. She remembered arriving at Lexington House around midnight after leaving Arthur's party earlier in the afternoon to rush home and warn Rebecca that Dunham knew where she was.

Dunham. Ah, yes, the earl had arrived at Lexington House not very long after her and demanded she produce his wife, promising to return with the magistrate and local authorities in the morning when she wouldn't. She had been too exhausted to worry about much of anything after his departure, so she had dragged her weary body up to an empty chamber and gone to bed.

Sleep had eluded her, however. She could not clear her mind of her troubles. She couldn't forget the earl or his threats, and worse, she couldn't prevent thoughts of Charles from barraging her mind. Every time she closed her eyes, all she could see was the look of complete disgust on his face as he broke off their engagement.

Before leaving Arthur's house, she had erected a stone wall around her heart to protect it from further pain. The wall was meant to stand forever, but now, as she lay here on this patch of grass battling a violent headache and wondering what to do next, the stones surrounding her heart threatened to crumble into nothing more than a pile of dust. Sentiments she had wanted to quash forever bubbled to the surface of this emotional morass and left her pining for him, despite the fact that he had rejected her on the basis of her sins. She longed for him to come back to her, if only to help her stand.

Get a hold of yourself, you fool. He's not coming back. You'll never see Charles Rodman again.

Fine. Just as well. She didn't want to see him again anyway. Ever. Moreover, she resolved then and there never to yearn for him again. She did not need him. She would figure out a way to stand on her own once her head cleared and she could determine where she was. Right now, none of that mattered because she couldn't think straight, so she closed her eyes once more and drifted away.

Hours later, or perhaps just minutes, she became vaguely aware of someone gently prodding her shoulder and speaking her name. "Julia?" It was a man's voice, to be sure, but whose? She kept her eyes closed, certain she was dreaming, until someone began shaking her shoulder more urgently trying to rouse her. "Julia? Julia?"

Charles?

Impossible. Though it sounded like him, the idea was absurd. Yet, when she opened her eyes a crack, a blurry form squatted beside her and greeted her with a tender smile as he caressed her arm. It could have been Charles for all she knew, but surely not. Surely, she was still dreaming. In any case, none of it made sense, so she closed her eyes again to return to the dream.

"Julia, Julia, wake up."

She opened her eyes once more, and this time, her vision cleared enough that the man's face came into focus. "Charles?"

"Oh, thank God. You're awake." He smiled sweetly at her as he knelt beside her. "How are you feeling? Are you alright?"

Was she? She didn't know. "Where am I?" She winced in pain as her voice croaked.

"You're on the lawn. In front of Lexington House."

Confused, she swiveled her aching head without lifting it to look around her. Behind her, what remained of the building still burned, while above her, a maid who hadn't been there before, stood wringing her hands in obvious agitation.

Julia attempted to speak once more but began choking and sputtering so much that her voice was nothing more than a raspy whisper. "How did I get here?" She continued coughing until Charles reached under shoulders and helped her to sit up.

He sent the maid to find her something to drink while he recounted the rescue. He explained how he, along with the footmen and Dunham, had found her trapped in the sitting room inside the countess's suite with Rebecca and the children. He told her that the footmen had carried Dunham's daughters out of the room and that Dunham had been assisting Rebecca and their son out to the hallway just as the art room below the bedchamber exploded. He said Dunham had been injured in the explosion by flying debris and that they'd had to leave him behind temporarily so they could evacuate everyone else safely.

"I don't understand," she rasped. "How did I get out?"

"You were unconscious when we found you, so I picked you up and carried you out."

Her mind could barely register his words. "You did?"

"Yes, and then after we escaped, I laid you here on the grass and covered you with your shawl before going back after Dunham."

She was utterly confused now, but the maid returned at that moment and handed her a cup of water. As she drank it, she tried to formulate the questions bombarding her brain. "Why was Dunham in the house with you? Didn't he start the fire to force Rebecca out?"

Charles nodded and then explained Dunham's remorse and how he had helped Charles and the footmen search for her and the others. He also recounted how Dunham had been impaled by a wooden projectile after the blast and couldn't go any farther, so he and the footmen had reentered the building after everyone else was safely outside and carried him out barely alive. "I left him with Rebecca and their children by the chapel and then came over here to make sure you were alright."

"I think I am. But I still don't understand."

"What?"

"What are you doing here in the first place?"

He hung his head and shook it in apparent shame. Then he sat beside her and pulled her into a tight embrace. "Julia, my love, I realized after you left Drake's party that I had been such a fool. I reacted stupidly and behaved like a heartless beast. I never should have ended it with you, so I raced all the way here to tell you how sorry I am. When I got here and saw the house on fire and then learned you were trapped inside, I panicked because I thought I was too late to tell you how much I love you. I'm so happy and grateful to God that you're alright that I can't even express my thanks." He sobbed a little as he continued to hold her firmly, resting his head upon hers. "I am so fortunate that we got to you when we did. I don't know what I would have done if I'd lost you. You are my life, Julia. That's what I came to tell you."

She leaned back from him, her eyes shining with tears. "Oh, Charles . . ."

He pulled her close again. "Shh, shh. Shush now. I want you to know that I don't care what happened in India. I forgive you for what you did. I forgive you for your affair and that you bore another man's child while you were married to your husband. None of that matters now. None of it. It's in the past, and I forgive you for it. I forgive you for everything." He paused for a moment to take a breath before continuing the speech he had rehearsed since leaving Drake's house. "All that matters now is that we marry and then sail as soon as possible to India to get Camille and bring her home to England."

He hugged her a moment more and then stood. He reached down and grasped her around her shoulders to help her stand also. He then held her at arm's length so he could examine her from head to foot. Her hair was an unkempt swirl of coppery curls, while her creamy complexion was blotched with soot and ash. As far as he could tell, though, she was unhurt. He pulled her to him and rocked her in his arms for an eternity, not wanting to break their contact.

She said nothing, but he attributed her silence to the fact that she had to be overwhelmed by the night's events. When she still didn't respond after a few more moments, he finally asked, "What do you say, my love? Will you marry me?"

She pushed her hands against his chest and pulled away from the embrace. She used the ends of her shawl to wipe her eyes dry before silently regarding him for several seconds. Eventually, she cleared her throat and spoke, but her voice was still low and raspy from the smoke. "Where did you say Rebecca and the children are?"

Confused when she did not answer his question, he

pointed behind her. "Over there. With Dunham."

Julia spun around and gasped at the sight of Rebecca kneeling over a shrouded figure and weeping
inconsolably. The children appeared lost and forlorn
as they watched their mother grieve. Julia broke away
from him and rushed to them. She knelt beside Rebecca and wrapped her in an embrace.

Though the sight of Rebecca and her children
despairing over Dunham was troubling, Charles was
more spooked by Julia's reaction to his renewed avowal
of love and proposal of marriage. Or rather, her lack
of reaction to it. She hadn't returned the sentiments
he expressed. She hadn't even acknowledged them.
In fact, she had said nothing about them and instead,
changed the subject to Rebecca.

True, the countess had been in great peril, as had
Julia. Perhaps she was just concerned about Rebecca's
well-being. And rightly so. But still, she had not said
one thing to him in response to his reaffirmation of
his affections. Perhaps she had been too overwhelmed
by everything to process his words. Perhaps tonight's
events were too traumatic for her and it was too soon
to discuss the future. Perhaps she needed time to re-
cover from all she had been through. Perhaps.

And perhaps not.

He strode over to them now. The countess looked
up as he approached. Her tears had made tracks through
the soot and ash on her face. "Oh, Charles. He's gone."

He crouched beside her and patted her shoulder in
an attempt to soothe her. "I'm sorry, Rebecca."

She nodded and wiped her face with a sodden black

handkerchief. "I know he was not a nice person some of the time . . . most of the time. He was awful to you. He was awful to me. He was awful to everyone, but I loved him in spite of how he acted."

Julia caressed the countess's cheek. "Even in spite of how badly he treated you?"

She nodded and swallowed before saying more. "It's crazy, I know. I can't hope to make you understand. But I loved him. He was really only horrible when he drank."

Charles refrained from disagreeing, choosing to comfort the woman with something positive rather than upset her with something negative. "And he loved you, Rebecca. He told me so before we went searching for you. He also said he regretted everything he did."

"Thank you, Charles. You are kind for not berating him, as you have every right to do." She wiped her nose and then took a deep breath. "He said he was sorry to you also, just so you know. Just before he took his last breath, he apologized and wanted me to be sure to tell you how truly sorry he was. About everything."

Unsure what to say, and more importantly, unable to form words, Charles simply caressed her arm.

Rebecca sobbed for a moment and then gathered her composure. "I know it's asking a lot, but will you . . . would you perform the funeral service, Charles? It would be a comfort to me if you did, and I think he would want you to also."

It was the last thing he wanted to do, but he couldn't decline the request, not when she was so vulnerable. So, he nodded and then squeezed her shoulder when she thanked him again.

Julia stood and called Harold over. Charles stood also, hoping to get her attention before the footman arrived. "Julia?"

She turned toward his voice but said nothing.

"Can we talk?"

"Not now, Charles. I need to get the women and children to someplace warm and safe."

"Let me take care of those details. I'll make arrangements for the women and handle everything here. You take your carriage and go with Rebecca and the children to the hunting box."

She nodded and thanked him, but her gratitude was not warm and genuine. It was cold and perfunctory. He helped Rebecca stand and then motioned for her to go with Harold after giving the man instructions to ready the carriage. Julia gathered her shawl around her as she walked away with the others without saying goodbye.

"Julia?" he called after her.

She turned back toward him, but once again, she said nothing.

"Julia, we need to talk."

She huffed slightly. "Very well then. Speak."

He eyed her warily. Was he mistaken, or was she angry with him? If so, why? "I'm sensing that you're upset with me."

She inhaled and focused her gaze away from him. "You are not wrong."

"May I ask about what?"

She shrugged. "I don't think it's important or relevant to anything."

He extended his arms in frustration. "It's extremely important. And relevant to everything. Our future. Our life together."

"Charles. Dear. We—you and I—we have no future. We have no life together."

He recoiled as though she had struck him. She couldn't have stung him more had she slapped him. "And may I ask why not?"

She turned to him and fixed him with her famous glare, the one that warned him he was about to be told everything he needed to know, whether he wanted to know it or not.

"You said you love me just a moment ago."

"Yes. And I do."

"You said you had reacted like a fool over my affair."

"I did. And it's true."

"But . . ." Her voice trailed off, and she turned her gaze away from him once again as she focused on some point far off in the distance. "Did you also not say you 'forgive me' for what I did?"

"I did. And I do."

She lowered her head and stared at the ground for a second. "Oh, really?"

"Yes, Julia. I forgive you. What you did is in the past. It doesn't matter anymore."

She looked up at him then, and her gaze pierced him like daggers. "And who are you exactly to forgive me for my sins? Are you my judge? Are you God? Do I need your forgiveness to go forth? I've committed no sin against you, except maybe a sin of omission, but I've done nothing to hurt you personally. I told you that back at Arthur's house, yet apparently, you did not comprehend what I meant."

"I'm not sure I do now either."

She shook her head with obvious impatience. "You told me just a few minutes ago that you wanted us to start anew, that you don't care about what I did in India. That my affair and the fact that I bore my husband another man's child don't matter. That none of it matters now. You said, 'I forgive you,' as if your forgiveness was required for us to move forward. It was almost as if you were implying that I had hurt *you* somehow in the past and you were forgiving me for it."

"Yes. And I meant it. I forgive you."

Her brows quirked together in obvious bewilderment. "Do you hear yourself?"

He nodded. "Yes. Do you? What don't you understand?"

She rolled her eyes and then refocused them on him. "I don't understand how I ever thought you could truly move beyond my past when you can't stop imagining yourself to be the victim of it."

"I am making every effort to move beyond my pain."

She pinched the bridge of her nose between two fingers as she sighed in obvious frustration. "You know what your problem is, Charles?"

He wasn't aware he had one, but he was certain she was about to prove him wrong.

"Your problem is that you're still so very angry with

your dead wife for betraying you that you're *unable* to move beyond your pain, and you're conflating her betrayal of you with my betrayal of Niles. You're acting as though I'm the one who wounded you simply because I had an adulterous affair like her, and you seem to be forgiving me as if I'm the one who needs your absolution. I'm not the one who hurt you, Charles. Arthur helped me to see this when I talked to him yesterday, and I wish I could make you understand it now. The person who hurt you was your wife. The person you need to forgive is *her,* not me."

He ran his hands over his face in exasperation. "You're complicating the matter entirely too much. All I'm trying to do is get us to reconcile our differences. Why can't you just accept my forgiveness so that we can move beyond this? I want us to get back together like we were before." He raised his hands to her in supplication. "Let's start over, Julia."

"Charles, let's . . . not." Without another word, she whirled around and walked away.

Bewildered by her attitude, he gaped as he watched her retreat, his only comfort being that she had not called him an arse.

"Arse."

Ah. There it was. Though faint, it was audible—and within earshot.

Two days later, Julia woke to the comforting smell of sausages, eggs, toast, and coffee, and the not-so-comforting memory of her last conversation with Charles. She was still annoyed with him, but at least she was not

still fuming with righteous indignation over his dec-
laration that he forgave her for her sins as though she
was the one who had hurt him and needed a pardon.

His inability to apprehend why this insulted her
also bothered her still. How could he not see that it
was his wife he needed to forgive, not Julia? His wife
was the one who had betrayed him with her infidelity,
not Julia. Yet, he was acting as though Julia's infidelity
to her husband had somehow hurt him personally and
he needed to forgive her for her past sins before they
could move forward with their relationship.

What he really needed to do was just accept the
fact that she'd had an affair before she met him and
come to terms with it. She needed him to understand
her past mistakes, not forgive her for them. If he could
just do that, perhaps they could move on afterward, but
not before.

She rose and dressed for breakfast. It was just past
five o'clock, much earlier than she was accustomed to,
but she wanted to be up so she could say goodbye to
Rebecca and her children before they set out for their
home.

She could make out several voices coming from the
dining room as she approached the door. Arthur and
Caroline must also have gotten up for breakfast. Much
to Julia's surprise, they had arrived at the hunting box
late last evening. She had sent him an urgent post right
after the fire, notifying him of the disaster and asking
if he would come to South Kindale when his party was over to help her sort through the chaos. True
friend that he was, he left the party yesterday morning

and arrived by nightfall. Caroline, who still believed her brother and Julia were engaged, had insisted on accompanying Arthur when she heard why he was leaving, hoping she could be of assistance in restoring order. Though Julia appreciated the woman's sympathy and willingness to help, having her there only served to remind her of Charles. And she didn't want to think of Charles.

Fortunately, she wouldn't have to think of him much in the weeks ahead. He was traveling with Rebecca so he could perform funeral services for Dunham. He would be gone a fortnight at least, so she wouldn't have to see him around town, which was a relief. She had a lot of work to do to and arrangements to make in order to relocate the women and children who were displaced by the fire at Lexington House. At Rebecca's insistence, they were all moving to Dunham Park near Dover in Kent to take shelter there until the new home the countess had pledged to build for them could be constructed. She alone was shouldering the blame for her husband's crimes. She alone was taking on the responsibility of making reparations to the women for what he had done to their home. He wouldn't have burned it down had she not been staying there, she had said, so she felt an immense obligation to make things right again.

Rebecca had also insisted on paying for Julia to move back to India to be with her daughter after learning that Dunham had also ruined her plans to sell Lexington House to pay for the move. As generous as it was, Julia had declined the offer. It was simply too much. She couldn't allow Rebecca to pay what it would cost to return to India and settle there forever with Camille. She was still determined to do it, but she would have to find another way. Rebecca then insisted on building Julia a new home to replace Lexington House, telling her that she could always sell the brand-new residence to raise money for her move to India. Julia had declined that as well.

She entered the door to the dining room and stopped abruptly at the sight of everyone seated at the table. She had expected Rebecca, Arthur, and Caroline, of course, but never had she imagined that Charles would be there also. He stood and bowed when he saw her, as did Arthur.

Caroline smiled broadly and waved her over to the table. "Good morning, Julia. Come sit." She smiled again as she pointed to her brother. "Look who's here. He arrived just a few minutes ago. Isn't that a pleasant surprise? I bet you didn't think you would get to see him before he left for Kent with Rebecca."

Julia arched a brow. "No, actually, I didn't. I hadn't counted on seeing much of him at all for quite a while." She strode to her chair. Charles pulled it out for her and helped her sit. He then returned to his chair. "In fact, why are you here, Charles? I thought you were going to wait for Rebecca's carriage to pick you up in town—at the vicarage."

"I was, but I decided to save her the trip into town by meeting her out here."

"You do realize that you have to go back through town to get to the main road to London, don't you?"

He smiled glibly and shrugged.

She did not return his smile. "Wasted trip, if you ask me."

"Oh, nonsense, Julia. He knew he wouldn't see you for at least a fortnight, so he had to come out and say goodbye. Isn't that right, Charles?"

"You are not wrong, Caroline."

"There was no need. We said our final goodbyes after the fire."

He flashed that impertinent smile at her again. "Well, my darling, I've missed you. And besides, there's something we need to discuss."

"We have nothing to discuss."

"We have lots to discuss."

"I don't think so. I think we said all there is to say after the fire."

"Would you give me five minutes to prove you wrong?"

"That's quite unnecessary."

"But I insist." Before she realized what was happening, he rose from his chair and went to hers to pull it out for her, leaving her little choice but to stand. "Would you excuse us, everyone? We won't be long."

He placed his hand on her elbow, sending a shiver through her body, and guided her out of the dining room, down the hall, and into the study. He closed the door behind him with a click.

She crossed her arms over her chest to show her displeasure. "Well? Speak. And make it short."

Saying nothing, he quirked his lips into another crafty smile and closed the distance between them. He didn't touch her. He didn't need to. Primal heat radiated from his body and nearly knocked her to her knees. The scent of bergamot and cedar wood weakened her ability to form coherent thought, while the heat in his aquamarine eyes obliterated all reason. Any thoughts of protest vanished into the ether.

He undid her arms without any objection from her and stepped even closer until his body touched hers. He cupped her face in his hands and stroked her cheeks with his thumbs. His hooded gaze reflected his desire and his intent as he bent his lips to hers and kissed her as if it were the first—and last—time he would ever do so. She whimpered in surrender and went limp, falling against him. He caught her in his strong arms and held her close as he deepened the kiss, pressing his tongue to her lips and sweeping her mouth when they parted. A feral growl escaped his throat when she slid her tongue into his mouth.

They kissed for years, it seemed, and yet when he broke contact, it felt like he had kissed her for mere seconds. She wanted more from him, but he let go of her and backed away.

Irritated with him for taking advantage of her sensibilities and with herself for succumbing to her baser urges as she always did with him, she crossed her arms over her chest again. "Is that all then? Have you nothing more to say?"

"I think I've said everything, except . . . I'm an arse, Julia."

Her eyes narrowed of their own accord. "Go on."

"Not just an arse. An unmitigated, insensitive, judgmental arse. I see that now."

Rather than ask the obvious question, she chose to remain silent, hoping he would elucidate his point on his own, without a prompt from her.

"I understand now what you were saying to me after the fire. I grasp what you were trying to make me see. And you were absolutely right. You've done nothing to hurt me. The raw truth is that I have been angry with Eleanor for years, and I was taking that anger out on you. I was punishing you for her transgressions and then forgiving you for them and acting as though I were some noble martyr for having the decency to forgive you for what she did. For two days now, I have dwelt in wretched awareness of the fact that I condemned you, the woman I love more than any other being in this world, for choices you made in your darkest hours."

He paused to breathe, while his eyes shone, possibly with tears. "I reacted like a cad when I found out the truth about Camille and what happened in India. I was wrong to judge anything you did, and even more wrong for having the audacity to forgive you as though I were the injured party for something that didn't even concern me." He paused once more. The sorrowful, plaintive expression on his face nearly undid her, but she couldn't yet respond for the emotions flooding her senses. He spread his arms in supplication. "I know I don't deserve it, but if you can forgive me, I want to make things right between us. Please, Julia. Please. Marry me. Be my wife. You make me a better person. Grow old with me and help me not to make judgments when I have no right."

Now she was just dumbstruck, awed by the depth of his self-reflection and perception. When she stood staring blankly at him, unable to speak, he lowered his head and dropped his arms as if in defeat. He reached into his pocket and pulled something from it. He took her hand and wrapped her fingers around the object. "I'm returning this, Julia. I can't keep it. It's too painful. It will always remind me of you." He let go of her hand and turned toward the door.

She opened her fingers to find The Lovers charm she had given him. "Charles, wait!" He turned back, and she rushed to him, wrapping her arms around his waist. "Yes. Yes, yes, yes, yes, yes, I'll marry you. I love you. I need you. I would be lost without you. You are the love of my life, the one Grandmamma said would come to my rescue. You are my King of Wands. Never leave me."

He surrounded her in an embrace as he kissed the top of her head. "And you are my queen. I won't leave you, my love. Ever."

EPILOGUE

*Four of Wands: Earthly and spiritual
blessings, joyous celebration of life,
prosperity and harmony in one's affairs . . .*

OCTOBER 21, 1818
ST. BLAISE'S VICARAGE, VILLAGE OF SOUTH KINDALE,
HAMPSHIRE, ENGLAND

JULIA STOOD IN FRONT OF the armoire in her dressing room at the vicarage trying to decide what clothes to take with her on her upcoming trip. She'd just returned to England three months ago after the long journey to and from Calcutta, and now, here she was hying off on another adventure in just two days, this time to Wales.

"I don't know what to take."

"You're over-thinking it, Julia." Cassandra sat on a nearby chair rocking her infant son David, Lord Margate, who slept contentedly in her arms. "Just bring everything."

"That's absurd."

"I agree with your sister, Julia," said Caroline. She sat at a small table serving tea to several china dolls and Cassandra's daughter Miranda and little Camille. "Just take everything. Then you'll have whatever you need."

"But why should I bring my spring and summer gowns, if I don't need them? I certainly won't wear them, not if it's chilly out."

Cassandra rolled her eyes. "Well, I didn't mean those. Just bring your fall gowns. And a few of your winter ones, too."

"How long will we be gone?"

"I'm not sure, but at least six weeks, I should think. Maybe even seven or eight."

"Seven or eight weeks! Surely not. You've gone barmy."

"Well, just think about it. It'll take us at least four days to reach Grandmamma's house near Llanfair and then another day from there to get to Rhaeadr Manor near Orllewin Dwr. That's five days. Then, we'll spend a week at Rhaeadr helping Violet prepare for her wedding. That's twelve days total, so far. Then, we'll likely spend at least a few days at Rhaeadr after the wedding to have a tour of the region, maybe even a week. That's almost three weeks altogether right there. After we leave Rhaeadr, we're going back to Grandmamma's house to stay with her and visit Uncle and Aunt Tremain at Chyfaredd Castle. That'll be at least another fortnight, in all likelihood. So far, there's five weeks. Then another four or five days back here to South Kindale will make it nearly six weeks all told. And what if something should muddle the travel plans slightly, like the weather or the roads? Or disrupt them entirely, like some unforeseen event?"

Julia groaned. "Oh, how exhausting. I would not even attempt such a long journey at this time of year, especially since we've only been back in England for three months, except that I wouldn't miss Violet's wedding for the world. And I dearly want Camille to meet Grandmamma."

"I know! I'm so excited for Miranda and David to get to meet their great-grandmother at last, too."

"I'm also glad that Grandmamma will get to see our baby sister finally get her fairytale ending."

"Humph. I'm not so sure it will such a happy ending for Violet."

Baffled by Cassandra's comment, Julia studied her sister for a moment in an attempt to decipher her meaning. "Why wouldn't it be? I've heard nothing bad about her betrothed. Have you?"

"No, but even so, I'm fairly certain she doesn't love the man."

"How do you know?"

"When I helped her finalize a few details before I left London last week, I couldn't help but notice how cheerless she seemed. She wasn't at all excited about her upcoming trip to Wales and appeared even less enthusiastic about getting married. So I asked her if she were looking forward to her wedding"

"And what did she say?"

"Well, you know Violet. She didn't say much of anything. She just shrugged and nodded, but I got the impression that she was merely going along with everything because she had to, as though she were resigned to her fate rather than happy about it."

"Oh, no. That's heartbreaking. I had so wanted Violet to find a love match."

"Ha. A love match? With Benthower playing matchmaker? Neither you nor I found our love matches until he was well out of the picture. And Phoebe and Bess *never* found theirs."

Julia heaved a sigh. She then stepped away from the armoire and sat next to her sister. "You're right, of course, sadly. But surely this Lord Breningreal isn't an awful fellow, is he? I've never met the man, so of course, I don't know."

"No, he's not at all horrible, and you have met him, Julia."

"Really? When? I don't recollect it."

"Nine years ago. During Bess's Season. He was friends with her fiancé's son, who was in the Navy."

"You mean he was friends with Lord Strawbridge's son, Captain Findley? I don't recall the captain having a friend called Lord Breningreal."

"He wasn't an earl back then. He was a captain in the Navy in those days, Captain Atwell. He only recently inherited the earldom after a distant cousin in Pembrokeshire passed away last December."

Julia tapped her chin for a moment. "I think I do remember him, now that you mention it. He was very handsome, wasn't he?"

Cassandra nodded. "Still is, though perhaps aged a bit in the past nine years."

Julia nodded. "Well, who hasn't? It's such a small

world, though, don't you think?"

"How do you mean?"

"I don't know. Have you ever noticed how certain people seem to wander in and out of our lives? Perhaps we don't pay much attention to them at first because they aren't very significant to our current reality. Yet, they end up playing enormous roles in our future lives. I remember Captain Atwell being everywhere in attendance at the balls during Bess's Season, alongside his friend Captain Findley. I even remember him dancing with Bess on many occasions. I can still see them together quite clearly in my mind, in fact. Who'd have thought that one day he would inherit an earldom and end up marrying our little Violet?"

Cassandra quirked her head to the side. "Interesting observation, Julia. And quite eerie when one considers it."

"Mama?"

Camille's sweet voice distracted Julia, and she looked down to see the girl's innocent face smiling up at her when she felt a tug on her dress. "Yes, my love?"

"When is dinner? I'm so *hungry.*"

She crouched down and hugged her daughter close, the smell of sweet spices teasing her nose as she sniffed the girl's hair. "Don't worry. It'll be ready soon, I'm sure."

"It's ready now actually, Julia."

Startled by the masculine voice, she looked up to see her dashing husband standing there in the doorway.

Camille broke away from her and ran to Charles and hugged him around his legs. "Papa!"

He ruffled the girl's hair. "And how is my little pop-pet?"

"Pick me up! Pick me up!"

Charles obliged and bent down to lift Camille in his arms, and she pecked him on his cheek. Julia's heart swelled and all but burst with the love she felt for both her daughter and her husband. She couldn't have wished for a better relationship between them than the one they had formed over the past few months. Camille adored Charles, and he adored her in return.

Caroline stood from the tiny tea table where she'd been sitting. "Do you happen to know where Wood-field is, Charles?"

"He's downstairs with Drake and Kingspointe. We just got back from our hunting expedition, and we're starving."

Caroline scoffed. "Expedition. That's rich. You've been gone less than an hour with just one gun among you, and you ventured no farther than the backyard. Did you manage to catch anything?"

Charles harrumphed as he scowled at his sister. "Only a slight chill."

Julia laughed. "Why don't you and Caroline go on downstairs? Cassandra and I will follow you after we get the children settled with the nursemaid for their dinner."

A little while later, after the children were situated with the nurse, the adults sat down to their own dinner, and Charles led everyone in a prayer of thanks for the meal. He also offered thanks for the safe voyage he and Julia had taken to and from India to get Camille.

Arthur raised his glass. "And may Caroline and Woodfield have a safe trip home to Chippenham, and the rest of us a safe journey to Wales."

"Yes, indeed." Cassandra reached across the table to clink her glass to his. "I'm so very happy you waited to go to Wales with us, Arthur, rather than going back in August with your parents when they headed to Chyfaredd Castle to see to affairs of the estate now that Percy's gone."

Julia sighed as a sorrowful pang settled in her chest. "Poor Percy. It was so tragic that he succumbed to that dreadful fever earlier this year. He was so young and had so much life ahead of him. I'm very sad I never got to see him one last time. He was such a sweet fellow. It must have been so hard for you and your parents to lose him, Arthur."

Her cousin sighed grimly himself. "It was. Father was devastated. Mother was inconsolable. They both took his passing very hard."

"At least they have you, though. That must be such a comfort to them."

He shrugged and flashed her a lopsided smile. "I suppose I did come in quite handy as the spare."

Julia smacked his hand at his attempted humor. "Oh, stop that, Arthur. They adore you as much as they did Percy."

He chuckled as he waved away her comment. "I know they do. I was just trying to lighten the mood."

"So, tell us, Arthur," said Cassandra, "now that you're *Viscount* Drake, do you intend to continue operating that publishing company you bought for little or nothing from Benthower when he came to you so desperately seeking money after William and I eloped and he wasn't able to get his hands on my dowry?"

"I don't know. It's an insanely lucrative venture. I'd be a fool to let it go. However, if Benthower is interested in buying back his shares, I might be convinced to sell them. But only for a shameless profit."

Julia laughed, as did everyone else at the table. "What do you suppose has made it so hugely profitable for you?"

"Not so much 'what' as 'who.'"

"Oh? Then *who* has made it so hugely profitable for you?"

Arthur gave her a cheeky smile. "A certain *genteel* young lady."

"Oh, yes. *Her.* I'd forgotten about her."

Cassandra was about to eat a bite of her boiled potatoes, but paused with them halfway to her mouth. "You're not talking about the anonymous author of *Confessions of a Genteel Lady,* are you? I adored that book."

"One and the same."

Cassandra set her fork down entirely. "Ooh, tell us who she is, Arthur."

He shook his head. "Can't. I promised the lady I wouldn't reveal her identity."

She clucked her tongue at him. "Well, that's just irksome. And such a shame. I would dearly love to meet her. She is such a clever writer."

Arthur nodded. "That she is. And *Confessions* was so wildly successful last year that our profits nearly tripled. Her new book is due out this Christmas, and I can't wait to see if it does as well as her first."

Julia raised her wine glass. "Though I haven't read her first book yet, I would like to propose a toast to the mystery woman."

Cassandra nodded vigorously and raised her glass as well. "Most definitely."

"Why's that?" asked Caroline.

"Someone who calls herself a 'genteel lady' has made substantial donations to both our refuge in East Welkin and the new one being built on the former grounds of Lexington House. We think it might be her."

"Well, then . . ." Caroline lifted her glass, as did everyone else. "To the Genteel Lady."

"Bless her generous heart, whoever she is," said Julia. "And may she know great happiness in her own life, wherever she may be."

"Hear, hear!" Arthur drank to the toast and then set his glass back on the table. "I will be sure to pass along your thanks and good wishes. If her next book is as successful as her first, then I'm sure she'll be contributing even more to your cause."

"What was her first book about?" asked Caroline.

Cassandra's cheeks turned a subtle shade of pink. "Well, it's probably a little too salacious to discuss here at dinner. Whoever she is, though, I would swear she's read the *Kama Sutra*."

"*Kama* what?"

"*Sutra*." Cassandra nodded toward Julia across the table. "It's a book Julia brought back from India when she returned four years ago. I'll lend you my copy when I return from Wales."

"Nonsense. Caroline can borrow my copy. It's around here somewhere, but I want to read this other book, the one by the Genteel Lady."

Arthur chuckled. "Well, you're in luck, Julia. I happen to have an extra copy with me. You may keep it. It's a great read. It's also very . . . oh, how should I put it? Stimulating?"

When the entire table laughed, including Charles, Julia turned her head toward him and met his seductive, hooded gaze. As he passed a dish of carrots to her, their fingers brushed together, just as they had done the day she showed him the picture on page forty of the *Kama Sutra,* and just like then, a spark of heat passed between them. He raised his brow suggestively and lifted the corners of his mouth into a shameless smile. No one but her seemed to catch it or the desire it conveyed, but the hunger in his expression kindled her own need into a slow burn. She arched her brow right back at him and returned his provocative smile as her face heated with thoughts of what the night ahead would bring. Warmth also filled her heart because, beneath his flirtation and the promise of pleasure, she knew there burned a love so bright, its brilliance would challenge the sun. And she returned the love of this man, her King of Wands, heart and soul.

The End

ACKNOWLEDGEMENTS

Many thanks to my proofreader, Hardy Garrison; my critique partner, Rachel Frye; and my beta readers, Julie Button, Amy Kenny, and Angie Thibault for their invaluable insight and constructive critiques.

ALSO BY ANNA DURBIN

<u>Kings of the Tarot Series</u>
King of Swords—Book 1
King of Wands—Book 2
King of Cups—Book 3
King of Coins—Book 4

For more information about these titles,
please visit our website at:
www.annadurbinauthor.com
Like us on Facebook at:
facebook.com/AnnaDurbinAuthor
Find us on Twitter at:
@TheAnnaDurbin
Follow us on Pinterest at:
pinterest.com/annadurbinauthor
Contact us via email at:
annadurbinauthor@gmail.com

ABOUT THE AUTHOR

Anna Durbin blends romance with the esoteric in her Kings of the Tarot series set in Regency England. Having grown up reading sagas of chivalry and romance, she began crafting her own elaborate stories in her imagination at a young age. It was only natural that she would one day write them down. Enchanted with the Tarot deck since her teens, she enjoys weaving the symbolism of the cards into her storylines. Her first novel, *King of Swords*, won WisRWA's Write Touch Readers' Award in 2018 for historical romance.

www.ingramcontent.com/pod-product-compliance
Lightning Source LLC
Chambersburg PA
CBHW070344260626
47161CB00001B/4